MAG

MAG

James Sorel-Cameron

HAMISH HAMILTON

London

HAMISH HAMILTON LTD

Published by the Penguin Group
27 Wrights Lane, London w8 5tz, England
Viking Penguin Inc., 40 West 23rd Street, New York, New York 10010, USA
Penguin Books Australia Ltd, Ringwood, Victoria, Australia
Penguin Books Canada Ltd, 2801 John Street, Markham, Ontario, Canada l3r 1b4
Penguin Books (NZ) Ltd, 182–190 Wairau Road, Auckland 10, New Zealand

Penguin Books Ltd, Registered Offices: Harmondsworth, Middlesex, England

First published in Great Britain by Hamish Hamilton Ltd, 1990

Copyright © James Sorel-Cameron, 1990

Quotation from *A Staffordshire Murderer* by James Fenton
reprinted by permission of the Peters, Fraser and Dunlop Group.

Printed in Great Britain by Richard Clay Ltd, Bungay, Suffolk
Filmset in 12/13pt Monophoto Garamond

A CIP catalogue record for this book is available from the British Library

ISBN 0-241-12800-5

For Mimi Klebinder

Every fear is a desire. Every desire is fear.
. . . Every victim is an accomplice.

James Fenton *A Staffordshire Murderer*

CONTENTS

BOOK ONE
The Three Stars

— 1 —

Being unlikely to survive, she did not take a name. She came twisting into the world, her back humped, rending the flesh from which she came; for which Mully, her mother, who had borne fifteen healthily and fluently, sliding them out in their time like skinned rabbits, never forgave her.

She was born in a big room on a cold winter's night at the heart of a vast old inn, the Three Stars. Mully, the lady of the Inn, lay on a great bed, splayed in tangles of soiled linen, screaming and cursing her. Two great fires roared in stone fireplaces at opposite ends of the room, the only sources of light. Five young whores, her mother's attendants, kept their distance in the darkness at the edges of the room, watching the great bed ablaze with firelight, alive with twisting shadow. They watched in mute horror the obscene and bloody struggle. It was a warning to them. Death they knew – it was like a candle caught by a draught; it was easy. They had not known that birth could be so fearful. At the end of the process, when Mully finally lapsed into the slow groans which carried her off into a sort of sleeping, they came forward. There was something there, something new, a hideous, hobbled thing that writhed about as if life were a hook in its bowels. They cleaned away the fleshly debris, brought opiates for their mistress. They found a girl lost in one of the barns who had been abandoned, brought to bed and bereaved of it quickly. She was taken on and given the wet-nursing of the little deformity.

This barn-girl loved the little monster with a thin little love for a year, became a figure of the kitchens and wash-rooms, the yards and stables, accepted there and ignored soon enough. Someone made sure that Mully never came across her, but that was not hard for Mully rarely left the big room now. After a year, for no apparent reason, the barn-girl went into a deserted store-room and slit her own throat with a stolen razor. Thenceforward the little monster was let loose to tumble about in the rubbish of the kitchen floors, attached to the society of infants, dogs, cats and the collapsed who lived at that level amongst trestles and troughs, inside great cupboards and disused chimney breasts. Someone, often Cloud himself, the master of the Inn, would instruct one of the women to clean her now and then; and she would be caught up out of the squalor, stripped and doused, towelled and dressed again; sometimes even loved a little; held for a night or two by a sobbing drab, then abandoned again, pushed away in a sudden waking revulsion.

She was allowed to exist, became a familiarity. She was called The Hedgehog by Gray, one of Mully's sons, a name which generally adhered to her, bringing her existence into an accepted fact. But truly, by the time she was able to make the distinctions, she did not know whether she was human or beast.

She acquired in time, mysteriously, the power of understanding, but never the power of speech: her tongue, like her spine, was humped and hobbled.

She would as an infant ramble for days in the complexities of the Inn. She would discover, at the back of a cupboard perhaps, a doorway to a tiny spiral staircase, dark and steep and wormy. She would struggle up and find herself in panelled bedrooms, unused for decades, where birds roosted and cats came stalking. She slept in enormous beds amongst fallen drapes and burst quilts. She awoke once in utter darkness to the scuffling of a cat and the sudden shriek of a mouse. After a moment of the purest silence, she heard the low purr, the slow breaking of tiny bones and the abrupt sounds of sharp jaws chewing. Later, she awoke again and the silence was as absolute as the darkness and both were rushing into her face like a sudden sea. She struggled against the dry drowning in her throat and gave out a cry of sorts which seemed to hold it off, to make everything suddenly sharp in the darkness. It was a moment of self-definition: she knew now, if not what she was, at least that she was.

Later, by way of broken panelling, by now bitterly hungry, she writhed her way out on to a long corridor but could find no end to it. A tall man in a black coat with tails that flapped at the back of his knees, an old man with a long face and long, fine hair, walked by her with a stick which he tapped ceremoniously on the floor as he went. She set off resolutely after him, but he was soon gone. Distant doors closed. She passed many doors, and she began to reach up and scratch at them, one by one, but none was opened for her.

A girl came hurrying past with a tray. She saw the little crippled thing and halted, stooped, offered her a chicken carcass from her tray, smiled secretly and hurried on. The child found a deep alcove with a table under which she crouched, sucking the oily bones for hours until they were dry.

She slept and woke and crawled on down the corridor. The tall man in black passed her again, going in the opposite direction. She did not attempt to follow him this time. She came to a wide flight of stairs which she ascended to another long, high corridor. She set off again, coming at last to an end, a wall where, impossibly high above her, was a window through which fell a brown, dusty light. She turned round and made her way back.

Later a door opened and two women came out into the corridor, tall, thin women, one fair, one dark, both dressed in spoiled golden gowns. They walked stumbling down the corridor towards her. As they passed, they paused and looked at her. Their cheeks were painted white, the texture now streaked and yellowing; their eyes and mouths and nostrils were wide, black gaps in their empty faces. The fair woman dropped to her knees before the child, took an empty breast from her gown and offered it, before being dragged away by her dark sister. They spoke no word, nor made any sound beyond the rustle of their gowns. They disappeared down the corridor. The child crawled to the door which had released them, but could rouse no one with her scratching. She crawled on, along interminable lengths of corridor searching for an open door.

She discovered one at last and found herself in a small, cluttered bedroom. Outside it was day but the curtains were drawn over it. The room's occupant was gone but there were signs of his recent presence. There was an unmade bed, a desk covered with papers and books in rough pilings. Many pieces of paper, some with writing, some with sketches and designs, were tacked to the damp, papered walls. A basin on a stool held stale water which she spilled trying to reach. She sucked some moisture from her sodden sleeves. She scrambled up on to the bed, and slept.

She was awoken by a young man with a bald skull and tufts of yellow hair sticking out over his ears. He was sitting on the bed and regarding her curiously, minutely, through dusty spectacles. She felt no alarm at his scrutiny. He took her from amongst the bedding which she had fouled, stripped the bed and pulled off her smock. He bundled the dirty linen out of the room and returned shortly with a pitcher of clean water. Having wrapped her in a towel, he gave her water to drink from a big cup and bread to eat torn into small chunks. The towel fell from her and she crouched naked on the floor, her back bowed over, cramming the bread into her mouth and swallowing it unchewed in thick lumps that hurt her chest but sank gratefully into her belly. Her host meanwhile had drawn up a chair and now sat with his head in his hands and his spectacles on the end of his little nose, continuing his observation of her. He reached forward and ran his forefinger down the nodules of her spine, traced her stark ribs, pondered her as she ate. She felt increasingly safe in the precision and objectivity of his examination.

When she had finished eating, shaking her mass of red hair aside to look up at him for more, he reached forward and lifted her to her feet, upon which she had not yet learned to stand unaided. Letting go of her, he watched her fall adeptly down upon all fours, her deformity showing like the spokes of a torturer's wheel set into her flesh. She felt a moment of apprehension here, but he sensed her retraction and laughed it away, caressed her. Lifting her, he spoke to her in a language, or dialect, which she did not know, but she felt a warmth of reassurance in his voice. He set her hands upon his knees and, thus supported, she submitted to his handling of her round head, his burrowing under her hair for the shape of her skull. He smelt strangely of some ointment or medicinal oil. His teeth were uneven with wide gaps between them.

He sat her down upon the floor again and gave her a blue

6

bottle to play with, a fat bottle, securely corked, that she could not get her fingers round. He found an old shirt, crumpled but clean, and fitted her loosely into it, folding up the sleeves to free her hands. He went and fetched clean bedlinen, brought more food – some fatty broth and a torn loaf of dark bread. He shared the food with her neatly. He made her a bed on the floor from a pile of old curtains which he also fetched from outside. He talked to her continuously, explained things minutely to her in his incomprehensible tongue, holding objects up for her, papers and books, bottles and pens; and small sketches, some of which she could recognise – a door, a fireplace, a cat, a face. He devised an arrangement of towels to keep her clean and he attended to them regularly.

Once, near the beginning of her stay with him, he drew aside the curtain, lifted her up and gave her her first, astonishing glance at the outside – a landscape of roofs and chimneys, towers and steeples rising up above them with the smoke and dust, rising up into a featureless, saffron sky. She clambered at the grimy glass in a sudden excitement, a desire perhaps for flight. He drew her away and lowered her sadly to the floor.

At night she would awake to hear him muttering in his sleep, rocking and writhing and shouting, at times, a fearful negative: 'Na! . . . Na! . . . Na! . . .'. She could understand that; it reduced her in the darkness. Once she woke to find he had come and had lifted her up into his bed with him. In his twisting sleep, reaching out to hold her, he had woken her. She extricated herself and tumbled down amongst the familiarity of the old curtains, in the safety of herself.

He taught her to walk one day, applauding her as she achieved her first stumbling balance, catching her up before it slipped from her, twirling her round. She quickly appreciated the advantages of this new skill, the first of which was the simple freedom of mastering the distortion of her spine, locating her centre of gravity and setting her deformity about it. His patience with her and his delight in her had lifted her to this and she laughed for him.

He was absent from the room for some hours every day, leaving her with small things to eat and to play with. He would always return with something new: a pitted wooden ball; a little horse of gingerbread which alarmed her as it dissolved upon her exploring tongue; a bag of small, flat stones, each of a different, intimate shade of blue. Often she stood below the window, trying to see out, willing him to lift her again; but he would not. He would shake his head, sit down and, holding her hands, give her a long, sad speech of refusal. She felt no desire to leave him, began to accept his little room as a world sufficient for her.

She stayed with him many days until, early one morning, she awoke to find the room full of strange men. Her friend had been hauled from his bed on to the floor where two of the men stood over him with knobbled staves, beating him, one after the other, methodically. He cried out, 'Na! . . . Na! . . . Na! . . .', and they beat him until he was silent. Other men, meanwhile, had set about destroying the room, tearing up the books and papers, emptying the coloured bottles, smashing them and splashing his inks and ointments over everything. As the men worked, she huddled up on her old curtains and they took no notice of her. When they had finished and gone, she crawled out and round to the other side of the bed where her friend lay. He was curled up, still. There was blood in his hair and all about his face, on the wall in wet splashes and trickled out on to the floor beneath him.

She tottered up, bewildered, and passed through the open door back on to the long corridor, back to a staircase down which she clambered, along another long corridor; until her sojourn in the strange room, like the rest of the small, closed scenes of her infancy, was gone from her into a blur, a distance from which she crawled and tottered.

A while later, the tall, old man with the stick came again into the corridor where she had wandered. She was standing propped up against a wall and, as he came to her, he paused, cursed her and struck her with a blow of his stick far bigger than she was. When she roused, with the thick bar of his blow swelling across her shoulders, he was gone. She crawled into an alcove and huddled there.

Old Mag from the kitchens found her there eventually and, gathering her up across her shoulder, carried her down with a bundle of soiled linen and restored her to her former life.

*

8

Here began her long attachment to Old Mag, who now took charge of her. She was given a permanent nest in the stable where Old Mag lived. Old Mag would lift her every night up into a manger full of bits of sacking and rags. At dawn, or before it in the winter months, she would be lifted down and would be hauled across the miry yard to spend her days in the complex lower chambers of the Inn. Late every evening she would be led back again, lifted up to her manger and swallowed in strange, patchy sleep invaded by dreams of rooms and corridors, images surrounded with terrifying darkness from which she would awake, gasping, to the noises of the night in the stables, the heavings and snorting of the beasts, the fierce conspiracy of rats, distant human mutterings and cries, to Old Mag's interminable chattering and wittering, to the great echo of the night in its silence above her.

Waking in the night, she would often peer from the rim of the manger down upon Old Mag, who hardly ever seemed aware of her. She never caught the old woman sleeping; perhaps she never needed sleep, living as she did in a continuous half-doze, dealing with the world in quick movements as if fending it off, never allowing it to come too close to her. Her little mangered charge was tended without the slightest expectation of response; merely dealt with – lifted, pulled, cleaned, replaced – moved through an impersonal routine that embodied a strong sense of certainty; for which, if for nothing else, she began to nurture an affection for the old woman.

She watched Old Mag with a growing fascination. She saw her, night after night, sitting awake at her lantern, swaddled in blankets, but always, at some level, active; whether sucking spasmodically at her pipe and blurring her head in billows of dungy smoke; or gnawing and worrying at a knob of hard bread; or fondling a great, black bottle that was as big as her head and from which she pulled mouthfuls of some sticky spirit, rolling it about her gums before swallowing loudly and gasping and belching as it bulged down her gullet; or if not satisfying herself in any of these ways, always moving, shuffling about the stall, rummaging here and there, or just huddling in slow, irregular shrugs.

She wore layer upon layer of old skirts, smocks, shawls and aprons which, on rare nights, very late, she would remove and wash, her nakedness wobbling fraily about her as she worked. Clothed, she seemed at times just a bundle; naked, she revealed herself reassuringly bodied. She was a tiny old woman then, squashed down into bulbs of flesh, breast and belly and buttock and thigh. Her head was round, her face red, her eyes small in her fat cheeks, her nose chubby and twisted. She always wore a grey linen cap, tight over her skull, flapping down about her ears and neck. The child saw what perhaps no one else in the Inn had ever seen, that under the old cap Old Mag was quite bald, her skull yellow and wrinkled like a melted eggshell. Washing each rag in a scummy tub, drying them one by one with a flat-iron heated on a small brazier and worked on a smooth board hidden and brought out only on these rare, ritual occasions, she would reinvest her nakedness with its many layers; or at least with those of them that had survived their purging.

She would relieve herself into an earthenware flagon which she burrowed up under her skirts and which gave out a brief, muttered chuckle in its darkness. She would then decant a small portion of her water into a wine glass with no stem, and would inspect it closely against the light of the lantern before going out into the yard to dispose of it.

She would sing an old song, only one and only occasionally. Suddenly the night would be possessed by her voice, thick and spluttered. The child learnt the words of the song long before she could have approached their meaning:

> *Poor Jenny's dead and gone*
> *That once was gay and free – oh*
> *Poor Jenny's dead and gone*
> *Hanged upon a tree – oh*
> *For th' murd'ring of her own sweet babes*
> *One, two and three – oh*
> *Poor Jenny's dead and gone*
> *In a cold countree . . .*

There were nights when Old Mag would sing this for hour

upon hour, falling into a rare stillness as she sang. And the child would peer down from the manger, emboldened, trying to find a voice with which to join in, but unable to, the barrier between her emergent consciousness and her disabled frame insurmountable, and in time felt to be so.

Once, when Old Mag dragged her across the broken cobbles of the morning courtyard, the child tried pulling back, catching the old woman's progress, causing her to turn and cuff the child instinctively. The child, her ear whining, persisted however and a second, more substantial and considered blow was raised, but held suspended as Old Mag found the child's eyes upon her, open eyes, perceptive eyes. The old woman winked a lopsided grin at her, let go her wrist, let her fall upon her rump in the mud; where she sat and, leaning her bent spine to one side, looked up at Mag, and beyond Mag up into the dark, dawn sky which dripped sour rain into her face. Old Mag hitched up her skirts and squatted down before her, chuckled and took lumps of her cheekflesh in both hands, shaking the child's face to see if the light would go out of it; but it would not go out. Old Mag tired first, sighed, spat aside, shrugged herself up and left the child to herself.

Around her rose the high structures of the Inn, a piling up of building upon building, propped, tumbled and re-propped, built higher; faceless windows and running walls; tortuous fractured chimneys leaking smoke; a precarious pile of architectural compromise and expedience exposing its nethers to the wide yard. To the child it seemed about to fall under the weight of the sky. It was a scary feeling but it swelled so tightly within her that she rejoiced in it.

Soon enough, sitting there in the yard became unpleasant. The slime seeped through her smock and began to ooze over her flesh coldly, claiming it. With an effort the child pulled herself clear, stood and tottered after Old Mag into the archway that led into the complex of the Inn's lower offices where her familiarities awaited her.

Old Mag spent most of her days in the washroom, a long room with a barrel ceiling lit by thin windows at one end, thin light which was blurred in the rise of steam from the long washing troughs which ran along the walls. There was an incessant dripping from the mass of white slime stalactites that hung from the round ceiling. Water, hot and cold, was brought in by kitchen boys, a pair of heavy buckets on yokes over their shoulders. These bucket-boys made their way down the long room, their heads bowed, watching their footing on the slimy duckboards, until one of the washerwomen would grab a bucket from the yoke and tip it into the trough. It was difficult, when one bucket was removed, for the boy to keep balance; and to stumble and spill the second bucket was a disaster, occasioning howls of execration and kicks which landed the luckless brat in the central sluice running the length of the washroom and into which, by the lifting of large wooden paddles, the troughs were emptied. The bucket-boys seemed to accept such humiliations: their faces showed no register of humanity.

Into the washroom came great stacks of crockery, baskets of cutlery and linen, sacks of vegetables, each allotted its area of trough for ablution. The washing of the crockery and glassware was the most prestigious, and also the most dangerous, since breakage incurred obligatory expulsion. There was a moment's pause when the trays of piled crockery, the racks of glasses, were brought in, by men not boys, and carried to the high trough where the élite of the washerwomen worked, a thinner, darker breed than the others, less rowdy, more precise, aloof. The only sound that could hush that great chamber completely was the rare sound of breakage from the high trough. The noise would occur concealed amongst the general cacophony, but would at once become isolated in its unmistakable sharp echoes, a silence falling back from it. In the silence, the washers at the high trough would step quickly away from the culprit to dissociate themselves from her. The culprit herself would look around in sudden panic, seeking a way to avoid or to share her tragedy; but it would always be too late.

Old Mag worked at the linen troughs, which were the lowest in the hierarchy of the washroom. Here was the centre of the cacophony, the slopping and slapping and loud incessant cycles of motiveless laughter. Here the women were uniformly old and shapeless, many-chinned and bearded women, features steamed into a raw ripeness, a bulbous similarity. The child could only distinguish Old Mag amongst her cronies from close quarters; and then essentially by her clothing, her peculiar smell amongst the folds of her many skirts where the child hid, below the great stone troughs, between warm, damp walls, her daytime nesting place.

The principal delights of those at the linen troughs were gleaned from close scrutiny of the various articles of bed-linen, a duty each of the washers performed minutely before immersing any article in water. If the linen bore stains, the discoverer of such would hoot the others into a cluster about her, and they would pore over the various discolorations. The prize stain was a blood stain, the discreet smear or the livid gush, each betokening some pain or shame that drew and excited the old hags. The child, noting these excitements among them, and once bleeding from her nose, offered Old Mag, in the palm of her hand, a few drops of her own, fat shining bloblets of the real stuff. She took much trouble to attract Mag's attention but the old crone was not interested, pushed her away after a moment.

The place to be was under the troughs of the vegetable-washers. Here was food, and the children of the lower offices of the Inn were brought up to fend for themselves; the child soon learned this. Here came great bushels of roots, great baskets of pulses, piles of thick-leaved greens. The more delicate vegetables and the fruits were dealt with elsewhere, as were the meats; into the washroom came only the brute food to be pared and shredded and piled naked into the kitchen tubs. The discard from this process was large and, at the completion of each batch, it was swept over the edge of the troughs and on to the floor. The rubbish lay about the feet of the women at the trough and a small cluster of children picked at the heap, sorting and snatching, making a continual, meagre foraging, gnawing and sucking the nutrients out of anything that fell.

The little Hedgehog found her way to the edge of this pack, watched them, and began to feed as they did; although she remained too delicate for the habits of one boy, a bald-headed, scabby thing several years older than she who sought diligently for the insects that lodged in the cabbage leaves, the slugs and beetles, and scrunched them up between savage black teeth, his lips drawn back, his eyes wide. She found her chief pleasure in the shards of roots which she took in her hands, caressed them clean of their dirt and then sucked until they were soft enough to yield to the warmth of her mouth.

She had not been with these children long when an incident occurred that was significant. At her first arrival, sitting at a little distance from them, she had attracted their curiosity. She knew her own strangeness by now and had outfaced this, soon sending them scuttling back to their feeding, establishing her own feeding on the edge of their pack. She did not participate in the scrambling that accompanied the first fall of a new load from the trough, being cautious and soon learning what was good, marking and waiting for it. Then one day she saw fall near her a half-root, neglected rather than discarded above. She wanted it and went for it as it fell. It was then that she came into conflict. She felt a pair of sharp claws lodge in her thick hair, was wrenched away, thrown aside, her head striking a stone support. Rousing and blinking, she saw her prize in the jaws of the scabby insect-eater who, she had realised, by virtue perhaps of his advanced diet, was the first of the pack. He eyed her with venomous contempt which she appreciated at once. Her head was grown large and bleeding from the blow. No anger rose in her, only a disappointment, a longing. She reached towards the boy in a gesture of offering, of sharing. He stopped eating. She came towards him, shuffling along the floor with her hand out. When she was within reach, he chucked away the root, grabbed her hand and bit it lustfully. She thought she was about to be devoured; had the circumstance been available to him, he probably would have devoured her. She squealed, and from the trough above came an unexpected intervention. One of the women, a thin, bony woman who could, like most of the others, have been the boy's mother, peered down at the disturbance and gave an immediate shriek of alarm. Suddenly a cluster of faces appeared below the trough rim, shouting and snarling. The boy was grabbed by the back of the neck, pulled out and slapped about the face until he bled from nose and mouth. Struggling to cover himself, howling, he

14

was beaten about the shoulders and shaken brutally. The child watched this, her own hurt gone, appalled. The boy, bleeding and blubbering, was then forced down on to the floor, his face pulled up to hers, his features twisted with wretchedness. The woman knelt beside him and, screaming abuse deep into his ear, she banged his forehead ceremoniously on the floor three times before the girl who cringed away from this homage. He was eventually discarded and fell coiling and covering his head, jerking as if he was still being hit. She did not dare approach him. She looked around the other urchins, a dozen pinched little faces, a dozen pairs of uneven eyes held upon her fearfully from the glooms and damps, a circle of fear of which she was the centre.

This retribution that had been taken for her was unique. As a rule the children were entirely ignored by the women; they lived in their own little anarchy, nursing their own little miseries and inflicting them upon each other quite apart from the world above them.

She realised that she had some inexplicable status here. When, in future, she reached out for a fat discard, the others drew back from her. One of the more timid ones offered her a whole turnip once, but was clawed back and pommelled. The turnip fell and was left for her, but she would not touch it. She tried offering her own treasures, but they were ignored. Her status evidently implied a separation; more than that she could not learn, not here at least. Its nature evidently lay beyond the world of the washroom. She would have to venture forth to find it. She made the decision to set out. She had begun, anyway, to develop a revulsion for the washroom and its inhabitants. Her status, whatever it might be, served at least to give her a distance upon her world.

Her particular horror in the washroom was the drain into which the central channel ran. This drain was a large iron grille at the far end of the room. The grille, far larger than she was, guarded a vast cesspit some way below the level of the washroom floor, a bottomless catacomb of effluence into which all the gutters and drains of the Inn debouched. At the end of every day, a pair of heavy men came through from the kitchen and, working a great ratchet-winch, raised the grille, allowing the muck to be scraped out from under the troughs, into the channel and down into the pit where it landed amidst deep bowel echoes after a hideous, black silence of falling. The children had to scurry quickly out of the way of the scrapers. She heard a story, presumably from Old Mag, of one of the bucket-boys who had slipped once, before they put the grille in, who had slid down the channel and over the stone lip into the Gehenna below. She was told, or had imagined, how he had laughed at the joke of falling and sliding along the channel, clowning; then suddenly the world had shot from under him, the light reduced to a shrinking hole above him. He had screamed twice and then had been gone. This tale bred nightmares. In winter it wasn't so bad; the air blew in through the grille icy and hard like the air outside. In the summer, though, the depth beyond the grille was appalling, embodied in its thick swaddling stench, lifting a veil of flies up to the grille-mouth. Last thing on the summer days the grille-men would light piles of yellow powder in old shards. These would be floated along the channel and would fall into the pit, roaring briefly, illuminating masses of rotten and broken stonework, masking the stench for a few moments with acrid fumes; it would soon swell back. The Inn would one day fall into this pit. Later, when she came to hear of hell, she had the image of it ready-made.

It was the presence of the great pit that finally drove her out of the washroom. Its stench tainted everyone. It invested clothing and seeped into the pores of the skin. It was in everything eaten and it was distilled in the belly. It was in the air and it fouled the lungs. It was the image of decay and death to which they had all succumbed. They were all dead in there; even Old Mag was dead as she worked at her trough. When someone died in the washroom, fell down purple and burst inside from working, they rolled them down the channel, lifted the grille and dropped them down into the pit. She imagined this but it was true nevertheless; and as soon as she had the understanding to articulate it, she knew she must find her way out before her turn came.

So, one day, dumped down at Old Mag's feet, making her way along the greasy stones beside the open channel towards the vegetable urchins, she went on. She passed out into a high lobby. To her left lay the courtyard through which she came every day; to her right a steep stone stairway rose out of sight; in front of her was another large archway opening into the kitchens. She went forward.

The kitchens were vast. Architecturally they were like four or five of the washroom side by side with the adjoining walls removed except for massive square pillars. All the walls and pillars had been whitewashed up to the level of the roof barrelling. At the far end of this multiple chamber, corresponding to the pit in the washroom, were the ovens, a battery of latched iron doors and stoking ports throwing a continual heat across the chambers. Light came in from a series of high windows on the left – the courtyard wall as in the washroom – and from clotted candelabra which burned in the glooms of the far reaches. On walls and pillars were hung clusters of implements: pans, skillets, griddles, ladles, long spoons, long forks, sieves, colanders, trays. From the ceilings hung bushes of dried herbs, congregations of onions, long smoked carcasses. Against the walls were tubs and sacks, barrels and crates. Within this crowded periphery, across the floors, were massive trestle tables, heavy blocks and stones about which the multitudinous activity of the kitchens was in constant progress.

The hierarchy here was soon discerned. The activity was divided into distinct areas, each centred about a large table dominated by a huge man in white, a beast of a man, each one distinct, each variously proportioned, but each out of the same mould of grossness. It was possible to imagine the whole activity of the kitchen to be directed at the feeding of these vast creatures. Each of them was surrounded by a horde of minions who were made on a different scale, dressed in a variety of worn greys and blues and blacks. The further these minions worked from their masters, the more importance and independence they assumed. At the bottom of the hierarchy were the hosts of pinched boys who plied between the sacks and the vats, who scrabbled up ladders, who scurried off to store-rooms and ovens, who scrubbed and scoured and stumbled about dazed with fatigue but never still, never waiting except in the immediate shadow of their master, always possessed by the blind energy of the place itself.

She encountered this new world with alarm, but was intrigued; not pausing at the doorway, but drawn in amongst the activity which was soon swirling all about her, oblivious to her, avoiding and ignoring her. Cast iron pans swung over her head, carcasses were rushed past her; a line of scrubbing boys advanced across the floor and passed either side of her like an incoming wave.

She found relative safety at last under one of the large trestles where upturned benches were stowed, amongst which she scrambled as the planking above her was cleavered and pounded, as liquids dribbled down upon her, blood and sauces, a loop of egg-white, a trickle of milk. She learnt to twist her head and to catch these on her stunted tongue, smearing her palate with their strange textures.

Under this uncertain roofing she settled, hedged by a moving barrier of legs, some booted, some slippered, some bare. She realised then the prime difference between the atmosphere here and that she had left in the washroom. There the noise, the clattering and chattering of the old women, had been unrestrained and ceaseless, pushed always to its limit, rising to fill the high space above it with anything so long as it was filled; here there was an abiding hush, an intensity of activity, not of noise. Occasionally, close or distant, loud cries sprang out, a command or a curse; otherwise the voices were low, urgent, functional and the abiding sound was the rhythm of work, the chopping and dragging, the pouring and pounding. It was a less reassuring noise than the chaos of the washroom. She huddled as the boards above her juddered with the hacking of meat.

Suddenly something fell off the edge of the table and a face fell down in pursuit of it. She cringed back but the face turned and lit upon her, a round, grey, greasy face with a lumpy, shaven skull above it. Seeing her, it made a swallowing sort of chuckle, bobbed up and then came down again, drawing with it all the other faces, a row behind and before her of pendulous heads, all with sweaty eyes, dry lips and jagged teeth. Hands reached out at her and, although she squirmed down as tight as she could, she was fixed at the ankles and wrists, snatched at and pulled from both sides. She writhed and bleated as best she could, then they worked it out. Some of the hands fell away and she was hoiked out and lifted all at once high into the air. She had a brief sight of the great kitchen spread out below her as she was buoyed up on uplifted arms, the focus of innumerable pairs of ill-matched eyes in upturned heads like so many mushrooms; then she was lowered carefully on to the table and she found herself placed ceremoniously on the chopping block of Mr Tow, the master of meat.

The chopping block was sticky with visceral fluids, and about it lay the day's offals, piles of minced purple organs. Above it loomed Mr Tow, his small, bald head atop a swollen body wrapped in layers of smeared, white aprons. His face was round in all its features apart from the nose, which was thin, a tiny pyramid of gristle with nostrils slit into its under-surface. Upon the nose was pinched a pair of round spectacles through which, rolling his head from side to side, he regarded this strange meat that had arrived on his slab. He held a long knife honed to stiletto thinness. She looked at him clearly. A mumble of laughter began in the faces around him, but he silenced it with a tightening of his mouth. He put down his knife and placed his left hand firmly but gently upon her hump, bringing his nose down towards her face. She reached up and felt the point of his nose with the flat of her hand; it was cold but the breath below it was warm. He lifted her chin and expertly squeezed open her mouth, inserting his middle finger into it and probing round her tongue. His finger was grainy and tasted salty, savoury. She could not have made an impression upon this substantial digit with her teeth even if she had wanted to: it filled her mouth too enormously to be attacked. She noticed that the top half of his forefinger was missing.

Removing his hands he reached over and produced, on the open palm of his left hand, a raw liver. This he nosed carefully and then offered it for her to do likewise. Expertly, then, he caressed it with the long knife and, putting the knife aside, he picked out a long, cut sliver from it, dangling it between thumb and middle-finger before her. She held out her hand and he let it fall. Finding its gummy rawness unpleasant on her fingers, she slipped it into her mouth where it felt much more natural, loosing its strong juices on to her palate and resisting the stamp of her teeth with its texture. After a moment's fierce punching between her jaws, it slipped down her throat in one, making her gasp and choke with surprise.

A small mutter of appreciation went up about her, and a jug of ale was handed in from the edge of the press. This was applied by an over-excited boy straight into her mouth, a sudden gush of foamy liquid that shot up her nose and made her splutter, causing the boy to have his ear turned in a complete circle by Mr Tow. She watched the boy's face bursting with pain as he suffered in complete silence.

She sat upon Mr Tow's table throughout that day, watching his work, watching him transform an interminable sequence of dead parts of dead beasts into manageable, cookable, servable foods. He chopped with the voracity of a machine, pounded with the blindness of a brick, filleted with the delicacy of a seamstress; and, that day, all for her delight; and she was delighted. The variety of size, shape and texture of the flesh and offals amazed her; as did the master's skill in knowing precisely how each mound of rawness was to be approached. He offered her many morsels to try, some raw, some from pans that were brought hot from the ovens for her approval. She preferred the raw morsels with their resistant textures and heavy juices. He would watch her eat with judicious approval, even when she screwed up her face and voided her mouth of some repulsive knot of substance. He patted her kindly and quickly sought something to please her.

At evening, Old Mag came to carry her away. Her arrival caused some sniggering amongst the minions, but Tow clumped together a pair of empty heads and greeted Mag formally. She reacted to none of it, swung the child down and hauled her across the damp yard in which, as usual, she paused to allow the child to relieve herself. The child squatted whilst Mag stood and muttered, watching, waiting. At first the child seemed constricted below, then suddenly the day's strange delicacies were bursting out of her, her bowels twisting and wrenching. But she knew about bowels now, had a definite image of all those strange parts packed inside her, working away in concert. This knowledge, now practically applied, made her feel larger and more complex than she had felt before. Old Mag brought a bucket, stripped and sluiced her, brought her into the stall, funnelled some black water into her mouth which filled her gullet with foul penitence, and put her to bed.

She wondered if she had offended Mag by her desertion of the washroom, not to mention her subsequent disgrace. Next morning, however, entering the archway between the two worlds, Mr Tow, with a clutch of the smaller minions, was waiting for her, and Old Mag relinquished her without a murmur.

'Just don't you have her squitting all over tonight, Mr Tow,' was all she said as she went off to her work.

'She is the lady of my table, Mrs Mag,' he roared after her, and bore the child in to her place to applause from the minions which he condescended not to notice.

So, a new pattern of days was made for her. A little chair was discovered for her, a high chair in which she sat enthroned, a tray fixed before her on which her little delicacies were placed. She was only occasionally now, surreptitiously, slipped something raw from Mr Tow's sausagey fingers, with a wink: little snippets of the real thing. So she sat and so she watched.

In the washroom, power had always been somewhere else. In the kitchens, the power was with the masters absolutely. The minions were of all ages, from sleepy little boys to wrinkled old men. The older they were the less work they appeared to do, the further from the masters they worked and the fewer of them there were. Often she would see a cluster of old backs bent for hours over something in a corner, oblivious to the rest of the activity about them. They were sour-faced and foul-tempered. All of them, young and old, had cropped skulls; none had any authority at all. All power was with the masters.

Mr Tow rarely gave orders. Everyone seemed to know what they must do and did it in an atmosphere on the edge of panic, of continual fear. Tow, unlike some other masters, rarely struck out; but when he did so, his blows were usually quite arbitrary. He would suddenly stretch out for a neck and shake the head above it furiously; or turn and stun a boy who scurried behind him with a blow on the back; or cover a face with his great left hand and twist the nose that was caught between his splayed fingers.

There was one ritual violence at his table, however. Mr

Tow would, periodically, emit profound and exhausting farts, at which the minions would fall into a sickening silence whilst he surveyed them savagely.

'Master Cobble,' he would say, having selected, 'do you dare to fart at my table?'

Master Cobble would make a sick apology whilst offering his palms upturned for Tow to lash with a stropping leather. Master Cobble would then curl down to the floor and be permitted, silently, to indulge his agony before being hauled up by two of his mates, the relief sparkling in their faces, who would prise open his swollen palms for Tow to inspect the efficacy of his chastisement. He would then apply to his guest for her approval, which she gave with a polite if uncertain smile.

One day, at a moment of Tow's most detailed concentration, removing the breast-flesh from a tiny bird in two perfect oysters of meat, she herself, inadvertently, half-excitedly, farted, quite volubly considering the size of her. Having committed it, she felt afraid, looked around the frozen faces of the boys who had instantly braced themselves. Mr Tow completed his operation, laid down his knife and swept round their faces, arriving at last at the culprit who sat unavoidably in the warm reek of her own bowels.

'My lady,' he said solemnly, 'I apologise.'

The minions subsided into little clusters of joyfulness and beamed up at her. She grinned and winked at them whilst their master sized up another little bird for his incisions.

She saw that each table had its own particular behaviours, its own disciplines imparted by its master. At the nearest table, where the bread was prepared under Mr Libbage, a dreamy, stodgy man who would lose himself in long rhythmic poundings of seething pillows of dough, there was far less control. The minions would fight and scratch and bite each other, steal corners of dough and munch them, hide and scurry about under the table to perform unpleasantnesses. Such outrages were perpetrated in strange silence and grew outrageous only when Mr Libbage was far, far away in his kneading. Suddenly he would explode in fury. His minions would pile under the table and cluster together whilst he laid about their sides and rumps with a long wooden spoon which broke eventually, signifying the satisfaction of his rage. The minions would creep bruised and groaning from their shelter. One would take the broken spoon, run off and return with a new one. Libbage would take it, inspect it, crack it experimentally over a head, return to his work and the cycle would begin again.

At the table of the pies, under Mr Allrig, there seemed the most perfect discipline. The minions there all seemed youthful and fit, spruced and pretty, their faces notably free from blemish, their behaviour quite superior. Allrig used no casual violence upon them, and they worked proudly, disdainfully, going so far as to kick or tread upon any minion not of their table who obstructed them. One of Libbage's minions, suffering thus and becoming loud about it, Libbage took offence, barged across to Allrig's table and slammed a fist down into one of Allrig's complex pies. Allrig merely lifted the hand away and blew into Libbage's face. Libbage, as suddenly as he had flared, subsided and went back to his own table. Allrig's minions were far too superior to crow.

Although for a long while she never saw Allrig so much as admonish a minion, she suspected him. She sensed in him a cruelty more profound than any she had yet witnessed here, and one evening these suspicions were confirmed. There was an unusual stir at Allrig's table and she saw his minions had formed a circle about one of their number who was in a state of some terror. A stillness expanded through the entire kitchen as Allrig took his place in the circle. He gave quiet instructions and the circle broke. A barrel was rolled over and the culprit, trembling greatly, lowered his breeches and bent over the barrel where a cluster of hands held him down. Allrig squeezed the proffered posteriors in what seemed to be a parody of Tow's handling of a haunch of meat, and then, producing a short stick, black and flexible, a specialised instrument, he proceeded to open the boy's flesh with a score of slow, strong strokes, each one carefully placed and distinctly applied. She watched the detachment of Allrig, the way he checked his instrument, flexed his arm, examined each blossoming weal on the boy's flesh before bracing up and slamming home the next stroke. The kitchen was filled with the report of these blows and their echoes, which were surrounded with a congealed silence.

At first the boy made no noise, or none that broke

through the slashing of the stick upon him. As the succession of blows mounted, however, he began to emit distinct yowls that quickly rose to a pitch that hurt her ears. The yowls were brief, sharp, and seemed echoes of the blows. Allrig waited until they were done before beginning his inspections and lining up to strike again. When he had finished and had nodded to the supporting minions to remove the victim, the yowls continued, at distinct intervals, as if the succession of strokes had established a pattern in the boy's mind that would go on and on. They dragged him and his yowls out, away to the far depths of the kitchen and beyond. The echoes boomed back from distant corridors. Everyone waited for the silence to return and, when it came, the barrel was rolled away and they all settled back to work.

She wanted to ask what he had done to deserve that. She did not believe that anyone so small, hardly bigger than she was, could have deserved that. It had set off a slow, rising panic in her stomach that she had no means of releasing. She looked to Mr Tow who had explained so many mysterious things to her, but he was dicing a large block of flesh into tiny, uniform cubes. He had begun this before the start of Allrig's performance and she saw that he had almost completed the long task; he had not stopped; his face was bland and indifferent, as they all were, even those who had paused and watched. She no longer wanted to be in the kitchens.

It was not the cruelty that appalled her, but their failure to have a response to it. They all seemed reduced to the level of the meat they chopped, the dough they heaved, the fruits they pulped, separated from them by a trivial act of nature. She searched, in the days after this, into the faces of the minions, but they looked through her, or winked lewdly, or grinned vacantly under her scrutiny. Although they could blabber and she could not, although they could limber and dodge about and she could only hobble, she did not see anything in them which she envied or would have been glad to share. She began to lose her pity for the flogged brat. She wondered if he had recovered and returned, but she could not have distinguished him from the others. The fear and the panic which had accompanied this pity, these went too and were replaced by an aching tedium. She had seen all there was to see here.

*

She did not entirely abandon Mr Tow. She would sometimes spend a day with him, lifted up into her chair. He was pleased to see her, would welcome her and treat her. He did not seem offended that she spent most of her days elsewhere now.

But the kitchens and the washroom, although central, were only a part of the underworld of the Inn, and she began to look about her for other possibilities, other explorations which, lying in areas more peripheral, darker and more darkly peopled, became alluring to her.

The large courtyard, faced on one side by the bulk of the Inn buildings which were entered by the archway that led to the kitchens and the washroom, and to the steep flight of stone stairs between them that was quite beyond her courage, was surrounded elsewhere by innumerable store- and work-sheds, barns and lofts, part of, or appended to, the central stables in a near corner of which was Old Mag's stall. To the left, emerging from the archway, was the enormous double gate and the wall in which it was set. Standing in the archway one bright spring morning, surveying the complexities before her, she noticed a number of sparrows hopping in the puddles between the disjointed cobbling. She looked up and saw clouds rushing high and white across the sky. She felt the stale air of the courtyard lifted and whirled about her tenderly. She made her way across the courtyard and towards the workshops in search of adventure.

She spent a day in the woodcutters' store where dark men in leather aprons split massive tree stems down into oven-staves, filling the air with leaping chips and the scent of bleeding sap. They eyed her when she first appeared, then ignored her, large men with shaggy hair tied in pigtails, and thick beards, and backs of lithe, moving muscle. She discovered the carpenters with their ripping and planing, a pair of elderly men, one tall and thin and pale, one short and round and red, both with spectacles and pens behind their ears. They would spend long minutes discussing a slab of wood, feeling its grain and its knots intimately before cutting and shaping and smoothing it, pausing after every procedure to examine and discuss and select the next implement and weigh and test it before applying it. She made her way into the blacksmith's den, with its furnace and its violence. The blacksmith roared madly to himself as he smashed bolts of hot iron into shape. He had boys, two dirty boys in trousers they had long outgrown, with bare, hollow chests and ugly burn-scars on their arms and backs; they lounged idly and moved sullenly to the blacksmith's hysterical commands. She scurried out and the boys stood in the doorway and lobbed old cinders at her as she fled back into the space of the courtyard, laughing and tumbling in the light.

Looking across she saw, for the first time that she could recall, that the great gates were open; some of the older kitchen minions, with some others of more outdoor build and dress, had hauled them apart. Through the gates an enormous wagon came, drawn by horses so large and slow that they seemed to belong to another scale of being. The wagon was loaded high with sacks, each of them about twice the size of a large man. She crossed the courtyard quickly towards the open gates, an impulse for escape tremulous within her. The enormous cart moved past her, its wheels turning slowly, crushing great ruts into the surface of the yard.

The cart passed towards the barns where a hoist waited at a high opening, manned above and below. She followed it shyly, keeping out of the way of the carriers and hauliers. She saw two men apart from the others, young men in smart coats and clean stockings. One held a bundle of papers and a metal box; the other swung a silver-topped cane. They were the directors of the operation, and they had noted her there. Their faces were lean and their hair was oiled and groomed, swept back and tied. They seemed to be related, brothers perhaps; but then everyone seemed related to everyone else of a similar station in the Inn. The one with the cane, who seemed a little less serious than the other, sharper, came towards her. He stopped and stood off from her in an attitude of contemplation. His companion kept his attention on the unloading, making marks on his papers. The man with the cane squatted down to bring himself level with her. He prodded at her with the cane, poking her over into the dirt.

'You're getting bigger,' he said, 'but you're still only a hedgehog.' His eyebrows raised. 'By God, you understand me, don't you? You understand. Do you know who you are? No. Let me give you a warning, Hedgehog; don't let anyone tell you who you are. Once you know that, that's the end of you.'

And, saying this, he swung back his stick to give her a great blow; but she would not flinch from him and, with a laugh, he lowered the stick, pushed himself up on it and sauntered off idly, slashing the stick about him, having revealed to her something else of which she was a part, and of which she knew nothing. It made her feel more lost, revealed a new way for her to be miserable. Before, everything had been self-contained, detached, comprehensible in its isolation; now she became aware that there was a plot and that she was a part of it: every move she made, every month she survived, contributed to it. It came upon her slowly, inexorably, the weight of it.

She turned to see that the great gates had been pushed shut. Beyond them she had seen, through gaps in the clustering houses, distant trees; low, hunchbacked trees and a low landscape beyond, way beyond. It was not a clear image, but it was a new horizon; or rather, the realisation that there was a new horizon; that the Inn was not the world.

And whatever the strange, cruel young man had meant, he had known her; and by his emphatic denial of her, he had, implicitly, established her.

On later days she ventured into the barns and stables, which had awed her in her earlier explorations with their height and depth and darkness. The workshops had been distinct, purposeful; the barns and stables were vague, mostly derelict and peopled, she knew instinctively, by the lowest levels of human and half-human detritus that the vast Inn supported, the finally discarded in their final little corners: the old ruined mumblers, heaps of rags that muttered and stank with the occasional corrupted patch of flesh visible, a twisted, emaciated limb, an eyeless face shaggy with hair and slime. She wondered if anybody knew them or tended to them; or came to clear them away at last.

There were also the lunatics, most of whom fled when they were approached. There was a group of young women, five or six of them, in tattered gowns that had once been fine, whom she watched clustering over a spot on the floor, restless and murmuring to each other, exploring, stooping, pointing. She came forward to try to see what it was that drew them. They saw her and broke, scattered like cats and were gone in an instant, disappeared into a strange, watching silence. She searched the spot where they had clustered, but there was nothing there; only her now, the centre of their hidden watching. There was a young man in the clothes of a boy which had burst about him, exposing his arms and belly, his legs and buttocks, thin and black with filth. He also ran off when he became aware of her, from a piece of wood he had been beating on the ground. When she moved on, he reappeared and began to follow her, dodging about, dancing or possessed, some three yards behind her. She stopped and turned slowly and there he was, dropped down on all fours, staring at her. She stared him out and he began to nuzzle under his armpit frantically, trying to gnaw himself. She approached him slowly, and suddenly he was speaking to her.

'It's over there. It hasn't got any smaller. You said it would. You said it would waste away, but it eats. It eats and eats and gets bigger all the time. Bigger and bigger and one day it'll be as big as . . . as big as . . .'

Then he deflated, defeated, getting up and ambling away. They were mostly silent, however: the sack or the pillar that turned out to be alive, revealing a face of hollows, a mouth that hung or gibbered, nostrils that sucked in rapid gusts, hands that twitched or dangled or clenched in attitudes of petrified prayer, eyes that stared forever inward into the vortices of shut minds. As she passed these, she always touched them to see if it made any difference; but beyond the occasional distant shudder it never did.

She wandered into and amongst the endless barns and store-rooms for day after day, and such encounters as these, although they were always occurring, always abrupt, blended into the background which was of grey, dusty spaces filled with the discarded clutter of generations, stacked and heaped. There were rows of stalls and staircases, rooms beyond rooms beyond rooms, piled high and spread deep, broken in and fallen together below the broken roofs which

28

leaked rain and powdery sunlight. There were birds and bats fluttering under the roofs; and across the floors the cats and the rats had a world of hunting and killing. But there was, above all this, above all else, a depth and a silence into which all was blended and made vague. It was a dream world, and to walk the old barns was to walk with the edges of perception blurred, the mind reacting to things within as well as without, equally. She was in most danger here simply of being swallowed. She had to stir herself positively sometimes to find her way out when her voracious little body, exerting itself over her mind, told her it was evening.

She made, however, one important discovery in the barns. She found a new way to Mag's stall. By ascending two stairways, going along a splintered catwalk, down another stairway and out perilously along a beam, she found herself directly above her manger with a view straight down into the boxed stall. It was strange to view it from this perspective. It looked dull and dirty from up here. One day she would be able to get down. One day she would find her way up here from the manger to the beam, and that indeed would be an escape. The idea of wandering the barns at night, when darkness muffled all the leaking light, appalled her. She sensed that nightfall would bring the barns and their dwellers into their own realm. Lying in her manger and knowing now, at least by implication, what lay in the barns about her did not frighten her; the stall embodied a security which nothing had ever shaken.

One day, worming her way along the beam above the stall, she saw something new. Although it was still only early afternoon, she saw Old Mag in the stall, lying back on the old straw bales, her skirt drawn up to expose the wallows of flesh above and about her knees. She was lolling from side to side. The child thought that she was ill and was about to cry out when she noticed another figure in the shadow at the edge of the stall, one of the elder kitchen minions, a little man, wizened and grey. He held the big black bottle up to his mouth; the slow lumping of his Adam's apple as he drank had drawn her attention to him first, distinguishing him from the murk in which he stood. She saw him lower the bottle carefully, belch thinly and leave through the stall door, fumbling at the bolts and then leaving it swinging behind him. Mag remained where she was until his echoes had settled, lolling on the straw; then suddenly she roused, pulled herself up, dropped down her skirts and burrowed in the straw beside her. The child could not see clearly, but she seemed to uncover something; there was a little clatter of coins and a scrabble to cover whatever it was up again. Crossing the stall, collecting the big black bottle and tucking it under her arm, Old Mag waddled out, closing the door tightly behind her. The child considered this scene which was beyond her penetration; although, as she thought about it, she connected it with several absences from the washroom, substantial absences which Mag had made to the amusement of her cronies. The child had once tried to follow Mag, but had been prohibitively dumped back under the trough and the incident had been forgotten until now. But the idea of Mag sneaking back into the shadows of the barn to secret meetings with strange people intrigued the child. She was again made aware of the manifold aspects of life which were hidden from her and which, once revealed, would take her forward in what had now become the abiding quest: the quest for secrets, the nature of which she did not know, but which she felt rising tangibly all around her, looming in the shadows she was beginning to invest.

So she spent her dawning years, moving amongst the lower life of the great Inn. She developed an intimate apprehension of large expanses of the lower offices of the Inn and of those who were bound there; but she had no conception of what rose above them all, by which they were all subjected. She avoided the places and people who communed with the world above: if the lower world had its constrictions, it also had its certainties. As she grew she became aware of the world above as a great weight pressing down upon the lower world, answerable ultimately for all its distortions and cruelties. She would dream of the cataclysm which would sweep that weight away in a moment, freeing them all, opening the barns and kitchens to the sky. The sky that was wide and wild above the blown courtyard would rush down and fill every dark space, releasing everything that was held down here, closed and secret and festering here, surging up and out in a roar of energy. This dream at times excited her, at times terrified her.

Meanwhile she slept in her manger above Old Mag's stall, and wandered through the chambers of her world, becoming their familiar as they became hers: the faces and figures, the spaces and corners, the seasons of light and the seasons of dark; the days when the mist smothered the courtyard and seeped into the buildings; the days when the rains came and ran shivers of water across the open stones and needles of leakage through every roof; the days when the sun held the courtyard static in heavy heat, intensifying and delighting the damp shadows about it; the days and days and days. And she held them all together within her bent little body, under her thickening mane of red hair that Old Mag eventually bound back in a thick plait that ought to have hung down her back, but which was thrown over her shoulder like a hank of rope. She scavenged from the barns a quadrilateral of broken mirror-glass the size of her palm, a lunatic's discarded nightmare, and spent hours gazing at her long features, her pointed chin, her pointed nose, her natural frown, her large round eyes which looked back at her secretly.

— 2 —

She could not have said precisely when she had first become aware of the music. It was no sudden realisation; it had been there a long time, caught at distances, across the courtyard or high up, away above her in the barns, always distant, perhaps even a natural phenomenon, a chance moaning which had incidentally turned into song. Then one day she caught it clearly, stopped and concentrated upon it, imbuing it at once with enigma, making it an object for quest.

It was, as far as she could determine, the playing of a small fiddle. It was a loop of sprightly melody that formed a shape in her mind; it had a steady dipping logic, with a moment of hurry and a shade of darkness before returning to its original even pattern. It had come as usual from high above her, standing as she was in the light that fell squarely into one of the barn entrances; but it came to her with a clarity that she had never realised before. She imagined, crucially, a humanity behind that music, a controlled humanity with, by means of the music, a reach beyond itself; as such it became remarkable, flowing clear of the forest of nightmares that tangled in the barn below it. The melody was repeated several times, then it attempted a variation of itself, became confused and vanished. In the moments after it had gone, it developed within her an emptiness, a longing.

She set off purposefully to locate the source of the music, but she could not find it, her search soon lost in the dark spaces and encounters with which the barns interminably surrounded her. She came into the barns every day after that, sometimes to wander, sometimes just to stand a little way from a doorway, a few yards out of the light and into the borders of the darkness, to listen for that music again. It did not come to her again for a long time. She woke up in the night, late, with Old Mag's mutterings down below her as eternal as the wind, with the barns creaking and scratching above her, but no music. She imagined sometimes that she had woken just after the music had ceased, its echoes seeming to fade in the darkness just as she rose to consciousness.

When she heard the fiddle again it was quite different, although she knew it was the same instrument in the same hands. It was a stormy day with thunder playing in the back of the sky and every ledge running with rain. She had stayed longer in the barn entrance than usual and the music came to her in a long meandering strain that had no pattern, long notes coming in a steady sequence, rising and falling, rising and rising and rising almost to inaudibility then sliding down again, slowly but steeply. It was a long way away now; she could not even be certain of its direction, and she knew she could never trace it. She went away before it ceased, running away before it could leave her alone again.

The next day it was there again. She almost dreaded it. It was not audible from the courtyard. She had to go so far into the barn to fall within its range. She dreaded its sucking at her and she dreaded its absence. It was the same as it had been on the previous days, a slow, gliding sound, a small sadness made formal. And today it caught her. She had been on the point of turning and running from it, had come to that point several times but the crucial jump from intention to action eluded her; and suddenly the music came to a rise, and fell and was over, gone.

In the sudden silence of that music, she felt afraid: she felt that she had been penetrated by the awareness and expression of another. It occurred to her, in the first shock of that fear, that she had assumed that the musician was aware of her specifically, had been aware of her from the first. The sense of absurdity that quickly subverted this assumption gave her no comfort, only a desolation – and she returned, wilfully, to the assumption in all its absurdity. She proceeded into the darkness conscious that she was critically observed and aware moreover that some sort of devouring creature awaited her.

It was a long day's wandering in the barns for her that day. She encountered more of the demi-ghosts than usual, drifting and scampering, crouching and standing. The fear which had come upon her at the doorway clung to her as she wandered. In all the figures she encountered in the darkness that day it was the eyes that dominated; in each dark face were two livid red slits with black centres, and each pair seemed to fix and contain her, pushing her away. She was careful not to react to them, to hold herself steady under them for they seemed cold and tightening. She had acquired a new vulnerability.

That night, waking in the manger, she heard the fiddle; not a tune this time, but a pulling at long, separate notes, a long way away. She scrambled to the rim of the manger to see if Mag had heard it. She was too hurried: Mag was looking up for her as she peered over. The fiddle had stopped and she found herself looking down into the fat, bunched face with nothing between them. She met there in Old Mag's face, for the first time, something distinct, an expression, a response. She had assumed Mag's face to be incapable of character; but now, in the eyes which met hers as if they were a trap into which she had fallen, there was a purpose, a grim malevolence. She thought of the man with the cane and she shuddered back down amongst her bedding again.

*

She gave up searching for the source of the music. She did not go back into the barns. She brooded on whatever they had in store for her, Mag and the other. The whole Inn seemed charged with an oppression to match her mood, or perhaps it just seemed so, reflected from her. She paid occasional visits to the kitchens, spent days back in the sweat of the washroom, where she was surprised to find herself the eldest by some way; but whenever the weather was fine, she sat in a corner of the courtyard, nestling in a heap of broken furniture near the carpenters' shop, pulling down a broken-backed chair and sitting upon it, curled and enclosed. People passed across the courtyard, but she paid them no heed. She was retreating into a dull cocoon within herself, and she was deprived of the energy to resist such a retreat.

One day, as she sat brooding, a large, black bull was led into the courtyard. It was held by a wide, tall man with dense red hair bursting out of his shirt and hanging like a wilderness from his head. He had a stick which was attached to a ring through the beast's nostrils. Two other men accompanied it, one on either flank, keeping their distance, armed with sharp goads which they hardly dared apply. It was an enormous beast; had it wanted to, it could have shaken them off and charged round the courtyard in the majesty of its energy. It did not do this. Its great black eyes looked far away and its mouth, dripping loops of saliva, was almost smiling. It submitted ironically to the men who led it.

A crowd emerged from the kitchens and washroom, some even from the barns, none of them venturing out from their archways or doorways, crowding together in a press. The child slid from her chair to run over and touch the beast, to smooth its warm, close flank, to blow down the silly little ear tucked behind its squat docked horn; but prudence overcame this impulse and she drew back, afraid of the men and their fear rather than of the bull. She was charged with an excitement but, as it rose to break from her, she looked and it was restrained.

They led the bull across and brought it to rest under the loading beam. Men had appeared at the upper doorway and were fixing a rope to the beam through a complicated set of blocks. They were intending to haul the bull up. This astonished her. How would it submit to that? The bull waited placidly below the beam, its nostrils dilating and its eyelids almost closed. Suddenly Mr Tow had broken from the crowd in the archway and was striding across to the bull with half a dozen of his elder minions keeping close behind him, sheltering in his bulk. He came to the beast, stroked it, whispered to it. She saw an eyelid raise and a glint of white flash. Perhaps there would be a battle between Tow and the bull; it would be a fairly equal contest, she considered. Tow patted its head and it responded by pissing a great, steaming puddle across the cobbles around his feet.

Tow turned to his minions who were suddenly in action. They ran forward with a large bucket and a large block of knives. Others had dodged round to the back of the beast and lifted its legs one by one into a broad noose. Before she could work out their intentions, they were running across the courtyard with a rope and the bull was jerked off the ground, roaring and thrashing, its forelegs clambering the air. Tow held the nose stick, pulled back the head and slit the throat deftly and deeply, the blood arcing out like a lash to be caught expertly by the two minions with the big bucket. As the bull writhed and the beam creaked and the crowd held silent, the bucket-minions danced about on the cobblestones to keep the mouth of the bucket under the gush which went on and on and, only after long minutes, began to pulse slower as the bull submitted, its eye now mostly white, its mouth open, the great teeth bared and the great tongue lolling out. At last it was still and the minions placed the bucket down under the final dribbling. Then they turned and presented themselves, spattered with gore, to the cheer of the crowd who now urged forward towards them, but still not too close. Mr Tow had not a drop of blood upon him. He glanced about the courtyard and saw the child standing, half-hidden, by the old furniture. He winked at her and she began to come forward, but halted, defiantly, not retreating, standing out on her own in the high sunlight that fell about the whole scene.

Mr Tow now began to undress. He removed his aprons which were caught as they fell by the waiting minions, revealing beneath them an enormity of white flesh, decency

35

minimally preserved by a foul loincloth which clung precariously under his belly, and was lost between his massive white buttocks. Thus stripped, Tow advanced upon the dead bull which, at his signal, was lowered slowly to loll upon the ground.

He took first a small knife and pruned the beast of its sex, laying the triple organ in a proffered bowl which was carried straight into the kitchens. Exchanging the small knife for one with a blade as long as his forearm, he slit the belly in a series of precise and deep slashes. He yelled a command and the carcass was once more run up off the ground. As it rose this time, its belly opened and a vast mass of pale innards burst forth, fell and splashed about Tow who stood and roared with achievement. Minions ran forward with a flotilla of receptacles which Tow filled with the various viscera, snipping and piling, losing his arms in the mass of it, cutting and slitting. The reek of the beast's black dirt came in a wave from the carcass and with this came the flies, a blurring swarm of them; perhaps they too had sprung from the darkness of the bull's bowels.

The stench finally made her aware of herself again and she turned away, nauseous. She had been lost in the ritual of the slaughter. It had been a ceremony, a triumph, a feat of prowess; and that seemed absurd now with it all reduced to the buckets of steaming offal which were being run back to the kitchens. She looked and she did not understand and, after a while, she did not want to understand. It was cruel and foul and trivial. She turned and ran from it into the open barn mouth, feeling betrayed and sick.

Her stomach settled in the darkness, but not her imagination. She found herself a corner behind a pile of fat sacks which had been forgotten there, had burst and spilled damp, dead straw in a deep mound. She nestled miserably down and felt the mice bolting away from under her through their labyrinths.

She sobbed herself into a little sleep, seeping tears of shame and self-pity into the dirt of her face. The sobbing released nothing; rather it was the articulation of an ache that would not let her go down into sweeter sleep. The heat of the day invaded the darkness, thickening the flies and maddening them; they fastened upon her to emphasise her inescapable corruption. She roused several times to free herself from a cluster of them. She struck out to catch a handful, but they were always gone, leaving her prickling and scratching as if they had got beneath her skin. They became part of her expanding misery.

She awoke abruptly from this little wretchedness and, mysteriously, it had gone from her. She must have slept properly. She felt quite eased, her body calmed and dreamy. The death of the bull had slid down into the indiscriminate tumble of her memory. It took her a while to become aware that there was something else, something outside her, a figure sitting on the sacks above her, watching over her, fanning her with a large, coarse leaf. She could not see who it was, only its outline against the dim light; and for the moment she did not want to know anything about it. She was simply grateful, associating the figure at once with her feelings of release. She stretched herself and felt light and clear in the moving air. She knew that she was not sleeping, but she had only felt like this in dreams before.

It was in the nature of things that this strange figure would soon be gone from her; she accepted this. When it suddenly slid out of sight, she was not sad. She lay still in the pleasant wash of feelings and wondered herself back into the present, thought about food and drink, discovering her mouth to be dry and musty.

Then he was back again, her watcher, scrambling over the mounds of sacks towards her, bearing a tin mug which he offered her. She put her hands out to take it, but he did not release it, guided it to her lips. She filled her mouth with cool, sweet juice, light and slightly fermented. She drained the mug and felt the bright weight of the liquid sink through her. Only then did she begin to concentrate on her ministrant as he wiped the mug on a white cloth which he had flicked out of a large pouch hanging from his shoulder, replacing the mug and the cloth in the pouch and burrowing about in it.

He was a boy with skin the colour of dark-stained wood. His hair was black and oiled, bound back in a little pigtail at the nape of his neck. His eyes were disturbingly blue, pale, watery blue. His nose was straight and perfect. His lips were fleshy and his face was long. He wore velvet breeches and an open black satin shirt revealing his pure, dark breast. He was strange and beautiful and she could only admire him.

From his pouch he drew a fat, blushed-orange fruit, a globe with a distinct fleshy cleft down it. He held it up and examined it. She thought he was going to do some trick with it, but he offered it to her. She took it and felt how its softness fitted into her palm. It was too delicate to do more with than hold. She offered it back to him.

'You don't want it? Go on,' he said in a low, congealed voice. 'It won't turn you. It's just right. Believe me. Go on. Don't you understand?'

She did understand but was so alarmed at his speaking to her that she could only hang open her mouth.

He took and lifted the hand that still held the fruit up to her lips and, before she had consciously decided to do so, her teeth had burst the furred skin and the honeyed flesh was filling her cheeks and bubbling down her chin. She laughed and he laughed too. She raised the torn fruit to his mouth and she felt his strong teeth biting into it, pulling away. They took turns and laughed, he finishing, holding the rutted stone between thumb and forefinger, sucking off the last fibres. He then took the white cloth again from his pouch, wrapped the stone, dabbed his lips and folded the cloth back. She who had smeared the juice off her face with the sleeve of her smock was embarrassed at his delicacy.

'One day,' he said, 'I will take you to my garden where the peaches grow.'

She could tell by the distance of his voice that he did not credit her with an understanding, but she did understand. She knew that things grew and were brought from their gardens into the Inn yard. She did not believe him, however. She knew he belonged in the Inn somewhere, and that that precluded him from access to where things grew in gardens. But she was happy with the fantasy, and she smiled to encourage him.

'I must go now,' he said. 'My mother will be looking for me. It's time I went home, see.' He turned quickly and scrambled off over the heap of sacks.

She scrambled quickly after him. On the barn floor, he stood and dusted himself down, unaware of her. He looked furtively about him and was about to go when he discovered her there behind him, watching him from the top of the mound with her tilted face. He pretended at first not to have seen her, looked over her and about him, the furtiveness replaced by a posed assurance; but she slid down, stood up and came beside him, and he was forced to regard her again. She reached up and took his hand between her hands, her gesture of affection. He looked suddenly alarmed and pulled his hand sharply away, nursed and chafed it.

'Who said you could touch me?' he demanded, his voice risen and outraged. 'You must not touch me.'

He began to walk away. She followed. He went out into the yard, his furtiveness taken over again, stooping him, his movements alert and bird-like. He went to an old pump and began to jerk at the handle, which shrieked. He pumped and pumped, but no water rose. The light seemed to hurt his eyes and he grew frantic. She went and snatched at the pump handle. He released it at once, stood back and let her pump for him, unbending her body as far as it would go, then bringing herself back down to her natural shape and bringing the pump handle with her. He withdrew into the shadow of the barn and crouched as she laboured at the dry pump and it shrieked and shrieked. All at once the shrieking was staunched by a gush of deep, cold water surging across the cobbling, spreading its dark, cold presence all around. She pumped on and on; it was easy now, rewarded, prolific. He came forward slowly, fumbling in his pouch and arriving at the pump with a stone of soap which he rubbed into a meagre lather, washing his hands and leaning back lest the water should splash his clothes. When he had done, she released the handle. He dried his hands on the ubiquitous white cloth as she watched the water-flow subside, the spillage gleam and still, turning brown as it seeped into the earth between the warm stones.

This procedure over, they straightened themselves and looked at each other. He began to move away towards the barn mouth, eyeing her. She began to move after him.

'No,' he said quietly, 'you mustn't follow me.'

She stopped. He continued to retreat slowly, then something occurred to him.

'You can follow me, if you like,' he said experimentally.

She proceeded. They entered the barn, he walking sideways, looking back to see if she was still with him.

'Stop,' he said. 'Stay there.'

She obeyed. He turned and ran off into the darkness, but she knew he hadn't gone far, that he was watching to see what she would do. She curled her legs under her and sat waiting for him. She had been back into the courtyard and she had not thought of the bull: that pleased her. She knew that sooner or later such things would begin to cling to her. She sat in the main entrance to the great barns with the light big and bright behind her and the darkness spreading up all before her and she waited.

She saw his eyes first, coming out of the shadow.

'Come here.'

She twisted herself up and approached, coming right up to him.

'You do understand,' he said. 'You do understand, don't you? I thought you didn't, couldn't. I didn't mean to . . .' He twisted about as if watched, as if unsure of what he hadn't meant to do to her. She smiled at him to help him.

'Would you like to meet my mother?' he said eventually, summoning his courage.

She smiled and jerked her head appropriately.

'Everyone's got a mother. I'll take you to meet my mother one day.' There remained an uncertainty in this, bred by his over-eagerness for her to believe in it.

She believed in it as much as she believed in anything in the ephemera of her world. She believed that he could take her somewhere new and she would be glad to go with him. She persevered with her smile and caught herself in time from touching him again.

Something caught his attention across the yard, and she looked across to see what it was. The two young men in smart coats were in the archway, talking and glancing about them. They noticed her and spoke of her, looking towards her. She had seen them occasionally and they always noted her thus, always generating an unease in her. She felt at once a need for protection against them, and she turned back to the barn, to the dark boy. He had gone however, and with an effort of will that hurt her strangely, she forgot him as she had learned to forget everything that came near her.

*

That night she awoke in the heat of her manger and heard the music. It came floating through the darkness like a thread of smoke, a dark, slow tune held tightly up in the fiddle's higher registers, edged with pain. It drew her from sleep. She awoke to the immediate realisation that it was the dark boy who was the musician and the music was, as it had always been, directed specifically at her, part of the plan, someone's plan for her. She sat up in the stall and peered into the darkness above her, trying to discern his shadow moving among the high, bulked shadows. The darkness was too much. Perhaps he could see her in the light cast up from Mag's lantern. She stood up to be more conspicuous, wanting him to see her and to know that she was responding to him.

'Get down!'

She looked down to see Mag standing in the centre of the stall, lit hideously from below by her lantern, hissing up at her venomously. Her cap was off and her bald head seemed raw bone.

'Get down, cripple!'

She obeyed, dropped down to the level of the manger-rim and watched Mag, who shook with fury; this was not, however, directed at her, but at the music which continued to drift and coil down around them.

'Stop that!' she screamed, stamping her feet and pounding her fists into her sides. 'Stop that! Stop that! I know who you are, you devil. I know you. I'll have you smothered!'

The music slid comfortably to a stop and the silence welled up again. Mag subsided, gasping and gripping her ribs. She was in obvious pain but the child could feel no pity for her; it was the pain of rage, of blind hatred. The child watched her coldly, and eventually Mag met her stare and was calmed by it, directed herself up at it.

'Don't you think you can fool Old Mag, you little cripple. I've watched you.' Her voice was cracked and spittled. 'Do you know what that was? Up there, squeaking and squealing? Do you know what it was? The little cripple eater, that's what.'

This did not move the child, who held her stare defiant.

'I'll tell you what he does, because I know, I've seen him at it. You listen now.' The voice went low. The old woman belched loudly and gripped her gut. She sat down and retreated into the shadows of herself again. 'You listen to me and I'll tell you. He puts his mouth here, here, where it's soft, here . . .' She pulled up her skirts and the lantern light flopped over her great white thighs, into the blotchy hairs about the vivid weal of her sex. '. . . Here. See, here. This is where he gets you. He puts his mouth here and he sucks and he sucks and he sucks and you feel it, you feel your guts being sucked out and running down his great big throat. And it hurts, it hurts, it hurts.' She rocked to and fro upon her stool. The flickering light seemed to set her lower self aflame, her bald head a rotten, falling fruit. 'Oh, it hurts, it hurts. No more, no more. But he won't let go. He sucks and sucks and sucks, and everything you've got goes sliding down his throat, his greedy dog's dirty throat. Now you know. Now you know.'

This had caught the child whose imagination was ravaged. She knelt at the manger-rim with her fists balled tight between her legs, holding on. Her face was open with distress. Old Mag was far away, closed in, and the tortured child was alone, feeling the lusts of the strange, dark fiddle-boy take hold of her.

Then Mag, quite unexpectedly, looked up and focused upon the wretched little head that hung in the gloom above her. The incantation of this nightmare had soothed the old woman. She dropped down her skirts and sighed. She stood up and came to the manger, mounted the old box on which she stood to lift the child up and down.

It was always a giddy swing down, growing giddier as the child grew and Old Mag withered. She feared dropping, particularly during her descents and particularly tonight when she was being brought down extraordinarily, with Mag unpredictable and suddenly more substantial to her than she had ever been.

'There now, there,' the old woman was saying to her. 'It's all right as long as I've got you. It'll be all right as long as you're here. You'll always be my crippled little thing now, won't you? Won't you now?'

She understood the idea of motherhood, had seen women with their babies in the washrooms and barns. She understood not only the fact, but the emotions that flowed from that fact. When the strange boy had spoken so intimately of his mother, she had understood. She had never considered for an instant that Mag might be her mother. Now, however, Mag had her sitting on her knee and clasped against her. Now she felt herself pressed into Mag's spongy body, her face swaddled in Mag's smell, a thick, dusty smell, dark as death and older than she could imagine. She tucked herself up into the curve of her own body, trying to harden herself to resist this monstrous cuddling; but Mag's limitless flesh was too much for her tininess to withstand. She submitted perforce but shuddered at the thought of this act of usurpation. She recalled deliberately the sense of horror which the old woman's nightmare had exposed in her, using it now to try to resist its obverse which threatened to overwhelm her to extinction. She wanted neither extreme, but the nightmare at least left her to her own damnation. She longed spitefully for the boy to come dropping down out of the roof-dark upon them, to carry her away, flying up into the distances with so much free space about her where now she was having to use her elbows to find a breathing passage through Mag's smothering.

It was obvious that she should stop writhing so, for Mag only hugged her tighter, assuming the writhing to be spasms of the nightmare. The child relaxed and subsided and Mag swayed her slowly. She thought, though, of the dark fiddler-boy, and she knew clearly that Mag's outrage against him was jealousy. The child grew in this knowledge, the knowledge of herself as a distinct part of the lives of others. She put her arms out across Mag's bulk and settled, freeing her face to gaze up at the old woman's mask, her moon-head, pitted and tufted with down, her little nose. If it was not motherhood, it might do as such for the moment.

She woke back up in her manger with Mag busying herself with breakfast, forking a knuckle of meat out of a boiling tub and blowing on it. The child felt a large need for such domesticity, the sight of Mag connecting directly with some impelling dream-emotion that had been with her just before she woke. She leapt up and swung herself over the edge of the manger, hanging on to its rim, her feet dangling and kicking, her back wrenched against itself. Mag let out a yelp, half-alarm, half-anger, and came towards her; but she dropped down, landing like a cat on all fours and springing up again.

Mag looked at her in surprise, then laughed. 'Now, get back up there, if you can, raggedy-brat,' she said.

The child considered the height from which she had dropped, reached up towards it, then looked about for something upon which to clamber. Mag caught her up before she could make the attempt and carried her over to the stove. The knuckle of meat had been dropped in the dirt in Mag's surprise

'Look what you did, raggedy-brat.'

Mag indicated and clouted her ear customarily. They busied themselves with the day, Mag dusting off the knuckle, the child finding the knob of black bread on which she would breakfast. The meat, she knew, was one of Mag's delicacies which she could not expect to share. So much was usual.

Before the breakfast was done, however, in its usual silence, the child became aware of a difference in the atmosphere of the stall. Mag gnawed on oblivious, but the child was halted: they were under observation. She thought at once of the boy and, turning slowly, casually so as not to alert Mag, she saw him standing in the light of the open stall doorway, standing straight and still, his hands hanging down, but the neck of a fiddle protruding over his shoulder, a broad, red strap coming across his body, a gash in the darkness of him.

The child turned back too quickly, causing Mag's glance to flash briefly aside, but she had fallen back to her crusts and the illusion of normality returned to them. The child had difficulty containing the apprehension that spiralled up within her. She felt keenly the boy's observations upon them. It was a feeling not specifically to do with the boy himself; it was a feeling of exposure, in the strong light of the morning, to another's watching. The boy's observation seemed to push between her and the old woman, making the child aware of her complete distinction from her. The unity of the previous night, their interdependence, was now turned, under this strange watching, into its reverse.

The child could not sustain his look for long upon her hunched shoulders in the climbing silence. She stood, turned

44

and faced him, taking Mag with her, drawing the old woman's attention to herself and then away to the doorway where the boy stood unmoved.

Mag leapt up at once, spitting with fury; but the boy stood his ground, exhibited no alarm even. She halted at the door before him, splintering with rage. The child struggled forward, her limbs grown suddenly lumpish, to place herself at the lintel, not actually between them but theoretically ready to spring out if necessary: she did not consider which of them she would seek to defend. Mag's shrieking was hideous but inarticulate and, after a while, meaningless.

The boy registered fear certainly, but he held still, as if trusting some invisible grille between him and the old woman. After a while he gave her a slow, unsteady bow, tilting the fiddle neck briefly down towards her. Old Mag's ravings were at last exhausted, remaining now only in a shuddering and a snarling that came into her rapid breathing. She calmed herself, held in her breath and became controlled enough to address him.

'Devil,' she said. 'Goblin. Obscenity. Abortion. Devil.'

'No, I'm not,' he said bravely.

'Oh, I know who you are,' she said. 'Everyone knows who you are. You shouldn't have been let live. Like her,' and she indicated the child without looking aside. 'Like that. Do you want it? I can't stop you, but they will. D'you know what she is? They'll get you. They suckle their own amongst their own, even the ones that come out twisted and half-done.' And with this she suddenly launched herself towards him.

He stepped aside quickly and she passed him. In a moment she was gone, and the child was left alone in the stall; it was a strange place to be now. The child felt afraid. The boy edged back into the doorway, watching her, coming for her as Mag had said he would.

'Can I come in then?' he asked.

She retreated fractionally from him which he took as a beckoning and stepped boldly in, walking into the middle of the stall and leaving the doorway clear for her to bolt after the old woman. He stood looking round, looking up into the roof. He seemed older today, more assured, more dangerous.

'She's not your mother, you know,' he said without turning to her. 'Do you know who your mother is?' He paused, distracted, intrigued by something in the stall, craning himself forward to see, but keeping his hands at his sides.

The child found herself backed into a corner down the walls of which she slid, into the shadows of which she cleaved. The fear of him was not a fear of something he might do to her, but a fear of herself, a fear of her own vulnerability, as if there was some exposed flaw in her by which he could enter and possess her; and, when he turned to her, with the deference he had inhabited since his appearance at the stall door, it exacerbated this fear, made her feel dark and aggressive towards him.

'Will you come and see the Ladies with me?' he asked. 'They're beautiful and kind and you might be a lady like them one day. Really you might, kind and beautiful too, when you're older.'

She crouched lower into her corner, eyeing him and clenching her fists.

'I'll play you a tune,' he said, unslinging his fiddle and untying the bow that was bound to it, 'I used to travel with the outlaws. They stole me away when I was a baby and took me far off, into the mountains where there are towns that are always in the mist, to the sea that rushes away to the end of the world, to the forests where it's always night and there's no difference between a man and a beast. I've seen the whole world. They brought me back after a while. After years and years they brought me back to my mother and went away again. But they'll be back one day. They taught me to make tunes. It's magic. You wouldn't be able to do it. No one here would.'

He tuned his strings as he spoke, plucking at each one, producing a dead little sound which he adjusted minutely. Then he ran the bow softly over the strings one by one, producing long, detached notes which filled the stall with layers of vibration. He stroked the sounds out of the fiddle like a purr from the throat of an animal.

'It takes a bit,' he explained. 'The tune has to be formed somewhere in the air, then it'll come out, just right, in a bit. Sometimes it's there before I begin and I just have to touch

46

it and it leaps out. Sometimes I have to wait and wait. Sometimes it won't come out at all. Here it is. Here it is.'

The fingers of his left hand began then to step amongst the strings like a spider and his right arm began to pump at the bow; and the melody fluttered out in the shape of a wheel that turned and turned and rattled over cobbles and cut down through water and bounced up into the air. She laughed and laughed, rocking away from her corner and back into it, bashing the wooden walls with her back. Her fear was gone. Perhaps he had outwitted it. She no longer cared. He finished suddenly.

'Let's go and see the Ladies now,' he said.

He led the way across the sun-bright courtyard to the archway. Here he paused, a little nervous. She came beside him and looked up curiously.

'Got to get across there without being seen,' he said, drawing back, ready to bolt if anyone should appear from either of the flanking chambers. He pointed to the narrow archway straight ahead, up which the flight of steep stone steps led. 'Up there.' He pointed.

Upwards, into the main body of the Inn, was a direction which had always, since the beginning of her days with Mag, been beyond her imagining. The prospect now of being guided up there was immediately exotic. She beamed at her guide.

She walked into the main archway, looking left and right, into the kitchens and the washrooms, the old odours of these places breezing briefly out at her, but they were nothing compared to the allure of the stairway. She went to its foot and stared up. The steps seemed to go up a long, long way into a faint light, the light of a higher world. She looked back to the boy who was watching her with eyes open and mouth tight. He indicated that she should proceed. She addressed herself to the task of ascent. There was a black, iron banister-rail, but it was beyond her reach. She began to ascend on all fours. It was slow and the stone met her flesh abruptly. It was a long, long way up, and the effort was great, and the higher she went the less secure she felt. The treads of the stairway were worn and shiny and she imagined slipping, tumbling and rolling down with every step she had conquered striking and breaking her. Above her there seemed no end to it. Her progress, a hand and a leg, then the other hand and leg, hauling the lump of her, was beginning to bruise her, each contact harder and colder. She wondered horribly how she would ever get down again. The motion of climbing had become automatic, each new step a positive effort against the awful fall she felt opening up, sucking behind her. She wondered where the dark boy had gone, why he was not with her. She imagined him now demonic, winged, hovering behind her, felt his shadow on her back. She turned, couldn't help it, and saw the fall rush up at her, saw the jagged stairway drop down into an infinity. She reeled and the rhythm of the ascent was dissolved. She jerked herself aside against the wall which hit her hard; but she managed to jam herself against it and the fall was cheated, for the moment. A cold, grey light filled her head and she sucked at the dusty air, closed her eyes and trembled and struggled vainly to reassert her sense of balance, her control over her jibbering limbs.

She heard him coming up eventually, running up the stairs towards her. She opened her eyes to see his dark shape obscuring the fall and, helpless, she reached out for him to catch her. He came up below her, but did not take her hands. He stood on the stair below her and gasped with achievement.

'Made it,' he said. 'Made it all right then. We've got past them now, don't worry. No one comes up this way, not from down there. They wouldn't dare. Come on then.' And he pushed on past her, opening that fall again, pressing on up, leaving her jammed against the wall.

A little further up he paused and turned, surprised. 'Come on then. What is it?'

She reached up to him, supplicating, and he apprehended her difficulty; but he fell into a difficulty of his own. He came down to within a couple of steps of her reach and stood looking down at her, wiping his hands on his jacket and looking at them, and then looking back at her. An idea came to him and from his pouch he produced a length of cloth, green and satiny. Stretching down, he dangled the cloth before her. She took it and wrapped it about her

48

wrists. Thus bound, she allowed him to pull her. He did so carefully, taking her weight.

'Not far now. Not far.'

She smiled thinly at his reassurance, not believing him, not trusting the taut cloth; but soon they were out on a landing, a horizontal walled floor upon which she lay and pressed herself, bringing the relief thumping back into her. She rose and wanted to embrace him, but he stood away, her strange boy, and bit at the edge of his lip. She glanced back at the stair mouth and gave him a little shudder. He understood and smiled.

'We'll get you down again,' he said. 'Don't worry. It's all right up here. Come on.'

He led her along a corridor lit by grimy panes still high above them. The corridor was long, making several curves, several abrupt turns, meeting other corridors. They passed endless silent doors. He clearly knew his way. She too knew this place, from long ago, felt a rising trepidation. She began to feel tired and hot, hobbling along beside him. He loped easily on, remembered her and paused for her to catch up. On she hobbled, going tight within herself, apart from him, not pausing when she caught up with him but pressing on. He slowed his lope down to move beside her.

Eventually he stopped and, having stopped to let her go on a few yards, called her back. 'Here it is then,' he said.

She turned to see him at an old curtain which he drew aside. She approached and saw a dark, spiral stairwell going down like a throat. She looked fearfully into it, but it did not go straight down like the other stairway; there was a banister of twined cord which was within her reach. Her fear was repressible. He was offering her the green cloth again, but she ignored it, grabbed the banister-cord and began her descent.

'Wait! Wait! I must lead the way.'

He squeezed past her and they proceeded into a darkness that was soon complete; but being so, it was easier than the light of the other stairs. The dark closed round her and she could hear him, just ahead of her, stepping slowly, his breath near, the jangling of the gear in his pouch regular. Down and down and down they went, turning and turning. There must have been an easier route to wherever they were going than this, and she began to resent his leading her through these mortifications. But she was not afraid any more, was buckled now tightly into herself, tighter and tighter as they went down and down into the darkness, and kept on turning and turning until the world turned with them.

Suddenly they came reeling out into a great low room, full of low lamplight and a sudden rush of smells, close, intimate scents of many conflicting sorts that overpowered her for a moment. She clung on to a curtain which he held back for her. The smoke of tobacco and of various candle-waxes was the principal constituent of this fume. As she moved forward she detected a shifting under-smell of flower-oils, of stale linen, of heavy flesh. It was a smell once richer, sharper and more subtly foul than anything she had yet breathed and, had it been conceivable to flee, she would have done so. What was this place?

She saw ahead of her a long passage leading to a wide doorway, also curtain-draped. This passageway was flanked by two rows of cubicles, some twenty on either side, each one shielded by curtains of various fabrics, all tattered, patched, of every imaginable shade of faded opulence. Most of these curtains were drawn; some appeared open but, from where she stood, she could see into none of the cubicles.

The dark boy advanced a little way along the passage and was peering from side to side at the various cubicles, approaching none of them. Without looking back, he beckoned her forward. She did not want to look. She came straight to him, ready to cling to him if necessary till he screamed and took her out. He bent down to her as she reached him.

'This is where the Ladies live,' he said softly. 'They are resting now. In the day they rest. In the night they rise up and become more beautiful than you can possibly imagine. You must be very, very quiet now. If one of them is awake, bow to her a little, like this.' Here he executed a deft movement down and up that would be quite impossible for her. 'You must be very respectful to them. Soon they'll learn to love you. They are the Ladies of Love and they love everyone. One of them, perhaps, will become your mother.'

She regarded his face, all bright animation, her mistrust swelling. She looked beyond him into one of the open cubicles. In it lay the long figure of a woman on a mound of deep bedding, her body draped in a robe of pale satin from which her long feet protruded. The robe fell open at her waist to reveal her breasts and belly. Her arms lay at her sides, palms open. Her head lolled upon her shoulder, her hair falling down in dense ringlets about her, brown and dull. She seemed on the edge of sleep, her mouth half-open with her tongue upon the lower lip. Her eyelids were low and there was no focus in the pupils. The child found her repulsive. She had never seen a human being laid out like this before, exposed and dredged in lethargy; but worst of all was the sickly pallor of the skin, white as milk, thin as tissue. Beneath it, the dark veins of her breasts could be seen, and the slow murmuring of the breathing that moved under her ribs. Upon this ungirded mass of flesh, the features seemed painted: the fat, red nipples; the black eyebrows on the white dome of the forehead; the nostrils like black bore-holes under the ridge of the nose; the thin lips upon which glistened smears of some sticky liquor.

The dark boy began to speak, close to her ear. 'That is my lady Sally Fly. She has a lover who is so great that he has no name. He comes to her from far, far away, and he loves her for days and days. When he is away from her, she sleeps. He takes her soul away with him and that is why she is so heavy. Isn't she beautiful? Wouldn't you like to be like her? Come on. I'll see if anyone is awake and would like to meet you.'

She stayed staring at the woman. The idea of her having her soul stolen away from her was real to the child, and it terrified her.

Then at the far end of the passageway a tall, elderly woman appeared, a woman who came swiftly and loudly down the passage. She wore a long, formal black gown which glistened. Her hair was black and swept rigorously back. At her throat was a gold disc tied with a black ribbon. Her nose was large, disproportionate, her chin pointed and jutting. She was the ugliest woman the child had ever seen, redeemed not by the slightest softness anywhere. She was so ugly that she was almost funny. She carried a cane with her and the child did not laugh. She looked around for the dark boy, but he had disappeared.

The child dropped down in the passageway at the advance

of this terror, expecting the cane to be plied upon her back. The ugly woman arrived above her.

'Whose is this cripple?' she called, but the silence held. 'To whom do you belong, cripple?'

The dark boy appeared, all sheepish grin, from a cubicle further down.

'I might have known she'd be yours,' the woman said,

'She's The Hedgehog,' he said.

'The family Hedgehog?'

The dark boy acquiesced smugly.

'Well, well, well. They'll pull you open one day, Tom Squit, and leave you out on the roof for the jackdaws.'

'My name is not Tom Squit.'

'What is it then?' she said, stooping down to examine the little cripple, not really interested in the boy any more.

'It's a secret,' he said, his tone rising but failing to rouse her.

'Hello, Lady Hedgehog,' she said kindly, quizzically. 'How much does she understand?'

'She sees through you like a bottle of piss,' he yelled.

The woman rose to face him and the child watched him fall into confusion under her glare. She turned back to the child, presented her with her hand which the child could not refuse and by which she was led away.

They passed the boy who was in the mouth of a red cubicle containing a dumpy woman with golden hair who, the child saw briefly, was stuffing a shawl into her mouth to stop herself laughing, her big breasts wobbling violently under the repression. They passed out of the long room, down a short staircase that led directly into a high, wide room, walled with dark hangings and filled with many couches of many sizes, all draped, some occupied by lolling, dreamy women, all here dressed finely. Beneath their lolling, as the child was led through, she noted a flicker of alertness cross their features. Still there was no daylight. The child began to believe they were underground, began to feel the structure of the Inn as a great weight above her.

The woman led her across this open room to a heavy door which she unlocked with several keys, opened and ushered the child through. Abruptly, the child found herself in a room full of daylight that came so suddenly that she was giddied for a moment. Long windows poured the light in from three sides and the child began to feel very, very high. This feeling was magnified by the smallness of the room; it was higher than it was deep and below and between all this window space it was so cramped with furniture that there was hardly any space to breathe in. At the centre of the room stood an immense desk; around the walls, below and between the windows were bookshelves, many-doored cupboards, many-drawered chests. The desk was stacked with papers, crowded with bottles, pens and strange ivory and steel implements, all arranged with a neatness that seemed cruel. On every surrounding surface there were strange objects: glass receptacles which gleamed, mirrors concave and convex, various polished bones, racks of phials precisely labelled. The woman had left her lost and oppressed amongst all this and had gone behind the desk, had seated herself there and was laying out pens and paper, was putting on a pair of spectacles, circles of thick glass in black metal frames.

'Now then, my child. Firstly you must be welcomed. I wonder how much you do understand.'

The child stared blankly, understanding quite enough not to betray anything unless it was to protect something more important.

'Oh, you do understand, don't you?' The woman was confident and persuasive. 'But you have no tongue, am I right? You see, I've always known about you. You are twelve years old. You were born in midwinter, in a room not far from where we are now. You will be taken back there one day, when the time is right. Old Mag looks after you, doesn't she? Listen to Mag, my child. She will tell you all you need to know, whenever you need to know it. She is old and grown loose, but Mag was Lady here before any of us here now were ever born. Now then, up on to the desk with you, my child.'

The child did not comprehend this instruction any more than she could have comprehended an instruction to fly. She stared at the woman, trying not to betray her real bewilderment but failing.

'Come now, you can find your way up there, can't you? You're a nimble enough little thing when you go hopping about in the barns, so I hear. You'll need to be nimble when you come to work with us here. Up you get now.'

The sense of betrayal which these words registered in her brought a rush of anger into her head. The woman sat with her chin still on her knuckles, the smile still in her teeth, waiting for her. She bared her own teeth in mockery and further, in rage; she beat her fists down upon the surface of the desk, sending a recoil of pain up into her armpits and producing only the dullest of thuds on the solid wooden surface.

'Good, child; good, good. Now, up you get.'

She summoned a little spittle in her dry mouth and she spat it across the desk-top, spattering the shine.

'Wipe it clean.' This was a command. The smile had gone and, without moving, the woman was suddenly violent.

The child looked about her for an escape. Around her were the slabs of window-light – she could have leapt into one of them, bringing the glass down with her in a million splinters, shattering enormously, flying out into the pure air beyond with the whole structure tumbling down behind her; but the instinct for this was thwarted as she imagined herself rebuffed by the hard glass, tumbling down broken amongst the black edges of the furniture.

'Wipe it clean. Dirty little girl. Wipe it clean.'

These reiterations were not necessary. They brought tears to her eyes. She stretched across and smeared her ragged sleeve over the desk-top, making it no cleaner, dripping great tears down where she had smeared. But the tears were acceptable; it was not cleanliness but humiliation that was required. The woman was propitiated.

'Good,' she said. 'Now. Up you come.'

And the child was writhing and swinging jerkily with the edge of the desk in her belly, her hands sliding about on the wood for a purchase. Then she caught her foot on something and pushed and was up, high above the floor, in the full light of the windows, crouched and reduced, with the woman's head on a level with hers, watching her.

'Stand up.'

This was done with difficulty and, once done, she felt hideously unstable. In the barns she was cushioned on all sides by comfortable darkness; up here, the light threatened to sweep her out. She could see through the windows now – roofs, courtyards, streets, the upper clutterings of the strange city beyond, multiplying into giddy distances; and the sky, an infinite hazy blue in which it was hard to breathe, like a sea. And down below her, the woman's ringed eyes watched with cold complacency.

After a while, the woman rose and went away to one of the side cabinets, her back to the child, selecting implements, noting things down in big books.

'I intend to make certain explorations of you, my child,' she said without turning. 'You will not be hurt.' She turned to find the child's face waiting for her. She smiled fractionally. 'Good. Now . . .' She advanced. She was carrying a small brass bowl, a brass syringe rattling within it, a small, white linen towel over one arm, and a small purple bottle in the other hand. 'We must have you out of those foul clothes.' She noted the child's alarm with the thin smile stretched like an incision. 'Hurry, if you please.'

She undid the ties of her smock and it fell from her, shuddered off. She stood and shivered, the coldness of the light peeling her. She bowed down under the weight of her bare deformity, falling down on her hands, her arse up in the air, but still not finding balance, going down on her elbows.

The woman laid a cold, flat hand upon her side to still her. The other hand came upon her buttock. The hands began to move across her, over her back and neck, into her hair to feel the shape of her skull, down her arms, under her chest and belly. The touch was hard and methodical, reading the surface and the structure below the surface. The fingers felt amongst her features, into her mouth, strange and dry and making her mouth dry. They kneaded at the numb lump of her spine and ran down her back to her buttocks which they parted and probed between. She felt them insinuated into the slit of her vagina.

'You'll do well enough,' the woman informed her. 'I will now draw off a little water, so we can be sure that you are wholesome.'

Peering underneath her, the child saw the gleam of the syringe and immediately felt its cold point pressed into her. A burning shudder went into her belly. It sucked with a sharp pinch and she lost control of her bladder. The woman held the bowl under her and she dribbled into it.

'You may come down now,' the woman said, moving to her cabinet again, leaving the child on the desk-top, paralysed. Little clinkings of glass and tricklings of liquid were heard. The child twisted her head to see the woman raise a clear glass flask into the light.

She began to weep, hard tears that twisted in her belly. She drew herself in upon her knees, wrinkling up under the exposure, the invasion she had suffered, the despoiling. She thought of Mag, and of her nightly self-examination and it came to her that she had been given, under the professional fingering of the ugly woman, her body. Before, it had been a pleasant lodging, a warm expansion of her straying thoughts, to be roused and eased, filled and emptied, moved with her small desires and responsive to her small pleasures, snug even in its distortions. Now it had been noted and examined, was at this moment being scratched with a short quill into papers on the woman's cabinet; it had become a part of the world beyond her. Her body was now an object and she was now its victim, its prisoner, condemned within it.

The woman turned and surveyed the object on her desk as if surprised to find it still there.

'Down you get and we'll find you something beautiful to wear,' she said briskly, going to the door, opening and calling, 'Here!' into a muffled noise of laughter that swam up into the room from the chamber beyond it.

The child slid from the desk, barking her knees and elbows and finally huddling into the dark of the floor, gathering her nakedness around her, looking dully up at the great furniture that towered over her.

A figure appeared at the door, she was indicated and a pair of eyes peered down at her.

'Something long and blue, I would have thought,' the woman said. 'Something loose to accommodate the ir-regularity of the shape. You see? The back? Good.'

The attendant left and the woman came and knelt down offering a small glass of yellow liquid. The child took it; it burned briefly down her throat and spread its fire into her chest like a pair of torturer's hands. The woman brought a blanket and covered the child, indicated a chair. The child, giddy now and a little nauseous as the burning had settled into her gut, submitted to being sat in the chair, high-backed, high-armed, polished leather, studded and hard for her little peeled body.

The woman, moving efficiently about the room, was talking to her, looking at her occasionally to see that she was attending, for they were things of consequence. But the child could not hold them. Her hearing fumbled the words and the meaning failed to cohere. She was asked frequently if she understood; and her look seemed to assure the woman that she did understand; and this, she later came to realise, was an achievement.

The attendant returned with a length of blue material, faded in pale streaks, but embroidered into a garment with tarnished silver thread.

'Ah,' said the ugly woman, taking it. 'That is the very piece. Good.' She then handed her out of the chair, removed the blanket and lifted the garment, billowing it out until it fell over her head like a dust-sheet. She felt the woman's hands tugging at it and eventually her head came through. Her arms were grabbed and shoved into the long sleeves and it was done.

'Come now.'

She was taken by the hand, firmly, towards one of the windows. She felt herself pulled towards that curtainfall of light and she closed her eyes expecting, quite irrationally, to be propelled through it.

'Don't close your eyes, my child. Watch everything.'

She opened her eyes and, as she did so, the woman swung open a long cupboard door and the child found herself framed in a sheet of mirror-glass, her stooped shoulders exaggerated in its cold fall, exaggerated in this blue sack that drooped down on to the floor round her. Only her head was free, floating within its wild aura of red hair, alarmed and open; the only thing she recognised, it was a betrayer, an intimate sister whose testimony had sold her, now brought to confront her with a cold wall of pain between them.

The woman behind her was part of the furnishings, looking over her, struggling amongst the child's hair to find the knots that had, some long while ago, been put in to tie back the mess.

'We must have this combed and oiled before you go back below. We want them in no doubt as to where you've been. They will leave you alone when they know.'

What followed was faint and faded. She had become lost

and she submitted to it, retreating into a distant part of herself. She was led down into the great room again and sat on a stool whilst the attendant woman combed out and oiled her wild hair, smoothing and straightening it into a long, perfect rope, ribboned and beaded, a heavy weight across her shoulder like a halter. Whilst this was being done the great room was slowly filled with women, all beautifully dressed in long, supple gowns, cut tight about their breasts and hips, in plain colours but of many shades: reds and golds, blacks and blues, deep blue and pale blue, pale almost to white. All had their hair swept back, combed and oiled, braided and bound up. They were each distinct, but they were all the same. They were all moving now, coming and going, settling, rising, none seemed still for a second. The movement seemed at first quite random, but she realised soon that there was some sort of game or dance in progress at the centre of the room; amongst the couches and chairs a pattern was being stepped out. The women were rising to join, or leaving it, all according to some ritual. There was music. There was the dark boy sitting in a far corner with his fiddle, sawing and sawing. The tune itself was so far away from her that she could not follow it. The boy was completely separate from her now. He was only a messenger, a musician, a servant. She didn't even want him to notice her. He did not. And the dance went on and on, the same, the same although its pattern never became apparent to her; she never had the satisfaction of predicting what one of them would do next. They laughed and talked as they moved, the beautiful ladies. She had the idea that they were all being wound up in this dance like toys, gathering momentum for the moment when their energy and beauty would be spinning free and they would be sent off into brilliant corridors, up stairways to unimaginable rooms where they would burn and glow and radiate their perfections. One day, she too; whatever it was. It was a mystery, but only superficially so. It seemed so fixed, so planned, so performed. If it was a mystery then these women themselves didn't seem to know what it was about. She wondered if they expected her to grow straight in time, to become like them. She would cheat them in that, and there was a strength in knowing this, even though she sat there in her borrowed gown, its fabric so gentle on her flesh with her hair tamed and tied down, and her posture, as if of its own accord, grown rigid, doll-like, waiting on the edge of the dance.

She felt a hand wrench at her and she turned to see Old Mag glowering at her, glancing about her with bared teeth, comfortingly familiar in her courtyard aprons and her courtyard reek. The child leapt to her, passed with her through the dancers who did not seem to notice them. Mag gripped her wrist and pulled. The music, as they passed near, did not falter a note.

Out of the great chamber they were back in the corridors, dark and echoing, past doors pregnant with voices. They came to a broad staircase and began to descend. Mag had not spoken nor looked at the child since she had taken her. Now, half-way down this staircase, she halted, gripped at the brass banister, shook the child free of her other hand and gripped her own side in exhaustion, her old face bloated with hurt. The child watched, strange in her new paraphernalia, sadly.

'I'm not dead yet,' Mag said, looking back up the stairs. 'They can have you when I'm dead. I'm not dead yet. Tell them that!'

Back in the stall, Mag undressed the child and sacked her more suitably, folding the blue gown up and stuffing it away somewhere in the mountain of her rubbish. She then undid the hair braid, sniffing the oil appreciatively, wiping some on to her own hair and chuckling, leaving the child's head disordered, tacky and itchy. Above all else, the child was weary; she reached up her arms, asking to be lifted up into her manger.

Mag laughed at her. 'Get yourself up there, my lady,' she said and left.

She tried, clambering on Mag's box, and dangling with aching limbs, but had no strength to swing her weight up. She dropped down on to Mag's bundles, burrowed and slept. She awoke in the night to find she had been pitched up into the manger, to find Mag muttering away in the lamplight below her as if nothing was changed.

But the change, over the succeeding days, the succeeding seasons, was undeniable. She moved among her familiar haunts but a sense of waiting now possessed her, surrounded her with a blur of dissatisfaction. She sulked now increasingly continuously, sitting in corners, under old tables in the courtyard stack, at a window high in the barns looking at the rain across the broken roofs, the interminable rain that returned every season, heavy and crushing, excluding everything else in its greyness; a mood from which the sunshine, the ice and mist were merely respites. The buildings dripped and, within, their darkness grew fetid. She was waiting for something that was coming inevitably upon her. She did not know what it was, and she did not want it; but she was waiting for it nevertheless, was locked into the waiting.

Then one night she awoke with Mag reaching into the manger and tugging at her, her face dark, the lantern down on the ground behind her and the two strange men waiting in the doorway. She was brought down, still mostly asleep. Her shift was removed and the blue gown was rediscovered and fitted over her. It itched on her sleepy skin. A cursory brushing and washing buffeted her head, tugging and slopping; but the men were growing impatient. Mag handed her over to them and they took her to her mother.

— 3 —

Mully, Lady of Ladies of the Three Stars Inn, lay dying in the bed in which she had borne her children, at the heart of her Inn. She had borne fifteen children, all healthy, and then The Hedgehog whose awful parturition had torn her inside and fouled her breeding forever. The years after this had been consumed in fits and violences, in immense drug comas; in the long, losing struggle to hold on to the rage for living that had, before The Hedgehog, made her feel immortal. Now, at last, defeat was upon her. They built up the fires in the wide hearths at the opposite ends of her room. Tiers of candles threw a glare over her sweated face, its black eyes and long cheeks, the bone structure pushing to the surface. Perhaps someone believed that the mountains of unusual light which streamed forth from the candles would keep the dark at bay; perhaps she herself believed that. Her black hair had been arranged on her pillows into a great black sunburst with her face, all sockets, at the centre.

In the middle of the pupils of the eyes a glint of the cold malevolence still waited.

In the room, keeping vigil in a high-backed chair, was the master of the Inn, Edwin Cloud, acknowledged as her husband but known to be father to none of her children. His potency was in the running of the Inn, the marshalling of the anthill about its queen who lived, who had always lived, entirely upon her enormous sensuality. The men who had been brought to couple with her, to supply the fluid necessary to her tireless generative machinery, had all gone, one after the other, quickly. There were legends that she had murdered them, devoured them raw. In fact, Cloud had sent them all on their various ways, some proud, some fearful, some destroyed; but gone, all of them. She thought of none of them, knew none of their names.

And now Mully was dying; and the news of her dying had entered every awareness in the place, a premonition of the end of the world. To most of those now living in the Inn, she was a creature of legend; but all knew of her and were touched with dread at the idea of her dying.

Edwin Cloud sat quietly now, awaiting the end, his fleshy face still, his small eyes alert. He had a long staff which he bore with him wherever he went, five foot of polished ebony tipped with a golden sphere. This now stood between his knees, his fingers folded around it. He would know the moment she was not there. What he would do at that moment was not known but was intensely thought on by the family, her children who were gathered at the ceremony of her passing, hoping for their inheritance, each expecting something special, something which would raise them above the others, each fearful lest they should be sucked into the coming vacuum.

Of the sixteen children she had borne, four had died in childhood, carried off by fever or accident, four great gaps of grieving in her remembrance. Three more had left the Inn in various circumstances: a girl with a lover; a boy seduced away by the soldiers to die; and sad Woley who had just got lost, aged thirteen, strayed off somewhere and never found his way home. The girl had attempted, years later, to return, but Cloud had caught her and sent her back where she came from. To leave the Inn was final. Nine remained – six parasites, two inheritors, and The Hedgehog.

The parasites were all waiting in the room with Cloud, watching not their mother, but him. There were the four tall girls brought down from their apartments, high and secluded in the Inn's highest and brightest corridors where they played endless card-games foretelling an infinity of fortunes for themselves and each other, nurturing their vanities, growing from children into women without noticing. After their elder sister's defection, they were shut away from all such advantages. Their mother planned for them to be perfected for hand-picked husbands who would be there when the girls were ready. As she had grown older, her ideas had drifted off into impossibilities whilst the girls grew selfish and spiteful with the awkwardness of childhood gone hard in their otherwise slack frames. They were called Deeda, Glarry, Mitte and Fintaniste, and they stood at their mother's dying exposed and alarmed, naked and lumpish in their fine gowns, all their high idiosyncrasies reduced, in the glare of death, to pathetic uniformity.

Apart from them, across four yards of clear floor, stood their younger brothers, Milon and Porsque, a pair of scalded adolescents who inhabited a hatred of each other so intense that neither could waste a fart that might offend the other. They fought each other like dogs. Milon had lost an eye to Porsque. Porsque limped permanently on the foot Milon had crushed. They always fought, never more poisonously than when they were still, as now, watching each other with the pus of their fantasies oozing visibly on their faces. The only times when they had ever been at peace together were when their mother had taken them, one under each arm, and had pulled them to her breasts where they could forget everything except her warmth and her soft, soft voice chiding them sweetly from a long way away. With the loss of this they were doomed to fall, locked together, into the pit.

The inheritors were the two elder boys, now the tall young men, Blade and Gray. They were the firstborn and, with Cullen, had been taken under the tutelage of Edwin Cloud from their first independence. Cullen had been the outsider, fast and mutinous; it was he who had gone for a soldier rather than face the combined and organised front of his two elder brothers for the inheritance of the Inn which, from their earliest discretion, each had seen as their sole birthright. Blade and Gray remained, the executives of Edwin Cloud, the initiates of the business. Both were tall, dark and taciturn. Blade, the elder, was entirely without discernible character; infinitely meticulous, precisely perceptive, absolutely alone in all he did or was. Gray had his brother's cold competence but also a strain of sensual curiosity that he exercised on selected Ladies from the great room, noting with a distant eye the motions of pleasure as they shivered through him. He was more voluble than his brother, putting their joint will into operation; he listened to Blade and conceded to his brother the virtues of minuteness and patience. Gray was, most importantly, the active force of the family. Cloud was only of the family by courtesy, not being a creature of Mully's loins. Gray was their mother's representative, always behaving as if he had come directly down from her, charged with authority: in fact he was the most formal in her presence, the one she took least often in her arms. Even the inscrutable Blade submitted to Mully's embraces, sleeping lightly on her bed, stretched out straight beside her restless sprawl.

Blade and Gray were not in the room with the others, having business below; namely the journey down into the stables to fetch the last of the family, the creature they never spoke of near their mother, and only to each other rarely; but this did not stop them, Gray especially, from considering her. They were under no instruction to fetch her, but Gray had known his duty at once and Blade deferred to his sense of family. However much she abominated it, Mully must be brought to face the creature once more, if only to issue the order for its disposal.

The six children who waited in the room nursed their own outraged selves, each bruised here under the impact of something bigger than them. They resented, one and all, the summons to this glaring, stifling room; and yet, the death of their mother was, for the first time in their selfish little lives, an event they could not avoid. They had suddenly been brought down to face a sense of duty which they had never before imagined existed for them. They shuffled, wishing at once that it would all be over and they could be loosed back into their claimless existences; and wishing that it could in some desperate way be averted, for they sensed, all of them, at one level or another, that what was about to happen would tear gaps in their shelters and admit something beastly. All of them willed it not to be, and all felt the impotence of such a willing, and none of them had any bastion of character with which to confront such an impotence.

Cloud sat silent, the thin-shanked man with the heavy globe of a head that contained everything necessary to the existence of them all. He alone waited with inscrutable calm. When Gray's cane rapped quietly at the door, Cloud's were the only eyes that did not turn. He watched the bed. The doors opened, both of them, noiselessly, and Blade and Gray came in together with The Hedgehog between them. The watchers, apart from Cloud, recoiled, some vocally, some physically, at the presence of their monstrous sister. The boys would have gone for her; Porsque even started forward, but the attitudes of Blade and Gray, and of Cloud also, were too firm to admit him such a release. They drew back, both of them, wincing as their violence was sheathed awkwardly. The four girls felt their sister as an assault upon their flesh and reacted according to which part of their sensibilities – skin, stomach, structure or sex – was particularly outraged by this visitation.

Cloud eventually turned to the child who was looking about the room for something at which she might direct herself. She was bewildered, sleepy and lost up here. She had expected the tall ugly woman.

'Do you know what we are?' Cloud asked her gently.

She advanced to look at him, looked back at the others, avoided looking at the big bed in which, she sensed, lay something fearful. She looked back at Cloud and met his gaze, felt it go into her.

'Do you know what we are, child?' he asked again, his voice small and liquid.

'She does not speak, sir,' Gray said.

'No. Her tongue is grown on to the bottom of her mouth,' Cloud observed. 'But she does understand. She understands very well. Come here.'

She came to him, offered her hands, palms upward. He was diverted by this gesture. He took the hands carefully between his long fingers, propping his staff against his shoulder. She noticed a black ring on his right forefinger, sunk deep into the flesh.

'These, child, are all your brothers and sisters. Blade and Gray brought you here. The girls are Deeda, Glarry, Mitte, Fintaniste. The young lads are Milon and Porsque. You are Mariole. We know you well here, better than you know yourself. Now then, Mariole. You must go to that bed over there. In that bed lies your mother, your mother and their mother. You must go and show yourself to her, and you must not be afraid. She is going to die very soon and she needs to have knowledge of you before she dies. You understand why this is so.' This last was a statement of fact. He released her hands and settled back, clasping his staff.

She held his gaze still, saw his eyes lift in a question. She turned and surveyed the general malevolence of her ugly siblings. One of the boys muttered something venomous, the one with the eye-patch.

'What did you say, boy?' Cloud asked sharply.

'If she hurts my mother, I'll kill her,' the boy said, clearing his throat as he spoke, a tremble in his voice.

'That will not be in your power,' Gray said. 'Be quiet.'

The child moved away from these exchanges, out into the middle of the room which was empty, a wide expanse of layered rugs. She felt herself propelled towards the great bed, four-postered, like a cage without bars. From the banks of bedding something moved, a sort of writhe buried a long way down. She looked back behind her to see if any of the others had registered it, but they had not; they were now only watching her. She was in a scene, playing a part which she did not understand; but it had to be played and a bubble of self-confidence rose in her. She would play well. She was suddenly in command.

She had come to the edge of the bed, her head level with the piles of bedding but unable to see over them. She reached up, grabbed with one hand, pulled up the blue gown with the other and scrabbled her foot for a toe-hold, found one somewhere between the mattresses and pushed herself off the floor, rising lightly and falling forward on her hands among the bedding.

There in its centre, small amongst its expanse, lay Mully, her mother, her eyes barely holding an ember of seeing, her hands above the covers, fists clenched, but without power, only with rigidity. Her hair splayed out from her head still jet-black, not a trace of grey. Her face was empty but for the eyes. Two minute dribbles of opaque saliva ran symmetrically from the corners of her clamped mouth.

Cloud had risen and had advanced behind the child, but not close enough to interfere, just to watch. She felt him there, but she did not turn. She shuffled forward and knelt over the woman. With the edge of her gown, she wiped away the saliva, wiped the mucus from the corners of the eyes, brushing delicately; but the material was rough against the fragile surface of that face, so she pulled it out of the way and touched with her fingers the pale features, the ridges of bone over which the creased skin was stretched tight. The eyes stared upward, unmoving. The child looked up at the roof of the bed and saw to her alarm that it was a mirror in which she was placed with a clarity that unnerved her, a cold, flat statement of her face and the face of the woman, both pairs of eyes looking down. Did the woman see her? Did she know her? This was her mother. Did she feel anything for her? The mirror had no answers, only its cold, flat statement of fact. What followed? She looked at the faces, side by side, to see if there was any affinity of features, but there was none that she could see. Her face was rounded out, the other was a mask. In the noses, perhaps. But dwarfing such a little detail was the contrast of form; the other so straight and long and fine, she so hunched and hobbled. But then she was alive and alert, and the other was nothing. She looked away from the mirror back at the reality, hoping that the mirror had distorted something, but it had not. She began to slither back towards the edge of the bed.

Something remained to be done. To slip away thus would be a defeat. She crawled back to the woman, placed her hands gently over the eyes and brought her face down, her own eyes closed, against the face below her, brushing her cheek against the other cheek, blowing softly across the mouth and nostrils. Then she left.

Cloud was there to help her down. She stood by him as he leaned over, then she crouched on the floor at his feet, tucking herself into his shadow.

A voice came from the bed, the woman's voice, her mother.

'What's happening, Cloud? What was that?' It was a voice deep with breath heaved up from the bottom of old lungs.

'That was your child, Mully.'

'Which one?'

'The last one.'

'The very last one?'

'The very last.'

There was a pause. Then, 'It's made me angry, Cloud,' the tone unchanged, 'very angry. I understood that she was dead. I ordered it.'

'I would have told you if she had died, Mully.'

'She should have died.'

'Once perhaps: at first. But it cannot be done now.'

There was another pause.

'Am I supposed to bless her, Cloud? Is that what she's come for? I refuse to bless her.'

'As you wish.'

'Are they all still here?'

'Yes.'

'All right, all right. Leave me now. You've done your duty. You've done enough.'

He straightened, looked down at the child, indicated with his stick across the room. She moved away, headed for a space near his chair where she would still be under his shelter. As she moved, with him behind her shepherding her from his discreet distance, she heard the voice from the bed once more, lifting out from its depths.

'I can't . . . I can't . . .'

The child reached her place beside the chair and stood there as Cloud settled himself back into it, not looking at her, looking across at the bed; as they were all looking, waiting, the time slowing down into a long, sustained ache around them with the roaring and falling of the fires the only animation, and that growing less and less real; larger and larger, and yet further and further away.

And in the bed Mully at last lets go, begins the final fall, feeling everything rush past her as she sinks and spreads, a dissolution that causes her to catch at her breath, but it's all going too fast; the gravity upon her is too great for her breath to be caught, the effort too much. She recalls briefly and brilliantly the form of that strange creature that climbed over her and touched her. It seems only now, at the very end, on the very lip of death, that the sensations of that touch come clear to her; before they were blurred and remote, now she recalls them precisely. The fingers move across her scaled eyelids, a warm, fat cheek pushes down upon her cheek, and breath, sweet, young breath blows across her, sliding down her throat like wine. She does not connect these sensations with a person, but with an abstraction of life itself. It seems that life itself has touched her, finally, making its farewell, warm and soft and breathing. It was never any more than that, but that was enough, that was it. It was intimate and clear and motiveless; and with the awareness of this, with its vow and its beauty, she flows out of this life and is dissolved into whatever follows.

She died so quietly that no one knew she was dead for a long while, apart from the child who sensed the change in the room at once. She felt quite suddenly that this ache of waiting and watching had become pointless; but she did not like to make a move, assuming they all felt it and that there was some other expected formality.

At last Cloud turned to her and raised his eyebrows, white smears above his thin, blue eyes. She found his look sad and tears came into her eyes, squeezed out of the weight of his look.

'Blade,' he said, turning his head; a signal.

Blade stirred forward unhurriedly and crossed the floor to the bed, leant across, looked back at Cloud and tilted his head down briefly.

The girls, Deeda, Glarry, Mitte and Fintaniste, at once set up a wailing, a low discordant unity of sound that seemed, for all its abruptness, as if they had been waiting for the signal to blurt it out to order. The boys, Porsque and Milon, turned to each other and muttered violence. Gray crossed to the bed, standing at the other side to Blade, and together they folded layers of covers over the corpse, straightening them out as if to tidy the bed, as if it contained now nothing. The unity of the room was imploded; the silence and the aching was now released in nervous confusions. Only Cloud remained firm and still.

The child was weary and bewildered and begged within herself to be taken back to the stable where all this might be swallowed up in the night and lost amongst the other dreams. She allowed her legs to fold under her and she leaned against the hard side of Cloud's chair, drawing up her knees and tucking down her head. Here she fell at once into a black sleep, her head throbbing and her limbs twisted. It was not a sleep that brought her rest, but a pit which digested her suddenly and regurgitated her into an awareness of the room full of muffled movement, full of legs and carrying a low, argumentative talking; then back down again into the dark; then up again with the room still and dark apart from the great beds of embers in the facing grates, and from the chimneys a distant, hollow booming.

She stirred herself and felt the aching in her joints as she shifted. She coiled and struggled to her feet, stumbling forward into the room, feeling all their eyes upon her. But between the two fireglows, the room was empty. She was truly alone. Except for the figure in the bed. She crossed to it. She had no fear of it. Her only fear was of the door opening, but she was soon in a position to dive for cover under the hangings below the bed should a hand touch the door.

The bed was now dark. She felt out but her arms did not reach across. She clambered up again and felt forward, through the layers and banks of bedding, reaching for that flesh, that coldness, if only to reassure herself that what she remembered of the preceding hours had been real. She stretched forward, edged forward amongst the dark bedding, and came to the other side. The relief was undeniable, and she fell back amongst the bedclothes which suffused her in their heady, sweet scent amidst which she fell into a real sleep, filled with quiet music and gentle touching.

They found the child in the morning and were frightened of her, the whores who came for the bedding to carry it down to the furnace. She appeared in the bed like some changeling, the spirit of their dead mistress returned in a cruel metamorphosis. Their squeals woke the child who sat up as the room filled with eyes, women's eyes. They were another breed of women here, not the thick-fleshed women she had seen in the long room, in their cubicles, the high-backed ladies who danced for the dark boy. These were older,

uglier, wall-eyed, scarred, hare-lipped, some with bald patches
and blotched faces. They stood away from her as she roused,
some muttering old charms, some shrieking intermittently.

Blade and Gray came and the women were sent scurrying
off. Gray closed the door upon them and locked it.

Blade meanwhile had come to the bedside and was standing over her, considering her. She looked up, looking for
some response in his face, the lack of which was beginning
to frighten her. Gray had crossed the room silently and
surprised her as he sat suddenly on the other side of the bed.
She turned but her inquiry was thrown back from the big,
cold mask of his smile.

She looked up and saw them in the high mirror stooped
over her, their heads down. She did not want to see their
faces, looked up between their heads to her own open face
in the mirror.

'Well?' – from her left, Blade.

'It must be done' – from her right, Gray.

'You say so' – Blade.

'You don't agree?' – Gray.

'I have no opinion. I am not the authority on family matters.'

'She is a perversion of the family, a cancer upon it.'

'You say so.'

'You are not going to oppose me in this?'

'I cannot see why it was not done at birth if it had to be
done at all. I cannot see that Mother's death makes it
necessary now. I lack your poetic appreciation of such
things. But no, I will not oppose you, Gray.'

'Will you support me?'

'Why do you need my support? Or my complicity, which
is really what you want?'

'Against Cloud. She made a mark on him.'

'Ah. Is that why it's necessary now?'

'Perhaps. Possibly.'

'Cloud is an old man. His turn is coming very soon. With
Mother's death, anyway, he ceases to be central.'

'You underestimate him.'

A pause. In the mirror she could see their brows, their
black, oiled hair swept back into small pigtails. They were
studying each other, confronting each other across her.

'Will you let this come between us? This little thing?'

'I cannot see its necessity.'

'Are you afraid of doing it?'

'Hardly afraid, my dear brother.'

'Something in your guts? Something turns you from it.'

'I do not think like that. I am not like you, Gray.'

'Let's do it then.'

'I will hold her. Do what you like.'

'You will be a part of it.'

'I will hold her.'

She felt hands pushed down upon her shoulders. She saw, reflected, Gray move, pull a pillow out from the heap at her head, hold it above her. She realised what was coming, but she was not afraid. She felt stronger than the pair of them, not subject to their desires. She drew in a deep breath as the pillow was pushed down on to her face, its texture coarse, the weight upon it heavy with violence. She held the breath within her tightly. It buoyed her up under the weight. After a while her chest began to hurt, her mind began to blur, a pressure began to swell her, pushing behind her eyes. She wanted to struggle, but remembered that her strength, her only strength, lay in her stillness. The grip upon her shoulders, the weight upon her face remained enormous.

Quite suddenly the grip slipped from her shoulders and, a moment later, the weight pulled from her face. She gasped quickly, sucking the air back into her, feeling its healing flood through her, her head giddied and her stomach turning; but all growing still again.

'Why did you let go?' Gray said, panting and angry.

'You could have finished it alone. Why didn't you?'

'You'll betray me in this.'

'How could I possibly betray you, Gray?'

'You are not with me, Blade.'

'Perhaps, finally, not. Your motives, perhaps, seem a little too personal for my tastes. There. Now you have it. But don't let it deter you. It will not rise between us. Come now, Gray, it's not important. Finish it if you need to, but quickly now. We have more necessary tasks this morning.'

Gray held his brother's face in his glare, seeking to overbear him, seeking to throw him down from this moment if he would not be pulled up with it; but he could not. He reached under the tail of his coat and withdrew, smoothly and abruptly, without looking away from his brother, a long-bladed knife. He held this up in the space between their faces.

'If you're going to slash her about with that,' Blade said, 'this is neither the time nor place. I will oppose you in that, brother.'

'You have no stomach for reality, Blade.'

'I certainly lack your sensual delicacy. I am a plain man, Gray. Now put away your toy.'

The knife was lowered to her throat. His hand he placed beside it, fingers spread over her neck. She met his eyes, his profound malevolence; but again her senses refused to fear him. It was a game he was playing with his brother in which she had become a token. If he was to slide that knife into her throat, she would cease to be an active token; she would gush blood all over his clean hands, all over his mother's bed: he would not do it. He did not. He gripped the collar of the long dress and ran the edge of the knife-blade down its length, ripping it open, pulling the fabric aside and sliding the knife adroitly back under his coat. He looked down upon her body, twisted aside to accommodate its distortion. He ran his hands over her, feeling the thickness of the flesh, the child-fat that covered her, pinching it to feel how it was firming.

'Ah. I thought your interest was more personal,' Blade observed, a detached relief easing his tone. 'A pity for you that she's family, isn't it?'

'That's no restriction, as far as I know.'

'You joke, Gray.'

'Fintaniste.'

'Now you're lying.'

'Am I?'

'You would never have dared whilst mother was alive, and you've hardly had opportunity since. Come on. We're wasting time with this.' He turned and walked off.

Gray continued to gaze down at her; she continued to gaze back, finding his face preferable to confronting the pale, peeled and twisted thing that hung above her.

'I'll be coming for you,' he said, 'one of these nights. I know where you are. Remember me. Expect me. I am the future here. You don't even exist.'

Ah, but I do, she thought, and you don't know where I am. I am here, safe inside of me and you won't ever be able to find me.

They had left her then, alone in the big bed. She heard a key turn in the door and she wondered why she was being kept there. She looked up at her exposure in the mirror. The women had lit the candles which flickered light across her face from both sides. She wondered why he had touched her like that, like the ugly woman had touched her. The touching had meaning, brought her body into play as something to be considered. She began to consider herself, to note the pads of flesh that gathered over her ribs, the incised cushion of flesh at the fork of her legs which she touched, found the space there, the entry into her which they had both sought and probed. It was an active place that prickled with sensation as she dabbled into it. It was a discovery. She saw herself make that discovery in the mirror and was another person looking down upon herself. She closed her eyes to come out of that scrutiny and the sensations spread slowly through her belly, a small bursting of delighted nerves. It was a secret suddenly given her. It was not, perhaps, entirely new to her, but it was, for the first time, explicit.

It was right that on her mother's great bed, in which all her mother's children had been got and born, that the latest of those children, the youngest and the freest should have found her way so far towards the centre of herself. Mully, indeed, had not got all that much further.

Cloud came in and found her later, huddled in blankets. She had deserted the bed for a warm niche by the faint embers of one of the fires. He unlocked the door, came in furtively, and was actually surprised to see her there. He had left at once, called along corridors and brought them running who had bundled her up and carried her down to Old Mag who had wept with joy to see her.

'I thought they'd done you away ... I thought they'd eaten you up ... They took all mine from me years and years ago and then they gave me you. I found you and they let me keep you ... and I thought they'd taken you ...' and so on, with variations, for many hours.

The child was glad of this effusiveness, curled up in it snugly; but she did not trust it. If it was meant, it was only there now and might not be there tomorrow; and if it was there tomorrow, if it was always there, it was no longer enough.

The death of Mully brought about changes in the family and in the Inn which all of them had sensed approaching that night, but which none of them had foreseen in any detail; except perhaps Edwin Cloud who saw and understood everything, or seemed to, sitting in his dark office, reduced to clerking the mundane complexities of the many lives under his charge.

Porsque and Milon, the vicious boys, were released at once by Blade from their childhood. Their room was taken from them, stripped, cleaned, given to other uses. They were provided with small, close chambers with bedsteads and bare walls, apart from each other. Blade dominated their lives, woke them early and dragged them behind him wherever he went, turned and slashed their faces with a short cane whenever they muttered, and often when they did not. They were at first cowed like dogs, hardly daring to go to sleep for fear of him appearing at their bedsides, demanding what they were doing, what they were thinking, what they had said when they thought he wasn't there. After a few weeks of this, they began to be drawn together, grafted on to each other's interests and united against the tyranny he exerted upon them. This was the first stage of their re-education. They snatched corners of time together and swapped obscenities upon him. They incubated a plan to kill him, to overhaul him with daggers and slash him to rags; but he was waiting for them. He confronted them one day with their secret, striking them at unpredictable moments in his long denunciation of them. He locked them in their rooms for two days and they fell into separate despair, each tormented by the certainty of the other's betrayal. When he released them, he was entirely changed. 'You are my brothers,' he said. 'We will be together now.' And they were. He began to give them tasks, separately at first, then together; menial at first, finding and fetching, first objects then people. At last he gave them his punishments to enact, firstly under his supervision, later on their own initiatives; firstly on a thieving kitchen boy whose arms they broke, one on each arm, simultaneously; later on many, many others. This at last was their true function, what he had bred them to, his dogs. They grew to love him, minded their manners when he ate with them, lived pure lives in emulation of his, eschewing every indulgence as he did. He moved them back into a room together and would come late at night to sit with them, to massage their perfections, to lull them to sleep with benedictions upon their fury, their cold, clean fury: the chastisers of the world. He began to speak distantly of one enemy against whom a great conflict would one day be fought. He did not need to specify this enemy.

Gray watched his brother's training regime with detached amusement. He assumed that the boys would turn on their new master in time; when he saw how Blade triumphed, he was forced to admire him. He was not without his personal apprehensions, but he could not imagine how Blade could see him as a threat. Let Blade have Cloud's position; he did not want that. He wanted power only in himself, pure personal power; not over any tentative empire, riven with paranoias. He did not want to create others in his own image, as Blade appeared to have done with Porsque and Milon. He wanted his victims to be revealed for what they were. He wanted to experiment, to watch and to learn, to satisfy his mind and body with the exhaustion of the minds and bodies of others. All others were weak in comparison to him, because he was able to expose and destroy them without a stain on his own mind. He would be able to take Blade, and Porsque and Milon, if ever they came for him, simply by turning them inside out, finding where their motivations lay quivering within them, and holding his hands over them until they were still. This was what he had inherited from Mully, the family heritage of which he was the sole possessor.

He began upon his sisters. He began to visit their apartments with elaborate and bizarre presents: a live dog-fox in a cage; an amputated human hand in a dark glass jar; enormous cakes in the shape of men and women with fantastic confectioned genitalia; a large sphere of black stone, veined with red, which lay immovable in the centre of their carpet; bottles of strangely drugged wine which turned them into monsters, turned the walls and furniture of their rooms into living, writhing forests, leaving them beached in sickly, grey convalescences. They grew desperate for his visits, his favours which suggested whole worlds to them. They huddled together in the expanses of soft furnishing that cocooned them, and were united more fiercely than ever they had been under the expectancy of his return; which, of course, he satisfied erratically, allowing their emptiness to proliferate for days, coming in suddenly whilst they were still buzzing from his last incursion, arguing over his last cryptic gift, a negro baby which they played with like a doll for two days before he returned and took it away calming them with tales of the prince, its father, part-man, part-demon, who had returned to claim it, who had heard with interest of its sojourn amongst the four pale virgins who lived up under the sky.

Deeda, Glarry, Mitte, Fintaniste. So far he had pulled them together. They could hardly be told apart at the best of times. Physically there were considerable differences, but emotionally and intellectually they were all soft and un-defined to the point of interchangeability. It was physically he separated them, sexually, as had been his design from the first, from the instant of his empty boast to Blade over the aborted affair of The Hedgehog's disposal.

He began with Fintaniste, for whom he had an independent desire; the youngest and most beautiful of the four, tall with long brown hair plaited into a tapered rope that hung down over the cleft of her buttocks; a long face with long features; long, open brown eyes; at the mouth, naturally haughty, at the eyes, naturally sad.

He brought her a present alone, slipped it into her hand, a lozenge of polished amber, ellipsoid, with a tiny black fly embedded in it. 'Secret,' he told her, and she kept it, withdrawing herself privately to examine it, holding it, caressing it out of sight of her sisters. Over his next few visits, he always found a particular questioning glance for her alone, towards which she rose to find him turned away again. At times she nearly cried out to him, remembering herself just in time. He brought a great baked fish, ten foot long on a garnished board. They set to it with their fingers, forcing wads of oily pink flesh into their cheeks. He withdrew a little and gave her his signal. She was quickly beside him. 'And have you kept our secret?' he asked. She nodded. 'And where is it? No. Don't bring it out here. They'll see it. Keep it close to you. Find some secret place upon your body, as close to your flesh as you can. Hide it there. Keep it warm.' When next he came, he brought opiates in crystal beakers etched with each of their names. They drank cautiously and slumped one by one into stupor; except Fintaniste who watched, waited for her effects to reach her, feeling cheated when they did not until she saw him there waiting for her. He drew her away to a side room and asked to see where she kept his secret. She revealed her strong white breasts with the amber lozenge incubating between them. He shook his head sadly. There was a better place, he said, much more secret. She must find it. He would come again in an hour. He stroked her breasts and kissed them to distract the sulky tears. He sucked the lozenge from her cleft into his mouth. He put his mouth to hers and ejected the lozenge on to her tongue. An hour later he returned to find her sitting with her breast still open, the lozenge still in her mouth, her cheeks pouted, her eyes bleared with frustration. He laughed at her, said she was a fool, said he would come back in another hour. She spat the lozenge from her and came at him, furious, screaming. He held her off, grinned. He told her to lie back and close her eyes. He would find the place. He would search her out and when he found the place she would know, she would understand the great secret. She submitted. He played with her long body, circling the secret, touching everywhere but there, until she understood. 'I know where,' she said. 'Here.' He affected a moment's amazement, pretended that she was wrong again, then broke into her all at once. She screamed and thrashed and he laughed. When she was still, he was quickly gone, leaving her bloody and bewildered and still mystified. She limped back to her dopey sisters and sulked for days. He arranged for her to come to a dark room. She lay in the darkness and he came to her again, regularly, fucking her at leisure until she became quite good at it.

For the others he concocted similar fantasies, peeling them off individually, teasing them, playing them off one against the other, bringing them to the point of submission

gladly, suddenly, completely. He gave them their individualities, created them in the parts of his fantasies, lost
himself for months, for years amongst their writhing sexu-
alities. It occurred to him to complete his set with The
Hedgehog who, disgusting though she was, was just about
of an age to have been interesting. She had, however,
already been claimed by Mrs Morrow and was to be put to
service; and he had no interest in her used. He neglected,
therefore, The Hedgehog, although he did find himself
thinking of her occasionally, determining idly to find and
finish her, never quite finding the prospect of this stimulat-
ing enough; she was a complexity and to kill her would be
to throw the puzzle away, not solve it.

— 4 —

One night, not long after her experiences with the family,
there was a large celebration in the washroom, a celebration
of indiscriminate abandon in which all the women of the
room were, for no comprehensible reason, liberated for a
day, drinking and singing and laughing until their pores
gushed and their stabilities were entirely abandoned. It was
a bewildering vision for the child, all these drudges suddenly
pouring strong ale and wine into their faces in obscene
quantities, spluttering and roaring, pounding about in their
rickety dropsical frames until the drink poured out again
from faces and arses causing immense hilarity. They sang
wildly, raging. The spites and tyrannies about which their
usual life was constructed were all miraculously and hor-
rifically absolved.
      Old Mag was at the centre of this misrule. The child nestled
under a trough alone, the other children having been drawn
out to join in; she was far too old to join them in anything
now. She rammed herself into an old niche that she had
long outgrown. She was cramped and miserable, wanting to
be back in the stable with Mag alone. She watched with
affected disgust as Mag went capering and rollicking about,
tumbling into the channel and being floundered out again,
wet and stupid, gulping down more sour wine and bellowing

execrable songs. The child wanted to take Mag home, felt that all this excess would cause Mag to fall and smash herself, to spill herself irrecoverably out on to the flagstones. And then the child would be alone. She had become afraid of being alone recently. She kept as close as she could to Mag, helping even at the trough which she could now reach, bashing out lumps of sodden sheet and enjoying the energy flowing out of her so directly, at times at least. She wanted Mag to notice her now, to stop this rioting and flopping, to come to her and touch her and take her back.

Suddenly, as if her wishing had made it happen, the party subsided. Serious voices were raised at its peripheries and taken up, carried amongst the revellers, stilling them one by one. They submitted resignedly, moving tiredly out of the whirling, collecting up their bundles and bottles. They began to leave, one by one, calling their goodnights behind them. The great washroom filled with emptiness and Old Mag found herself isolated in mid-song.

'That's all now, Mag,' someone yelled.

She rose up, turning on a moment of outrage but, like the others, subsiding. She sat on the floor and held her head. The child crept out of her shelter and came to her, putting a steadying hand on her shoulder.

'Just a bit, my little knuckle,' she said, turning away and vomiting efficiently into the channel beside her. 'That's the most of it now,' she said, turning back, spitting, wiping her mouth. 'Now then, knuckle. You'll have to help me home.'

With a tight claw upon the child's shoulder, she made several attempts to set herself on her feet. With the child shoving on her rump, this was finally achieved and they set off, zig-zagging down the centre of the room, lit by failing candles, and out into the dark of the archway. The child steered leftwards and they were out in the courtyard, the clean, cold night air swimming round them, rousing them sharply and making them conscious of the little warmths they maintained. The child wrapped her arm round the old woman to support and direct her, but also to draw comfort and warmth from her.

The old woman tottered and meandered and eventually sat down like a pudding on the stones, bringing the child to her knees beside her. There was a big, stone moon, full and close above them. Mag looked up at it as if surprised by it, afraid of it momentarily; then she gave a little dog-like bay and chuckled sarcastically.

'I've been here forever,' she said, 'ever since that moon was a little knob of chalk no bigger than my head.' She struggled to regain her feet. The child took her arms and heaved. Old Mag rose slowly at first, then toppled forward and fell on top of her, smothering down upon her and roaring with laughter. She rolled off and lay on her back in the courtyard, the laughter coming in hoots. The child sat beside her, immune to the cold now, looking up at the moon and feeling it growing larger and larger, coming towards them with its pale, cold light.

'Old Mother Moon,' said Mag, serious again, sitting up beside the child. 'Old Mother Moon who has no children. Poxy old bitch. Barren old cunt-sucker. She feels nothing. You see the great gates there, child, you see them? There used to be a fine arch above them, cut from great beams of oak and carved. Look, you can see where the stumps of it are still. They cut it down after the soldiers had gone. The soldiers. There was a time, you see, when the town was full of soldiers and there was a battle fought out there beyond the meadows. We could hear it from here, the thump–thump–thump and the crash–crash–crash of it all day, rolling in from out there like a plague wind. We waited. We waited. Then they came, the soldiers, in their fouled coats and their metal plating, with their burnt, black faces and their knotty arms. Their skulls were made of steel and their hands were claws. They weren't young and they weren't old. They didn't smile and they didn't sing. They drank our wine and they ate our meat and they laid us down wherever they found us till we were bruised from knee to knee and our bellies were bloated with their slime, but they never smiled and they never sang. They brought in prisoners, twelve men in rags and blood, and they kept them for three days and three nights standing in the middle of the courtyard, here, where we're sitting now, twelve men who never sat down, who stood with their eyes closed and their mouths open, parched and fly-clustered like old meat. Then they hanged them from the gate-arch, from the oaken beam. They bundled them into a line in the gateway and noosed them

80

up, and they stood there, shoulder to shoulder, blocking the gateway, roused at last, looking at us with big eyes, asking for mercy, asking us, the women, girls as we were then, all drawn and draggled and hopeless, but still girls then; they looked to us for mercy. Out of their ghostly faces the big eyes came begging. Then the soldiers pulled them up, all twelve of them, all at once, just two feet into the air and those eyes rolled about and swelled and swelled, and their mouths were open like pits and great black tongues lolled about in them and their thin, bare legs kicked and leapt, all twelve of them dancing with the sun behind them and the dust thick in the air and the smoke hazing the sun; and one by one they went still and the light went from their faces and they grew dark, long, dead shadows, twelve shadows swaying in the dusk. And the soldiers said they had to stay there, stay there until they rotted, and that anyone who took them down would go up in their place. And there they stayed, growing stiller and stiller, and blacker and blacker in the heat. At midday you couldn't see their faces for flies. At night the breeze creaked the ropes and each had a different little dead squeal as it strained and turned. They blocked the gateway there for two weeks, stinking and rotting, with the bones showing through where the flesh rotted off. The soldiers were gone, said they'd be back, said they'd know who had touched their corpses. And we spent days out here in the courtyard, just looking at them. And then, at last, someone said, 'They won't come. They've gone for good. They're all dead.' And we went up and cut them down. They fell in a great heap, rattling, stiff. And we hewed down the gateposts and the great cross-beam. And we made a fire here, here where we're sitting, here where they had stood, and we burnt the gateposts and the cross-beam and the bodies, and we danced round the fire pretending that the soldiers were dead, gone, never coming back, but they did come back, they always come back, always have done, always will. Everything will be smashed down when the soldiers come, everything will be pulled down and taken away. Everything you have, everything you are, will suddenly belong to them. It's the law. It's the law. You get quiet and you get cosy, somewhere to sleep easy and then the soldiers come and down you go, down you go. They

81

know everything and what they don't know isn't allowed to be known. They know everything and they push you down with it. And if you argue, they say, this, this, this is everything, this is my right, this is my sword, this is my fire, this is my fist, down you go, down you go, down, down. You can't hate them because they're not soft enough to hate, not until afterwards and then it's too late.'

And in the moonlight the child saw the old woman's face, her round, pocky, moon-face, silvered with tears, glinting like an old, weathered stone in the frost. And the child clung to her with a fear that was grown very big. She looked at the gateway and could see now the amputated stumps of the arch, and in her imagination, above them in the darkness, she saw what had been there, the uprights, the cross-beam, the twelve ropes plummeting down to the twelve weighted corpses, the twelve ropes like bars, like the strings of an obscene harp played in the wind which, in the moaning of the long nights, found that sound still. Death. Death. Not the death of that strange woman, her mother, who had died within herself; but death like the death of the great bull, here in the courtyard where they sat, the life checked in full flood, the quickness halted, the flesh become weight. There was such a sudden finality in this that oppressed the child hideously.

She took Mag back to the stall and sat with her through the night, dozing for disjointed lapses of time whilst the old woman keened and groaned, far away in her distant hurting. The child watched pitifully, tried to grip the old woman in some sort of embrace, at which she was pathetically inadequate. At dawn, at last, Mag yielded and took the child in her arms, and lay down with her amongst the bales and quilts and boxes on the stall floor.

She never again, after that night, slept up in the manger. She was now with Old Mag constantly, her child now more than she had ever been. She retained her freedom from the washroom, wandered as she had always done, but was never far from Mag, never went beyond the light of the courtyard now. She grew active for the old woman, not merely dependent upon her. She came back and tidied the stall, found coloured things, bits of cloth or paper, or even a flower, to temper briefly the abiding darkness. Mag herself always greeted her now, always talked to her. They were together for a long, easy time; during which the child began to grow.

She marked her growing carefully, groomed her body as much to examine it as to keep it sweet; although, incidentally, she discovered the pleasure of cleanliness. She marked the swelling of her breasts, the shadowing red hair at the forks of her body. She marked the sweet ache of bleeding that set her in play amongst the moon-phases. She greeted these changes with intense curiosity, kept them secret and treasured them in her solitude. Her body was warm and pleasing, womanly now and soft, and she could roll up tightly and create tensions and little pleasures that flowed and flourished in her. It was a happy time. She laughed a lot and found others who would laugh with her – Mr Tow, the women in the washroom and, above all, Old Mag who seemed to know what was going on within her, all her secrets, and to take a personal pride in them.

She saw the dark boy now and then. He too was changing, growing tall and thin of face, looking cruel and high, wearing a dark blue cloak and carrying a small cane with an ostentatious green stone as its knob. He did not carry his fiddle now. He would come down that long, stone stairway into the archway, stepping now fearlessly between kitchen and washroom, although the child, when she watched him closely, could still see a spark of fear at the corner of his eye. She watched this exhibition of himself, this bravado. Was it for her? He had assumed new power, new dignity. He came across in her direction as if passing casually, and he bowed to her. She did not like his new dignity. It reeked of proliferated betrayals, hers amongst many others. He strode past her into the barn as if expecting her to follow him. She forgot him.

Then one day the soldiers returned to the Inn. Coming out of the archway to consider the sky which was emitting a thin, sharp rain, she noticed them first as a larger than usual crowd at one end of the courtyard, near the gate. They were not initially imposing, a bedraggled assortment in bedraggled finery: their uniform bedragglement was the first thing that drew her attention to them. They all wore red jackets and breeches that had, long ago, been white. They all had big bushy hats which they held under their arms, or which lay on the ground at their feet. They all wore swords and pouches, belts and buckles. It did occur to her that they were soldiers, but she resisted the idea as inappropriate; they had none of the violence that she knew must come with the soldiers, the fire and the torn flesh that soldiers feed upon. She could not see their faces through the sweaty mist of rain, but their attitudes were tired and despondent. She observed them perplexed and apprehensive. Then she became aware that she had attracted their notice, found herself caught suddenly in a bewildering isolation.

One of them was approaching her, walking roundly, heavily, jangling his sword and pressing down the puddles with his cracked boots. His face fixed her, a skewed face with stone eyes and broken teeth, and a white scar from his eye to his lip. He came upon her and considered her. He looked back at the others who laughed.

'Greetings, beautiful virgin,' he said. 'We are my Lord Hasham's Regiment of Foot, or the flower of its manhood, guaranteed free from all manner of prick-rot, and most desirous of finding a welcome suitable to our pluck and vigour. All debts chargeable to His Majesty whom God preserve. Are you at home? Sergeant Tobb Slunt at your pleasure, ma'am.' And he clicked his heels tightly.

The others had spread forward, behind the sergeant, and were pressing over his shoulders and each other's.

'There'll not be room for me in that,' one of them said. 'Look at it, then – humped out of shape already.'

'Go and fetch Old Mag,' the sergeant said. 'Unless she's dead, in which case fetch someone else.'

'Unless she's only just dead, in which case we'll make do.'

This was a joke and the child was shoved away in a push of sour laughter. She ran in, bouncing herself off a wall and stumbling over a doorstep. She found Mag who was amused by her panic, but kind, kneeling to catch her. She asked the child what was wrong and the child tugged at her, but she didn't take it seriously.

'I'm all busy now, knuckle. Get yourself down there and I'll be with you in a while.'

But someone had peered into the courtyard and yelled across, 'Hey, Mag, it's Tobb Slunt and he's a sergeant, and he's got his army with him.' This initiated much delight.

'You're not taking on the lot, are you, Mag?'

'I'll do a couple for you!'

'Poxy–poxy–poxy!'

Such an avenue of encouragement was made for Mag as, with her mouth lipped in a deep smile, she progressed the length of the washroom with the child beside her. Mag left them to it.

The soldiers had moved away from the archway, were sheltering from the continuing rain in the barn mouth, near the stall door, in an expectant cluster. Mag stooped to the child.

'I'd better go and tend to them before they come over and kill someone for their supper. Off you go now.'

The child stood in the archway and watched Mag cross to them. They greeted her loudly, parted for her and closed round her. Mag had gone into the stall and the soldiers were unbuckling their belts and taking off their jackets, all animated now. The child moved round the edge of the courtyard towards them, towards the barn entrance. She had to make her way past them and into the depths of the barn. She felt Mag was at risk and she wanted to be near. She would scramble up into the rafters and peer down, ready to drop amongst them.

But it was not fear for Mag: it was simple curiosity that impelled her. Since Mag's tale of the hanged men in the gateway, the idea of the coming of the soldiers had gathered in her. She saw them with their faces of burnt brick and their eyes of splintered glass, breaking everything, bringing the Inn down around them and, at last, finding her there. She imagined herself splayed down in the rubble with metal spikes driven into her, nailing her hands, bursting her head, finding the heart of pain below the soft flesh of her breast. These were soldiers and yet they were not like that. She watched them, a scruffy knot of skinny, blotchy men, standing about in boots and braces, scratching and twitching, coming out into the yard to empty their bloated bladders. And yet there was something that did connect them with her nightmare, something hard and cruel, irreducible below their evident mortality; and it was connected with the secret business they had come to do with Mag; and that she had to see for herself.

She came to the barn entrance where they were clustered and paused, trying not to pause, trying to will herself quickly through them and into the darkness beyond. She pushed through and created a sudden burst of activity about her.

'Hey, hobbledy, show us your arse then!'

She dodged a hand that swiped at her and a laugh that might have struck her down, and she sped into the depth, not looking back until she was deep enough to turn and bolt. She looked and saw they had lost interest in her. They stood in a huddle and were taking a decision, drawing straws to cheers and groans. One of them stepped out and went to the stall door, knocked and entered. She heard the bolt slide and she scampered on into the damp heaps and splintered inner walls, searching out the old way she had found to clamber up into the roof space.

The depths of the barn were strangely deserted and silent that day. It gave her no comfort, this possibility of being the only thing moving in the barn. It gave her a sense of her own movement that she did not want. She wanted to be invisible.

She found her way up soon enough, after some confusions, and was soon out amongst the roof-beams and fallen floor-joists that she knew would lead her to the vantage she sought. She paused to calm the hurry of her movement lest she should be seen, which would be appalling, which would be a betrayal of Mag; nor indeed did she want to fall.

She saw the glow of the stall-lamp rising up into the dark. She was edging along a beam just broad enough to allow her to crawl. Below her were other beams which would break her if she lost her grip. Gradually the stall came directly below her, lit, garish; and, lying back, facing the door, propped on bales and bundles, was Mag, the grey cap obscuring her face viewed from above, her skirts drawn up to her knees and her dress pulled open to expose her tumbling breasts. Her knees were wide apart and between them lay a strong stave. At her right hand was a lantern, unshuttered and filling the stall with a jumping glow. She was, as the child saw her, alone, lying quite still, breathing heavily as if asleep. Was it all over? The child, caught in a strong suspense, held her breath, gripped her beam, and waited.

Eventually the door opened and one of the soldiers entered, closing and bolting the door, looking about him before addressing his gaze to Mag. As he did so, he slipped the straps of his braces off his shoulders and advanced.

'Pence first,' said Mag, in a voice of such sudden practicality that it startled the watching child.

The soldier burrowed in his breeches pocket and advanced his hand with a small clutch of coins upon it. Mag took the coins, one by one, bit them, leaned over to one side to peer at them in the lantern-light. Satisfied, she hid them away somewhere, and took up the lantern, bringing it towards the soldier who backed away.

'What've you got to be ashamed of, soldier boy?' she said.

The soldier looked perturbed, the sweat glinting in his eyes as he again glanced about him but, as he glanced, he also fumbled at the fastenings of his breeches, stooping to tug them down around his knees. From under his tattered shirt-lap up popped a fat and peeled lump of flesh that the child had by no means expected. This Mag, by the lantern-light, inspected minutely. The child was meanwhile postulating that this flesh was something extra that the soldiers possessed, and that this was what made them different from the others. She could not, in her life around the courtyard, have failed to have been aware that men had a complicated cluster of parts which permitted them some facility in urination; but this thing was something different. It looked uncomfortable, unhealthy and bloated, strutted out from the soldier's thin white thighs.

'We'll give it a try, soldier boy,' Mag said, replacing the lantern and hoisting up her skirts.

The soldier dropped to his knees at once and shuffled up between Mag's legs. When he had shuffled up as far as he could, he stretched himself out, laying his body over hers and pushing his legs out behind him. His head lolled on her shoulder. The child could see the greasy top of his scalp, balding, the small pigtail half-untied. His arse, two long and grimy mounds of pale muscle, lifted and dropped a few times. He then grunted and a visible lassitude came upon him; he slumped on Mag as if he had suddenly fallen asleep.

'There's a good soldier boy,' she said. 'There's a strong little man.' She pushed his shoulders and he slid from her, folded up on his knees on the ground. As he struggled to his feet, the child saw that the lump of flesh was gone, retracted into a recognisably usual male part, up over which, with some caution, he pulled his breeches, buckling himself up and shaking himself out into a grin.

'The bottle's over there if you want to replace your strength,' Mag said. She was wiping between her legs with a rag.

The soldier applied himself to the bottle, gave Mag a final nod, still grinning; then unbolted the door and was gone. Mag scooped up the coins from where they had been temporarily concealed, burrowed aside and reburied them into a chinking heap. She then composed herself again and was as the child had first seen her, reclined and waiting.

A minute or two passed, then, with a brief rap, another of the soldiers slipped into the stall and the whole procedure was re-enacted: the giving of the money, the inspection and acceptance of the offered stub of flesh, the lying down, the shuffling, the relaxation, the disengagement. It took a little longer this time. This soldier seemed more confident, laying hands upon Mag before she pulled him down to it; but the cycle was completed soon enough and he was gone with his lumped flesh eased back into its proper shape.

A third soldier, a fourth, a fifth came in and were received in the same way. The money was offered, the risen flesh was inspected and admitted between Mag's thighs, emerging in a little while reduced and retracted. The bottle was applied to and the soldier left.

After the fifth, Mag roused, went to the door, and bolted it. She then went burrowing about in the straw, from which she extracted a small, stout box. Unlatching and opening it, she exposed to the watching child, dancing in the lantern-light a whole bed of coins over which the new coins were shot. Mag ran her hands briefly over this hoard, withdrew them quickly, closed and latched and hid the box again deeply.

And then she glanced up and, to the child's alarm, met her eyes directly.

'Come down now, little knuckle,' she said. 'Come down and let's see what you've made of all that.'

The child shrank against the beam, tightly, plotting escapes, closing her eyes to recover the darkness in which she had imagined herself to be immaculate.

'Come down. Quickly now.'

She had to submit. Although she had felt it quite possible to drop down into the stall from above, she had never actually done it. She looked down to the plankings which crossed below her. There was a way down, three drops from beam to beam and then an easy fall into the manger straw. She contemplated it and it frightened her; but she couldn't go back: it would look like running away and she had decided, somewhere, not to run away. She had been seen; she had been part of the game from the first. She hung her legs down, clung with her arms and found the first beam below her, planted her feet upon it, releasing the beam above, stooping, balancing; growing bolder, excited by the gravity that drew her down. She jumped to the second beam, swayed and stumbled and went down on all fours. The danger came at her, but she jumped at it, bouncing against the last beam and plumping painfully into the old manger which groaned under her fall and powdered dust about her face. Sucking back her breath, and coughing, she rolled over the edge and was down beside Mag who whooped with laughter, who cuddled the child, who burrowed a hand under her skirts and inserted a finger into her sex which was open and glowing: it was an alarming but most instructive contact.

'Your time will come soon enough,' she said. 'Don't you be in any hurry. I'm too old to have monsters put into my belly now, but you're just beginning all that. Don't you rush. Take care of yourself. Hug me now, hug me. I'm full of jelly and I'm so old, so old. If I could have one year of your childhood, hump and all . . . If I knew where you hid it, child, I'd tear it out of you with my teeth . . .'

How could she help wondering about it? It appalled her and

it fascinated her. Not understanding what Mag meant by monsters in the belly, she did not believe in them, could put them aside. She began to size up the kitchen men, to wonder what it would be like for one of them to put his part to her in that way. She began to interpret certain looks that lolled at her. This initial curiosity did not impel her very far; the minions were, by definition, poor specimens. They sniffed at her and itched at her and showed wet mouths and scraggy necks. She found them absurd at a distance and repulsive nearby. If they had not, by their positions in the kitchens, been bred to servility, she might have been afraid of them. She kept out of the deep barns now.

There was, though, a fear attached to it: not of the monsters, in which she could not believe but which she could never entirely forget; it was a fear of proximity. The idea of another person entering her body was an idea she could not contain within mere physicalities. To be covered and entered, to be coupled thus, would be in some way to become the subject of a larger possession. The soldiers who had come to Mag, each in his way, had been propelled by an energy which they had driven into her and had left in her. It was perhaps the secret of Mag's nature to receive and to feed off this energy. The child had no idea how she would be able to contain such energy. Mag lived with the fierce self-awareness which the child knew to be her first strength. When she had been taken up to that high room and subjected to the ugly woman's probing, she knew her strength was being tested, her centre exposed. It was, she realised now, in practical terms, an examination in preparation for her use in this act, which was merchantable obviously; this intrusion of masculinity into her that would bring her to the centre of the Inn's functioning. This was what waited for her.

Turning such thoughts around within her, feeling herself at times eager for it to happen, to be done suddenly, longing to lose herself in it, feeling at times the summoning of every resistance to it straining to the point of rupture, she became aware of the dark boy again hovering about the courtyard, fixing himself distinctly upon her. She did not trust him, not at all, kept herself at a solid distance from him, ignoring him when she could not actually avoid him. But from this distance she watched him, tall and clean, delicate in his movements and aware of himself in a way that had outgrown awkwardness and had become, with his manhood, graceful. With him, perhaps, she thought, it might be possible. She had recalled his loathing of contact, and that was now intriguing. She recalled his music, now a part of her receded childhood, and she recalled the sad expectancy it had generated; and that sad expectancy she now recreated within herself, physically, sweetly.

She dreamed of his coming to her as he had come once, to lead her away. She dreamed of leading him, of enticing him into her. They were forbidden dreams, magical with secrecy and guilts, Mag grunting and restless, eternally Mag, full of soldiers' energies, going off muttering to herself as the child pretended sleep. She dreamed, abstractedly at least, of a completion that would free her from all this.

— 5 —

My Lord Quillan was possessed of a fascination for virginity, for that moment of physical and moral rending when a girl became a woman, when all her possibilities were open and were closed with one thrust. This possession rose in him like a tumour and, when he felt it swelling in him beyond repression, he would send for Bayne, his physician; and Bayne would journey to the Three Stars Inn to take spirits with Edwin Cloud and to make arrangements.

At the designated midnight, my lord would enter the Inn and would climb small staircases to a bright but closed chamber. Bayne would attend, and only Bayne. He would help my lord's disrobing, none but his physician fit to see him in this condition. My lord would sit in a chair by the fire drinking wine which he had brought with him. The girl would, meanwhile, in an antechamber, be examined by Bayne for her perfection, and for a degree of physical maturity which was also necessary. The creature would then be brought before my lord who would look briefly and would always agree. Bayne would then assist her to her position on the bed, on all fours, her sex exposed; he would then leave and wait at the door. My lord would wait, sometimes for an hour, then rouse from his chair, clamber up behind the aching girl with increasing unsteadiness, and would insert his sex very slowly into her, feeling minutely for the resistant membrane, savouring that one perfect moment before he became aware that he was falling, holding himself at the point of it, second by second with the tears streaking his dusty face. When he could hold out no longer, he pushed home. The girl would emit a small squeal as she had been taught; a token squeal only, nothing hysterical. My lord would withdraw at once and ejaculate into a white silk handkerchief; Bayne would later see to it that this cloth and its deposit of noble seed was burnt. My lord, discharged, would call at once and women, under Bayne's direction, would come in quickly and bundle away the girl. My lord would spend a further hour alone, dropping down a spiral of despair, his vitalities of mind and body vanished, his loathing for himself superseded only by his loathing for the thing he had paid to despoil. He wanted, to complete his evacuation, to have the thing dead, finished with absolutely; he wanted to watch Bayne at work professionally with his knife upon the fouled flesh, reducing it to specimens. The suppression of this final lust skewered him. There could be no final satisfaction without it and he could never bring himself to enquire for it. He was afraid of the finitude of his power, afraid of reaching the limits of the boundless deference, the obsequious openness to the drip of his gold. He nursed, in the aftermath of his little ecstasy, a sense of petty injustice, of the restriction of his instinctive rights. After this hour's lassitude, Bayne would knock, enter, attend to the handkerchief, assist my lord in certain ablutions and in dressing, would guide him back down to the waiting carriage.

As he grew older, he had expected this particular need to abate. It did not do so. It lay more dormant during the summer and winter, but it returned in due season inevitably. Without it he might have ceased to believe himself alive. Sometimes indeed he fancied that he had died in the night and that hell, his inevitable bourn, was for him to go on as he had always gone on, into eternity.

*

There came a last time, however. It was a blowy, stormy night as he travelled to the Inn. Cloud, he found, was now fixed in his chair and my lord, who insisted on paying his respects, found him a shrivelled and repellent figure. But Cloud informed him that today there would be something extraordinary, something unique. He only hoped his lordship would not think his motives any but the highest.

'Let me confess, my lord, that I have a personal interest in what we have for you tonight.'

'This exceeds the terms of our understanding, Cloud.' He was uneasy at the twinkling eyes in the old man's reptile head.

He went to his preparations determined not to let Cloud's insinuations affect him, and indeed, they did not. After a glass of his wine and a meditation upon the operations of his body, he found himself ready as ever for his necessary exercise.

The door was tapped and opened and a little hunchbacked girl in a plain white shift appeared, surprising my lord with her wide, curious eyes set within a wild mass of red hair. Meeting his startled response, she frowned and looked over her lumped shoulder at her two attendants, a tall, ugly woman in black whom my lord had seen before, and a dark, evil-looking youth. Bayne was there too, standing back with a hint of a sneer suggested below his customary mask. My lord was immediately suspicious; more than that he was afraid; more than that, his fine phallus wilted.

'Bayne?' he said.

'My lord?' Bayne came forward to receive his master's words privately.

'What is this?'

'This is Cloud's little mystery, my lord. Are you not intrigued? Home-bred and hand-reared, so they claim.'

'Get rid of them, Bayne.'

Bayne turned and signalled. The attendants bowed and were gone. The girl remained. Bayne crossed to her and put his hand at her neck, jerking her head back, pulling down her jaw.

'The tongue, my lord, is grafted to the mouth and quite incapable of coherent speech. I have ascertained her essential suitability, my lord, but if you are not absolutely at ease, I will ask Cloud to do better for us.'

'Be quiet, Bayne.'

'My lord.'

He studied this fiery little cripple and, skewered and humped as she was, he could see nothing womanly about her at all. She was not human. They had brought him an animal to mock him. Then it occurred to him that, being an animal, she might perhaps be subjected to his final desire. This possibility re-aroused his purpose, a situation he could not conceal from the attentive Bayne.

'My lord is intrigued?'

'Show me.'

He expected, under the shift, a pelt perhaps, some sign of her animality. He saw, when Bayne had razored off the cloth, a pretty little form, albeit twisted aside: fat breasts and a fierce little sex. Bayne turned her round and bent her over to give my lord a view of her functional end. She seemed more natural on all fours which reassured him – animal after all.

'Make ready, Bayne.'

He led the girl to the bed, and patted the spread sheeting. She jumped up agilely and he adjusted her positioning, instructing her as he did so.

'My lord will approach you. You must keep very still. You must clasp this bolster. You must close your eyes and you must not endeavour to look. If you fail in any particular you will be whipped.'

'Blind her, Bayne.'

'Blindfold her, my lord?'

'What you will.'

Bayne laughed, but uneasily. He blindfolded the girl, as he had done sometimes before; but there was something new here. Bowing, watching his master closely, he retreated through the side door.

Quillan tottered to the side door and locked it. He tottered to the central doors and checked that they too had been secured. He looked around for a weapon, a knife: it must be a knife. He had no knife. He posited a great blow, a throttling, a smothering, but he could not clearly see his way to any of these. He skittered and lurched about the room looking for an escape; but the obvious escape, the obvious purpose, was too strong in him. He clambered

94

quickly up the bedside and addressed his flesh to the little pink halter offered between pale, full hams, below the pursed and disapproving anus. He found her receptive to his intrusion, and he thought, they have cheated me. But soon enough he touched the little resistance that delighted him so. He could not concentrate, however, and had shuddered straight through before he knew it. She made neither sound nor movement. He did. He cried out in alarm lest she should rob him. He jerked away quickly, painfully, as the thin deposit blobbed out of the end of him. One short wince and it was over. His victim remained motionless, bound blind and dumb, the dark blood slipping down her thighs.

He no longer needed to kill her. Once he was completed he had no stomach for any more. He could only have done it if he had been able to do it at the very moment of breaking her. Why did the act itself not kill her? Why did he not have that final potency? Why had he barred them out? Why were they not here to remove that soiled rump which seemed to glare at him, a blinded bloody cyclops. He shuddered and groaned. It was worse now than it had ever been. He felt his bowels turn to cold muck. He felt his mortality drag in his guts. He tumbled off the edge of the bed and regained his chair. Turning he saw, at an oblique angle, the hideous mound of her back, the breasts dangling cow-like below her.

'Foul,' he said aloud. 'Foul . . . Foul . . .'

The creature stirred. Its ability to do so alarmed him.

'Come down,' he called. 'Come down from there.'

She fumbled at the blindfold and exposed an eye which quickly sought him out and which seemed to comprehend him at once. Why had she not been drugged? He had assumed that they were always drugged. The idea of this thing alert, aware, participant, disgusted him.

'Come down,' he said. 'Come here.'

She eased herself down, off the bed, her movements a little wary, her legs apart. She looked down at her ruination and, grabbing a loose edge of the bedlinen, she wiped herself. She addressed herself to my lord then, this strange, nude thing which had no shame, which had no fear; which had no more reproach than a kicked mongrel; who only stood there and waited for him. She did not belong there, not in this place, not at this moment. She inhabited a reality above her sex and above her deformity which he could not accommodate. She was not a creature less than he had assumed her to be, but more. She smiled fatally at him.

'Come here,' he said, although he did not want her to come and she seemed to sense this, approaching cautiously, keeping a vital distance. He made a sudden movement at her, saw her tense but hold herself still.

'Do you know who I am?' he said. 'I am the Lord Quillan. I am the last Lord Quillan. You are only here because I have need of you. You only exist because you are useful. You only exist because I choose to enjoy you. Learn that of the world tonight.' But he could sense the absurdity of this posture even as he struck it.

She put her hands to her breasts. He thought she was going to cover them, but she held them, touched her nipples, still looking at him, still smiling.

'Cover your shame,' he said, feeling increasingly ridiculous with every reaction to her. He felt for one horrible moment that she was going to laugh at him. 'Cover your shame, damn you!'

It took her a moment to understand what he meant by this. She returned to the bed and pulled off a coverlet, a glittery, embroidered weight of material that she hung from her shoulders, draped herself completely, turning back to see if she had done right.

It was no good. He could not confront her, not in any guise. He had seen her but he could not understand her. The attempt to understand her opened abysms in his mind.

After a while she squatted down on the floor by the bed, then sat, still watching him, although he could see the sleep beginning to flow in her, a sweet sleep which left him far away, quite alone, abandoned, dead effectively.

Bayne had heard the door being locked, but he had his own key. He expected to find something grisly in there tonight. He waited the hour and then went to the door and rapped firmly, but there was no response. He wasted important seconds working the inside key out of the lock before he could use his own.

Inside Quillan sat rigid in his chair, his face bleached, his chest heaving slowly and heavily. He's done it, Bayne thought, although he could see no immediate evidence, no carnage dripping everywhere. If it had been done discreetly there was the chance of a quiet withdrawal. He locked the door behind him and went to his master.

Quillan raised a finger towards the edge of the bed.

'I understand, my lord. All will be attended to. It is of no consequence.' He did not want hysteria. Satisfied on this point first, he addressed himself to the object of Quillan's indication.

The girl lay asleep, breathing deeply, tousled and snug in a mass of coverlet. Bayne was puzzled.

'Do you want *me* to . . . to have her removed, my lord?'

'You cannot remove her, Bayne. She's escaped. Why was she allowed to escape? She has destroyed me.'

This was beyond the limit, insanity. He took the old man by the arm, raised him firmly and led him carefully, swiftly, to the door, opening it, moving out into the anteroom to which the dark servant boy had returned. He shouldn't have been here. Bayne grew aggressive.

'You be careful what you take notice of, boy,' Bayne warned.

The boy shrank back.

'Open the door, damn you.'

He took the old man out into the corridor, still driving him at the elbow, feeling the inertia gathering against the movement. He was afraid that the old man would seize up completely before he could bolt him down the stairways and into his coach. He began to urge forward as the old man began to drag back, leaning against his propulsion, his broken face open, the eyes rolling. The spasms of some sort of distant fit began to take hold of him.

'May we help, sir?' Blade and his two dog-like companions stood across the corridor before him.

'You may get out of my damned way,' Bayne said, pushing the old man at them, but he was beyond his endurance; he crumpled and vomited suddenly, a purple gush of fouled wine. 'Get my lord's coachman up here, quickly,' Bayne said, dropping beside his master.

Blade looked at his companions and they went at once.

Bayne produced a phial and squeezed open the old man's mouth. He poured in the liquid, held the nose and mouth shut, and the drug made its uncertain way down the up-struggling gorge. The effect was almost immediate. There was a shudder and a collapse. It was as if all the bones had been dissolved. The clump of the approaching coachman was heard distinctly. Bayne cradled the old head until they arrived, then helped to lift the wasted body. The coachman who carried my lord proceeded whilst Bayne turned to confront Blade and his brothers.

'You have witnessed what you should not have witnessed,' he said.

They remained a solid mass across the corridor, dull and brutal.

'Have that little abortion put down at once.' With this, he turned and went to attend to his responsibilities, feeling that he had given them a direction, feeling unusually and pleasantly powerful.

Porsque and Milon looked to Blade for the nod. Blade, strangely, was undecided. He frowned and moved to the door of the antechamber. Passing through with the others at his heels, he came into the bedroom. The child, still in her coverlet, sat by the fire, looking into it. The dark boy stood beside her, watching her.

'Get out of here, you,' Blade said.

The dark boy moved across warily, coming between the child and her brothers. The child looked up with bleared eyes, roused from her sleep too soon, not comprehending.

'Get out.'

'I've got to take her back. I'm to look after her.'

'We'll see to her. You do what I tell you.'

'No. I've got to take her back.'

The child rose and moved sleepily forward, past the dark boy, towards the doorway in which stood her dog brothers, closing their shoulders, lopsided, revelling in the strength of their ugliness. She approached them as if they did not matter, stood still and waited for them to part or not to part, as they would. The dark boy moved suddenly close in behind her.

'You can't hurt her. Master Cloud sent for her himself. I'm to take her back to him,' he blurted, his words clotted with fear.

The child turned and looked at him, aware for the first time of his attendance, unaware of the significance of what was happening but suddenly full of pleasure in his being there with her against the brute louts who stood in her way. She took his hand. She felt him wince and she remembered, a long time ago, his revulsion at her touch. It was more important now: he did not repulse her.

'Let us go through. Please,' he said pitifully.

'All right,' Blade said.

The brothers subsided with a mutual hiss, but obeyed.

The dark boy and the crippled girl passed through, hand in hand, and the three brothers remained.

'Cloud is dying,' Blade told them. 'We will have her soon enough. We must not move into the heart too soon. It would make us vulnerable.' He had the feeling that they were not convinced by this. He threw them a sop. 'The fiddler boy,' he said, 'him we will, of course, have at our leisure.'

— 6 —

Once out in the corridor, the boy extracted his hand from hers and had to stand still whilst his bowels went weak at the release he had received. The child stood and watched him, hitched the coverlet about her shoulders and pulled at him with smiles. He recovered himself soon, and led her to Cloud. He told Cloud of the outcome of the night's work as he had seen it. Cloud seemed grimly pleased with her, patting her cheeks with his dry fingers. The boy mentioned, stumbling, Blade and his brothers, but Cloud was not interested in them, and certainly not in him.

Then the child did a strange thing. She stood back from Cloud's chair, shook the coverlet from her shoulders and stood naked amongst it, her arms at her sides, looking at him. The boy saw the old man's eyes fill with a sudden delight. There was a moment from which the boy was helplessly excluded; then Cloud told him to cover her up and take her back to Mag.

He took her down, afraid of every shadow, but conscious

of her, nevertheless, as something new, something important, something with a hot beauty that made him unhappy. He had always felt that she was a little thing he could honour with his interest; she was gone far beyond that now. He was vulnerable and frightened of her too.

Mag was waiting for her in the barn doorway, silhouetted by light coming out of the stall. She rushed to recover the child, to hug her and take her inside. The stall door closed and the boy felt the shadows surrounding him. He scurried away quickly to his room.

The room he had colonised and occupied now for many years was a small garret above the Ladies' great chamber and connected to it by a steep, hidden stairway. There were other rooms up there, but all were unoccupied. He had cleared his one room of its debris and maintained it in a pattern of neatness and cleanliness which reflected him directly. It had a bed, a chair, a table and a skylight. He could only stand upright just inside the door now he was grown. He had gathered up there objects and pictures, stones and smooth fragments of coloured glass, straight-edged scraps cut from old books; and a circle of mirror-glass as big as his head. Everything was arranged precisely in its place and into a pattern in his mind which comforted him as he lay there in the darkness, asleep or awake, with his own little perfection surrounding him tightly.

He was musician to the Ladies; and their messenger too, their intimate messenger; with ambitions perhaps to become their chancellor as he grew into his maturity. They knew him and trusted him as they knew and trusted each other; not far, but further than any other man, for he maintained a hard and consistent recoil from their big, warm bodies. Occasionally one of them would reach out for him and he would shudder off the touch. It was not that he was without the edge, the bitter longings, the sour dreams; it was the idea of contact, of physical intimacy, that disgusted him. He was terrified of the flesh's corruptions, terrified of disease. His body was a sanctity, an integrity, held tight whilst the world slipped and slithered and rotted down about him. He dreaded the loss of that integrity, dreaded the corruption surging over him.

He had acquired the fiddle from a travelling man who

had crept into the barns to die. He had a perfect, instinctive comprehension of music. Any fragment of melody that drifted by him he could catch and retain exactly, reading it and transferring its pattern on to his fiddle where, once established, he could reinvent, invert, embellish it at will. It was a gift: he knew it and was grateful for it. Without it he would have been nothing, a kitchen catamite; with it he was able to make his space and to inhabit it clearly. It had been his credential when he had first approached the Ladies. He could make them laugh and dance and weep, and this power he loved because it was such a pure power, demanding no equality, no bartered emotions. He loved to find dark, high corners of the Inn from which to scatter his music, or at least he had done as a child. Growing older, he reserved himself more, was anyway well-known now and had to take his mysteriousness about with him rather than peeking it out of the darkness. He knew that there were some, in the kitchens many, who loathed him and his music. He was careful to avoid all such, but he feared them constantly; they were beyond the reach of his music. Recently he had begun to play for Master Cloud himself. The old man sat rigid and dormant under the weaving of the boy's most intricate lines, but he would call him back occasionally. The boy was glad to go, dreamed of acquiring some essential position in the heart of the Inn, colonising its emotional ranges, marshalling and expressing them. The thought of such power made him glow.

Taking up his fiddle that night after returning the little hunchback to Mag, he felt a personal need of his music. He closed the door tightly, hoping that none of his music would escape. He played without thought, tripping his fingers and pumping his bow, looping endless melodies around each other with indissoluble energy. He was attempting to exorcise a need in himself which he did not understand but which was embodied in the image, the idea, of the little, naked cripple girl whom he had been following for so many years now. He knew what they had done to her tonight and it disgusted him, physically, brought bile into his mouth. But she had endured it and, enduring it, she had somehow enhanced herself for him. She ought to have been diminished and reduced, but she had not been. She was not drugged and degraded as the others always were. Somehow, he came to realise, the little cripple had survived it.

The child herself, after the effusions of Mag, after examination and anointing with strange unctions, powerfully sweet and stinging to the inner flesh, lay wrapped in a new coverlet, warm and sore, beyond sleep, in a pale exhaustion that, in the dark, with only the far-away glimmer of Mag's lantern, was strangely pleasant. The act itself had been at first frightening, then absurd, then pathetic. The preparations had frightened her, the hush and the hurry that had surrounded them, the special mysterious logic that was applied to her over and over again. Then to be perched up on that bed with her arse in the air whilst that old, bony man had fumbled into her, that had been absurd. It had hurt at the point of rupture, but her flesh had eased quickly round it and was prepared to welcome it when it had been sucked out of her; it had been trivial. Then the old man lolling in his chair, looking at her as if she had felled him, a melting old skeleton shuddering and trying to summon up some potent curse against her whilst she had been stood there waiting for him to ask something of her, to put her to some use at least. That couldn't have been all there was to it. But he was all bone and no flesh and he had begun to set hard, and she had been so sleepy. Of her passage to Cloud and back to the stall she had only the ghostliest of memories, mostly of the dark boy who, by contrast to the old man, had been all sinuous flesh and actively desirable. She went on wanting.

Over the succeeding weeks she waited impatiently to be called into service again, but was not called. She had a strength and an individuality which she wanted to be put to use. A sense of accumulating disappointment settled in her.

She did try, one windy afternoon, making eyes at a couple of minions at work on a stack of logs near to the carpenters' shed, trying to draw them into the dark barn with her. They noted and understood her, considered her as she leant against the wall and touched herself, smoothing her body to make them imagine it. They were imagining, but she could see that she had made them nervous with her provocations. They whispered together, looked about them, but decided to ignore her.

Mag got to know of this and was severe. 'You go putting yourself round down here, knuckle, and I'll make your fat little arse so bloody raw you'll scream at the thought of a kitchen-boy's prick.' And she shook the child until she cried.

Then one day she heard the music again, singing deep within the dark barn, and she roused entirely and rushed into the darkness to find him. She did not find him and the music ceased. She sat and cried for herself.

Months passed and she grew morose, sulking when Mag tried to tend her, inciting a reciprocal rage in the old woman who slapped her frequently. The stall began to reek of ill-humour.

'You're a wretched little thing,' Mag said at last, 'a wretched and ruinous little hedgehog. You're even beginning to smell like one. D'you think they'll call for you when you stink like that?'

She took this last advice at least, drew herself together with a regimen of cleansing, washing and grooming, aggressively, to take out on her flesh the spite she felt within, a prickling hedgehog thing indeed, all greedy nose and dirty spines.

Eventually she was called up again to be of service. By the time it came, her dissatisfactions had settled so resolutely into her that even this call for which she had longed gave her little release. She was grown bitter and surly, had become possessed of deeper desires now. Perhaps if what they had used her for had been of any importance, it might have been different, but she knew by the lack of mystery with which she was collected and prepared that she was merely filling an absence, doing a chore.

She was led to a sordid room where two boys, fuddled with drink, were allowed to maul her nakedness. They were clumsy and painful, only one of them achieving his purpose and that perfunctorily and awkwardly. She lay on the smeared sheets and had to listen as they congratulated each other, boasting of how brave a thing it was they were doing. Above all, these lies revolted her. She sat up and watched them, but they would take no notice of her, had done with her, or were afraid of her more likely.

She left them to their own regard, snuggled down and slept, in a real bed at least, amongst real sheets, in which she could imagine herself waiting for the whole world to lift its energies up and come to her.

In the morning she woke to find the room full of light and the dark boy by her bed.

'Good morning to you, Lady Mariole.'

She was so riotously glad to see him, she leapt up in the bed to embrace him. He stepped away, grew confused and grim. She too drew back, insulted. She looked at him and became aware, calmly, of the hard physical divide he insisted on maintaining between them. She pulled the blankets about her nakedness and this seemed to reassure him. He looked around the room and saw the gown she had been wearing for her arrival. It lay on a chair where she had draped it. He brought her the gown and she struggled into it; he did not help her with this.

Dressed again, she slid to the floor before him, forgot the bed behind her and was prepared to be quite submissive. Such submission was put on with her gown and, suddenly, it seemed fitting, natural, exciting for her. She did not want to cling to him, must not, not yet; there were perhaps other satisfactions; she wanted first to be with him.

'Would you like to see my room?' he asked.

She played coy, which was precisely right.

'Have no apprehensions, my lady. I am not without respect. I will play for you. It would give me pleasure.'

She recalled his old betrayals of her, but the memory could not hold up against her edging pleasure. She went with him into a draughty corridor, along to the great room where the Ladies had danced, round the edge of it and through a curtain, up a steep and smelly stairway, ushered by him, going where he indicated from just behind her, breathing upon her warmly.

In his tiny room she sat upon his bed, her legs tucked under her, her sex beating quietly as he played, winding and circling her round and round. He was playing for her purely and directly and it was a pleasure that consumed her. Tears ran down her cheeks. Her body glowed and hummed. She rocked on the edge of a laugh that never quite broke. She watched his thin body standing awkward by his door, the fiddle under his chin, his fingers arching and moving, his bow diving and jumping, stroking and sawing. The music had no particular shape or colour to it; it was too close for that. It was a whole atmosphere. It filled the room and it filled the light that fell into the room. It was perfect. She was entirely happy at that moment, entirely embodied in her sensations, entirely free of herself. She was his entirely.

She loved him and, afterwards, back in the dreamy, dusty reality of the stall, she longed for something to give him back, something she could trade for the music which he had bestowed upon her. But what did she have apart from the humped little body, which he did not want? Her tongue was tied, her hands raw and unskilled. She could think of nothing, she was nothing. It made her sad. If only she could have sent that sadness out of her in some comprehensible form she would have been free; but she was alone.

One night, not long after this, she woke to find the stall full of strange lights and hard shadows. She had come abruptly to the surface of her sleep and various panics clutched at her. She recognised the brute brothers, Porsque and Milon. She saw Mag rise up to face them, dwarfed by them; Old Mag dwarfed and afraid, a shrivelled old woman pleading hopelessly. They were looking at the child who pulled her bedclothes about her and backed herself into a corner of the stall, braced herself against it. She felt afraid of them as she had not been before. Before, they might have killed her; now it was only pain they wanted of her. And more than that, she found herself wanting life suddenly, aware of the grip of her heartbeat within her, aware of the black rising of her fear. Had she been able to imagine any sense to it, she would have leapt up at them; but their faces were too hard, too full of readiness, their mouths too set, their eyes too sharp. They came towards her.

She saw that they pulled a weight between them, a tattered, wet bulk which they lugged towards her. She knew it was some monstrosity. She assumed that she was to be required to offer herself to this monstrosity. She grew at once defiant, contracted herself fiercely to keep whatever it was out of her if she could. A stench of blood and filth wallowed at her as they approached. They reached down and pulled up the head. It was the dark boy, or the remnant of him, his face gone, mangled and puffed with their violence.

'Your prince, my lady,' one of them said.

They dropped him before her and turned away. She screamed, the sound rising like a thorn through her throat. They stopped, turned back, laughed and left.

In the minutes following their departure, held still by the stun of her scream, Mag and the child were immobilised. Then the child came out of her corner and went down on her knees before the boy, not knowing how to touch him, not knowing whether he was even alive. Mag came into action, bustled forward and began pulling at his ankles.

'We've got to get him out of here. Quick. We'll pull him into the courtyard and leave him there. Quick now. Come and help me.'

The child was lost for a moment, but as soon as Mag began to move him she flung herself forward on to the boy's back to halt the old woman, glaring fiercely up at her. The boy emitted a groan of shifting agony and both the old woman and the child drew back. His being sensible, his being alive, opened new dimensions to their problem, making each more determined.

'Now, now,' Mag said, 'don't you go stupid on me now, girl. Shake him out of here. It's too much for us now.'

The girl bared her teeth and clenched her fists and Mag, who had always before solved any differences between them with a cuff and a wrench, saw now what she was facing, at last, and drew away, looking instinctively for something with which to arm herself. The child, however, was possessed of a superior determination based upon a new, hot loyalty. She was suddenly proud that he had been brought to her; and Mag was impotent to fight with her. Even as she advanced with her stave, Mag knew she would be defeated, or that victory would be so messy as to be pointless. She threw the stave aside, knelt down and wailed, at the limit of her resources, having always known that this little deformity would one day be too much for her, as life itself would one day be too much for her in spite of her incessant wakefulness and the shrivelled impermeability of her heart and soul. She knelt and stooped over and wailed and wailed.

The child, watching Mag's infolding, waited. She did not

trust it, assumed it to be merely a ruse to take her off guard. She watched for Mag's eyes to flick up from her wailing, to pry out her opportunity. The child waited, covering the boy, tensed for resistance, wondered where her teeth might find their deepest hold upon the old hag's flesh.

Time passed and Mag did not change, nor did she let up on her wailing which began to grate upon the child's nerves in a spiral of mounting violence until she could stand it no longer. She sprang forward at the old woman, hissing and hitting out. Mag squealed and fled with the child's fists about her head and shoulders, with the child trying to clamber up on her back and pull her face apart. Once out in the yard the child let go, sped back into the stall and bolted the door. Mag bundled herself down in the dismal night air and continued her wailing, quieter now, aware of the Inn which rose above her and of the darkness which rose above even that.

The child meanwhile had taken the lantern and had settled down by the boy to begin the long task of reclaiming him, if that were possible. His hair was matted with blood and his clothes were ripped apart from within and without. She ran her hand over his torso, but he gave no indication of sensitivity. His head, badly cut, was puffing up. His nose was broken and handfuls of his hair were missing, his scalp patched with blood. But these were superficial. He breathed easier now, sleeping. He would be all right in a while. They had not hurt him profoundly, had frightened him out of his self-respect, but that was easily convalesced. Then she saw that they had broken both his hands, had crushed them into a meaningless mess of bone and flesh. She wept for him then with a misery that flowed through her like the darkness.

When she had cleaned him and roused him, forced some of Mag's spirit into his broken mouth, she wrapped him in a blanket and took him from the stall across the courtyard and into the Inn. She refused to glance at Mag as she passed. It was very early, not yet dawn, and even the first stirrers had hardly begun their sleepy ablutions as she took him on his way. She fastened a blanket over his shoulders and draped it hood-like over his face. Such a figure would not be remarkable amongst the first movements of the Inn. He walked on his own, steadily, but without direction. She directed him, through the kitchens where the fires were being raked and revived, up the stairs which were wet and slippery with scrubbing, along corridors where the nightdust had settled and staled. She was resolute and unafraid until they came to the lobbies of the great room.

She paused there. But she could not go back now. She moved through the quiet lobbies and through the curtains into the great room which was empty. She had never seen it empty and it alarmed her thus. The figure beside her was unaware of anything and she did not consider him, just steered him on, down the steps, across the expanse of rugged floor, boldly across the middle of it. There was a dead stillness around her. The candles were spent into great mounds of cold, sickly wax. There were glasses and bottles and plates of congealed discards. But there was no one. She hurried him on but he was loathe to be hurried.

Eventually they came to the curtain that led, through the small alcove that stank of cold urine, to his stairway; but as they reached this curtain she felt a presence move behind her. She turned to see the ugly woman far across the room, fixing them, coming hurriedly towards them.

The woman approached, looking from side to side, apprehensive. The child had never seen her without her assurance before, and did not know whether to be relieved or afraid.

'He'll be safe up there,' the woman was saying, 'for a while at least. Don't let him come down. They'll not come up there after him. If they had wanted to finish him, they would have. They might forget him up there. I'll do what I can, but if he comes down here, I'll denounce him and you. Go now.' And she pushed them both into the alcove, tidied the curtain closed behind them and was gone.

Up in his attic, she found it had not been invaded as she had feared it might have been. A sense of safety grew round her. She barred the door with a chair as best she could, and guided him to the bed, laying him down carefully. She felt then quite exhausted. She lay down beside him and slept up against him, trying to spread the warmth of her body into his. He lay still on his back, wound in the blanket, set hard against a deep, internal shuddering. She curled herself to him but he had set himself against her, against all of them. She wondered whether he was awake or asleep, sometimes sitting up to see. Usually his eyes were open, glinting within their puffed sockets, wet but black and distant. She resumed her sleep, for her own sake finally, enjoying the stretch of his body if only in her imagination.

She stayed with him for many days up in his room. Food was left for them daily in the stinking alcove whence she collected it. He sat up to eat, doing so dutifully, receiving with difficulty the broth-soaked knobs of bread she broke and pushed between his lips. She attended to his cleanliness, washing him, swabbing his torn skin and rebinding his mangled hands which hurt him fearfully. This was a futile operation: they would always be cramped, dead claws. She feared infection in them however and she remained assiduous; glad when the threat of sepsis seemed to be past. The swelling and the pain seemed to grow less; she could bind tighter in a fiction of healing. He closed his eyes, would not look at his hands unbound.

At first she tended him dutifully and thoughtlessly. He was hardly real to her in those first days, no more than some strange creature she had found abandoned and was endeavouring to keep alive out of blind humanity. Later though, she began to look at him, to see again what had caught her imagination in him. She touched the dark skin, smooth and finely textured, dry, without the pale fleshiness which characterised her own surface. She regarded the long limbs, the tight torso, the lean head. The face was beginning to deflate and to lose its blue stains. It would be scarred and distorted, but as such badges lost the immediacy of pain which distanced her from them, they would seem noble etchings, fine individualities. His eyes were dark and clear now. His hair, which she groomed so carefully, so gently, was beginning to give pleasure to her touch. And underneath all these various surfaces, animating them all, was his life which, when she had first brought him up here, had been panicked and threshing about below the clamp of pain, but which was now growing calm and strong. She would lie at night with her head over his heart, listening.

She thought of leaving him now that he was growing stronger. He could lift a cup to his lips now, held between the pads of his hands, steadily, drinking easily. She could have left him, or would soon be able to leave him. But she would not. Her ministrations were not selfless nor had they ever been. She loved him and she wanted to be nowhere else. As his strength amassed, so did her anticipation. She laid her body beside his and rejoiced in the tension of her pleasure. She was careful to lie very still, to resist the temptation to complete her pleasure in any obvious way. It was enough to be beside him. Every day drew her nearer to the day when he would turn and respond to her. And when that happened there would be liberty. They would be free to rise and leave the Inn. She realised that she had, quite suddenly, begun to imagine a world beyond the Inn. She had no independent images that might people such a world. She felt it rather as a space, a place of uncluttered light and air, a place where movement and expansion would not be restricted, where she, above all, would be able to stand straight. She waited for him with a steady energy and willing that was as certain as morning.

He would never meet her eyes. Not once did she catch him watching her. When she came near him to tend him, he closed his eyes tightly. At first she accepted this, but as the days passed it began to rankle in her. She felt that his avoidance of her was deliberate. He was ungrateful, spiteful, cruel to her. She came to want only his look, only his recognition of her. She would not leave him until she had this from him, only this, only this.

But when it came, at last, it brought with it everything else. She was washing him, sponging down his body, engrossed in her contact with him, glancing up without thinking to find him there at last, clear and full, with her at last, the eyes engaged and sustained upon her. She jumped within herself and had to draw back from him to contain and direct the jumping within her. He lay before her, long and naked, his face blemished, his hands in ragged mitts of bandaging, but perfect as she had dreamt of him. He followed her with his eyes, raised his mangled hands in supplication. She approached him carefully, held his glance, but flicked her eyes once down his body and back. She placed her hands on his face and the eyelids dropped down. Her hands were cool and wet; his face was burning, the emotion masked by his darkness. She put her mouth on his mouth and breathed into him. She smoothed her hand down across his chest and belly and covered and held his risen sex.

'My lady,' he said, his voice broken but the words stamped out precisely into the silence in which they had been locked for so long. And three seconds after he spoke, the tension sprang in his sex and the fluid leapt across his stomach.

She kept very still, allowing the moment to diffuse about them. His eyes were open now, looking wild. She was afraid of what she had done to him. She drew away eventually, intending to undress quickly and clasp herself over him.

'Clean me!' he said. 'Clean me and cover me! Help me.'

She obeyed, subdued, her own pleasure grown elephant-ine. When he was wiped up and wrapped again in his covers, she waited for the sleep which she knew would soon come to him, which it did quickly enough; then she attended to herself, unable to resist it now, hoisting up her skirts, kneeling on the floor beside him and touching her centre, dreaming that it was his touch, swelling and breaking with a shudder that woke him.

'What are you doing?' he asked, struggling up to look over at her.

She withdrew her hand quickly, guiltily, looking up at him for forgiveness.

'What were you doing? What were you doing?'

She raised her skirts and showed him. He trembled at the sight, wept; and she wept too, not daring to approach him.

She busied herself taking down the slop bowl and endur-ing the foul alcove in which one of the Ladies moaned and stank, abandoned there. She wandered off into the corridors for a while, needing to be afraid, needing to be at the mercy of the cruel, impersonal Inn for a while. She returned to him after nightfall to find him standing at the foot of his bed, peering through the skylight, bundled in his blankets but shivering nakedly.

She lit a small candle and set out the food she had brought up, a bowl of meaty soup with sops of dumpling. The ugly woman had kept her promise. She turned to him, looking for him to come and eat. He stood still, watching her, his face grown puffy again, his eyes dark, his mouth open. She waited for him.

He shuddered and shook the covers from his shoulders.

In the small light she could see that his sex was again risen out of him, a dark curve of swollen flesh. He was looking at her resolutely, pleading with her.

She untied her laces and the tight, plain dress she wore fell from her. He did not seem at all concerned with her nakedness; which hurt her. He made as if to approach her but the slope of the roof prevented him. She climbed on to the bed and knelt herself as they had taught her, presented her sex to him under the ridge of her back. He made his way awkwardly to her, stumbling and groping out, crying in pain at every jar. Once behind her he began to probe clumsily and she had to reach under, between her legs, to direct him. She felt him suddenly pushed into her, felt his bound hands steadying him on her back, felt his legs trembling against hers. She buried her head down in her hands to treasure these peripheral sensations constructed about the enormity of his intromission of her. He began a sequence of irregular shoves which activated her but produced no continuity, none of the cyclic swell of pleasure that she required of him. She grew angry with him, clenched her fists and beat upon the bolster. She felt his completion within her; the melting of his sex was soft and liquid and sweet, but small and he pulled away quickly, struggled off the bed and found the mug of broth which he drank greedily and messily, clasping it to his face and swallowing the greasy dumplings whole.

She sat beside him, followed the style of his feeding, although she took her time, not wanting to be awake all night with gut-cramp. When he had finished he lay back on the bed, closed his eyes and slept, or appeared to. She shuffled her body against his and drew the covers over them.

So began a long, long struggle. It was her fault. She had raised the fiend in him. He lived in a state of pitiful slavery under it. Most of the time he lay deep in a languor. Once, twice, sometimes three times a day he would twist all the desolation into a strut of perverse energy which bloated his cock. She would kneel dutifully down and he would sink himself into the sleeve of flesh she offered him, push himself irregularly against her lean buttocks, sometimes for ages and ages, until the tension shot and he discharged his little strength into her, lapsing immediately into the depth of his lassitude.

She began to nurture a growing anger at his inability to

attain anything beyond this dog-like act, this succession of imprecise shunting and small discharge, leaving her increasingly numb and hardly even aroused; not that he would have noticed. At first she had turned aside and attended to herself, but soon the sheer monotony of their situation wearied and withered even this. She began to loathe him, above all for his silence. He hardly spoke a word to her. He indicated his need by pushing her, or sometimes just showing her his cock. She was all cunt to him.

She did not know how long they had been at this, saw no progression in it, wanted to be gone from him. And yet every time he approached her, a corresponding glint of hope sprang in her, a glint which kept her submissive, just, kept her there, her anger holding. Nor did she ever acquit herself of blame for what was going wrong. There was something she had not learned, something she did not achieve in him, as he in her. If only, like a real person, she had been able to go down on her back, to open her whole body to him rather than just her sad little rump, her knotty little hump.

The room began to stink, to reflect their disorders. Their bodies inhabited a closing chaos, static and degenerating. Half-eaten food lay about the floor, soiled linen, broken objects. Only his little circle of mirror-glass remained untainted, on the wall, above; but they never looked into it. It hovered above them like a moon, perfect and distant.

But waking one night before he awoke, with a pale silver-blue light coming down upon them, making them of one luminous texture, she found him aroused and knew that he would awake soon and make his demand. She kept very still, listening for the sounds of his body which would indicate his surfacing. He breathed on, the deep pulls of sleep with a little shudder at the back of each exhalation to indicate his permanent, essential tension. She examined her feelings at this moment of stillness, the dread of another bout of dog-love, the grain of hope that something real, something truly potent would break from him into her. Upon his body, tiny droplets of moisture glittered. She knew again his beauty, after everything, his long, supple beauty.

He gave a little splutter to signify his imminent waking. He groaned and she heard his eyelids flick open. She lay still. He reached down at once to his sex, his maimed hand upon it and whimpered, stirring and shaking at her. She remained obdurately still, a concept of defiance forming in her and strengthening as it formed.

But then she had a much better idea, was suddenly all awake and moving. She straddled his body and sat on his stomach, pressing her weight down upon his forearms.

'What are you doing?' he asked. 'Get off me, will you? I can't breathe. Get off me, you cripple!'

She showed him her teeth and she saw him grow afraid. This gave her strength. She lifted up, reached under her and fed his sex into hers. At last she had him, spread out below her. She rode him slowly and evenly, leaning down over him, brushing her breasts against him.

'I don't like this!' he cried.

But she did. The hard protrusion of his sex nubbed against hers which flowed and opened and closed around him, spreading pleasure down her thighs and up into her belly. Her completion was sudden and violent, twisting her up about it. She felt his release, warm and small within her. She lay upon him finally stilled and covered him with kisses which he was too weak to resist, his mouth open, his head held tight against hers.

She slept eventually and, once convinced of this, he extricated himself from her quickly and carefully. He was in a state of held panic, had to get from her. He gnawed at the binding round his hands and released them. They were numb but not entirely unusable. Through a fog of pain he found trousers, a shirt and a jacket, pulling them on. He was woefully thin. He could not manage shoes. The thought of trying to manage shoes made him sick. He would flee her quickly. He burrowed in his little wooden chest which he kept under his bed and found in it the knife that he had hidden there. He had stolen it a long while ago and, although he had cleaned it and sharpened it and handled it regularly, he had never had the courage to take it out with him. He struggled to put his fingers round its haft, struggled to make it his weapon, the key to his freedom. He left the room and made his way along his corridor, into one of the deserted rooms, through old panelling, into roof-spaces, down to the level of the ground, yard-level, street-level, by a maze of a way which only he knew of. He knew where he was going.

7

Edwin Cloud had been dead several days. Gray knew about it and was working quickly and secretly. Blade was now, ostensibly, with or without Cloud, the only power in the Inn, with his two bludgeon-boys to express his power, and a growing cluster of satellite minions who were drifting in for a share in the new order. Gray knew that their first absolute move would be against him. Only he, however, knew that Cloud was dead; and his, therefore, was the first move.

Now he must consummate his power. He was the inheritor of the Inn. He would find a partner as sexless as Cloud had been, to run the business. He had hoped it might be Blade, but Blade was not sexless. No one as cruel as Blade had become, was sexless.

He was moving now. He had Porsque and Milon poisoned, not fatally yet, just enough to keep them squirming over their own anuses for as long as he needed. He went to visit his brother who, he knew, was uncharacteristically unguarded, visited by a dental abscess which Gray had not instigated, but which was a gift. Fortune was evidently with him.

He came upon his brother in his room, brooding, looking up at him as he entered unbidden, trying to narrow his watery eyes.

'Brother,' said Gray cheerfully.

'What do you want?' Blade said, through a mouthful of pain, reaching for a stick. 'Go back to your women.'

'Women,' he said largely, 'have always possessed what is most valuable in the world. You are foolish to have ignored women, Blade. It has made you narrow.'

Blade slashed with his stick which had become a sword. Gray, expecting this, lifted a chair to receive the sword's point and broke it. The brothers faced one another.

'Cloud's dead,' Gray said.

'I don't believe you.'

'Yes, you do.'

Gray watched his brother then slowly submit, his face

going pale with the finality, the stupidity of his defeat. 'There can be no compromise,' he said.

This might have been a question; it came as a flat statement. Gray had hoped, sentimentally, that there might have been a compromise; but confronted with the reality of his sickly brother, he knew there could not be. He produced a small black bottle from his pocket, placing it on the table before Blade.

'Some medicine for your toothache.'

Blade took up the bottle, glanced at it then threw it down into the cold fireplace where it shattered.

'You'll have to do it personally.'

'Ah, I thought I might.' And he brought a pistol from his pocket, raising, cocking and discharging it in one movement. Blade jolted briefly, the ball making a ragged hole in his forehead above one eye. The hole smoked then gushed blood then, as Blade fell, began to discharge foul matter.

Gray watched this with a real sadness. He had not meant to kill his brother. It seemed from a cursory glance that he had meant to do so; but he had meant merely to prove his supremacy. He had naturally come armed. He had never planned to kill Blade.

It seemed as if events had taken over and that he was no longer personally, individually responsible. It is Fate, he told himself, regarding his brother's upturned fish eyes and smashed forehead. He felt free of any restraint, propelled upon certainties, riding the crucial moment. He left the room and locked it, dropping the key down a drain-shaft as he passed. It would be another of the Inn's many sealed rooms. He knew of a dozen such doors which were locked on long-forgotten secrets. Blade, amongst his first commands, would have had them all opened. He, Gray, would never open them. He had an instinctive understanding of the Inn and its binding mysteries. That was why he, and not Blade, had inherited. The time would come when his sisters, too, would have to be locked away permanently. His next decision must be upon the fate of Porsque and Milon; but his instinct to finish with them at once was deflected as he turned and resolved to do it. Without Blade they were done for in one sense anyway. They still might be dangerous, but it was a predictable danger.

He considered The Hedgehog next. Blade had provided an imaginative, if temporary, fate for her; but it was a fate dependent upon the fiddler-boy who was also Blade's creature in that Blade had worked his destruction as well. Now Blade was gone, the fiddler-boy became an unknown factor once again, and consequently The Hedgehog needed to be seen to. As he walked the corridors thinking of this, Gray became convinced of its urgency and he set his course for it directly.

As he rose on to the landing where she and her fiddler-boy lived, he became aware of the light falling on to the attics. The day was foggy and a dense white muffling clung to the glass of the skylights, bright and sharp, but completely opaque. It gave him a claustrophobia which blurred him. He must find her and kill her quickly. He had his stiletto sewn tightly into his coat. He would twist her head aside and open her throat. He would lock the door on her.

He saw that the room was open. He went in, knife out. The room was empty. It reeked of copulation, a sour, stale smell that, not being his own, disgusted him. The fog oozed close on the window-glass and seemed to be leaking into the room. He caught a sudden image of his face in the circle of mirror-glass on the wall, and he saw the cruelty, the mad cruelty in which he dwelt, briefly held there before him. That's not what I am, he told himself. That is only what it is necessary, under the pressure of the time, for me to become. He turned and went out into the narrow corridor. He searched the adjoining rooms and he found the other way out and down which he ought to have known about, but which he had not known about. Blade would have known.

And suddenly the moment of his destiny was gone from him, blown out like a candle. He turned sickly and did not know whither to go. The Hedgehog was loose. Had he come up an hour earlier he would have caught her and killed her; but she had escaped, and with her all the secrets of the Inn were out. The ironies of all this seemed so inevitable that he did not even bother to consider how a dumb cripple could spill the Inn's secrets. But she could and she would. And indeed she did.

She had woken after her triumph over the dark boy from a

sweet dream. She had woken and he was gone, and that at first did not matter to her; the achievement was complete in itself and perhaps it was better that the pleasure established was not yet cloyed by another layer of his reality. This was her first reaction, coming clear from her sleep. Soon after she began to remember his danger down there and her heart began to tighten for him. She rose and dressed herself hurriedly to seek and to retrieve him. The futility of this soon overtook her. If he had not already fled the Inn, then they would already have him. The reality of losing him came upon her. She would never see him again. Somewhere down there they were completing the obscenity they had begun. She curled herself up on his bed and felt the bitterness of their cruelty. Nothing happened that was not cruel, that was not the exercise of power by the strong upon the weak. She raged at the injustice of it, the injustice which she herself personified in her mute and crippled and used body. She was the symbol of the Inn, of what it did to those it owned. She had been born a slave, an object of use and, resisting this, she felt the heat of rebellion rise in her. She rose with it, off the bed, through the open door and out into the narrow landing, nurturing this spirit before the futility of it overwhelmed her once again. She considered ways in which she might effectively throw herself against the weight of the Inn. She could think of nothing, only of hurling her tiny strength against one or other of them. But they were not the Inn, not the cruel brothers, not the ugly woman: they were the creatures of the Inn as he was, her dark lover, as she was; they were all of them in and of its systems forever.

She decided nevertheless to follow him; to see, at least, what he had done, what had been done to him, to see if it had made any difference. She would return to Mag, if she would have her. She would learn to offer herself to men in pleasing ways as Mag did, to become only her child, at last, as perhaps she was always meant to be. These had merely been the days of adjustment, the days of learning before the inevitable submission.

Out in the corridor again, she noted an open door into one of the other garrets. She followed through and, amongst the piles of jumble, discarded furnishings and mouldy bundles, all furred with dust, she found an open trapdoor in a wall which she had not known about before, but which was obviously his way out. She burrowed on and the darkness of the high roof-spaces surrounded her.

Shown her way by fractures of light, she descended through the darkness. The beams here were older and fatter and dustier than the beams in the barns; and she was enclosed by a sense of the Inn which, unlike the barns, was alive, murmuring and secretive, ticking and plotting. She found her way, through a split panel into a bare room with windows whitewashed. In the centre was a table on which was a pile of papers tied tight with thin straps of black ribbon. She glanced at the papers, at the yellowed writing upon them. She fingered the lettering and longed to be able to read it. She lifted the bundle. It was light and bursting with dust. There was a rectangle of dark wood where it had lain, a deep shine in the ubiquitous stratum of the dust, like a black mirror. She felt that she was holding a great secret to her heart although that secret was closed to her. Systematically, she ripped the papers which crumbled to dust in her hands. She scattered them about the room, and went to the door which was locked. She set her weight against the lock and felt it break with a sudden but easy splintering; she was out in one of the great corridors. Pulling the broken door to behind her, she proceeded.

As she advanced along the corridor, she felt in the muffling stillness that people were scurrying behind the closed doors, were keeping very still and waiting for her to pass. This feeling puzzled her but gave her courage.

She came at last to a small staircase which she recognized definitely, and which took her down into the kitchens. The kitchens were, for the first time in her remembrance, still. The minions and their masters stood by their tables in silent groups. The ovens billowed out heat, but nothing was in progress. She looked for faces she recognised but strangely found none. Glances were sneaked at her, but mostly turned away from her to let her pass as if she was an irrelevance. She looked for Master Allrig but his place was taken by another master, old and wizened, outweighed by his apron of office. She looked for Master Tow, but he too had been replaced by a parody of himself. As she passed the table of meats, however, she realised that this was Mr Tow himself, although what had befallen him she could not begin to imagine. She caught his eye and paused, looking to him for a sign, a word, as she always did, but he did not seem to recognize her. Something was happening, something was over. Realising this gave her a new energy.

In the courtyard the mist was so thick that the barn was mere darkness ahead of her. She crossed the cobbling and the mist enclosed her. To her left she saw a light move, gleaming through then vanishing. She deflected herself towards the light and she found it had passed on the road outside the Inn, that the gates were open and there was no one in attendance. The secret parts of the Inn were open. She could slip away. She would. She would go and give a farewell to Mag and then she would be gone.

She came to the barn and saw light falling from the stall mouth. There was something wrong about the way the light danced. She became afraid, began to regret turning away from the open gateway. It would be better just to run and be gone. She turned to the courtyard again and saw the stillness of the fog, its solidity, the way it pushed everything into the distance, held her where she was with something horrible at her shoulder, glowing there in the shivering lamplight. She turned back to it, hoping to beat down her fear in her confrontation of it.

It did not go down. It came out strongly, like a stench. She advanced, a step at a time, and saw the familiar objects of the stall, but saw no reassurance in them. Things had been smashed, rifled, torn apart. Some savagery had come here. She saw Mag's legs jutting out from under a covering of straw. The whole stall was decked with blood. A great puddle of it seeped from the straw. It glistened black in the lantern light. She knew what had happened. She saw the box where Mag had hoarded her earnings open and empty. She knew who had done this.

She fell to her knees. She cleared away the straw, the covering of the crime, the hypocritical modesty over the obscenity. She would at least uncover it.

The old woman had been stabbed repeatedly. Her clothes were rent and her fat flesh burst through them, torn open, congealing. Her head was missing. This seemed to the child the most awful thing of all, to deprive her not only of her life, but of her self. She looked about her, now herself drenched in blood, having to breathe harder and harder to retain her strength. She saw an axe-haft amongst the straw. She scrambled amongst the debris and finally, suddenly, her fingers were playing helplessly over Old Mag's face. She closed the eyes, smoothed her hand over the bald skull, so small in death, avoiding the severed stub of neck, touching the features as if they were still Mag's; but the coldness and the weight of death was set upon them. She raised the little round thing and faced it. The eyes were shut, the mouth open, slack; the thing was nothing. Mag was gone.

She submitted to a terrible grieving then that rose up in her and broke her. The finality of death was like a stone wall into which she had been thrown bodily, only now recovering her senses, only now hurting. She sobbed and choked, retched and raged and curled herself down, smearing herself with the filth of the stall, Mag's filth; living and dead, Mag's filth. She crammed the filth into her mouth, ground it into her flesh and raged.

She searched for a strong cloth, found an old childhood smock that she had not worn for years, but which at last she had outgrown rather than outworn. In this she wrapped the head and, tucking it under her arm, she left the stall.

About the courtyard were many figures, tall and obscured in the greyness of the mist. When she appeared they were moving; as she proceeded they stopped, stood still, went solid in the mist and against the fury of her movement. Bearing with her the head of Old Mag, she crossed to the gate and passed through it into the narrow, squalid lane that ran along the back wall of the Inn and the back of other buildings, equally tall, dark, silent, a gigantic graveyard in the sticky fog. She proceeded.

She followed the lane which was long and filthy and squeezed tighter and tighter between high, dripping walls, until suddenly it debouched on to a thoroughfare, much like the lane in composition and environment, only broader, more mirey. Here, for the first time, she saw people, people not of the Inn. Everyone she had ever met had been of the

Inn; even those whom she had seen with the freedom to leave the Inn had, for the duration of their stay there, been digested by it; as she had been. But here, at last, were the fabulous people who had not been touched by the Inn. They were shapes only, so far, in the fog, dark shapes but moving. The Inn she now thought, as she moved away from it, was frozen, solidified, waiting only for the earth to shudder to bring it all down. Out here, above all, there was movement. She was moving; her body beginning to succumb to the cold, her extremities numbing, but she kept moving. The more she kept going the further away from the Inn she would be and the more anonymous she would become. She assumed that it was obvious to anyone who happened to glance at her that she was from the Inn. If she walked on long enough she would arrive at a place where the Inn did not exist; except in so far as she brought it with her, would always carry it, a part of her deformity. This awareness weighted her. She trudged on, her feet swelling and growing thick with icy mud which caked its way up her calves. She still clutched her token, a severed human head.

As she walked the people grew more frequent. Some of them passed quite close to her, high above her with a scuffle of clothing, a thump and squelch of boot-soles. She set her head down and pushed onwards, clasping herself tightly together. She was soon amongst a crowd, moving and milling along a dark, wide street which revealed a solid level of cobbling beneath its slimy surface. Lights appeared at irregular intervals above her, round, orange balls, flaring out. She heard swaddled voices calling. Leaps of laughter jumped into the air above her and were gone. Around her moved people, all formless, wrapped in heavy cloaks and dark coats, pushing and packed. She began to have to negotiate a way amongst them. They shoved and jostled against her. She felt one or two of them caught, regarding her. This impelled her onwards, pushing energy and purpose back into her rapidly shrinking self. Her mind was beginning to slip and slither in its weariness. She walked and staggered, stumbled and pushed herself, thumping into people, bashing into walls and posts and crates. She became aware of herself as a small, drifting mote in a turbulent flood, noisy and full of cruel purpose and blind momentum. Doors opened and gushed light and smoke and voices. Still she pressed herself on until she could hardly move, had to struggle to squeeze herself forward through the formless movement of the crowd. She began in her desperation to imagine that she was being borne round in a circle back to the Inn, that she would suddenly fall through a doorway and be grabbed, taken back, that this strange new world was no new world, just the external, liquefied substance of the old world.

Suddenly she spun out of the crowd and was in a tiny blind alley with house backs rising up over her on three sides and the fourth, behind her, the mill of the street. There were boxes and barrels, old and decayed, at the blind end of the alley. She fell into them and burrowed down amongst them and fell into a black sleep that ate her whole.

When she woke it was night and the world was filled with a vast downpouring of rain. She woke to hear her own feverish shudderings rattling the box-slats about her. She broke free of them desperately, still clutching her treasure, the token that would buy her her freedom, although she could hardly now recall what it was. She fought for breath and shoved herself forward, out again into the street. It was dark and deserted now although, through the rain, she could still see lights glinting. She was stripped of all purpose, shivered and shaken of direction.

She hobbled onward, stumbling and falling often now, her knees and elbows barked on the cobbles that gleamed in the rain like great, black knuckles. She moved just to keep moving, knowing that if she stopped she would be finally overcome. This began to matter less and less. Let me only see an end to this night, to this downpour, she thought, then I will give in. She grew delirious; strange forms, bright and sickly, appeared at the edge of her thoughts. She did not mistake them for anything external, knew they were freaks of her own imagining, that they were the attempts of something strong within herself that sought to overcome her. She struggled on, her arms cramped rigidly about her burden which had now become physically part of her.

With a sigh that she thought at first she'd imagined, the rain ceased and the blackness of the night glittered and chilled about her. The silence of the sky brought her new clarity. She heard the water rushing away across the stones, down gutters and drains. The light grew stronger and steadier. She heard footsteps, tipped with iron, clattering away into a distance, a stillness, a concealment. She heard the ghost of a song sung by many voices deep within a house.

She came to a low wall beyond which ran a great, dark river, a moving mass of water edged with tidal debris, full of eddies and rushes that gleamed in the night. She looked down, mesmerised by this great, uncertain movement, appalled by it: so strong, so quiet, so violent. She walked along beside the river, against its direction. On the farther bank the town continued. Over there the houses were larger, stately, ordered. They were an indication of the breadth of the world the Inn knew nothing of.

She began to grow weary again. The river entered her thoughts like a drug. It would be alluring, easy, to lose yourself in such a river, to become certain, moving, strong, quiet, violent. She came to a wide bridge. It rose up, this bridge, lifted the way up on an arch over the river, but she was afraid to venture on to it, afraid to have the river running below her. She would not be able to resist that. She paused on the road, facing the bridge, clutching herself, numbed, faint.

Looking up she saw the dense mass of running cloud, catching gleams off the city below but running strong and heavy like the river, a parallel of it. She found no release there. Above and below flowed these enormous oblivions. She faced the bridge again, determined to throw herself upon its back, the only available response.

Suddenly, as she looked, the clouds opened and a patch of night sky, alive with stars, opened above her, changing everything, bringing every shadow into a sudden definition, holding the movement of the river and cloud, still with its perspective of immensity. She gasped.

She steadied herself and crossed the back of the bridge and, as she did so, a glow of light appeared, a slit in the sky far away on the river. She paused and watched as the landscape was suddenly activated, as buildings and water and sky began to glitter with their own colours and the stars faded above her. She was going downhill now, across to the far side of the bridge and the new city.

BOOK TWO
St Thomas's

— 1 —

The Three Stars Inn had been established originally at the centre of a small market town, and was for years bound with quiet and order. The town stood some few miles south of a quiet city for which the Inn was a first, or final, staging post, but from which the town maintained its own little dignity beside the willow-fringed river that meandered about the countryside, grew fat and aldermanly, flowed into another, broader version of itself and then through the city of which it was the basis, the artery of its solid commerce.

Then came a new age, and the city swelled and exploded. Its southern reaches were cleared and colonised. The factories grew there behind high walls, great brick piles which bellowed and roared and sucked, which battered brute metal, brute stone, into brute objects which slid out oiled and gleaming darkly, turned into machinery from machinery; going into the furnaces raw and going from the furnaces molten and stilling into weights of perfect, mathematical importance; a cruel, synthetic virginity, subjecting those who forged it hour by hour. They came to work willingly in these new cathedrals of industry, drawn in by the regularity of the machines, the masculinity and the air of new importance exuded by their new masters, men who had taken the world by its vitals and were shaking it into a new intensity of direction. It was later, but soon enough, too late nevertheless, that the men realised that they were not the liberated converts of the new age, but its slaves; just as they had been slaves before but, now, slaves on a deeper level to a more potent force; and without the landscapes to console them, the turning of the seasons to whittle them down cleanly. All around them now rose the walls, twenty-foot up without relief. Honeycombed and catacombed, the streets spread in new lengths, tagged on to the old at odd angles, the roads unmade, unconsidered, the random yards traps for breeding mire, every corner a fulcrum for sleet or dust, every crevice a slit for vermin, nature reclaiming the streets with its hardiest, its most brutal manifestations; every wall running with tears and sweat and shit, the oozings of the pressed lives within. At night a darkness and a silence came. Lights smouldered deep behind occasional windows; most only reflected more darkness. The night would thicken with fog and coal-smoke, the damp rising and settling and passing through walls and doors and partitions deep into flesh and bone and brain. Children huddled at the edges of rooms about their parents struggling together in acts of generation that had all the implications of murder.

The city had spread relentlessly, enormously outward, engulfing, amongst many other things, the Three Stars Inn. The Inn began to gather a reputation which drifted northward, and beyond, out into the wide, blowy landscapes. People began to be aware of the Inn as a place in which a strange twilight was sustained and, if the shadows of such twilight were ever needed, then you could go there, briefly and cleanly, or forever if necessary. As the northern reaches of the city grew rich, so they grew virtuous, renouncing many things, rising above them, constructing prohibitions and silences. South of the river was merely a sewer, palpable when the wind was contrary; the Three Stars lay beyond that. It was unacceptable, north of the river, to know of the Three Stars; but it was known to all, available to all; all, at least once in their lives, willingly or not, at least imagined such a place and their own particular place within it. The actual industrial areas did not come quite so far south, but the people did; seeking perhaps a way out from the centripetal force of the factories, subsiding defeated in alleys and yards around the old Inn, many being sucked into its agelessness, its silent acceptance of all defeats, all abominations that crawled in and huddled out at the back ends of existence. In the proliferation and energy of the sprawl southwards, the Three Stars remained, enclosed, a black space, blurred on the new maps, dangerous and uncharted.

North of the river, the awareness of the Inn began to be a cause of concern. Individuals, hearing the stories, some of the stories, denounced the Inn vehemently, braced as they spoke by the shock an admission of awareness of such a place induced. The authorities, at times, were petitioned. But somehow it all came to nothing. The Three Stars Inn remained: it is better to know where such a place is, to have it defined and surrounded than to pull it down; for devils dwelt in it, were pensioned off in its chambers, living fat and atrophying, who once expelled might prove a threat to the multitudes who lived in their unreflective ignorance. Such rationalisings, like all the most comfortable hypocrisies, were never articulated. Years passed. Those who demanded action against the Inn grew louder, more defined; those who held back from such action grew more defensive and concealed. When the end came it was foreseeable from a great distance in spite of the drama of its actual occurrence. It came then as an inevitable and long-willed act of purgation; and when it was done and the Three Stars was no more, many felt cleansed, eased of a weight upon their moral sensibilities. A space was cleared into which might fall a pure, sweet light; but such a pure, sweet light has its own intoxicant, and a space cleared is still a space: fill it with the purest light and the light will take on the shape of that space, will react to the pressures that made the space in the first place. It is never simple. Nothing is ever final.

One bitter winter's day, in the cathedral, at the centre of the formalities of the city, old and new, an act of desecration took place. The cathedral was not in formal service at the time, although there were always devotions in progress in one of the small chapels or sanctuaries, or even in the silence of a figure standing alone below the immensity of the roof or before the great west window, a wheel of many-coloured glass which seemed to turn slowly if watched for long enough. An unseen organist laboured in a dark, formal counterpointing which echoed out, struggling into the great stone chasm of the nave from far away and dispersing; too intimate finally to take hold here. About the long nave small groups stood talking quietly, some walked in pairs, some walked alone, looking about them or just pacing the calm space. Their clothes were dark and sombre but their voices, though muted also, were swollen in the grey light that came as much from the stones as from the windows. It was a place of manifold seriousness and solemnity, a place that embodied the highest achievement and the profoundest doubt of its age, which aspired to be all ages.

The senior cleric present at the time was the Most Reverend Josiah Tamber. He had lunched frugally but finely – a bowl of clear broth, clean bread, dark wine and subtle cheese – and stood now with five ladies, each the widow of a senior cathedral clerical officer, discussing the ideals that might infuse an episcopal mission into the southern suburbs. The widows were attentive whilst the Reverend Tamber spoke much of light and revelation, of scriptural invigorations, of the first importance of making men, and women too it went without saying, aware of the soul as a living organ of their bodies. His zealous metaphors touching biological matters, the five widows grew imposingly silent; shocked, and shocked at being shocked by such a man in such a place upon such a matter. The Reverend Tamber was not displeased to have shocked them thus; although he too was shocked, subtly, by the sudden vigour of his own ideas.

'The soul', he said, 'is a vital organ as the other vital organs. It is healthy or corrupt, abused or enhanced within the life of its possessor. But, unlike the other organs, the fleshly organs, it is not subject to the final corruption. Imagine, ladies, if one's . . . one's spleen was to be preserved into eternity, with the secrets of its chemistry revealed at last to the All-seeing . . .'

At which point he noticed a strange figure advancing up the central aisle towards him. He looked quickly at his five good widows, but they were still looking up at him expectantly. He closed his mind to what he had just seen and tried to remember what he had just been saying, but could not. He had determined not to register what he had seen; an act of instinctive dishonesty which he justified by faith in the higher beauty of God's world and its purposes.

The five good widows, however, were lost in his sudden blank; their expectancy began to cloud. Suddenly they were aware of the most terrifying stench which took them by the throats. They choked and backed and turned. The mild intellectual shock with which the Reverend Tamber had been teasing them was made vengefully palpable, made flesh, abysmal corruption advancing upon them.

A small creature, hunchbacked, ragged and fouled, stood amongst them, regarding them with a face that, below its filth, burned red with fever and infection – eyes, mouth, nostrils issuing disease. It clutched a disgusting bundle to its breast. It shuddered and lolled its head. It fell to its knees.

The five widows backed stumbling through rows of chairs, emitting high cries of distress. The Reverend Tamber was fixed before this incarnation. A centre of disturbance was established and the attention of the quiet edifice was soon alerted and focused upon it. People were drawn into this focus almost involuntarily, a dark cluster forming about Tamber and the monster. A moment of revelation, of high conflict, seemed to be in progress at the heart of the cathedral. People appeared who had not been evident before. The news ran out into the precincts of the cathedral, into the streets beyond, and more people came running in, noisily as they came, then hushing as they approached the heart, pushing surreptitiously to see, standing on chairs, a dense circle of awed respectability, spontaneously drawn to witness.

Josiah Tamber was aware of the crowd as it gathered, a great and tightening pressure of the world about him, before which he was dressed in uprightness.

'My child . . . ', he said, as quietly as he was able; but his words were taken up by the crowd in a great buzzing which roused his anger and frustration. He glowered about him and they stilled respectfully (ironically? expectantly?) and waited for him. 'My child. What is it you want with me?'

It occurred to him, by the way the creature stilled at his words, that, before he had spoken, she had not even been aware of him there. Nevertheless, he reassured himself, she is an instrument of Providence; it is not necessary for her to be aware, only for me to be. She had stilled at his voice, however, her head trembling, her lips tightening. She was offering him something, wound in a disgusting cloth, a spherical thing. It appeared like some foul boiled pudding, perhaps offered in some grotesque parody of a charitable submission.

'What is it, my child?' he asked, fearful to lay hands upon it.

She said nothing, but her arms were weak and sagged. He had to accept it. He tensed himself and took the burden. It was surprisingly light, but sticky, smearing his fingers at once. He held it at arm's length. It stank, also. Having delivered her burden, the child sank to the floor at his feet.

The crowd about him stirred, lifted in expectation, and yet seemed to edge back a fraction. Tamber remained with the foul thing held out, unable to take a realistic decision, fearful lest it should drop from his hands and burst defilement on to the floor of his cathedral; or this was what he tried to believe. Really, he did not know what to believe, what to do. Having, he felt, achieved enough in accepting the thing, he felt it was the duty of someone else, higher or lower than he, to take responsibility now. His pose of heroism was receding. He was prepared now not to be as elect and worthy as he had thought himself.

'What is it, sir?' asked an urgent young man in the inner wall of the circling crowd.

'It is an offering,' Tamber said clearly, regretting it as soon as he had said it.

'Show us,' another called, less mannered.

Tamber turned and offered them the bundle.

'Show us! Show us!' they cried.

Tamber looked down at the creature who was gibbering and feverish, and beyond taking any further part. He prayed for courage, for strength of mind and for strength of stomach. He cautiously removed one hand from the thing and balanced it upon his other, picking with the very tips of his fingers, like a conjurer determined to show the probity of his operations, at the ragged material which adhered to the object, peeling it away.

He knew what it was before it was clearly revealed and he clenched his teeth and set the muscles of his stomach in which his fine but frugal luncheon suddenly grew mutinous. He prayed again, fiercely and briefly, for strength and received it. He revealed the head of Old Mag to the gathered people in the city's cathedral like a great mystery, the final answer.

They fell back smitten, tumbling, shrieking and stumbling away from the centre. The impact of the outrage shoved them back physically from this abomination. What had they expected? Something precious? Something consoling? Something quietly and politely ambiguous? Fools.

In the chaos that followed Tamber put down the object

on the floor of the aisle and, to steady himself from the uproar, and before he realised what he was doing, he pressed his defiled hands into his face which felt at once as if it was dissolving slowly in acid, the flesh of the fingers melting into the flesh of the cheeks. He remained, kneeling on the floor, his hands clamped over his ruined features, unable to proceed any further.

At first he felt that his faith, the entire structure of his life, had been swept away, the emptiness cauterised in an instant. But reassuring hands reached him and he felt their weight upon his shoulders lifting him, not physically but spiritually, from the maw of his despair. He had fallen from a terrible high place but a miraculous wind had caught and held him. He heard the organ which had gone on playing through the whole revelation, distant and eternal, working out its patterns and counter-patterns oblivious of anything but its own solipsistic perfections, and he wept with gratitude for it.

It was never ascertained how, precisely, the crowd who were in the cathedral that afternoon, nor those who caught the news of the incident as it flooded back through the streets of the city, came so quickly to connect the little hunchback and her severed head with the Three Stars Inn. The police who came and took her, and it, away, who proceeded logically and circumspectly through the forms of evidence and investigation, arrived at the Inn some long time after it had been invaded and sacked by popular outrage. They were left as usual to tidy up the detritus of spilled emotion. The people, however, had known the provenance of that horror at once and had congealed into a torrent of outrage which rushed south, shaking off the cautious and the sensitively respectable as it went, gaining the energy of the mob as it crossed the river and sucked its way through the workers' tenements.

They carried fire and iron with them. They tore their way into the Inn at every known vantage, and in those first few hours, those first few days, they destroyed everything, simply and completely, smashing and rending and burning. They did no intentional harm to any of the inmates of the Inn, those who remained; most had already fled, had blended into the surrounding slums, or had sped out into the countryside, or perhaps had become absorbed into the mob itself. Those who remained to be apprehended were fragile, terrified, mad, and were taken from the buildings as prisoners released from some great tyranny. They were drawn carefully through the destruction and were taken into a nearby church, a wooden shack by the river, where they were fed wholesome broth and where a minister read to them for long hours in a great voice from the Psalms and the Prophets. Meanwhile, the destroyers had their will. They did not regard what they destroyed, did not relish or marvel at it; their rage was a puritanical rage that sought only to bring down and to scour out this festering place. If they found positive evidence of particular abominations, even corpses, they did not pause over them, but committed them in bundles to a vast bonfire which they set up in the courtyard with everything that would burn: furnishings, floorboards, beams, rafters. A great glow filled the city's southern sky. The police gathered in regiments to this beacon, but they kept back on the edges of the crowd with no thought of attempting to halt the course of the destruction which was so methodical, so orderly, all passion sublimated into the vast blaze which roared up in a great torso of flame from behind the black walls. The police stayed to witness and to prevent the enthusiasm spreading into any more important properties, of which there were not many in the vicinity of the Three Stars Inn.

Then gradually the fire died down and the crowd began to disperse. A bout of heavy winter rain doused everything, turned most of what remained into mire and slime. Then the police moved in with much precision and effectiveness, cleared out the stragglers, sorted through the rubble and pronounced the place unsafe. By the spring, workmen had been deployed to dismantle the broken walls, to clear the area. Within a year the whole sprawling site had been levelled ready for redevelopment to put a great stone stopper on that pit in the earth's solid surface.

It was certain, though, that the ghosts of the Three Stars Inn had escaped the conflagration and were at large in one form or another. How could they not be?

— 2 —

The creature who had initiated the great purge of the Three Stars Inn was taken to the city's hospital and became the subject of great academic and moral interest. She was very ill, beset with fevers that ate at her very bones. She was placed in a small high room and a nurse sat by her at all times, watching the struggles of the fevers to gain a final possession of her. She herself seemed to lie quite still underneath the twistings and sweatings which visited her. She did not seem to be present at all sometimes, just an object tossed about in the darkness in a small, white room. The most eminent doctors, of the body and of the mind, came to consider her; stood afterwards in dark, furnished chambers offering diagnosis, prognosis, treatment. Some of this was attempted upon her, watched with intense curiosity: none reached her. Leading figures from many walks of life, the great and the respectable, the fashionable even, came to be with her for a little while. She was famous, a sort of heroine, the only survivor from a great wrack the contemplation of which awed them all.

The fevers eventually abandoned her. She grew calm, seemed to have moments of consciousness, of awareness; it was hard to be sure. Her calmness was not recovery. It was assumed finally that she would never recover, that her existence would at best be quiet, self-possessed but vegetative; and probably brief. She remained in her room, calm and floating in a layer of light, lying always on her side, facing the window, her eyes open and her pupils unfocused. She submitted to the medical probings. She allowed herself to be sat up and fed, and washed. She had grown thin and womanly. Her face intrigued those who studied her. It had an implicit watchfulness somewhere within it that belied the debility. She did not speak and it took them a stupidly long time to discover that she was unable physically to do so.

An artist called John Stone, a young man with fashionable connections and a vaguely disreputable way of life, spent a week sketching her, sitting in a corner of her room and filling a small portfolio with studies of her face which gazed steadily at him throughout. He tried talking to her, but his easy words found no purchase upon her silence. He showed her the images he had made of her and she studied them, or seemed to. He asked her to move, to adopt postures for him, but she lay still and disregarded him: he knew, or he thought he knew, that she understood him. He wanted the nurse to leave the room so that he could slip off her smock and sketch the lines of her nakedness, the bowed back, the breasts which he saw plumping out the shapelessness of the hospital linen. After a week he had grown bored with her and he left with a sense of failure and frustration. He wanted finally to slap her face to generate a response, but the stout, starched nurse-chaperone doused his energy in all directions and he gave up.

He had an aunt and uncle, this John Stone, a vicar and his twin sister who lived in a large rectory in the south-west of the city, in the new suburbia that was flourishing, where the enterprising mundane were establishing a social altern-ative to the contrasts of north and south which had erstwhile possessed the city: the Reverend Clarence Clack and Miss Clarissa Clack. John was the son of their late, younger sister who had married a taciturn and romantic man some years her senior, who had turned out, after the wedding, to be a brutal country squire of whom John's mother had soon died, leaving her son to grow up neglected and spoiled and sensual. His aunt and uncle were of a different stamp entirely. John maintained his connection with them in a spirit of sardonic humour, knowing that his life and profes-sion affronted them and knowing that, provided he retained his façade of decency, he would always be tolerated as the only child of dear, dead Charlotte whom they pitied for the passionate brevity of her life, girding thus the constriction and endlessness of their own.

When he considered their life, the iron and whitewash of the rectory, it was really her life he thought of, Aunt Clarissa. She was a tall woman, composed, he imagined, mostly of bone. He visualised her ribbed and hipped vastly with thin, pale flesh trembling over the structure. Her face was trian-gular, a sharp chin and a great sharp nose – a family blemish which John shared but, in his case, considered erotically, a fleshy beak quite unlike Aunt Clarissa's bony crag. Her hair was grey and stapled under white caps that were starched into angular helmets. She was a woman reduced about a knot of impregnable ideas, religious, moral, social. He had learnt to probe and expose these ideas over the years to his own cynical satisfaction.

She had knotted her life about her brother, Uncle Clarence, her twin and other half. His frame was like her frame, tall, large; but where she had ossification, he had a jovial, vague weight of flesh that one would, John imagined, strike only to have one's fist lost and cause the man to beam with the merriment that, beside his sister whom he was always beside, always seemed on the point of breaking out and never did. His face and her face had begun the same, but where hers had been constrained over the years, his had expanded; the lines on her face were graven, in his they were folds; the blue of her eyes was the blue of cold mornings, his the blue of distant hilltops.

He was an appalling preacher, rolling away in the immeasurable beauty of Christ the Saviour, the overwhelming love of God, the truth of mercy and the mercy of truth. His parishioners purred like cats before a stove under his long addresses, left comforted if they could avoid the prickling of Aunt Clarissa's eye as they passed from the waxed darkness of the church into the morning air. He was, at heart, a musician. He sat at the new organ in his new church and spread himself out across the manuals and pedals, swaying and rolling as the music swelled him and bore his rejoicing into the hands of his Creator. Clarissa would sit in the church, upright and still, as her brother played; a lump in the church's sonorous throat that would not be swallowed.

They had been together since childhood, this brother and sister. He had gone away to school and had come back to her each holiday. He had gone on to university where, after a year and the death of their parents, she had come to set up lodgings and to minister to him. They had lived an uninterrupted mutual existence for forty years, from parish to parish, even to a spell in the colonies amongst the heathen, and had excluded the rest of the world. For either of them to have married would have been unthinkable.

One Sunday, their nephew John arrived for luncheon, an

affair of boiled mutton and stale, strained vegetables which Clarence ate with relish, Clarissa with mortification, and John with a satisfying sense of everyone's absurdity.

'I've spent a frugal and instructive week, Aunt,' he said into the silence of the tablecloth.

'Good,' she said incuriously.

'Working, John?' His uncle accepted the conversational offer.

'Oh yes. In the hospital.'

'Ministering to the sick?'

Had he not known her better, he might have suspected her of sarcasm. 'No, Aunt; I have been visiting the child from the Three Stars Inn,' he said and filled his mouth with food at once.

The shock upon Aunt Clarissa was immediate and delightful. His uncle did not follow the reference at first, remembered eventually something of it.

'Ah yes. A sad tale, I understand. You explained it, I think, my dear.'

The thought of Aunt Clarissa explaining the Three Stars Inn to Uncle Clarence caused a difficulty in his swallowing. A look at Aunt Clarissa who was walling him up with her eyes, made his swallowing at once effectual.

'She is as beautiful as she is alert,' he said to his aunt, 'behind a veil of complete silence and complete stillness. I spent a week trying to bring her to life, but I failed. I have the drawings with me.'

'I noted your portfolio in the hall.'

'Are we to see them, my boy?'

'I would like you to see them.'

'Are you pleased with them?' his uncle continued.

'No. Not in the least.'

This was, as far as Aunt Clarissa was concerned, the correct response.

'They are not,' she said, 'intended to shock us, John, I hope.'

'I hope, Aunt, that I'm grown out of that by now.'

They exchanged a balanced smile.

Afterwards, in the drawing-room that was furnished so barely that the warmth of the small fire seemed insolent, he presented his sketches. He drew them, one by one, from the

138

tissue paper and handed them to his aunt who looked and passed them to her brother. He held them at arm's length whereas she peered down into them. John awaited their response, but a strange, functional silence settled between them as they exchanged the thick sheets of cartridge. A maid glided in with the tea and glided out again. John glanced across to see if she was pretty, but the girl kept her face down, her shoulders stooped. He looked at his aunt and uncle as they looked at his work and he saw only their masks, sour and bright, the matched pair. He felt uncomfortable in their silence; and hurt, for he had lied to them – he did feel a considerable satisfaction in these sketches. They were not vigorous, lacking the energy of imagination to which he aspired as he painted; but for that he could not have expected their appreciation. This work, though, had a different quality: a classical impersonality that was new for him, and for which he had expected to find approval here. He realised that he had brought these pictures down in an attempt to court the approval of his funny old aunt and uncle. He blushed. The last sheet went out, round and returned to his portfolio. He tied the ribbons and sat back, looking glumly into the heap of glowing coals, a little image of hell lest they should neglect its omnipresence. He tried to pluck up the final courage to ask if they had liked them.

'Do you . . . approve of my new style, Aunt?'

'I know nothing about style, John, nothing whatsoever.'

'Will they sell?' his uncle asked.

'No. They are not to be sold. They are done to develop my eye, exercises in observation, exercises in honesty. I have a portrait to undertake next week, Lady Glandon to be painted as a gipsy girl. I will make her look very wild.' And so he slipped away into his usual level of discourse. The moment had gone.

Shortly he left, taking his portfolio with him. He shared a narcotic pipe with a friend, a young doctor. They discussed in great detail various delights of the flesh, intending to go in search of them; but the night grew late and they lapsed into lethargy.

The next morning, Monday, Clarissa Clack arrived, without

appointment, at the office of Sir Marcus Gossiter, the senior physician of the Free Hospital. Gossiter knew of the Clacks. His brother, the bishop, had them in his diocese and was continually worried that they would inaugurate some dreadful outbreak of enthusiasm, of primitive religion or of moral scouring, Clarence floating like a cloud and Clarissa the cast-iron anvil to which he was tethered, lifting as he rose and coming down again like a demolition hammer on the ecclesiastical equilibrium. They had been tucked away in a safe, bourgeois parish where the aggressive respectabilities of their flock might absorb and smother them. Gossiter was apprehensive, however, when this strange, tall woman was shown into him.

He offered her a chair, sat behind his desk. She was out of place in the soft leather of the chair, landscaped with dark, polished panelling and heavy bookshelves. He interviewed here for senior appointments, explained points of medical ethics to discomposed politicians and churchmen, softly admitted tragedies to those they claimed, dictated his decisions: it was a place of power and this woman was not under his authority.

'And what is your business with the Free Hospital, Miss Clack?' he began distantly.

'I will be direct, Sir Marcus, since I am here so abruptly. You have under your care . . .' she paused deeply, '. . . a girl.'

He knew at once which girl of the hundred or so under their care she meant. He remained, however, still, waiting for her to articulate it.

'A girl, a crippled girl, from the Three Stars Inn.'

He recalled the connection. The artist nephew had been in last week.

'Yes, indeed, Miss Clack. A pitiful case.'

'I would like to offer to take her under my care, under the care of my brother and myself.'

'That would be quite impossible.'

'Her medical treatment is complete, I understand.'

'Certainly not. We may not have effected as complete a cure as is possible, and we must continue to endeavour to do so.'

'Her malady is, so I understand, no longer physical, but spiritual.'

Sir Marcus contracted, jabbed by this. 'Of that, Miss Clack, we cannot be sure.'

'I would submit, Sir Marcus, that a minister of religion has a more profound resource with which to heal this child than a doctor of medicine.'

Sir Marcus did not agree at all, was indeed convinced of the reverse, but it was a flaw in his impeccable respectability and he could see that she sensed this; he could not challenge her on these grounds.

'It is a medical matter, Miss Clack,' he said flatly.

'I disagree.'

'You are at liberty so to do.'

'You reject then my offer? Out of hand?' This was an ultimatum. Where would she go next? Gossiter knew that he was only a first stage, a first avenue of approach. Who next? The bishop? The government? The monarch? The mob? The woman was determined and without the first scruple, armed with her own monumental righteousness. He paused before her, looking at her and trying, by his silence, to baffle her into believing she was out of her depth: a futile aspiration.

'You are aware, Miss Clack, of the nature of the Three Stars Inn?'

'Yes, thank you, I am well aware of it.'

'And this girl, this young woman, for she is not a child, Miss Clack, was a part of that place, was born and brought up amongst the most merciless depravity.'

'Do you have, Sir Marcus, a treatment for prolonged exposure to merciless depravity?' She permitted herself a tight smile. 'I do.'

'You may not know, it is not generally known, Miss Clack, but she was with child when she came to us.'

'That I did not know. The child was lost?'

'It was. You know of her deformities?'

'Yes.'

'You know that she is unable to speak, physically unable?'

'No. That too is new information for me.'

'One of our most experienced surgeons has a plan to operate upon her, thinks it possible, possible to free her tongue. That at least must be explored before we can consider her future.'

This caused her to think. She bowed down her head. Perhaps she prayed for guidance. Sir Marcus dreaded it.

'So you see,' he came in quickly, 'we cannot set her loose into the world yet. I do not reject your offer out of hand, Miss Clack. I thank you for it and will consider it with my colleagues. I will write to you within the month . . .'

'She must not be . . . operated upon,' Miss Clack said suddenly, raising her head and accusing him. 'I am shocked that you should even consider it. What do you want to unlock in her? Her silence is a gift, and it must be respected. I will not allow you to operate upon her.'

'Miss Clack!' he said. 'I will not be addressed in this manner. You have a perverse idea of the ethical proprieties of my profession. I think my colleagues and I might be trusted to make the best possible decision in this case. Now, I must ask you to . . .'

He had made not the slightest impression upon her.

'She must not be operated upon. She is not an animal but a child of God, as you are yourself, Sir Marcus. She has a soul and the hope of salvation. If you will not release her into the care of my brother and myself, then you must release her to some other moral authority. She must not be left here to be experimented upon. That must be clear to you.' She rose. 'Now then, I would like to be taken to see her.'

'That is out of the question, Miss Clack. Please be seated.'

'You are a busy man, Sir Marcus. I do not want to take any more of your time. If you would just give an instruction to one of your employees.'

She was as certain of victory as he was of defeat. She showed nothing of this in her tight face, however; although he did not meet that formidable article for more than a moment.

'Please sit down, Miss Clack. You cannot see the patient.'

'My nephew, a man not noted for his medical skills, nor indeed for his moral probity, was allowed free access to this girl for a whole week. If you refuse me permission to visit her, I would insist on a written statement of that fact with such reasons as you may care to adduce. I will wait.' And she sat down.

He rose from his chair, felt himself trembling up in the air above her.

'I will inform the bishop of your visit, Miss Clack, of

your request and of its tone, which I am bound to say . . .'

'Your brother is not *my* superior, Sir Marcus. I have only one superior, and Him you are welcome to consult, at length; in fact, I would seriously recommend it.'

Sir Marcus eyed this female with a hatred that was suddenly perfect. He luxuriated in the sudden image of her at his surgical mercy, her knotted body released into its bare biology, her arrogance and whalebone cut away as they would be one day. He smiled upon her to reduce her, but her reality asserted itself again very quickly, quite unaltered.

'Very well. I will take you to see her, Miss Clack. Perhaps when you are faced with the reality of what you only imagine so far, you will be amenable to reason.'

'Perhaps I will,' she said, almost amicably.

On the way up, along the high, dark corridors, acknowledging the respectful bobs of nurses and orderlies, Sir Marcus felt that, perhaps, they would be well rid of the girl. It would have to go through the senior committee but he would not actively oppose it. There was, in truth, little more they could do for her. The surgical liberation of her tongue was a doubtful project which he was, in fact, opposing. She had become the subject of morbid curiosities and they were better free of her. Let this madwoman have her: they would probably be good company.

They arrived on the top corridor where sheets of glass had been inserted in the slope of roof, one of Sir Marcus's own innovations. The light was startling after the dark below, and unreal. The mental patients, those who did not need close confining, were roomed up here. Sir Marcus had always noted the healing properties of light upon the diseased mind. The effect of rising into this light from the darkness below was of coming into a strange place. Here the struggles seemed to have been resolved, the darkness of pain transfigured. It was no triumphant place, however, no triumphant transfiguration; more a rising into silence and cold calm. Sir Marcus, who did not believe in an afterlife, would, had he believed in it, have pictured it as a place such as this: cold, clear, quiet, full of chastening light. The pace of their progress slowed to accommodate the calm that such a place seemed to require of them. Beside him, the tall woman kept in step, the dark material of her skirts scratching.

He did not look at her to pass any of the solicitations and gallant assurances that he might have offered to a regular lady visitor.

They came to the door which was at the very end of the top corridor. He rapped and opened the door, holding it for Miss Clack who moved in past him without looking at him. A nurse rose in a starched shell from a chair, bobbed, her face cowled. The girl lay with her back to them, curled on the bed, dressed in a brown smock, stockinged in black with canvas shoes, her odd back and her cropped red hair distinguishing her. Miss Clack moved at once around the outside of the bed and stooped down to peer into the girl's face.

She lived now in a white space. Movement only happened on the periphery of that space, a long way away. Sleeping and waking, dreaming and being, were aspects of a continuous flux of existence, all of it reduced of its potency, an easy, distant life which demanded the nothing she gave it. Into this suddenly dropped a woman's face, a carving of a face with a bird's eyes. The woman was touching her face. She had long been immune from contact. The woman took her hand between her own hands which were gloved in black, were warm, strong and enclosing. The woman knelt down beside her and began to murmur to herself, an incantation, inaudible but definite. The girl could hear its rhythms and cadences, feel its precision and force. Behind the woman was the great window, a slab of roaring light with thin bars restraining it from floor to ceiling. After a while the woman was done, drew away her hands and stood back. The girl meanwhile had become intrigued by the window, by the light. She stirred and slid off the bed, her feet coming into abrupt contact with the floor. She pushed herself upright, but her legs would not hold her. She fell to her knees, went down on to her hands. She felt hands upon her shoulders. She knew by the texture that they were those same black, gloved hands. She rose and the hands supported her. She went to the window, reached forward and gripped the bars.

Below her, revealed in the haze, lay the city, streets and roofs, people moving far below in grey light, horses and carts, birds clustering and circling, smoke lifting and hanging, a horizon vague and gleaming, the river like a trough of lead twisting slowly through the buildings. The hands supporting her dropped and she clung to the bars, pressed herself against them and felt a great weeping fill her. For what? She did not know. A great thawing filled her and she wept.

Some days, weeks, later, the strange woman would come again and take her away. She took to getting off the bed, watched by the impassive nurse, a shadow of a face within the starched cowl, and attempting to walk to the window. She clung to the edge of the bed until her feet grew used to her small weight, until she gathered her awkward balance again; then she tottered across to the bars, gripping them and staring, each time, into a new sky, the city's upturned face relit, sombre or glorious, dank or gleaming; and always there was the thick river, lead or gold, but mostly brown and heavy, a permanence. She grew aware of having crossed that river. It was the only one of her memories she could handle firmly, plucking it from the chaos, a little triumph which strengthened her. By the time the woman came for her, she could walk freely, if slowly.

Holding on to the woman's forearm, she left her cell into the free light of the corridor; then down the stairways, dark and stony and foul, an atmosphere it was difficult to breathe; but it was only a fog through which they would pass. She shrank into herself and blocked it out. And suddenly, from a small side door, they broke into the street which ran with light and tinkling and the heavy shift of horses and vehicles, the mill of many people. They climbed into a carriage which creaked upon its springs. A marvellous sense of motion came upon her, a sense of moving without having to exert herself, being carried along, lying back on smooth, shiny leather with the world pulled past the open window and warm summer air, thick with the scents of the new city, blown in. The tall woman sat beside her, a handkerchief to her face, watching her as she laughed and shook herself with this multitude of sensations.

Suddenly the crowding of buildings and people, windows and noise was gone. The carriage rumbled and seemed somehow to lift up and she saw they were crossing the river. She gasped and went to the carriage window. The woman's hand came upon her shoulder protectively. She gazed out at this slow wonder of water, this infinity of slow, glossy power, and she shivered at it; a shiver of fear, but also of recognition. Then they were over and the carriage swung and turned and busied itself in streets, quieter, tree-lined, the trotting of the carriage-horses rapid and precise upon the cobbles.

Soon they entered the gravel drive of a large, heavy house, the rectory of St Thomas's, Longfield; which was to be her new home.

The rector of St Thomas's, Clarence Clack, stood in the portico of the house as the carriage door was opened, as his sister stepped down and handed down the girl, their charge, the little, crippled mute whom his sister sought to rescue. Clarissa brought her forward, stood below him.

'This is Magdaline, Clarence,' his sister said.

'Magdaline,' he repeated, coming down, placing his hands upon her head which was warm.

Between his palms, her eyes rose to him. Her mouth tightened and he saw a spark animating the features that he had not expected, a gleam of perception. He recalled briefly the horror of her past and he looked to his sister, whose set mouth and strong eyes reassured his faith once more against the corruptions of reality.

— 3 —

At St Thomas's, her life was subject to a regime that caught her up at once. At first it bewildered her, but soon she was enormously happy within it. It was tight and inflexible. She rose and washed and dressed in the first light of morning, at first to the chivvying of Sal the housemaid; but soon she herself had taken control, was up and bustling before Sal could get to her. Sal assumed a great superiority over her, all fuss and teeth-sucking and boundless condescension. But she submitted to Sal, working her out and feeding her self-esteem surreptitiously. Sal buzzed and flustered and had to find something every day to put right. Nevertheless, quite rapidly, she grew independent and Sal preened herself on her achievement.

Her room was small, high and light, as her room in the hospital had been; but there the light had been of high spaces, windy, large and indeterminate. Here it was sharp light, thrown off white walls and off the surfaces of bowls of cold washing water, and off the whiteness of the many layers of underclothing in which she now had to bind herself, surmounting all this whiteness with a plain, brown dress. The whiteness, she quickly realised, was to show up any spot or blemish, any error of uncleanliness so that it might be seen and purged. This above all was the secret of her new world.

Breakfast brought her into the presence of the brother and sister. They were always there before her, sitting at either end of a long, oval table: at one end, with the window behind him, the rolly brother who beamed brightness upon her; at the other end, with the door behind her, the pinch-featured sister who frowned perpetually, but admitted tiny gleams of commendation to show through, now and then, at things done properly. She sat between them, in the middle, amidst a spread of white crockery and heavy silver cutlery on a thick, white tablecloth. Sal served. The girl wondered why she too was not a servant. She felt she had the status of a child here, wanted a chance to prove herself. There must have been some purpose in bringing her here, some preparation for something beyond; but she had not divined it yet. She looked forward to it nevertheless, something new to apply herself to, to expand herself within. Thus she thought in the moments of protracted silence, in which brother and sister would close their eyes and draw down into themselves, muttering, that preceded every meal.

'Did you sleep well, Magdaline?' the brother would then inquire.

'Cormey tells me you were prompt this morning,' the sister would then offer, or something of the sort. 'Cormey' was Sal. Sal had told her at the beginning, 'Cormey's me upstairs name. Sal's what I am. You know me as Sal, only don't let Miss Reverend hear you.' 'Cormey' didn't match her, certainly, any more than this lumbering 'Magdaline' thing matched herself.

In answer to their breakfast solicitations, she would look at them and open her face wide, a gesture which seemed to satisfy them. They would signal to Sal who stood back, attendant, and who would then ladle hot, thick porridge into all three bowls. They would wait for her to start, which discomforted her at first, for her instincts told her that this was a place to sit and watch and imitate. She would succeed here by ascertaining what they wanted her to be and by being that. This was no defeat for her, for it embodied a tremendous and desired safety for her. At breakfast then, every morning, she had to begin. She learnt soon not to be tentative, not to show reluctance; this inaugurated a prickling concern for her that she must avoid. She ploughed in her spoon and filled her mouth with the hot, glutinous mess. It had a dry, dead taste and the consistency of vomit. She longed to be sucking the juice out of a bone, to be flaking off roasted flesh between her teeth; but there was no point in such lusts here. She swallowed the porridge then and felt its warmth oozing along her throat and down into her stomach. This was the function of the meal, she assumed. It was also a part of the life of the place, she discovered, to be kept hungry and cold: not cruelly so, bracingly so; not so that it hurt, but so that there was a constant sharpness and awareness through which it was necessary to strive onwards. The substance of the breakfast was therefore quite appropriate, palliating solidly the essential cravings. The bowl of porridge was the entire meal; it was a substantial bowl but she could have sunk at least two more of the same. But to desire anything here, she soon learnt, was to have it denied; first by them and then, soon learning, by herself. She began to understand and accept this. The strange brother and sister had no more than she did, perhaps less. Sal dolloped out the helpings with pre-arranged precision.

Some mornings she would be taken visiting by the sister. This involved a quite unnecessary rewashing and regrooming, the wearing of a specially stiff gown of dark grey satin which had been sewn for her by Miss Clack herself. It fitted tightly about her and, if anything, extenuated the rise of her back. She would sit opposite Miss Clack in the carriage and be rocked and jolted through strange, moving scenery which she always wanted to hold and watch: strange houses and streets, strange, sudden faces, and most strange of all, expanses of trees and bushes and lush grass without even a perceptible trace of a human being. She had never imagined that such places could exist, she wondered how people were kept from claiming them, longed to run free in them. But she had learnt to sit still on her side of the carriage, under the incessant observation of Miss Clack who never looked out of the windows. They would disembark before some impressive portal and be ushered up broad stairways into rooms clogged with furniture, clotted with dark velvet, white statuary and great, gilt clocks that knocked ominously and would break suddenly into choruses of sharp clanging. She would sit on the edge of some hard sofa, her knees together, her gown spread out tidily around her, her back pushed as straight as it would go, the material tight to bursting, her hands clasped in her lap. Around her were strange women who talked and squinted and smiled tightly as they tried to react to her. She was evidently a strange object for them and, although they discomforted her at first, she could tell from the slit of a smile on the face of her guardian that she was meant to be strange; furthermore, that her strangeness had its own power.

'What will you *do* with her, Miss Clack?' they asked.

'Bring her to an intimacy with Christ,' she replied, so quietly and finally that they fell silent and simpered. They gave her tiny cups of tea which she took in tiny sips, following their custom; which was difficult in this instance, as her hands felt large and flabby on the tiny, china shells, and they were watching her all the time, expecting her to fumble and drop the cups. She spent much time in these places holding in her breath and feeling, after an hour, a tightening constraint upon her which began to become difficult to contain. Miss Clack always seemed to sense this tension and to take her away in time, alarming the women by sudden decisions, taking the girl by the hand and pulling her swiftly out into the air where the tension would be released at once. She would breathe deeply and stretch herself out in her gown until the seams creaked in her armpits.

Returning to the rectory, there would, by way of more washing and brushing, be luncheon, a meal as fraught with ritual as breakfast, the porridge replaced by a watery stew with tantalising hints of meat in its savour and in some of the strange gobbets that floated in it. Most of these gobbets were floury hunks of vegetable or dumpling which clogged her teeth and, if they yielded flavour, yielded only sourness. She endured this, and endured the second platter that offered her another doughy lump that had a tinge of sugar and sometimes a bloated raisin in it, and which dried her mouth and left a congestion in her gut that took most of the afternoon to dissolve.

After luncheon, however, came the crown of the day – an hour's release into the yard and gardens of the rectory itself. The rectory was surrounded by a high wall, solid on three sides and with a strong iron railing at the front. There were various gates, but she never attempted these. Between the house and the walls, a square building within a square perimeter, was her territory, overlooked by the dark windows of the house from which, she knew, she was always watched, would have been disappointed not to have been watched. To the rear of the house were stables and sheds, of no interest to her; she had known stables and sheds before. A gravel drive filled the front garden and swept around both sides of the house, linking in the stable yard. Between this drive and the wall was the garden, a strand of uneven lawn, tended but not nurtured, lumpy and mossy. Beyond that were the flowerbeds, with their sparse shrubs, thin borders. The gardener, a decrepit called Abraham, prodded at the beds with forks and spades and hoes, bending his ill-hinged frame to tug up dead roots and living weeds. He was quite oblivious to her as she watched him. He seemed to pick at the surface of the earth as at a scab. There was a tree to the left of the house, disproportionately mature and sturdy, a great mass of tree which had thick, leathery leaves and a dense, wrinkled bark. It creaked and muttered continuously in the wind; it still caught the copious rainfall and dripped it at its own will long after the skies had cleared. But most intriguing of all was the way the growth of the garden insinuated itself through the fabric of the rectory and its surrounds, in spite of all old Abraham's scratchings. She saw how grass blades speared up through the grey mass of gravel; how faint cracks in walls grew moist and green; how mould spread over anything neglected, anything not wound up in the daily living – grey, feathery mould like a beard, of great delicacy and complexity, a minute undergrowth. Spiders colonised corners; mice established fanatical communities in straw and under skirting boards; birds wedged nests and smeared the walls below with their excrement. Sal and Abraham and the cook would go through days of purging fury – scouring, trapping, pulling down in dust and filth all the evidence of the invasion. The girl laughed secretly at the futility of all this. What they obliterated were only the traces, the faintest smears of a great proliferation that was far more pervasive than they would ever be.

As the clocks, of which the rectory possessed many, struck three, she came in from her hour of liberty, drank a cup of tea in the drawing-room with the brother and sister, and was then taken up to the top of the house to a room where she was, by Miss Clack, subjected to formal schooling. She gripped a chalk and made tortuous shapes on a slate imitating shapes in a book. She listened to Miss Clack reading her distant places and distant people: not real places or people, but shapes conjured out of the emptiness, larger than life but hollow, in the tightening band of tedium that these hours pressed round her. She wanted to comply in everything, wanted to do all that was required of her, but this was beyond her. She could only feign attentiveness. She felt ashamed of herself, but could not do it.

Out of the schoolroom and when not on display, however, in all other areas of her new life, when Miss Clack was not pressing directly upon her, the girl could not withstand her affection and concern. Her emotions were quickly engaged. She loved this strange, knotted woman who jerked through her days, always alert, always dominant, always alarmed by the jump of the life within her tight clothes. The girl marvelled at the patience with which she was treated, even at her most clumsy, at the intimacy and infinite solicitude with which her life was supervised. If only I was still a child, she thought, if only I was brand-new. But there would be a way to respond to, to requite this love. She would find a way. For the moment, the barrier remained. She would have loved to have slept in this long woman's bed. She imagined her released from all her constrictions, a long, fragile form, cold but warmed by the soft body beside her. This was a wild fantasy. Such a scene was impossible. Everything Miss Clack was would be lost in such a context. That was obviously, now, not the answer to anything.

*

There was another dimension to her new life, the strangest of all, the most alien and yet, perhaps, the most promising. After supper every evening – her favourite meal, coarse bread and cheese – Miss Clack would lead her, through a side gate, across a dreary graveyard and into the church to hear her brother at his office. On one day in seven, there would be three visits to the church – early morning, mid-morning and evening. There were also days when the routine was abolished for further long sojourns in this strange, cold vault. Sometimes the place was almost full; not very often. Sometimes there was a scattering of old, stiff people there. Sometimes they, Miss Clack and she, would be the only ones there apart from the Reverend. It made no difference. What happened, happened, however many there were there or were not there.

She noted the way that Miss Clack, whilst in this place, kneeling and muttering, standing and singing in a thin and hideous warble, would become rapt and intensified, would depart in some sense from herself and be spread out in the draughty spaces, the dark roof, the rising presence of damp and dust, and the sealing calm of echoes which took even the hiss of your breathing and spread it out in multiple spirals of sound that wreathed endlessly about. The girl watched the woman with fascination and wondered what was happening to her, wondered whether it was good or bad, a freedom or an enslavement: she could not decide. It was beyond her comprehension. Far away, amongst platforms and daises, rails and candlesticks, embroidery and stonework, the Reverend Clack moved and murmured through his rituals. He wore long, white robes which were obviously his natural attire. She saw him in the house as a vague and distant figure, kindly, soft and a little lost. Here he belonged, moved with grace and sang out in a voice of sweetness and passion. He bowed and bobbed, raised silver goblets to the roof, read from great books in humming tones. He did not impose himself upon the place, but became a part of it, filled himself into it, expanded until the atmosphere swaddled him like a cloud across which he played like the sunlight. Between the two, brother and sister, was a mutuality that was apparent at all times, but which, here in the church, became central. Here they were quite separate, never more so physically, yet under the prevailing atmosphere of this place they were absorbed in the same process; still, but moved by the same energy. The more she watched, the more she thought, the more the mystery became explicit; not soluble, but plain.

It was a mystification that at first awed her, then made her resentful. She could see no point in her being subjected to these great, open hunks of time in the cold and the damp and the darkness. It was not like the tedium of the school-room, nor like the constriction of the drawing-rooms; it was large and seamless and there was no stance she could take apart from it. She tried to listen to the words that burbled out about her, from him and from her, sometimes together, sometimes in set responses, but she could not hold the ideas which were moved about here, could not relate to the talk of pain and peace and joy in a place that seemed so far removed from any of these. The other words that seemed to token much here – sin, grace, praise, worship – she did not begin to understand; they fell like heavy stones, jarring the air about her.

The unease and the resentment were, in time, dulled. She felt the atmosphere of the place, although still beyond her comprehension, beginning to seep through her resistance. She began to be taken over. It concerned her. When she was away from the building she felt as if something was smother-ing and digesting her; entering the church was to be devoured, the high, dark roof a rib-cage, the palpable mys-tery a digestive organism. She shuddered as she walked the grey gravel and crossed the moist flagging before the west doorway, sunk into herself as Miss Clack forged on beside her, drawing her along. Once inside, however, the shudder-ing was soon eased and the strange absorption took her. She seemed to be becoming aware, here, of an aspect of experience which she had not been aware of before. It was an awareness of herself, distinct from the whirl of sensations in which she lived most fluently. She began, it seemed, to be growing a new perspective upon herself, to see herself as if from outside. She saw how pains, pleasures, frustrations and releases dominated her with an acute simplicity that enabled her to flow through life gladly and positively, activated by contacts, by the certainties of her quick biology. To realise this about herself was made possible, in the church, by a sense of something else, a sense of the physical surfaces of life becoming stilled, neutralised for a time. It was like sleep in that; but unlike sleep, in which everything was abandoned to a riot of dream, or to an utter darkness, here she was still in control, clear and still vibrating with awareness. She began, in this strange new context, to recall her days at the Inn. The memories were still far from distinct, the faces distorted and unreal, the sensations so large that they still swallowed her up; but she strove to reclaim them, to rehearse them in her mind, setting them out in order to examine them for their significance and, ultimately, for their value.

In the church stillness, against the mutterings and creak-ings, the broken singing and the swish of long garments, the sudden memory of her brief ecstasy with the dark boy returned to her and rushed in her so that she almost cried out with it. Only a sudden grip of awareness, a sudden consciousness of Miss Clack, rock-like beside her, enabled her to surface in the quotidian before, slowly and carefully, letting herself out again into the stillness. The memory was crucial, however, and she had to learn how to control it, value it, ascertain its truth. She returned to it gradually, recalling the room, the moon-mirror, pale light, dark skin; at first all still; then the movement, the sequence of feeling, the rise of pleasure to the point where it broke and flowed through her. It was sharpened and perfected in the memory. It seemed, here, to be given back to her. In the stillness of the church she had felt it come – the tremulous re-opening of the world within her. She accepted it as given because it freed her if it was given, and because she could not conceive of any other way it could have come. It was a part of the strange love she found around her, in the strange sister and brother and in what they represented, which was what they were, which was worshippers of God.

Theirs was a new species of love for her, a love not of body and person, but of the moving force behind body and person, above it. This new abstract stillness was, super-ficially, challenged by the push of her nature; but in both there was power and purpose that was balanced. She saw herself suspended between these two powers, spinning slowly like a planet, but of no fixed orbit, spinning out in the night with a harmonious whirr of gravities about her. It was a triumph of feeling. It made her bristle. It sent great urgencies rushing up in her to burst silently and run like light through her. There were moments when she was possessed, quite consciously, of enormous happiness. Beside her knelt Miss Clack who also had her joy, the joy of warm steel. Before her the Reverend Clack had his joy, the joy of music across bright water surfaces under low willows. And between them her joy was balanced, but moving.

This was the difference between them and her. They had learnt to hold still their joy, to fix it and to become subsumed within it. The nature of her joy, however, every rise of urgency, pushed her forward and told her there was to be no stillness yet. She was not yet free as they were free, nor set as they were set. She was still moving, although she could see no clear direction as yet. When she found her direction, would they stop her?

— 4 —

At this time she began to be troubled by dreams. At first she could not recall them, but awoke, thrown from them as from a violent animal, gasping in the cold darkness of her bed. She felt afraid, invaded by something that would not come clear to her, which fled from contact with her conscious mind. She grew afraid of sleep itself. The darkness waited for her, attendant, malevolent, aware. So far, these visitations were infrequent and, although they often dogged her mornings, they soon evaporated and her life ran fluently again.

One night, waking from such a visitation, she found herself able to recall the dream, or a part of it. She had been in a great wood with trees that grew as she watched them, twisting and writhing their branches together above her, their roots churning the soil below her feet. There had been violence in this growth. She had been fearful of losing her balance, of falling to the earth and having the root-knuckles scramble over her and, proliferating, pull her down as they sought nourishment in the soil below. She had awoken and her panic was real, her gasping against an actual force.

This nightmare began to recur clearly. Sometimes it was night in the wood. Sometimes there was a thin winter sun to be seen at which the branches clawed. Sometimes there was hot, sticky fog. Sometimes there was only darkness, utter darkness in which she could only feel the clambering and scratching of the tree roots. She would have night after night of easy, sealed sleep; then this would break back upon her in one form or another. Sometimes it was hard for her to awake, although she knew it was only a dream even as she dreamt it. Her struggle then became a struggle for consciousness. At the worst time of all, when she awoke, she found that the dream remained within her in a physical coiling and wrenching of her own bowels that seemed to have taken over the silence of the dream forest. What was clear was that something was occurring within her of which she had no control.

Another dream began at about this time, although its substance was not, at first, clear. It was the obverse of her first dream. It was a dream of solitude and clarity, colourless and motionless. She was held together in the midst of a great void that seemed to want to envelop her. She was not unwilling, in her dream, to be enveloped; nor did she desire it. The void swelled about her until she felt the edges of herself to be a thin membrane, smooth and taut from the pressure from without. She waited for the membrane to be split, for the void to flow in and absorb her. She awoke from such dreams more puzzled than afraid, her body recovering its reality strangely.

She found herself, in the midst of this cloying void, as it pressed most closely about her, longing perversely for the forest; and when the forest came to her, the next night perhaps, or even the same night after an uncomfortable gap of consciousness, she was glad of the opportunity it gave her to struggle, to fight against a force that was unequivocally destructive.

After a while, this dream-life established itself as the dominant part of her existence. Every night she was entered by one or both of these states; and they began to claim her waking hours as well. The dreaming and the waking were blurred, the days flicked mechanically by and she was swallowed within herself in a mind that was not entirely her own any more, that was at the mercy of dreams, submissive, dulled. The world's reality began to drag about her. She felt weary and unhappy again. She seemed to have reached a point of understanding beyond which she could not go, within which she was stymied, defeated.

She began to develop a pain under her ribs, a distant ache at first, hardly noticeable. It grew, and some days it was a great lump pulling her forwards, a great stone which diminished her breathing and caught her moving with sudden angles of sharpness. Its dullness though was its worst manifestation, a solid grey weight upon her at all times. It was a pain bred of her silence and flourishing in her silence. Some days it went entirely and then she felt a bewildering release which flowed through her hours with a detailed pleasure of awareness. Then the damp weather set in, the dismalness, and the pain would return to her. She struggled at her breathing, not knowing whether her continual brooding awareness of the pain served to shrivel or to breed it; probably the latter, she thought, but could not stop herself brooding.

There was, one night very late, an arrival in the rectory which was kept greatly and ostentatiously secret. Sal knew but would say nothing, and the girl's curiosity was aroused by the trails of footsteps, mutterings, men talking, cigar smoke drifting in empty corridors like whisps of damnation, doors being closed with the fat metal thunk of bolts and locks. The house itself seemed to brood, seemed to have its own dark tumour. After a while there was a baby crying, and ceremony suddenly broke the spell of the brooding. They all went, one dark and windy evening, across to the church which was at its darkest, only a few candles flickering around the open font. A baptism was performed upon a tiny child. Miss Clack stood godparent and her brother performed the office. She and Sal stood attendant; and there was another, a pale, shivering girl with a face hollowed down to its bones. She was wrapped in shawls which shuddered as if themselves palsied. She stood apart. The child was named 'John' and handed by Miss Clack to the lonely girl, and they all trooped back to the rectory and the doors were closed and locked again.

She knew instinctively what this was all about. She waited to be allowed to go down to the child and her tragedy. What did they know about it, any of them here? She felt the opening of death down there below her and felt bitterly impotent. It came and there was a moment of its passing through the house, an awful bolus of blackness. She struggled to scream and did produce a sort of cry, but it was lost in the weight of the house. Next morning there was only pale silence, fragile hush.

At breakfast she saw their faces lined by their vigil and sagged by defeat. They were too tired to think beyond it towards meanings and rebirths in a place beyond the vale of pain. After breakfast they seemed to be lost for activity, to walk hesitantly out in the daylight. She took her opportunity. Miss Clack sat at her writing desk, sharpening a pen and pausing it over a white space, the thought jammed in her wrist, her mind ungeared. The girl came beside her hardly noticed, not noted. Miss Clack began to write rapidly but the impulse died. She sat back and looked at the girl and frowned. Her long bones seemed to be folded uneasily under the small escritoire. Her cap and gown, all black, seemed penitentially uncomfortable. Her whole existence seemed an awkwardness. She regarded the girl blankly, not knowing how to look at her. The girl reached and took her hand, held it between her own palms, a stiff bunch of fingers, cold and dry-skinned, and so absurdly small for the woman's length. She caressed the fingers and watched the old woman's face, saw it contract instinctively, then hold its focus far away; then the attention gathered and returned to the girl, a smile and a tear edged into it briefly and were allowed to remain.

She rose from her chair. 'Come along then, Magdaline,' she said. 'You must see. I'm sorry. We have had scant time to think of you over these past days.' And she led her by the hand upstairs, along a far corridor to a closed door. 'It's very sad, my child, but it is a terrible mystery and you cannot be hidden away from it.'

In the room was the coffin, on trestles. In the coffin was the sad child with her baby, both in white, waxy-fleshed, the mother's arms arranged statuesquely to hold her child.

'There is peace here now,' Miss Clack said.

She did not feel peace here, but a burning pain in her throat and face that was nearer anger than anything else she knew. It seemed to her deceitful to say that there was peace here. Whatever spirits had been held within the dead child and her scrap of baby were gone, into nothing or into some new domain, but gone absolutely. It was ugly to dress them up like dolls and to talk of peace over them. She wept and Miss Clack comforted her with contact, holding her shoulders and allowing her to muzzle her face into the deep, black skirts; but she could not even imagine the flesh beneath them.

After the funeral, a needlessly protracted affair performed against a massive stone wall in bitter drizzle, she was rewarded by being allowed to sit up in Miss Clack's drawing-room on a stool, by a fierce fire in an iron-basket grate. She was brought a mug of hot broth which revived her with its vapour and its strength as she took it in scalding gulps which numbed her mouth. Miss Clack sat above her in a high-backed chair, drying her damp skirts, lifting up the hem to expose layers of grey petticoat, a sight which alerted the girl with a remote hint of intimacy. There was, she sensed, a purpose in this scene, and it forbade her simply to relax and enjoy it. She waited for Miss Clack to speak, waited a long while, but was conscious of words rising to her lips and never quite finding the clarity to come forth.

'My child,' she said eventually, finally, 'my child,' then she paused. 'I would not allow them to give you speech. Was that wrong of me? Do you understand what has happened here today? Probably better than I do. She spoke, poor little Judy. . . She spoke of its beauty. I cannot understand that. I cannot understand how so foul, so evil a thing could ever be beautiful. What is it? I am terrified of what you cannot tell me, of what you know that I can never know. I do not understand it. As I watched that little girl, Judy, die, I thought all the time of you. You survived. There was purpose in that – you must trust in that purpose, you must believe in it. You can tell me nothing. You cannot deceive me though. I have always been deceived, always will be, by anyone I trust. And yet I must trust. It is my calling to trust. It is my burden to be betrayed. Except for my brother, of course. You mustn't think I meant my brother. He is, as I am, certain. You must learn to love my brother;

to trust him and to love him. There is more love in him than you will find in me. That is his side of things. Mine is . . . mine is to . . . to press myself into the harshness of life, perhaps . . . It seems inconceivable that either of us should have ever married. It was always unthinkable. I could not bring children into a world that is so sad, so flawed . . .' Here again she paused substantially. She had not yet come to the point, was filling the room with the twistings of her conscience, trying to bring forth the real issue. 'When you came out of that place, you brought with you something. Do you remember that? You must remember. There had been murder. You brought it out into the world. Yes. You do remember. It's painful for you, child, and you must forgive me for causing you pain, but I must recall it now, briefly, once and for all. You must try to understand in order that you may forgive. I cannot understand, and I could not forgive it if I could, but you must. It has not been given to me to suffer as you have suffered. But there is something else.' And this was it. The girl was alerted by the arrival, at last, of the issue. 'When they took you into the hospital, you were with child. Did you know this? Did you?'

No. No. She had not known it. Her first instinct was of outrage. They had taken her child from her, pulled it out of her, smothered it before it had even been born. This was what had been missing all these months. The absence opened at once in her womb, and it hurt her. She doubled over with the pain of it. Hard cold hands were placed upon her shoulders. They were intended to reassure, but they pushed her down below the surface of her pain. She shook herself free and shot herself up, her jammed back wrenching. She cried out.

Miss Clack's face was scarred with two parallel runnels of tears. The girl saw her fear of her, but she could not console that fear.

'Forgive me, child. I'm nearly there. I'm coming to it directly. I need to ask you about your child, about its . . . about its making. I need to ask you, my child, and you must try to tell me as best you can. Be patient with me, I beg of you. I need to ask you this one thing. Was there love? Was there? Was there love?'

She wanted to cry out in affirmation, defiant affirmation;

but she did not have the power; not only because of her lumpish tongue, but because of the weight of the question. It had been given to her loaded with a new implication and she could no longer answer it in herself. She stared up at the hard old face that loomed over her and met it nakedly.

'Was there love?'

The door opened and Clarence Clack came in. They did not turn to him, the question held between them. He kept his distance, waiting upon them. At last the girl turned and saw clearly in his face what his sister wanted to see in hers. His face was old and puffed, sad and helpless, watery; and yet in the very softness of his features, in the spring of his white whiskers and the shiny pad of his baldness, in the folds of his jowls and the blear of his eyes, there was a love so boundless that it absorbed them both. It did not answer the question taut between them, it dispersed it. He stood with his hands under the tails of his coat, his feet apart, waiting upon them.

His sister rose stiffly, her skirts settling back into position. She approached her brother who watched her. He took her hands and clasped them, a sternness, almost an admonition, coming into his face, not of his own making, but in reflection of her face. The girl rose also, wanting to see what his face had for her. She approached and as she came to him, he reached out and laid a hand upon her head, a soft, meaty weight. She searched his expression which softened upon contemplation of her, opening to her and then, just for a second, he tipped her a wink with his left eye, a gleam and a flash of a wink that jumped her and brought up an urge to laugh which she suppressed, shocked at herself, and at him.

She bobbed a little curtsey which she had learnt from Sal, left and went to her room, closed the door and sat upon the edge of the bed.

That night the final dream came to her at last. It came only once, but its presence was so large and so clear that she needed no recurrence. It did not surprise her, as the other dreams had, coming as they seemed to from outside of her, taking possession of her; on the contrary, she was waiting like a bride for this dream.

She was afloat on a river, drifting on its surface, buoyed

perfectly on a moving swathe of clean, blue water between green banks. The landscape was soft and endless, the sky a flawless dome above her filled with light. She floated so easily that she just had to lie back and feel the strength of the movement that bore her. There was both a peace and a purpose in the movement and she submitted to it. Then she found she could turn herself, direct herself, shift her position so that the force of the flowing water could be made to act upon different parts of her body. Its pressure came upon her thighs and sides, caresses, soft and cool. The distortions of her body were absolved in the fluid power of the water. She turned herself round until the pressure of the current came between her legs which she opened to allow the eroticism of the contact to find its best purchase. The flow was running between her open thighs and she felt it move in small ripples across the surface of her belly to disperse against her breasts. After a while, she became possessed of an urge for self-denial, for disconnection. She turned promptly on to her stomach, brought her legs together and sent the flow up over her buttocks, pushing her down. She swam with long, sweeping strokes, her body fantastically long and lithe and full of liquid freedom. She came suddenly to the bank and found her feet on soft, warm silt, her hands gripping tufts of grass. She wriggled and was free of the water, standing in a soft meadow scattered with brilliant flowers, an enormous meadow undulating and lush, rising some long way away to form a horizon. The warmth of the air girded round her, making her flesh feel firm and tautened. She began to run, her dream-body perfection still with her. She ran with leaping, tireless strides across the grass, knowing it all to be a dream, knowing she would wake with all her distortions, but delighting, nevertheless, in her otherworld freedom, the reality of which was intense. She ran for the pleasure of it at first, feeling the ground rise against her, causing her to toil a little; then it would dip and her legs grew light again as she sped down into a soft declivity to meet the next rise with a marvellous momentum. She was running to a certain place, to a certain person, to a place over the next rise, or over the next, where she would be met by someone who would still her, who would hold all this energy that was running through her and would reflect it back into her where it would make her strong and whole again as she had always been deep within herself. She bounded over the meadow-hills and the swelling of the expectancy grew and grew within her.

She awoke breathless and full of an awareness that was stronger than the night which enclosed her, and so bright. She felt clear and purposeful. She clambered out of her bed and sat on the chamberpot which sharpened her awarenesses with its circle of icy porcelain. The warm hiss of her water, its release, its diminishing echo, its sour reek, all existed brightly in the new awareness that the dream had given her. She knelt by the bed as they had taught her to and prayed for the reality of her dream. Let me have a use for myself, she prayed; let me out of this silence; now that I know, let me out in some way.

— 5 —

Next day, the girl was taken out again by Miss Clack. They did not, however, go in the carriage, nor did they dress starched for company. They dressed plainly in coarse working dun. The girl had submitted to having her hair bound tight under a yellowed length of linen. She was being dressed for another part but, unlike the dressing for the social visits, this was not dressing to be seen, but to see: this excited her. They packed food – bread and cheese and brown bottles full of water. They set off on foot, early, after a hurried breakfast taken before the house was up. They walked from the back of the house and let themselves out through a little gate behind the stables. They came into an alley at the back of closely built houses from which the muffled clatter of pots and crying of children could be heard. The stench of cold, morning privies was strong in the rising warmth of the day.

The alley led to a street of small but neat houses, dark, curtained windows and shiny front doors. They passed little corner shops and began to meet the men who stepped out into the morning, sleepy-eyed and stiff-collared, in cheap suits and boots that were polished but dull.

But she was hurried past this world of sad respectability. Miss Clack walked strongly and evenly. The girl beside her could sense the strong, thin legs moving under the heavy skirts. She had to urge herself onward to keep up, her bundle of provisions unbalancing her gait, which was anyway lopsided like a little dance-step. She hummed a tune in her head to accompany her movement and to take her mind away from the beating of cobbles on her feet and the pressure of the heat upon her head. She ceased to observe the passing houses as she grew wearier, burying herself down amongst the relentless progress that was demanded of her.

Eventually Miss Clack slowed, and the girl raised her face to the street through which they now moved. There were high houses on both sides, too high for the street between them. Their form was regular: steps led up to the doorways and down to basements; large windows were spaced between the doors and in uniform shape but diminishing in size up the faces of the buildings. From these dark regularities, however, spilled a great, untidy mass of livings. The doors were all opened and clustered with children and old men. The windows were open and uncurtained, bedding was slung out to air through them, and women leaned and shouted, could be seen washing, came to tip out slops into the street. Some of the windows were closed, were curtained, dark, and these, in the context of the cacophony, the sprawl of the others, seemed ominous.

The street through which they again began to move was, she saw, crowded. Urchins ran about the legs of horses, the wheels of carts; clusters of idlers, men with trays of broken knick-knacks, women sitting with baskets of limp provisions. It was not a busy scene, just a crowded one. And there was filth everywhere, mounds and gulches of filth which seemed the natural element of the place. The urchins, who were the nearest to the filth, slopped through it and played in it, seemed its creatures, spawned from it and made of it.

As they passed deeper and deeper into this world, they were increasingly ignored. Such glances as they attracted glided over them. When a fight or a pursuit, or a stumbling old drunken woman, rushed towards them, they were, uncannily, avoided. They were untouched and, it seemed untouchable; and as they moved through this squalid place, their distance from it seemed to grow. It became dream-like, insubstantial. Sudden details loomed up at them but were disconnected, ephemeral. A small boy sitting on a box vomiting bloodily into a chipped white pail. An old man standing dumbly as a group of women threw gouts of filth at him and roared with laughter. Two young women dancing formally, bowing and turning, lifting their trailing skirts and pointing their raw toes delicately. A boy with a deep-pocketed jacket full of eggs which he clutched, reaching surreptitiously, drawing one out, deftly breaking it in the fingers of one hand and dropping its substance down his up-turned throat. Two women counting out a pile of dried peas, sharing them equally, on a space in the street scrupu-lously cleared of its muck. A row of women lining up to have their heads shaved by a greasy man with an old razor, nicking and scraping them whilst they sat forlornly, taking the few pence he pushed into their hands without looking, and going away with white domes above their burnished foreheads and grimy necks, as if touched by some sickness. A small, wiry boy, stripped to the waist, his buttocks showing through torn breeches, punching a boy a foot taller than he, a fat boy who reeled at each blow back into a crowd of other boys who pushed him away irritably into the gutter where he struggled up, the smaller boy stepping over to him and hitting him again, in the face, in the belly, on the ear, a precise bolt of his fist which flung the fat boy down again. A man who entertained a small crowd with a puppet-show gallows, a trap and noose and a stick-like figure with a great head, great popping eyes, that dropped with a crack and, at the twiddle of a string, jerked at the end of the rope. A quintet of girls, sisters, stamped with an identical, flat, family nose, the oldest almost a woman, the youngest almost a baby, standing in a row, howling out a song in a rough but exact unison: *The fields and the flowers and the pretty, pretty birds-o, All on a summer, summer's day-o.*

They passed through these streets untouched and untouch-ing, towards a destination that the girl began to fear; for, although she saw all this from without, the cumulative effect of it all, of the helplessness and meaninglessness, yet the importance of every detail to those they involved, and the utter insignificance of her observations of them, carried her back brutally to scenes she had forgotten, or had wanted to forget. She grabbed Miss Clack's hand and struggled to bury her face in the woman's skirts; but there was to be no slackening of pace. The woman's face was almost closed, the mouth tight, the eyes thin, the face propelled by a purpose that was held hard against pain. The girl knew that she could not reach that pain, could not share it; that if the woman relaxed for a moment to share it they would go no further, but halt in this place and be lost. The pain was a reassurance then; it told the girl that what she felt was real, seeing it in the woman's face also; and thus she was strengthened.

At the end of the street they were in, shutting off the end, was a large, low building, with wide stone steps leading up to double doors. As they approached, it became apparent that this was their destination. The girl noted that the nearer they drew to it, the thinner grew the crowds. They climbed the steps. The girl turned and surveyed the street, was alarmed to see how short and small and mean it seemed. As they had travelled it, it had seemed interminable. Now, some feet above it, the length was meanly foreshortened, the people shrivelled. She felt the woman's hand upon her shoulder, turned and was led into a long, wide hall, bare boards, high, small windows, a long box of dusty air. The place was empty, not a piece of furniture in it, except a heavy pulpit built into the far wall. Towards this prominence, Miss Clack strode. The girl stood near the door and watched her recede, reach the pulpit, mount it, turn and confront the empty space between them.

'Come here, Magdaline,' she called, her voice enormous, carried by the echoes and gripping the girl tightly. She scurried over to the pulpit and stood before it, looking up, aware of the space behind her and frightened of it. 'Closer . . . closer.'

The woman was directly above her. She had to twist her neck right round to look at her. The face seemed mad, hanging there above her, the breath hissing through clenched teeth.

'This is our mission, child,' she said. 'We must bring them here and we must offer ourselves to them.' She reached down into the pulpit below her and drew out a large hand-bell. 'Ring the bell as hard as you can. Go on, child.'

The bell was heavy. She stood out on the steps and surveyed the street, but not too closely. She shut her eyes and swung the bell up, letting it fall of its own accord. The sound was piercing, painful to her, but she did not think that it would carry far. It was a shout in a roaring, a candle held up against the mouth of a furnace. It was pathetic. She wept at it. When she was exhausted she stopped, sat and curled up on the steps. Eventually Miss Clack came to her, sat by her and roused her to eat. They ate in silence. A few of the children ventured a little way towards them, drawn by the food, but only half-drawn. They waited for an offer but Miss Clack was only offering herself and the children soon drifted back into the street.

They sat and stared along the street for a long while, until the afternoon shadow filled the gap between the houses; then they journeyed home. The rectory when they reached it tired and silent seemed strange. Its security which had seemed so strong only the day before, was now temporary again. She had seen too much to be at ease, more than would rest within her. As she made her way up to bed after an evening of implacable silence, Miss Clack followed her to the foot of the stairs, leant on the banister.

'Tomorrow,' she said.

Day after day, the tall woman and the hunchbacked girl passed along Victory Street to the Victory Mission Hall. The doors were opened and the hunchback came out and rang the bell. The doors of the hall remained open upon an empty space, like the mind of an idiot, full of dust and turgid airs, moving only to far distant echoes. Day after day, through a summer that weighed interminably hot, they waited with the street bustling and bursting in its long perspective before them. Their perseverance was, however, eventually rewarded.

One day a small girl, running in terror from some violent game, scrambled up the stone steps, past the woman and the hunchback girl and into the space of the hall. The woman rose slowly and followed her in. She was standing in the hall, looking about her, becoming afraid. She crouched down, shrunk into a tightening spring as the tall woman approached her, stood over her and then passed on towards the pulpit which she mounted.

'I bid you welcome,' the woman said strongly.

The child sprang up and ran back towards the door, straight through it to the rim of the top step. Below her, on the street, were gathered her pursuers. The hunchback was beside her, watching her indecision, seeing below her the rat-grins and gog-tongues of a crowd of about twenty boys who clustered together, reaching up their bare forearms and calling for her obscenely; but holding back. The child faced them, panting and knotted. The hunchback saw how gradually the fugitive girl regained her breath and became aware of the balance which held her. Below her a mob sought, predictably, to defile her; behind her was that great unknown space. The mob pushed and jostled forward, stumbling on the bottom step. The child tossed up her head with its tails of black hair and began to retreat, her arms spread, feeling behind her; grown strong now, taunting them to follow. She backed clearly through the doors of the hall, deep into it. The boys, with a sudden communal whoop, came leaping up after her. She turned and ran into the middle of the hall, stood still in the centre of the floor, arms at her side, facing the woman in the pulpit. The boys, in their first rush, spread out as if to encircle her, but up in the pulpit was the tall woman watching them, each one of them. They all went still, aware of the space and the stillness, looking about them, looking back to the doorway in which stood the hunchback; but, catching their eyes, she moved to one side to show them that the way out was still clear.

'I bid you welcome,' the tall woman said. 'You who suffer are the blessed ones of Christ. Your suffering frees you. We have come to honour you.'

The ragged children shifted uneasily. The fugitive girl acted first, jutted her chin in the air, turned and strutted to the door, breaking into a run as soon as she had passed into the open air. The boys whooped and piled through the doorway in a mass after her.

The hunchback remained in the doorway, watching them merge back into the street.

'We have begun, child,' the woman called to her.

A couple of days later, the children suddenly returned, a whole pack of them this time, forty or fifty. The girl who had originally broken the taboo now lolled against the shoulder of a tall, sinewy-looking boy in a long cloak. She had ribbons in her hair now and had daubed a pasty whitening on to her face. She seemed to be fêted in some way, at least by those nearest to her in the cluster. On more detailed inspection, it seemed that they were all in some sort of celebrational array – loud, laughing, pushing and sprawling about. Watching from the top of the steps, the tall woman and the hunchbacked girl did not see them appear as a body, but watched how they gathered, almost at random, about a moving point, giving it momentum and taking momentum from it, as it became the surge of a crowd, as it came clear of the concourse of the street and was distinctly approaching them; although, strangely, none of the children seemed to be looking ahead. The direction was held within the group and all, as they clustered into the centre, were moving forward. When they came near the bottom step they halted, hushed each other quickly and at last looked up at the tall woman who stood waiting for them.

'Welcome!' the woman said, opening her arms briefly, then turning to stride through the hall to the pulpit.

They lingered on the street, restless and muttering, as if about to disperse, but contained, focused upon the hunchback who remained to usher them. One of them took a step up from the mass, a boy with a shaved head and globed eyes that seemed incapable of closing. When he spoke, his voice spluttered through toothless gums.

'Can'a marry 'in'n'ar? Can'a? Can'a?'

He came up to the hunchback, rose over her, hands on hips, head heavily to one side. As he repeated his question and received no response, she could sense a simple anger mount in him. She stared into it, but it was quite unreflective and she had no opposition to it. She pointed inside, but he did not step past her, stood twitching, his eyes swelling and his hands slipping off his hips and hanging by his side nervously. She dropped her eyes from him and turned, walking slowly through the door, expecting him to grab her and pull her back. He did not. She walked steadily into the hall and heard him behind her, coming forward a few steps at a time. She left him near the door and wobbled across to the pulpit, taking her position beside Miss Clack some half-way up the steps of it. When she looked back the boy had not come far in. Behind him, though, the doorway was filling with the others who urged forward into the hall, surrounded the boy and filled the whole width of the door end.

'Come forward, children,' the woman called. 'There's room for all of you. Don't be afraid.'

Her words stilled them. They looked at her seriously. From the vantage of the pulpit, they did not seem menacing at all. They seemed bewildered, estranged; desperate but with an empty desperation too sunk in their thin and ragged bodies to be more than seldom and stupidly active.

The boy stepped forward and pitched out his question again. 'Can'a marry 'in'n'ar, miss'ss?'

His words were thinned in the echoes of the space. He turned and grabbed at the girl and her attached, cloaked boy, and pushed them forward a little. They stood together, embarrassed, looking around them, anywhere but straight ahead, holding hands. They were so young, so wizened and tattered beneath their fiction of finery, that the idea of a marriage between them was pathetic; it was without the energy it would have had had they been older, or the innocence had they been younger. It seemed as they stood there, beneath their embarrassment, an insult, a gesture of defiance against some sort of preconceived idea of respectability which the woman in the pulpit perhaps embodied for them. It was impossible to know how they might be answered. Miss Clack looked up at the ceiling and her eyes filled with tears which spilled down the sides of her head.

She was roused by a touch at the hem of her dress. She blinked and blurred and looked down through the blur to see Magdaline looking up at her, asking her. She looked at the children, misty shapes of many shades across the long floor.

'Why do you want to be married?' she asked.

'Don'ya know, eh? Don'ya know tha'?' The bald boy played to his crowd who hooted for him, moving forward, the others came forward behind him with a surge that settled as he settled.

'I cannot marry you,' she said, rising over their row, but going unheard. 'I have no blessings for you. I have nothing for you,' she said, holding her open hands. 'Nothing.'

They urged slightly forward as if pushed from behind and having to come forward a few steps to gain a purchase to resist the push.

'I have come,' she said, opening herself out, 'to honour you. I am glad to meet you. Bring me your suffering. Be proud of your suffering for it makes you strong in the sight of God. He loves you. He notes your pain and He will recompense you. I live under the hard stare of His censure. He has given me much and it is heavy for me to bear it. You are free. If only I could teach you to celebrate your freedom and to become aware of God's love for you.'

They had heard all this before, or words as like it as to make no difference, and they were visibly disappointed. They muttered and moved about, turning to each other, loosened up now they could see through all this. The bald boy who had led them felt something of the responsibility for their being in this blind alley and, the hunchbacked girl saw clearly, he was urgent to find some way to reassert himself, which meant a gesture, which meant a violence of some sort.

She moved suddenly from the shelter of the pulpit and came, in her uneven way, towards them, towards him in particular. As she advanced, they backed but she was amongst them, upon him before any general retreat had developed. She stood squarely before him ready for whatever he might need to do. She dreaded a shout of protection coming from the pulpit, a shout that would force them. She was surprised by her height above them. She became afraid of them; she felt she had something which they could take away from her. When she had pushed herself out into their malevolence, she had thought only of offering herself to distract them from Miss Clack: it had been an instinct bred in the old life, a leap into the mouth of the storm to meet it unabashed, to let it go where it had to go. Now she felt afraid. She looked back at Miss Clack but hardly saw her, a dark shape on a high pulpit. 'You are free,' Miss Clack had assured them, had offered them this as a cause for celebration. She had been free once, as they were free, but was not so any more.

They were steadily closing round her. Again the movement was individually imperceptible. Whenever she actually saw one of them moving, they seemed always to have been shoved forward by others. She looked around for the bald-headed boy but when she located him, he was amongst the others, one of the crowd, not leading anything anymore. She could not distinguish the young lovers at all, although she turned herself one way and another, moved about in a decreasing circle trying to establish them. When she realised how much she was moving, she held still, not wanting to show her fear. She shuddered and felt her muscles beginning to lose their grip. She lowered her head. She could not imagine what they might do to her. The brutality of these wretched children was entirely simple; it was innocent as she had once been. Now there was a price to pay, a loss of freedom, a desire to live that was also a fear of death; and more than that, a fear of pain, a fear of shame, a fear of not being what she wanted to be. She bunched herself and allowed herself to drop down on to her knees. They closed about her, fetid, darkening. They touched her clothes, dabbing, grabbing, caressing briefly then snatching away, handfuls of the material wrenched at, pulling her in different directions as it gave and tore. She put her face in her hands and knelt lower, to present them only with the alp of her back. She felt a gasp of exposure as her shoulder was suddenly bared, her round flesh touched and nipped and clawed. Their purpose did not yet seem to hurt her; rather to explore her. She submitted, afraid of both resistance and compliance, became a doll for them, a strange mute beast. Their proximity was noxious, clouding her. Where they touched they seemed to imprint dirt and bruising, an exposure to an inimical element.

Miss Clack saved her, came down and they eased away from her, forming a wide channel down which she flowed. The girl shook herself to free herself from the cloy of their touches. She opened her eyes to the black monolith of her protectress. She was white and half-naked, trembling woman-flesh, full before these weasily children. She stood up straight as she could, her back and breasts open. Miss Clack placed a confirming hand upon her shoulder.

'You see,' Miss Clack said to them, 'she is as you are. She

too has her suffering. Do not be afraid to look at her. She cannot speak, but she understands. If she could speak, she would shake the walls with her words.'

The girl took Miss Clack's hand and pulled upon it to attract her attention. She was wrong about these children: they understood nothing of this talk of suffering and freedom. Miss Clack surveyed them from a great height. Miss Clack looked down upon her kindly, squeezed her shoulder.

'You will forgive them, Magdaline.'

She looked round the vacant faces, saw smiles edging into them, tedium, disengagement. She saw the bald boy, caught his eye. He peered at her through lowered lids, half-winking. She broke from Miss Clack and advanced upon him, her breasts jumping. His friends parted and he, under the fixing of her eyes upon him, stumbled back and hit the wall behind with the back of his head, solidly. She was upon him at once, staring into his face. He looked afraid at first, then recovered his leer again, dropped his eyes down to rest upon her exposure. She hit him with a closed fist upon the side of his face and sprawled him along the wall. He blinked and held his balance with difficulty. There was a gasp and a movement amongst the others, whether away from her or towards her she did not care to notice. She waited for the bald boy to regain himself and raised her fist to him again. He fell to the floor without being touched, suddenly collapsing as if his bones had fallen in a pile within him. She stepped over him and reached down a hand. He took it and hoicked himself up. He regarded her, up and down, looked about him, nervously at first, and then laughing.

The laugh was taken up all round. The girl returned to Miss Clack, pulling the bits of her dress stiffly about her. Miss Clack looked bewildered. The girl hugged her about her middle, burying herself in the copious black satin. She felt Miss Clack's arms about her shoulders. She heard the children cheering and clapping. Holding the front of her dress together, she took Miss Clack by the hand and led her to the door. The children made an avenue and cheered them out, reaching and touching them as they passed triumphantly into the street. She felt Miss Clack pulling occasionally, wanting to stop and draw back, wanting to say something; but the girl pressed on and they left Victory Street and made their way back to the rectory, the girl fearful lest her bubbling laughter should break out and her modesty be outraged.

The next morning Miss Clack at breakfast said, 'I think we have done all that can be done at the mission, child.' But the girl rose up at this, stood down from the table with the outrage in her face. Miss Clack smiled, defeated.

'Very well, very well. We came away without locking the hall yesterday. That must be attended to, at least.'

It was a cloudy day. The air was sweaty and the rain would seep through sooner or later. They walked the length of Victory Street and attracted more regard than usual from the elders – curious, suspicious recognition. The children, however, broke into activity as they passed, gathering and following, or running off to fetch others. When they entered the hall, a multitude of children burst in behind them, surrounding them noisily. They were smothered in wreaths of celebration as large as it was inexplicable. She saw that Miss Clack was confused by it, troubled. She delighted in it. She laughed and gave them her hands to hold, allowed them to bear her about amongst them, touching and greeting her in a continuous uproar, leaping and cartwheeling about her. Miss Clack, meanwhile, had struggled to the pulpit, and was calling to her from its safety in a stern voice. She went and took her place beside Miss Clack, looking up and trying deliberately to muster and reflect all the resonance and joy about them. Miss Clack frowned down upon her and said something which she could not hear for the noise of the children who still poured enthusiastically into the hall in scores. They were all in motion, all in full cry. Games and dances formed in spaces, were crowded out and dissolved. Tiny acrobats leaped on to the shoulders of others or turned upside down, their legs writhing, vaulted over any back that bent for a moment. Trials of strength were made with chains of the children gripping wrists, gripping waists, pulling against other chains, the participants yelling for support, more support, until the whole struggling centipede overbalanced and half the room seemed to be on the floor for a moment, then up and into the next game.

A group of girls, some of whom she thought she recognised from the day before, came to the pulpit and pulled at her. She resisted at first, looking up at Miss Clack; but their pull was too strong, their eagerness too insistent, and she was propelled into the midst of the revels with a roar of approval rising around her. She was lifted off her feet and borne high in the air above the tangled mass of bodies. She floated freely, flew about the room, passing from hand to hand, a multitude of upturned hands above the upturned faces.

Suddenly they released her. She found her feet and raised her face steadily, to see before her an emaciated boy with long, straight, white hair, pale, almost translucent skin, and delicate, sad features. He registered a distant alarm at being faced with her. They propelled him towards her and began to titter. His lipless mouth began to tremble and his beautiful eyes to blink. He wore a jacket and trousers that he had long outgrown, but the body revealed beneath was clean and pure. She shook her arms free of their support and she reached out to greet him. They gasped, and those at the edge of the space were pushed forward by those behind, urgent to know what was happening. He came forwards then, turning himself sideways, and she took his hands which were unnaturally long and bony, but were also soft and fragile. She could have ground him so easily between her fingers. She wondered how such a frail thing survived down here. He came close up to her and looked at her, then about him, receiving a loud surge of encouragement. He looked back at her and his strange mouth widened its line into some elemental smile, his cheeks tinging the most delicate, floral pink.

She lifted herself up, lifted her head clear of them, looked through the cloud of dust that rose over them. Their eyes were upon her, but she looked over them, the prickling points of light below the dust, looked across to the pulpit where clung poor Miss Clack, her face drawn tight, her body ossified. She could not have broken the game to please Miss Clack. The game was the point of their being there. They had contained all that wild street energy within this building and had turned it into a celebration. The pale boy was to be her lover. She tucked his twig-like forearm under her arm. It was strange to be so substantial beside him: her bulk could have encompassed several of his. She led him forward, the crowd opening like a miraculous sea before them, closing behind.

They came at last to the base of the pulpit. Miss Clack leaned down, her breath coming quickly, a cough suppressed.

'What are you *doing*?' she asked. 'Who is this? Who are you, boy?'

'She's mine,' he said, his voice as thin as water, tears rushing down his face.

The girl took him, knelt and embraced him. He sobbed in rapid spasms and nuzzled himself into her breasts. She looked at the press of faces around them and, as she looked, they began to draw back, pressing away from her and her lover. From the rear of the press murmurs rose, protests; but these stilled and she could hear their feet upon the steps, hear them draining out into the street. They receded like a tide, fulfilled and easy, and soon the long hall was emptied; its echoes still bustling, its dust in a turmoil, but empty apart from Miss Clack, her lover and herself.

His sobbing had shrunk into a steady trembling against her. She lifted up his face which was full of alarm. She kissed his forehead, kissed his cheeks, kissed his lips but he had no knowledge of such kissing and she stopped, held him closely. When he stilled, she rose with him and, holding his hand, walked with him across the hall to the open door.

Outside the sky was dark, purpled, and rain was dripping down over the street. The street-bustle went on under many-coloured awnings, all makeshift and precarious, all gleaming their old colours out into the wetness. He was looking up at her. She smiled and released him like a bird. He ran down the steps into the empty space before the hall, looked about him. From nowhere, it seemed, a small crowd of the children sprang out and clustered round him, bearing him off.

She turned and walked back into the hall. A gust sprang up from the street, caught one of the doors and moved it with a groan, blew a blast of dampness into the vacancy. She came to the pulpit. Miss Clack had come down, awkwardly, her joints stiffened. She came to Miss Clack and leant against her, put her arms around her. The old woman patted her wearily. They began to move back towards the doors. It was early but the day was surely over now.

'I don't think,' Miss Clack said as they heaved the doors closed behind them, 'that we should come here again. I wanted to show you, child, and you have seen, I think. I wanted also to . . . to say something here, and I think I have said something . . . or, if not, then I think it does not need saying anymore.'

They had finished shutting up. The door was locked with a great iron key and they faced the way home tiredly. They had to come again. They had begun something which could not be abandoned. But a new day for that. Now she must attend to the old woman who was bewildered and tired to a depth she sensed but could barely, personally, imagine. She took her hand and they travelled back down the dripping street.

They went back the next day, and every day, Sundays only excepted when their attendance in the parish was unavoidable. Clarence did not enquire where they went and, the girl assumed, knew somehow what they were doing. She sensed, or at least imagined, his implicit approval.

Entering Victory Street, they were now always greeted by the children. The children anticipated them, clustered round them, crowding them up into the hall. Miss Clack, at a distance – whenever she could find one – conceived plans for a school for these children, or at least some attempt to give them the basic stories of the Saviour. Such plans never found a reality amongst the swirling, promiscuous energy of the children themselves. It was Magdaline whom they loved and greeted, placed always at the centre of their dubious games. Miss Clack was only her attendant. She no longer mounted the pulpit, sat now on its steps and watched in a blur of bewilderment as the games were played out.

They danced and they sang. They squabbled and they screamed. They fell silent and let the silence grow to bursting point then exploded it with a sudden, terrifying clamour. She did not know whether this signified joy or fury, or some pagan amalgam of both. At these climaxes the ragged children became united, and, after them, they subsided and fragmented into their separate clusters and solitudes, some quiet, some lively, some turned in on themselves, some still spinning and colliding with unspent energy. She would study one such cluster to see if she could determine any sort of purpose to its activity. The games could hardly be said to begin, they just started up somehow; and their ends were sometimes determinate, a triumph of a punch, sometimes indeterminate as if the game had not succeeded or, if it had succeeded, she had missed the point of it.

Her only point of reference was Magdaline and the strange little monster boy. They were always together, at the centre of something whenever they came within reach of her observing. They were treated by the others with a deference and care. They were continually brought things – scraps of dirty food in dirty cloths, birds and mice, dead and alive – to touch, broken bits of things to handle and examine, perhaps even to bless. It all reeked of paganism, of sacrilege; she broke from her fascination frequently with shudders of revulsion. They were brought arguments to resolve, the protagonists shouting and slashing out at one another before them, allowing Magdaline to touch and calm them, allowing the monster boy to pronounce upon them; the pronouncements always seemed to be accepted. The ragged children performed for their chosen pair, dancing, walking on their hands, leap-frogging round them. The whole hall hushed as songs, sweet and frail, were sung, pipes were played, hideous knives were juggled, fire was eaten in massive quantities and blown about singeing hair all round. Miss Clack's greatest moment of horror occurred when a chubby boy was hustled forward and coaxed into exhibiting an enormous penis to them, a sight of much wonder and serious appreciation amongst the older children. Miss Clack had wanted to spring out and denounce this, but she realised with a weird opening and sinking feeling within her, that it was a token entirely within keeping amongst this strange confusion. She did not know whether this realisation resolved the obscenity, or revealed the essential obscenity of everything else there. She was neutralised, and could only attend the ending of the long days when at last, as the evening sunlight poured in through the doors almost horizontally, the confusion began to drain away, slowly but perceptibly, out into the street, until only Magdaline and her monster were left, hand in hand, standing in the doorway, watching the others go.

When they had watched the street drain before them, they

178

turned and came back to Miss Clack, hand in hand, walking slowly but looking at her as they came, Magdaline smiling and easy, the boy furtive and abashed. She could not look at Magdaline whose easiness upset her; she looked at the boy, so pale that the sun almost glowed through him, so frail. She wondered at his provenance and shuddered to think of the inbreeding that must have spawned him. He seemed subhuman in a way that Magdaline and her deformities never did. Beside him she was robust, womanly, beautiful; she was beautiful, Miss Clack felt this strongly now.

'You bring 'a back 'amorra',' he said when they reached her. 'You bring 'a back 'cuz 'e's mine, y'know. Humpty-back, jumpty-back.' On the surface of his fragility he wore a pathetic assertiveness. He shook his twiggy finger up at Miss Clack, prodding at her, baring his loose teeth.

She turned to look at Magdaline again, for a cue how to respond to this, and she saw that a sadness had crept upon the girl. She touched the boy's head and shoulders and she looked to Miss Clack to say something for her.

'Don't worry, child,' she said to him. 'It will all be done well for you.'

She held her hand out for him. He took her fingers, examined them quickly and brought his teeth round them. There was no strength in his bite and she did not, therefore, know whether he meant to hurt her or to apply some strange caress. She submitted. His mouth was dry and his breath seemed cold, clammy. She shuddered and slipped her hand away. Magdaline turned to him and headed him back down the hall to the door, kissing and releasing him.

Miss Clack envied Magdaline her freedom, but grew strong in the pride of having given her that freedom, set her to work in the world; and here she was flourishing amongst the sadness and the pity, moving actively amongst it, never outweighed by it; not solving or healing, that was too great a task, that needed heroes and fanatics, that needed fire and anger; no, here they witnessed and, in witnessing, ministered. Watching Magdaline, the silent hunchback moving amongst them with her faint consort, she felt herself a flame burning brightly amidst the darkness of past and future, a flame of faith and hope, pushing back the darkness, clearly and purely, however briefly. This felt good.

— 6 —

The summer bloated, swelled and burst into a drenching, misty autumn that clung to the stones and seeped into every crevice and every throat. In Victory Street the burden of the season was heavy. First they saw how the faces sagged, the eyes gumming, the throats thickened with phlegm; then they became aware of the sickness in a more malevolent form. Undertakers in high, black hats, their raw, blue faces and their soggy overcoats, moved up and down the street outside, in and out of the tenements with a careless heaviness that frightened Miss Clack and Magdaline, not only in itself, but also in the apathy, the resignation it seemed to slam into the people.

They came one day to the hall and noted the sombre faces, sensed a change, wondered what it would be. There were less of them that last day, but there were some new ones, older, adolescent, their lumpish adulthood intruding into the spirit of the place, restricting the others. The children tried games, tried to lift some music, but it would not rise from them. The adolescents seemed surly and disapproving. Miss Clack viewed them with apprehension, sat tight under the pulpit whilst Magdaline passed amongst them, looking for her lover. She came to the adolescents who stood at the edges of the hall in knotted groups, muttering when she was out of reach, tightening when she approached. She came to them and looked at them, questioning them. They stared back dumb, or turned away. Occasionally she roused a moment of aggression and approached expecting some blow to come at her; but she came too squarely at it and the violence was pale and defeated too. She did not like facing them out like this: it closed them up and she wanted them to open to her. She went to the doorway and looked out into the grey, gleaming street, looking for him.

She had seen the undertakers, had listened to the unaccustomed precision of their bootheels, watched the fearful ease with which they hefted the boxes high up on to their black shoulders. She sensed the presence of death at that moment. She knew at once that her boy lover was gone and that these elder children had come to tell her, or to blame her. She turned back to them with this new knowledge and their observations of her quickly confirmed it. She wept for him, for she found that she had come to love him. When she had first been given him, it had seemed a mockery, but she had grown to see the beauty in his frailty. He was so thin, so insubstantial that touching him she would touch the life of him so near the surface. It had been so pure, uncomplicated by anything he might have built upon it. Any skill or any strength he presented could only have been painted on. There was only the pale translucence, the gentility that was beyond any assertiveness. She had realised in him an exact balance for herself. His fragility made her strong. His attenuation gave her purpose. It was all so full of possibility. She had dreamed of his growing into a perfect, child-like manhood, imagined him honed to a point of sexuality where she might have met him equally. How minute and perfect such a moment would have been, almost too much for him. The danger of it had caught her, late at night, in the dark slot of her rectory bed, at the edge of panic, at the edge of release. And now he was dead.

She went down the steps and on to the bare street, allowing the clammy air to enclose her. She knelt on the cobbles and beat her fists into her thighs. The lump of her back throbbed dully.

When she looked about her, the adolescents had come down and grouped round her. She rose, glanced about them and then ran as fast as she could, up the steps and back into the hall. Miss Clack saw her approaching and rose, puzzled but ready to defend her. She snatched Miss Clack's hand and pulled her away. Miss Clack knew better than to resist. They came back down amongst the crowd who clustered and led them, herding in close, down along the street.

People came to look at them from doorways, stopping as they approached, held back. The houses were full of eyes; in every darkness, over every ledge, faces watched. These gazes were not to be dwelt upon, for they were possessed by their own uselessness, a gaping insensibility which opened a giddy human chasm on either side of them as they turned off the street and approached, for the first time in their many weeks of passage through that street, the wall of house fronts.

They climbed the hard street steps to a doorless doorway and went into a crowded corridor, dark and gleaming with filth. The walls were obscured by strange shapes that were piles of rubbish, falls of the fabric of the tenement. They were pushed through amongst the crowd that bore them, closed around them, shifted them on. Their progress was a struggle through a press of writhing bodies which obtruded their bones into them as they proceeded. Often they were halted entirely, clotted to a standstill, stifling.

They came to a stairway and ascended. The stairway was stone and had no banister, and they rose, it seemed, to dangerous heights, a hideous fall to one side of them, glimpsed spasmodically where glints of daylight came in, or where a lamp flickered. The steps were steep and punishing, uneven so they stumbled, clinging on to each other, and making alternate progress, weighting each other against the push and pull of the crowd below and above them.

At last, abruptly, they were propelled into a room. The crowd remained at the door, peering in on them, pressing tight, but keeping out. The walls were raw and fractured, the window gone entirely, its gap covered by falling sacks. The thin boy lay on the floor in the middle of the room, naked and dead, his arms and legs thrown out crookedly. Miss Clack held back, retracted, but the girl went to him and closed his eyes, drew together the sticks of his limbs. He did not appal her in death: he was a mere skeleton with the thinnest strippings of flesh about him. The stench of his consumption filled the room. Miss Clack fought it and spluttered, but the girl breathed it in like a drug, daring it to grip at her, outbraving it. She knelt and took an attitude of prayer beside the body, head down, hands clamped. She made no words within her, just submitted briefly to the attitude as a seal upon him. Whatever he had been, he was not now.

She rose and joined Miss Clack. They went to the wall of faces in the doorway which parted and they came to the top of the stairway. Gripping each other tightly they made the perilous descent, the crowd opening for them and closing behind them.

As they descended, the people seemed to draw back, to breathe in. A silence congregated about them. The whole tenement, the whole street seemed to swell with the silence. They came down and out into the iron daylight, longing to be free of the silence of the house, only to fall into the silence of the street which was worse, glutting the chasm between the houses and lingering there like a smog. The people stood silent and waiting, their eyes upon Miss Clack and the girl. Everywhere about them there were eyes, still unfocused, characterless, accepting, waiting. Miss Clack rushed her down the street, through the morass of watching, through the silence, afraid of it.

At the end of Victory Street, by a fire of old furniture and broken crates, a dozen undertakers warmed their thin, black bodies, shifting about and muttering, passing a large bottle about and hawking into the fire. They took no notice of the fleeing women, waiting for some signal, some appropriate moment to move in. A large van stood with its doors open, two black horses harnessed to it with their noses in feeding bags. Inside the van was a stack of cheap coffins of a uniform size. Smaller carts with single horses awaited as hearses. The undertakers with their long faces and bored eyes were like attendant torturers. The girl paused, wanting to rush amongst them, but Miss Clack hurried her on.

The next day, and for several days after, they returned to Victory Street, but didn't venture beyond its entrance, beyond the station of the undertakers who grew in number, brought a whole conglomeration of vehicles to the mouth of the street. The girl and Miss Clack stood and watched the black figures carrying the empty boxes in and moving amongst the still people, withdrawing with the boxes replete, loading up the hearse-carts and sending them away. The people were lost in the apathy and silence. There was no will in them at all, no will to raise even a voice of mourning or of pain, no will to register the departure of their dead. Perhaps they were all condemned and waited only for their turn. The girl and Miss Clack stood and watched, witnessed and registered and mourned for them.

Then one day there was a dispute amongst the pack of undertakers, an argument, it seemed, over money. A coffin was slammed down and the men discarded their professional solemnity, raised red knuckles across the box. It seemed that there was an understanding that each firm of undertakers should only collect one corpse at a time, in strict rotation. It appeared that they were remunerated by something called the Institute which paid them per capita. One of the firms, returning with their load, had been challenged. The others had gathered round, had pushed the actual bearers aside, had pushed back their flailing colleagues, had prised the lid off the suspicious box in which were exposed the corpses of three children, a boy and a girl, possibly twins, heads at opposite ends, and a tiny baby, hardly born, nestling on their legs. The perpetrators of this fraud defended themselves with counter-accusations and with furious outfacing, their accusers thus inflamed even further. They did not stand still, but edged away, the frauds shuffling towards any open space, their accusers wheeling about them to cut off their retreat, a movement to the edge of violence.

The girl watched the progress of this little whirlpool of contention. The contentious coffin was left lying in the street, its lid flung off, its cargo open. The steady, misty drizzle had begun to settle on the little faces, giving them a drowned, washed-away look. The boy's eyes had not even been closed. The girl knelt to attend to this.

It was a sight beyond sadness, beyond anger. It drained her. Looking at the unwholesome, spongy, grey flesh was like looking into nothing, an empty space that absorbed everything about it. There were the thin limbs of the boy and the girl, the sunken bellies and the ridged ribs, the bare, black feet, heels at each other's knees, the toes flat and slightly splayed, the hands with their nests of lines lying open. And between them, cradled on their calf-bones, was the baby, bald, naked, purple-skinned, tiny-featured, fingers bunched with minute white nails. For one mad moment it seemed easy to breathe and blow the life back into them; the moment after, the impossibility of this came like a dull persistent nausea.

'Enough,' Miss Clack said, standing over her. 'Enough.'

She rose and they moved away.

The next day they dressed in their Sunday finery. Their carriage came to the door and awaited them. They were borne away, back over the river. They arrived back at her new beginning, the Free Hospital, and rose through its high porticoes.

Miss Clack spoke fiercely to tail-coated attendants and they were shown into a formal room, all polished, soft leather and walnut, with the underlying smells of caustics and unguents which the institution of the hospital poured over the corruptions with which it dealt.

At last he arrived whom they had come to see, Sir Marcus Gossiter. It was plain that he did not welcome them.

'Miss Clack ... young lady ...', he said, inclining fractionally to each. 'What brings you back to my hospital?'

'What do you think might have brought us?' Miss Clack said sharply.

He paused to blunt the sharpness. 'I really', he then continued, 'have no idea at all. Perhaps you have some scheme, some improving idea? Or do you, Miss Clack, merely wish me to register my official approval of what you have achieved upon that girl?'

'Do you know Rackerly, Sir Marcus?'

'Rackerly? The district beyond the factories, over the river? Not well, Miss Clack, I must confess. We have little need to go and seek misery. It finds us faster then we can attend to it as it is.'

'Do you know that there is an epidemic in Rackerly, Sir Marcus?'

'I don't think "epidemic" is a term which you are qualified to use, Miss Clack; I hope you will forgive me. There is always sickness where there is squalor and ignorance.'

'There is an epidemic in Rackerly.'

'An epidemic of what, precisely?'

'You do not know?'

'Miss Clack, the Institute appointed by the State provides the machinery for all such eventualities, and, such as it is, it provides. We do not live in a perfect world. If you would crusade, Miss Clack, go and teach them in Rackerly the meaning of cleanliness, of regimen, of self-respect. These are not my specialisms.'

'Go to Rackerly. Go to Rackerly and do something. They are bringing out the dead in scores. We saw three children in one coffin.'

'Oh, I can show you far worse, here in this building. I can show you pain and madness and hideous deformity, diseases that eat and bloat, corrode and corrupt the organs for no apparent reason. We can only hope to help those who seek to help themselves, Miss Clack. Life is pain and misery. Surely your faith confirms this. There are those who succumb and there are those who struggle. I have nothing for those who can only surrender.'

'How high does the tide of corpses have to rise before you will see it, Sir Marcus?'

'I assure you, Miss Clack, that the procreative energy of these people will soon make up for any depletions. Forgive my inability to wax sentimental. They overcrowd themselves and they turn their adequate and sturdy tenements into great sewers, and the harvest of their sin, Miss Clack, is death. I refer you to the tablets of your faith. If they cannot direct you to an understanding of life, I am sure that I, a mere scientific rationalist, cannot. Good day to you.'

Miss Clack rose and, in almost a whisper, said, 'You know you are damned, Sir Marcus. Your soul is deformed. I will go and I will send them out to you. I will tell them to rise and to throw themselves upon you. They have more right to life than you do.'

He smiled. 'Your charity seems in short supply today. May I show you some more deserving cases. Perhaps you will be moved to adopt one or two of the more hopeless, make some more space for us here.'

Miss Clack went to the door, her face so hard it seemed as if it might shatter, her eyes knots of pressure and her mouth so tight it was almost invisible in the sheerness of her face.

Out on the entrance steps, Miss Clack paused to search for the waiting carriage. The coachman had seen them and drew carefully across the busy courtyard.

'To Victory Street, Rackerly,' she said as she handed the girl up into the carriage, clambered in herself and they jolted off.

In Victory Street, the carriage made its way with difficulty down the rubbish and the ruins. The day was held in a bitter, grey fog, not dense but pervasive. The street seemed in the last stages of decay. The clutter seemed the final gutting of the tenements. The people carried heaps and heaps of broken furniture and rags out on to the pavement. The carriage, its solid, black body struggling through, drew little attention. Eventually it halted, unable to proceed, rapidly enclosed amongst the clutter.

Miss Clack emerged, helped the girl down and then pointed up, to the roof; they were to climb on to the roof of the carriage. The coachman lifted the girl bodily and set her upon the curved and lacquered surface which seemed precarious and fragile, bending under her weight. She did not stand up, was certain that with Miss Clack's weight the roof would split and rip them as they fell through it. It did not. Miss Clack rose majestically, stepped up lightly and drew the girl up to her feet. They stood together above the street, surveying it.

The people began to notice them, perforce, and, although they instinctively looked away again having glanced up at what they had bumped into, they recognised the woman and the girl and their gazes came back. They seemed to be held, to be drawn in, not too close, not too distant, ready to deflect and to blend back amongst their broken dwellings once more. But as the girl gained the confidence to look away from Miss Clack to whom she was clinging, she saw how the street seemed to be filling with the dark figures with pale faces upturned, a pale mist settling round them, binding them in, blurring them into a mass. Miss Clack seemed only to be waiting for them. The girl looked to see her face lifted up, rising into the grey sky, dark and determined.

She placed her hands upon the girl's shoulders and stared into her face. She is mad, the girl thought: it was an exciting thought, full of possibility. She turned the girl round and they faced the same way, turning slowly, looking round the waiting faces. The carriage roof shrieked under the strain. Around them the people were gathered – the poor, the condemned, the pitiful – faces blank, not hoping, and looking, to the girl's desperate and fanciful eye, as if they wanted no hope. Miss Clack would not let them off so easily. She began to speak to them.

'Children of God, children of suffering, why were you

born? Was the hour of your birth an hour of celebration of the release of a new, free soul into the world? Was it? Or was it rather a day of lamentation for the binding up of another object of pain and misery? You are the playthings of disease, of cold and hunger. That is why you exist. You are they who go without that others may be satisfied. You are the dispossessed of that which others go lightly in. You are the human gutter that allows others their little dignities. Oh, you are crucial to the well-being of the world. Every sin that is bred here burnishes the virtue of others. You must suffer, my children, that others may go free. But do not be deceived as they are deceived. It is not your sin for which you are punished, but their sin. They call you sinful, but they are deluded. Only you can see clearly. The sin is theirs and you redeem them. You are the image of Christ himself. Here is the Christ. Here is the second coming. I worship you. I beg you to know this of yourselves. You are holy. You are perfect. You can go out into the corrupt world that surrounds you, and you can perform miracles. The world is yours to be turned into gold. You must leave here now and spread your light out into the city. Go on. Go on. You are purified by your suffering. You are perfect. Go on. Go on.'

The listeners did not move, but something moved through them. The girl doubted that many of them heard what had been said: none of them surely could have understood it; or perhaps they did understand. She understood. She had an image of them streaming out into the city aflame with light and joy. She submitted herself entirely to Miss Clack's vision, which seemed to enter her directly through the hands clamped upon her shoulders. A profound energy filled her, running from Miss Clack out into the crowd and rising back up through them. Their faces registered no perceptible change but, in the light of her vision, they seemed to become alive in a way that they had not been before, each growing strangely distinct. She could focus now upon faces, male and female, young and old, features that suddenly gained precision and character, eyes that could wink, mouths that could curl in laughter or contempt, brows that could squeeze into intensity. The girl wanted to leap from the roof of the carriage in the certainty that they would surge forward with a cry and lift her as the children had lifted her. She urged forward but Miss Clack restrained her, tightened her fingers upon her shoulders with a gripping pain that writhed pleasurably through her. Freedom was waiting here. It would come at any moment in a sudden rush. Any second now, everything would be flung open and set loose.

Miss Clack's oration in Victory Street that October afternoon was not, after due and careful consideration, held to be criminally responsible for what followed. Amongst her audience on that afternoon had been several police informers but none of these could agree to what she had actually said, and an attempt to compile an indictment and to distil a composite report, which the informers could memorise for the public courtroom, was aborted. For a woman of her connections to have been arraigned as some sort of revolutionary force was not thought to be in keeping with the official attitudes to the disturbances, which held them to have been spontaneous, random, prompted, if at all, by foreign agents and other peripheral social outcasts and fanatics. Miss Clack was relegated to the status of harmless crank. The prospect of her loose in a courtroom did not attract anyone. Senior officials visited St Thomas's and endeavoured to throw alarm upon her, which was a futile proceeding; and upon her brother also who was held responsible for her good behaviour; but he observed their serious demeanours with a detachment that did not allow them to establish any understanding with him. He kept asking them what it was, exactly, that his sister was accused of, and simply would not be involved with dark shadows cast from high places. They posted watchers about the rectory but, as the riots ran their course through the gathering winter, Miss Clack remained tight in the bounds of the house and the watchers grew very cold.

The mobs were sporadic in both their fury and their size, spreading and thinning out, gathering force then melting away as the occasions arose, as focal points were established, targets for their fury were identified and brought down. Massive damage was done to the factories. The great machines were expertly unpinned and released their vast cogs and rollers down into tangled heaps of scrap. Children systematically smashed the panes in walls of windows. Enormous fires were started, rushing through the high machine-room chambers and bursting out the walls. In one factory the furnaces were stoked up to crisis point and beyond and an enormous explosion obliterated its perpetrators and most of the surrounding tenements. It was as if the monster had risen up and struck back.

Those who owned and ran the factories had removed north in good time. Those who were caught were hanged from their factory gates; but, apart from one defiant old steelmaster, the victims were little men, office clerks and section managers who exhibited bewildered loyalties in the face of death. They died proudly, most of them, finding moments of heroic dignity way beyond anything their life had offered them before, hauled high above the brick dust and the hooting of the mob below. One old man who broke down and squealed for mercy was let off to hobble away home.

The new residential areas were not systematically attacked. They became an outlet after the factories had been sacked, more often for those plundering for food. In certain small areas, political committees established heady fictional states, setting the bourgeoisie to work, abasing and abusing them, setting up noisy tribunals to try them for exploitation of which, being property owners, they were all, by definition, guilty. Some were even executed – a whole family in one instance, a man, his wife, his old mother, his three sons – an old grudge paid off. The man had been a notorious slum landlord and many flocked to take a part in his suffering. A cold fury arose around this act which grew out of proportion and became the destruction of the dozen little tyrants who had incited it, for it left a disgust and lethargy after it that drained the ideology of its power. Mostly, however, the residential areas were not submitted to this sort of rage. Stray packs of rioters, drunk with freedom, made forays, but the neatness and quietness of these streets, and the bewildered gentleness of their inhabitants, clouded the ardour of the invaders. These were not, after all, the real enemy. Their doctors ministered to the injured and plagued from the slums. Food was given freely. The slums had been a living scandal for a long time and the new bourgeoisie had no loyalty to the powerful who sat secure across the river. The slums were, to most of them, a living reminder of the pit they had struggled out of and which yawned always to suck them back should they ever relinquish the tedious struggles of their petty new world.

Then, when the first snows fell, in the last days of the old year, the riots were over, exhausted, frozen out by the winter. The slums suffered hideously that winter and were, in part, allowed to suffer. In the spring, a new administration took control with pledges of reconciliation and reconstruction and much was achieved; not enough to make profound changes, to cut to the root of the problem, but enough to restore, enough to set it up again with a new spirit, a new concern which the nightmare of the riots propelled. In the long perspective of history, the city had been let off lightly.

The rioting never directly threatened the rectory although there were tales of it bursting into respectable houses not far away. There were occasional knots of brutish men to be seen about the iron gates, but they were usually police. Once there was shouting and breaking within earshot, but only just, not close.

The arrival of a squad of soldiers in the rectory drive, at last, one morning when the overnight frost again showed no inclination to thaw, was at first a fearful sight. The Reverend Clack went out to the soldiers. His sister and the girl stood at the drawing-room window watching. He spoke to the officer who did not dismount. An adjutant with a sheaf of papers made notes, looked about, and then the troops left.

'We are to ring the bells,' he said, returning to his sister.

'One bell,' she said. 'One bell tolled for death.'

He kissed her, placed a hand on the girl's face and went to organise the statutory peal of victory. Miss Clack wept, cold tears that ran straight down her face and which she made no effort to restrain or dispel.

The one place south of the river that the riot had failed to penetrate at all was the Gunwall Prison. The mob, in force, made one advance upon it, some of its individuals being fired by history and symbolism; but the prison was not an object of communal loathing, unlike the factories, and the assault, failing to find an easy way in, was abandoned. The factories were far more enslaving than the prison. Those who were caught up by the law, those from the slums, found usually that their disorganised, snatching existences were regularised by the prison in a way that many of them actually took to. Here at least was an institution that identified them, if only as malefactors, unlike the factories which simply used them by the mass. In prison you had a particular place, a particular reason for being in that place and a particular duration, after which you were released, legally purified.

The Governor of the Gunwall Prison was at this time a retired army major by the name of Thomas Bosker. A fire in a colonial quartermaster's warehouse had disfigured him. He had, with a set-steel bravery of which the fire could only melt the surface, gone into the blaze to bring out the regimental account books and a whimpering native boy who had submitted to the will of his cruel, heathen gods. Bosker was left hideous. The left side of his body was destroyed – the ear gone, the eye blind, the arm shrivelled, the leg withered. He wore his disfigurement sternly, like a badge of office. He was righteous to the point of tyranny. Addressing a prisoner out of the strict line of duty was forbidden, as was striking a prisoner, as was rewarding a prisoner for any personal favour. The prison under his regime became a place of absolutes. He was everywhere.

He knew the name, number, offence and sentence of all four hundred prisoners, would interview them, one by one, on their arrivals and departures, knew of their attitudes and behaviour whilst serving sentence, weighed them each with a detached impartiality that shrivelled them. He was present at their midday meal in the great dining-hall. He would read to them, in his slurred, burned voice, from the Bible, would lead them in prayer, praying for submission and for repentance, for gratitude and for mercy.

Bosker had apparently foreseen the possibility of the riots to the extent of providing the prison in time with enough, on half-rations, to endure the siege. He refused to acknowledge the violence beyond; the gates remained locked for the duration. Those whose sentences expired during those weeks were given the option of staying on, and all took it. To those within, seeing the glow of the burning factories, hearing the distant clamour and imagining the worst, the prison became a place of sanctuary and security, and Bosker's virtues were seen in a new light. They could all relax under his unflinching autocracy.

After the riots, Bosker became celebrated. The government needed heroes and he was much spoken of. Legends of him going out of the prison gates and sending the mob about their business were worked up in patriotic ballads and prints. He declined to countenance one moment of celebration personally. Duty alone had been done. The day of the arrival of the troops, a cheer was raised for him in the dining-room, which he suppressed at once.

'That you are here,' he told them, 'and that we are here is a matter for lamentation. There will be no celebration within these walls. Nothing has changed. Nothing will ever change whilst I am governor here. That is your certainty and your punishment.'

He was unable, though, to restrain the curiosity that was bred about him beyond his walls. He was visited by many notables who sought publicly to admire him, but felt that they only succeeded in affronting him. Their meetings with him were always one-sided and uncomfortable, but they all came away with tales of his presence and fortitude. They came looking for someone to admire and he was unable to disabuse them of this comfort.

He found a way to deter these polite visitors soon enough, and that was to take them down from his rooms, from the models and designs and statistics, down into the actual prison. He would invite them to dine in the prisoners' mess, to tour the cell corridors, and particularly the modern sluicing and latrine arrangements, to meet random house-breakers and manslaughterers with shaven heads, mouths full of bloated tongues and hands that jerked and quivered under the Governor's questioning as if seeking something to grapple with. Bosker was careful to note any inclination to prurience in his visitors, pursuing it relentlessly. He caused something of a scandal when he treated a delicate and philanthropic young earl to the ritual of a flogging: he did not enjoy his edification. After this, the flow of visitors was staunched.

Then one day, eighteen months after the riots, he received a letter which expressed a zealous and detailed interest in his work and a desire to encounter, under his model conditions, those who had fallen from the acceptable behaviour of society. The tone of this letter was lucid and avid and it impressed Bosker. After all the fools and voyeurs he had received, at last someone wanted to come and see the prison as he imagined it – a tight, constricting tunnel through which his malefactors were forced, stripped of everything, to be purified fit for re-entry into the world, if they proved strong enough. It concerned him that so few did prove strong enough. In this letter was promised the possibility of someone with whom he might discuss the abiding concern of his. He read the letter twice with mounting enthusiasm before he realised that it was written by a woman – Miss Clarissa Clack. Realising this he recoiled, caught himself, then hurriedly fixed a date at random, inviting Miss Clack and the companion of whom her letter spoke, to visit him on the morning of the seventh of September next. So great was the impulse under which he had responded, that only when the letter had been sent out did he realise the significance of the date. He had failed to consult his appointments book and when he did so he saw that he had invited Miss Clack to visit him three hours after he would have had to preside over an execution. He drew up another sheet of paper and began to frame the words of an apology, a deferral of the visit: but he halted. The execution would be well over, the prison would be subdued and Miss Clack, whoever she was, would come in on the end of that great ritual conclusion of all of the processes of the law which the prison represented. It would be fitting, if she was half the woman he imagined her to be. Let her come. Let her be appalled out of her sensibilities if she would.

The malefactor, on this occasion, was a man called Slite, an old, knobbled man who had lived all his life in a clump of mud hovels which didn't even have a collective name, in a hole under the downs some fifteen miles from the city. He had a reputation for misanthropy, kept pigs and scrabbled up a foul and petty livelihood from them. He had a wife, as old as he, but contrastingly large and lardy. They said he had married her because she was the nearest thing to a pig the parson would read the banns over. They had lived in taciturn intolerance of each other and of the outside world longer than any of their neighbours could recall. One morning Slite, according to the testimony which was toiled out of him, decided that his wife was an idle slut of a witch woman. He had watched her guzzling the fat off a hock bone at breakfast and had decided against her. He had stood up, fetched a griddle iron of massive weight and had knocked her skull open at a blow. None had witnessed this act and he could have claimed provocations enough to mollify any reasonably misogynist judge and jury, but he seemed neither to comprehend nor to care what they ranged against him. He lugged the carcass out of his hut and dumped it on a dungheap in plain sight. When they came to take him away, he cursed them but came without difficulty, saying he'd have to be back to see to his pigs by sunset. The processes of the law bored and irritated him and, although he seemed to recognise why he was locked up and, superficially at least, in what peril he was held, he could not be brought to any real sense of responsibility for his crime nor appreciation for the law which took him to task for it. At the assize he interrupted and argued, created something of a figure in the vulgar mind and the court had to be cleared on both days of his trial due to the hilarity which he evoked, but which he himself took no part in. The court was much affronted in its dignities but, apart from my lord himself, could hardly take Slite seriously. My Lord Justice Walland was emphatically unamused by Slite, who looked him squarely in the face and showed him not one iota of deference.

'Your crime is the most heinous known to man. That you

seem to have no sense of its enormity, makes it unmitigated in the eye of this Court. You have taken life as casually as you might have brushed an annoyance from your sleeve. Our society has no meaning if it shows the smallest fleck of indulgence towards you. There is only one sentence . . .' But when he had passed it, black-capped and sonorous in the majesty of his office, he paused, looked at Slite and asked him, 'Are you aware, Slite, of the penalty you have incurred?'

'I'm aware that you're an old sow-fucker like the rest of us, in spite of your dressing up like the squire's maiden grand-mother.'

A scurrilous enemy had a beribboned sow delivered to my lord's chambers the next morning, and the profession unbraced itself in laughter. My Lord Justice Walland made it known that any reprieve for the man Slite would be taken as a personal aspersion upon him. He was not without influence. Slite would suffer.

Living out his last weeks in prison, Slite complained about everything – the food, the bed, the warders, the confinement. He could never accept that the doors were closed absolutely for him. He would suddenly set up a clatter and demand to be let out for a bit to go and see his pigs. 'They're my living!' he roared into the stone nights. He seemed to understand what was to be done to him, but it made no real impression upon him. He lived hour by hour, grumbling and grousing. The chaplain was told he'd 'an arse too idle to fart'. Bosker was told his 'mother didn't know the difference between you and the squits'. The warders appreciated such gems and grew very fond of the old brute, especially when he turned his wits upon them. The days passed.

Bosker visited Slite on his last night.

'Do you know what we must do tomorrow morning, Slite?' he asked.

'Spin me on a rope's end, spin me on a rope's end,' the old man said as if bored by it. 'Stand a few down below me, eh? So's I can drop me guts on 'em.'

The chaplain appeared and Bosker observed the horrible uncertainty which riddled the poor man's face. He left Slite a handful of cigars and went. Out in the corridor he passed the hangman, a bearded ox of a man, incongruously besuited for the dignity of his solemn office. Bosker exchanged a formal, knowing nod with the man.

He did not sleep that night, stayed up with his Bible, read and re-read Christ's beatitudes to the suffering and wretched. Before dawn they brought him tea. He shaved, aware of the bright weight and keenness of the blade as he scraped his twisted face.

At seven-fifteen he went down to the ante-room before the condemned cell. The hangman and the chaplain were already there waiting. The hangman worked with a delicacy and solicitude that Bosker marked with admiration. Slite was greeted formally, introduced to his executioner who strapped his wrists and patted him on the shoulder, supervised his leading-out lest the flanking warders became too narrow and pushing. Out they went into the yard.

The morning was clear and fresh, the day strong and unblemished. In the yard grew grass and daisies. Birds flew up from the grass and found perches on the barred window ledges from which to bubble out song: the quiet procession of humans did not alarm them. The execution shed was a two-storey building, the gallows beam jutting out from the upper storey with waiting noose above a trapped platform. On the ground floor double doors were open, through which the warders and the executioner led Slite, whilst Bosker and the lord sheriff, the doctor and the other dignitaries waited out in the yard. All were hot and uncomfortable in the closed sunshine. Bosker insisted on full uniform whatever the weather.

The little procession disappeared into the double doors. This was the crucial, difficult moment. The prisoner, having seen the waiting noose, led from the light into the dark suddenly, was most prone to panic. Bosker's attention strained for noises of struggle and despair which would destroy the dignity of the man and of the ceremony, plunge it from quiet, inevitable ritual into gross butchery. He relied at this moment entirely upon his hangman, on that calm bulk which had, in truth, never let him down. The man was almost an imbecile to talk to, but he had this presence within his office, this delicate authority at which Bosker marvelled. The hangman cared for his victims like some tender parent. Bosker had no specific fears that morning. He had watched Slite crossing the yard, his wiry little body moving unevenly and haphazardly as it always moved. He had not even cast his eyes up at the platform.

At last they appeared. The hangman moved the warders out of his way, a sign of his confidence, and in a matter of seconds had strapped Slite's ankles, had bagged and noosed the old head. A glance at Bosker, a nod back to the hangman and the traps flew open. Slite fell straight, snapped and, for a horrible few seconds, burst into a writhing and coiling on the end of the rope, doubling and kicking and thrashing. This was not supposed to happen: the man should be dead at the rope snap. Bosker glanced furiously at the hangman whose face registered a massive rage. For a second Bosker expected him to turn on one of the stiff-faced wardens who stood either side of him, staring straight ahead, pale and removed.

'He's bodged it,' said the doctor gleefully at Bosker's right hand. 'It'll take twenty minutes now.'

Bosker turned on the man, finding himself also raging.

'Thank God!' said the sheriff from his left.

Bosker turned back to see the body stilled, turning slightly, the rope creaking. The stench of Slite's bowels, his last message to the world, wafted across and the doctor, with a professional shrug, crossed the courtyard, mounted a small step-ladder held ready by two warders, ripped open Slite's shirt and with a nod confirmed the completion of the punishment. Bosker turned at once and left the yard.

Later that morning the hangman presented himself at Bosker's office for his fee. In the office he seemed more than ever displaced, large, strong, the suit tight at every seam, his tiny, piggy eyes soulless in the burst of black beard that engulfed his face. Bosker searched, ritually, for the envelope with its guineas which had been placed ready precisely.

'All correct, hangman?' he asked.

'Sir.' The confirming nod.

'Any thoughts on the movement of the body?'

'Spasms, sir.'

'Spasms.'

'Making a mock of me, sir,' the hangman said resentfully. 'I expected something.'

'You failed to mention it.'

'My problem, sir. My responsibility.'

Bosker studied the man for some insight into him. Did he enjoy his office? Perhaps he did. Did he feel any pity for his victims? Hardly pity. And yet how could he give them that comfort, that support at the end?

Bosker found the envelope and slid it across the desk. The hangman leant forward, picked up a steel pen, inked it minutely and wrote his name in the open space that awaited him on the official form, 'Catch – Hangman'. He rose, touched his forehead, collected his envelope deftly, slid it into his waistcoat pocket and left.

On his way through the outer office the hangman saw, to his considerable surprise, two women waiting there. They sat together on high-backed chairs, one tall and thin and hard, one short and bulgy, hunchbacked. He paused and caught himself viewing them as potential customers. The hunchback would be interesting to drop: he wondered if her thickened neck would pose difficulties. He smiled to himself.

The little hunchbacked woman met his gaze, blushed and looked away. The hangman endured an unusual moment of self-consciousness at this reaction to him, looked instinctively behind him where there was only a big window which gave out on to a roof-space, the regular, long, grey-slate roofs of the prison, and above the flawless sky into which, he fancied, fluttered the soul of Slite, a man who had cheated him comprehensively, not only by that disgusting dance he had performed at the rope's end, but by failing to consider him at all as more than another faceless official. He was Jasper Catch, the hangman, the craftsman, the expert. He gathered his indignation and strutted out of the outer office with the eyes of the hunchback, he was sure, firmly upon him. He would have liked very much to have the professional pleasure of her. Such a thought was decidedly off-limits, but it came to him forcefully as he descended and passed through the multiple locks of the prison.

*

Bosker rose from his chair to greet Miss Clack and her companion, who alarmed him by her deformity. He had put the anticipation of them out of his mind as he had dealt with the business of the morning. Now they were approaching him with eyes fixed upon him firmly, Miss Clack's eyes hard and penetrating, her companion's soft and welcoming in a particularly feminine way which upset him further. He addressed himself to Miss Clack and tried unsuccessfully to ignore the other.

'You come, in fact, on a difficult morning, Miss Clack,' he said, having greeted them and summoned tea. He looked at her closely. Did she know what was echoing in the prison air that morning?

'You have hanged a man this morning,' Miss Clack said flatly. 'I hope you have achieved your purpose, Major. And I hope you know what that purpose was.'

His social unease evaporated. She was everything he had hoped for, jumping straight to the heart of it.

'Do we ever know our purposes certainly enough?' he said.

'We ought to know our purposes certainly enough, Major Bosker, if we wilfully take human life; in that case we ought to know them very well indeed.'

The tea arrived, which was fortunate, for this was too heady a discussion to begin with. Bosker glanced at Miss Clack's companion, but glanced away again.

'Now then,' he said amongst the tea-tinkle which did something to obscure the previous weight. 'Now then, Miss Clack, what is it that I can do for you?'

'We would like to see your prison, Major Bosker; and to talk, if we may, with some of your prisoners.'

'And may I, forgive me, enquire what your purpose is?'

'Our purpose is to see and to learn.'

'And to teach?' There was an aspect of her that might have meant sermons and pamphlets and he wouldn't have that.

'Not to teach, Major. I have nothing to teach any more. That is the wisdom of my old age: I teach nothing. You see Magdaline, my companion?'

Bosker nodded in her direction without really looking.

'She teaches.'

Bosker looked again, seriously, wondered where he was being led by this. The little hunchbacked woman had deflected her eyes as if in modest embarrassment.

'But you need not be afraid of her, Major. She is dumb, you see, and has been so from birth.'

Bosker did not know whether this was supposed to be a joke or not or if the woman was mad. He rose from his desk in a somewhat aggressive mood, determining to give this good lady and her attendant grotesque what they wanted and more, if he could.

'Let us proceed then, Miss Clack.'

They stood on a small iron gallery above an enclosed hall some forty feet below. In this hall, a file of prisoners walked round and round in silence. They moved together step by step, but not firmly, dragging their feet, shuffling, but all precisely in step. Their shaved heads were bowed, their faces in shadow for the only light came through a lantern window high above. They were all dressed alike in loose prison khaki stamped with the prison motif. Two warders stood in the centre of the circle, long chains hanging from under their blue-black tunics, thick staves dangling from their wrists, stiff-faced in their awareness of Bosker and his guests.

The girl was appalled. This was not a place of neglect and deprivation: this was deliberate. She had known cruelty before, but never on a scale such as this. She wanted to clutch Miss Clack's hand but that gesture was out of place here. She wanted to turn away but felt it her duty to look. The men moved in a slow whirlpool of futility that seemed too intense even for death to affect it; if one was to fall, to crumple and die, the others would just go on and on, new ones coming in and feeding the machine.

'And is this intended to be part of the punishment?' Miss Clack asked loudly enough for all to hear. No one below reacted visibly.

'Everything here is part of the punishment.'

They proceeded to a workshop – a long room, high-ceilinged and lined with men in clusters, in pairs, singly, at work, each one quite enclosed in his work, the face concentrated upon the labour and drained of all else. A bench of men unpicked the threads from old blankets, dropping them, long grey worms of worn wool, into wooden boxes at their feet. Elsewhere the boxes were placed near machines and other men picked out threads and fed them into the machines which other men turned slowly, winding the wool slowly into spools. There was a machine which pressed out thin brass badges: a man held a sheet of metal whilst another leant on a lever and the badges dropped one by one out into a box. Elsewhere a small brazier heated an iron with which a man dabbed solder on to the back of each badge and another, holding the badge in a small grip, applied, by means of a small pair of tongs, a pin on to the molten solder; then dipping the badge into a bucket of acid which hissed violently but briefly; then dropping it into another box. All the men, at all the tasks, worked in complete silence.

The girl watched them, but they did not notice her. She reached into the box and picked out a badge: it was oval, decorated with symmetrical, idealised leafage, had a noble head profiled in its centre and, underneath, a large-lettered legend. She wondered who might earn the wearing of this sharp brittle token. She was going to drop it back into the box but instead offered it to the man with the tongs. He took some while to notice her offer and then, sighing at the interruption of his rhythm, he took the badge from her hand with his tongs, dipped it automatically in the acid again, and dropped it back against the others. The solderer paused in his rhythm too, held as if by a malfunction of the machinery within him. Neither man registered her presence at all. She turned back to see Miss Clack and the Governor behind her, watching her, making her feel awkwardly important.

'And what have you done with their souls, Major?' Miss Clack asked, taking the question straight out of the girl's head.

'We have cleaned their lives of everything outside,' he said confidently, 'in order that they might become aware of their souls in the silence, in the certainty of their lives here. It is here that they may discover their souls, in most cases for the first time. But it is a very hard lesson, Miss Clack, and, to be honest with you, not many of them have the final honesty and strength to learn it. We should have them younger, and for longer.'

There seemed to be nothing to be said to this.

'Is it possible to speak with them?' Miss Clack asked after a while.

'Not in the workshops, Miss Clack. I will have one brought to you.'

'May we choose any one?'

'Please.'

Miss Clack looked to the girl, wanting her to choose. The girl looked helplessly back, unable to contemplate any of these thickened faces individually. Miss Clack continued to look at her, trusting her, deferring to her superior instinct, a faculty the girl knew could not operate amongst such as these. She stabbed blindly out with her finger and indicated the tongs-holder.

'Very well,' Bosker said. He went to the senior warder. 'At meal-break, seven-twelve-thirty-seven to the second interview room.'

They left the workshop, Bosker grown sharper in his movements, more precise, more confident, more resentful of them. They saw the dining-room, its long tables and polished vats, deserted but for the distant clatter of preparations.

'I supervise the midday meal personally,' Bosker said, indicating a large lectern.

'You read to them?'

'From the Holy Bible.'

'Trying to teach them, Major?'

The girl listened to this futile parrying, studied the distorted face of the Governor. He was as much a part of this place as the prisoners were although, unlike them, he seemed to believe in this nightmare; they had no chance to believe in anything here, just to endure. The claustrophobia began to make her giddy.

They were shown at last into a room with an interviewing table and two chairs on one side of it at which they were invited to sit.

'There is no chair for our guest,' Miss Clack observed.

'He will not understand any attempt at informality, Miss Clack.'

'We would like to speak to him alone.'

'I cannot permit that.'

'Because we are women?'

'Because you are vulnerable, yes. And because, more than that, you are outsiders.'

A warder-clerk appeared with a bound file of papers. Bosker took them, undid the ribbons and glanced over the papers briefly.

'Shall I tell you whom you have selected?'

'Seven-twelve-thirty-seven. That will be enough, thank you, Major. We will meet him on your terms to begin with.'

'Good,' he said, handing the papers back to the warder.

'Can I ask that you be absent during our meeting, Major?'

'If you wish it, I will be absent.'

Bosker left and the two women were, for a few minutes, alone in the interview room. A stone silence surrounded them. A high, barred window threw bright light into the upper air, but the brightness did not survive the brown walls and scoured floorstones around where they were seated. They sat separate, the girl begging Miss Clack to speak to her at least, if touching was not possible here.

'This place is the end of the world,' Miss Clack said drily. 'The end of the world, we learn, is not to be the collapse of godless man back into his animal state, as I had always thought it would be, but this. The end of the world is man deprived of his soul – systematically deprived by men who believe they have his highest interests at heart. Pull yourself upright now, Magdaline. Here is your friend coming to meet us.'

He shuffled in slowly, became conscious of them and of the warder at the door behind him who had brought him and who would take him back in a little while. He put on a parody of standing to attention. They studied him. He was young, hardly twenty. Under the prison shadow that pervaded his face, the flesh was still firm, the eyes clear. There was a monstrous scar running across his cropped skull, down his forehead, over the bridge of his nose and into his cheek; as if someone had tried to cut his head in two, or had succeeded and stuck the two halves back together again – they did not fit exactly.

'Who are you?'

'Seven-twelve-thirty-seven, ma'am.'

'What is your name?'

'We leave our names behind us in here, ma'am,' he said obediently, after a tiny pause in which his eyes flicked aside to locate the warder.

'How long have you been here?'

'Four years, three months, two days, ma'am.'

'How much longer?'

'Five years, eight months, twenty-nine days, ma'am.'

'Ten years. For what offence?'

The eyes flicked back again. 'For wrongdoing, ma'am.'

'Robbery? Violence? Murder? Cheating?'

'Yes, ma'am, only it can't've been the murder else they'd've topped me, wouldn't they?'

'Do you suffer here?'

A pause for thought, then, 'Oh yes, ma'am.'

'How did you come by that fearful scar?'

'What scar, if you please, ma'am?'

'You have a great scar, across the top of your head, coming down across your face.'

'Can't say that I've noticed it, ma'am.'

There was a bounce in this answer which the warder noted and stirred at. The prisoner flicked his eyes back and then surveyed the faces of the women: first Miss Clack, then the girl at whom, very quickly, he winked.

'Will that be all, ma'am?'

'God bless you.'

'Thank you, ma'am. And you, ma'am.'

The warder was already advancing into this exchange. He clapped a hand on the boy's shoulder and he shrivelled at once into facelessness.

'One moment, warder, if you please.'

The hand dropped, the boy faced them again, his eyes suddenly filled with tears which broke down his face in a gush.

'Pity poor John Bone, lady,' he said suddenly.

'Are you John Bone?'

The warder had his hand back on the boy's shoulder and was pulling him to the door.

'Not me, ma'am, not me,' he muttered, frightened at once into recovering himself and submitting to the warder who quickly had him out.

'John Bone,' Miss Clack said decisively as soon as they were alone. 'We must find out what he's convicted of. We will not let them do this to him. We shall hire a counsel to go over his case. I know of a man, an acquaintance of my nephew . . .'

But the girl knew it was all futile, saw the hours of waiting, the confrontations with sardonic officials, the whole tedious toil of it before her. She felt herself retract, looked at Miss Clack as she went on and on, her resolution rising and rising. The girl longed to be free. The love she had felt for this woman was used up, was weighted down whilst she needed to lift up and go on. There was for her a limit to this weight of suffering Miss Clack wanted them to bear. She took the old woman's hand and stilled her talk, but Miss Clack smiled and patted her and bustled her up and out.

There was a brief interlude whilst Miss Clack exchanged final formalities with the Governor. The girl drew away, not wanting to be party to these dry moves, stood and watched the moral wrangling of these two sexless fanatics. Yes. Yes, this was what was lost here most of all, the acknowledgement of sexuality. She strutted past them, walking free of this hideous institution as if it had no walls. She passed into the brightness of the day with Miss Clack beside her. It had been too long. She would find a way out of this life. She grew defiant and proud of herself. All paths in Miss Clack's world led only to death, with a frantic urging at something beyond death that none of them could even imagine properly. She knew better.

Pity poor John Bone who would lie awake in his prison cell and dream of the warmth of a woman, a saddle of flesh and bone in which he could be child and be man, held and rocked tightly, striding out into the world again. Pity poor John Bone in the long years ahead of him, the stone nights, the iron nights in which he would shrivel and grow useless; unused, unrealised, unmanned.

In St Thomas's Rectory, whilst his sister and her child were off in their search for human realities in the Gunwall Prison, Clarence Clack, sitting in the drawing-room by the window, looking out over the lawns, began his dying.

Firstly there was a physical process to which he had to submit. He had been expecting it. It had been a subject for contemplation all his adult life and now it became real. He experienced its onset with curiosity. So this, at last, was it. He had felt this tightness in his chest at various times over the preceding months. It would catch him at moments and make him gasp, a sudden stubbornness of something at his centre, an unwillingness to proceed. Before, it had always eased after a while, after a moment or two, after an hour's quiet, a good night's rest. Now it was coming with a dominance that would not be denied. He recognised its approach, a lightness of being, a gaiety of body that was fragile and delusory; the last inner dance of his flesh before the onslaught. He had taken his position in the window; in an easy chair, his hands upon the arm rests, his back leaning slightly. He awaited the inevitable assault. By keeping calm he could appease it a little, he felt, be ready for it when it came, meet it squarely, be perfectly aware of what it did to him.

He believed unequivocally that his death would release his immortal soul into the presence of Almighty God. He would be judged and he would be rewarded or condemned according to how he had lived. He did not believe that his salvation was certain. He had lived a life that had failed to engage fully with the twistings and tanglings of reality. He had been distant, culpably so. He prayed for remission but he did not believe that he had any absolute right to it. It did not, at this moment, trouble him: he had perfected his acceptance of God's will as he had perfected his acceptance of his own nature, too readily perhaps, too long ago. He was not better than most of those he had encountered, in whatever worldly depths they might have been; but he had, unlike them, been blessed with a quietude of soul, a simple pleasure in his life and in his faith and now, at the last, that was too firmly what he was for him to articulate any final upsurge. He would greet death like a visitor, a guest – without courage because he was without fear. Life was a confinement within the complexities of the flesh; from which confinement he was about to be released, grateful that, for him, the complexities had been so few.

Such thoughts were not, however, dominant in him as he

waited, as he felt the first stirrings of tension within him, as the presence began to rise in his breast in slow urges, testing him to see how much resistance it would have to overcome. He knew that he only had a few moments of mortal clarity left him, and he spent them upon his sister upon whom his dying would be an inconceivable blow.

They had seemed at times two halves of one person. He had always imagined that they would face this moment together, change together, and be united thereafter absolutely. The surprise of this moment was its solitude. As the edge approached, as he knew it was approaching, he knew that he was about to be separated for the first time in his life from Clarissa. She had always been the active part of his life, deciding and doing for him, keeping the life about him straight. She had protected and sustained him, allowing him to dwell in the clear, airy spaces of prayer and music, allowing him to articulate the joy of his faith and taking upon herself the hard tasks of reality, tending the parish, activating the dull congregation and drawing them at least in his direction.

Now he was leaving her. The knot tightened within him. All his physical power was suddenly, instinctively, sucked into the assault in his breast. His muscles were powerless as every fraction of his strength rushed to confront the dark catastrophe at the centre of his being. There was massive pain and he would have cried out if he had had any strength with which to cry. The pain was a great spiked object set in him, pulsing and wrenching him from within. He prayed for release but he knew that he was not yet ready: he still had things to settle in himself before he would be freed. In answer to this need, the spokes were drawn in, the pain became an inert, attendant lump. He was quiet again, powerless to move, given a few moments before it came again.

He cried out for his sister, silently and helplessly. If she could walk into the room now it would all be right. He could go easily with her touch upon his arm, her kiss upon his numb brow. Why was she not here? Why had she abandoned him? Over the past months he had lost touch with her. She had rushed off into maelstroms that he could not even imagine. She had become possessed of something he did not understand. Had she, at the last, betrayed him?

He thought, inevitably, of the strange hunchbacked girl and finally, he could not answer the question of Clarissa's loyalty. A moment of irredeemable doubt came upon him. Was the girl a force for good or for evil? He had known the world, his world, so clearly, so simply. His duty and his joy had been to share this simplicity, as far as he was able; in every situation in his entire life he had been able to apply this principle and, although he had not perhaps often succeeded very fully, there had been a completion in the offering. But the hunchbacked girl had eluded this simple calculus. He saw her as a victim, but he could not pity her. He saw her as a demon, but he could not fear her. He saw her innocence, but he could not see through it. He saw her defilement, but it did not repel him. Her complexity, more than anything, appalled him because it seemed bigger than his simplicity which he had taken to be the greatest truth in the world. He looked up to find himself, at the last, in a strange game, foxed and mated; and very soon, very, very soon, he was going to have to account for his play.

His last image was of the strange girl coming into the window-bay where he sat, rising over him and touching his face, closing his eyes as the life flickered out of them, and he did not know whether she had come to see her evil consummated or to bless him on his journey. One might, from a hypothetical safe distance, propose that it was a moment of perfect doubt and that finally saved him. Within that moment, however, there was no pain, only a final collapse into the darkness, a complete and effortless surrender of the flesh.

The girl who had come in whilst Miss Clack had gone into the church to pray for a while, had found the brother dying, had gone to him and had seen the disjointing of his limbs in the apoplexy, had seen the nakedness in the eyes and had touched the old forehead at the moment the life had left it. She felt that moment like a charge up her forearms, into her shoulders and lifting into the back of her skull, she sensed his lifting up out of his body, was certain that this was the moment of his soul's departure.

So, she thought, we survive death. It was something to

bear in mind in her new resolution to go out and assault life once again. There was no need to grieve for this old man. There would, she realised coming quickly back from the moment, be a need to grieve for this old man's sister.

BOOK THREE
Cutchknoll

John Stone had long withdrawn from the full-time pursuit of his art into his family inheritance, Palmead Hall, a small and decaying estate which maintained him as a minor country gentleman who washed delicate landscapes on long afternoons. He had married a serious-minded spinster some years older than himself, the daughter of a brick manufacturer. She had brought him financial independence and he lived an easy life now, gratifying his extravagant city tastes in rustic self-indulgence. They had no children and they dwelt together at Palmead in different worlds.

The marriage was disappointing. His wife, Edwina, grew hypochondriac and spent much time studying the workings of her body under the dubious tutelage of a Doctor Gollonia, a foreigner of outrageous manners who took up residence at Palmead for long weeks, who ate noisily and expostulated semi-coherently about the movement of the waters of the moon and their influence upon the political economy, attempting to draw Stone into discussion. Stone treated him with an enervated contempt which he had not the subtlety to detect. Edwina hardly spoke to anyone but Gollonia now, and to him only in private. Rumours crept under doorways, but Stone cared not a whit for them. He doubted whether Gollonia had the substance with which to cuckold him; and he would probably have rejoiced for Edwina if he had been able to convince himself that this was afoot. Edwina showed no sign of rejoicing. She never left the house now, lived amongst dark furnishings in a miasma of salts and embrocations. It was a formal marriage only.

Returning from his Uncle Clarence's funeral, Stone told his wife over dinner that he intended to invite his aunt to make her home at Palmead. Edwina became very alarmed at this news. She had met Clarissa Clack a couple of times and considered her insane, viewed her arrival as a hideous chaos about to fall upon her tightened life. Gollonia was away, on a tour of the Continent to view notable freaks and to claim a share of an inheritance which rapacious kinsmen in some southern city were denying him. She had grown less tractable in his absence.

'How long will your aunt be here?' she inquired, having digested the news of her intended arrival for some fifteen silent minutes.

'She has nowhere else to go. I expect her stay here to be permanent. It's not as if we have no room for her. She is greatly defeated now, Edwina. She is to be pitied, not to be feared.'

'I will not abide alterations. I will not abide any interference in the domestic regime of the house, John. You must make that clear to her.'

'She will fill a very small and very quiet corner.'

'That is not my recollection of her.'

'You have not seen her since Clarence died.'

She remained silent, chewed perfunctorily on a crust of warm bread, swallowed it down painfully and thought of the knottings of her recalcitrant bowels – sulky and spiteful children who would not obey her.

'She will, of course, bring her companion with her,' her husband said, pouring himself a third glass of the cold, bitter wine she could not drink.

'What companion?'

'You don't know of Aunt Clarissa's companion? Surely you do, Edwina. The hunchback girl. The goblin.'

'You are being facetious.' But she knew he wasn't. He was plotting against her.

'I found her in the hospital. I made some sketches of her. My aunt was moved by the sketches, or by their subject I should say. She took her up and turned her into a little penance. They're quite inseparable, have been for years.'

'I am not well enough. You are only devising things to plague me. You are cruel. You have always been cruel.'

'You know nothing of cruelty,' he said firmly, silencing her, diminishing her as he always did.

Her brother's death had struck Miss Clack a blow that was fatal to the central purpose of her life. The girl had gone from the drawing-room window, had found her in the hall removing her bonnet and had led her to him. Miss Clack

214

had known, before she had seen it, to what the girl was leading her. She had gone to him and had knelt at his side, bowed beside him as if receiving his benediction. She had not wept, had not spoken. She had remained there for some minutes. The girl had kept her distance, waited. Miss Clack rose suddenly and looked out of the window, abstracted. The girl had gone then, had taken her hand, had turned her to her and had seen the vacancy in the face that was immediately final.

Miss Clack had stirred herself, had given directions, had made arrangements, had dealt with all the complexities of closing down the household and preparing it for the next incumbent. Amongst all such stuff, the interment of her brother had passed almost hurriedly, in a blur. The girl had shadowed her throughout, prepared at any moment to be freed from this strange woman, freed in fact as she was now in spirit; for Miss Clack had no consciousness of her, nor of anyone. She had relinquished all her obligations at St Thomas's as if slipping an awkward robe from her shoulders. The girl saw her distantly, calmed as she had never seen her before. It was all effectively over. She had accepted her nephew's offer with formal gratitude.

'You will come and live with us at Palmead, Aunt Clarissa.'

'Thank you, John; if Edwina is well enough.'

'And Magdaline also, of course.'

'If we will not inconvenience you.'

So they came. So they sat on the sofa of the dusty drawing-room at Palmead that afternoon. The room, like the rest of the house, was dominated by the style of John's father, a dabbler in natural history and an avid field-sportsman. The trophies of his science and his sport adorned walls and cases, dusty and decaying. Neither his brief wife nor his son appeared to have asserted themselves in this place. An aura of fading imbued the house with a sad weight. The two women in black waited for their host and hostess to descend and greet them.

The girl had never met Edwina Stone, had glimpsed John only occasionally over her years at St Thomas's. She had been imagining exotic and dangerous possibilities to them. When the door at the far end of the drawing-room at last opened and the couple advanced, she was entirely surprised, rising from her seat.

He was grown old, his long, fair hair thinned and tarnished with grey. He walked precisely, held himself stiffly; but this aspect of him was belied by his face which was wild, angry, like a beast's, burnished with deep vertical lines running up his forehead. Beside him, balancing him, was his wife, a short woman incredibly fat, her bloated little body supporting a bloated head stacked with dull, brown hair drawn up to reveal jutting little ears. The girl was reminded abruptly of Old Mag and that memory was a mad memory in this place. If he looked as if he had recently been brought in from the moors, she looked as if she had been in a hot bath for several years, her skin puckered and pallid.

They advanced towards her, walking lopsidedly, she lolling on her husband's arm as if drunk. They both looked at her, not at Miss Clack, focused upon her as they came. He paused by a high-backed chair and guided his wife down upon it, looking to her briefly before returning his gaze to the girl. He selected an armchair, flicked up his coat-tails, sat and leant back. She realised that she was the only one standing and, having been caught thus, did not feel she could sit. She looked aside at Miss Clack who was gazing abstractedly out of the window to where the lawn reached into a haze of flowerbeds and trees beyond.

'Welcome to Palmead,' John Stone said, addressing the girl.

She dropped him her lopsided curtsey and he laughed, throwing his arm across the chair back and looking at his wife.

'My wife, Edwina,' he indicated, 'also welcomes you to Palmead.'

'How long is it, child,' the wife said in a voice that sounded on the edge of tears, 'that you have been with my husband's aunt?'

The girl looked to John Stone who allowed himself a moment's amusement before answering, 'My dear, Magdaline is, alas, unable to talk. I promised you quiet guests. Aunt Clarissa? Aunt Clarissa?'

'Yes,' she said eventually, part of a discontinued conversation, 'thank you, John, for your kindness, and Edwina.

Especially. How are you, Edwina? We heard you've not been well.'

'Better, thank you, Aunt Clarissa, a little better.'

'We will not be staying long. We will just rest here a little and then move on.'

'Please stay for as long as you like Aunt Clarissa,' she said desperately. 'Please think of Palmead as your home. Please.' Here she began to emit the tears until her husband glowered her into self-control.

They gathered, thereafter, once a day for dinner, all four of them at a large, round table with a servant ferrying food to them. The table could have seated a dozen; at it they were separate. Edwina Stone struggled out pleasantries from the edge of her pitiful self-control. John Stone presided over her, noted every inflection and judged it silently, deflecting at the girl glances of sardonic inquiry that she found unpleasant. Miss Clack remained a long way away, occasionally settling in the present like a bird probing a stone yard for food, finding none, flitting away again.

During the day the girl's business was to attend to Miss Clack, to help her dress and breakfast, to settle her in a small, upper drawing-room where she would gaze out into the woods and fields and skies. At first the girl stayed dutifully with her, but soon it was apparent that this was quite futile. Miss Clack was dying and wished to be alone in that most intimate of bodily processes; she would take years over it. So, once again, she was released to wander and to explore a new world. She avoided the servants of the house who regarded her with suspicion and dislike, being new and strange. The house with its manifold galleries and rooms full of decaying mementoes was claustrophobic. Every room reeked of a past which belonged to no one, and even when she identified something personal, a worn doll, a card covered with looped writing, different colours, different hands, the plastercast of a child's face, a box full of scented, ribboned hair, such things dispirited her with the silence that surrounded them and made them pointless.

Outside the house, as the winter began to be unleashed and the rain began to sweep in wave after wave across the low countryside, was another world, limitless at last – a world of growing things and wild creatures, the dead masks of whose ancestors sprouted from the halls and stairways and which became creatures of fantastic savagery in her unguarded imagination. The sharpness of the fox's teeth, bared in its muzzle, the clawing of antlers, the blunt menace of the crow's beak amongst its deep, dropping plumage, the adder's coil afloat in its thick jar of green fluid – each frightened her, entered the dreams which, in her solitude, began to crowd her again as they had done in the early days of her life at St Thomas's. She kept inside, even on the clear, calm days.

Months slid away. It was a long winter. Nothing seemed to change. Few visitors came and those only to see John Stone. There were occasional domestic eruptions to be heard from below or from behind doors, but she had established no way there. Miss Clack grew more substantially still and silent day by day.

Winter brought a ubiquity of blown brown tones to the landscape and a bleak grey to the sky. Occasionally the world outside was held still in a brilliant white frost which brought clarity and light alarmingly into dark places within the house. It was bracing to shiver, to see a skin of ice upon the water bowls, to see the steam flowing from nostrils and mouths. It brought a few days of vividness to a long, dark season.

Miss Clack, in the cold weather, had shrivelled and had given up attending dinner, sitting now like a guilty secret, shut away in the far reaches of the house, passing days, weeks sometimes, without speaking. The winter dragged on long into the new year and nothing seemed to change. Spring would come and she would have to break free somehow. Meanwhile she wandered through days and days that were full of chills and draughts and long hours of rambling about the house just to keep warm, with her mind finding less and less to take hold of. Even her dreaming grew distant and dull.

Edwina Stone never overcame the shock and disgust that the hunchback girl generated within her from the first moment. She assumed that the girl was one of her husband's monsters, one of his harlots brought to Palmead as a cruel

218

affront to her, awaiting her demise ready to take over. Edwina found it impossible to think rationally of this creature. She strove hard to liberate her thoughts from speculations upon her, but could not; and yet she struggled not to consider too deeply about her lest her emotions burst out of her and rode her to chaos; which was what they wanted.

She determined at last to kill the creature. She would entice her to her room and give her poison. She drew from amongst her many phials one containing a noxious brown oil about which Gollonia had given her dire warnings. It had the property, so he had said, of numbing the most violent aches that racked her. It was only to be used in the most absolute necessity, and then minutely, and never near any broken skin nor any of the openings of the body apart from the mouth. Gollonia had bestowed it upon her as the ultimate mystery of his craft, his parting oblation to her. It had been kept deeply secret and it had thus accrued further potency. She had thought often of suicide, the final escape from the weight of her being, the lumping of her flesh about her. Gollonia, who had understood her better than anyone, had given her this little, sealed phial perhaps with this last eventuality in mind. She took it out regularly, fearfully, expecting John, or her maid, or some unknown authority to burst in upon her as she held it and denounce her. She would grip the little phial in the depth of her palm and feel its potency, feel it coming alive as the warmth of her clutch infused the glass.

The monster he had brought into her home was the latest testament to his cruelty. They spent hours in depraved mockery of her. But she was not impotent. The world would exonerate her. She would stand in the courtroom, not as accused, but as witness, testifier. He would be on trial and she, gathered up at last, would bring the judgement of the righteous down upon him – fornicator, adulterer, degenerate, tormentor. Let him maintain his cruel smile in defiance of that torrent of truth.

She worked with stubby fingers at the cork of the little phial. It was very tight and she shook with the effort required before, all at once, the resistance gave and the phial was open. She sniffed – a foul reek, brown and oily, rushed into her head, giddying her. She had to catch herself from lurching and spilling the precious elixir. She replaced the stopper, wrapped the bottle in a silk handkerchief and lodged it deep in the pocket of her gown. She composed herself in the small chair beside her tea-table, having drawn open one of the heavy curtains to admit a grey mass of light, bringing the shadowy geography of the room into a clarity that made it strange, loosing its warmth, becoming larger, the familiar bulks of chests and chairs and hangings growing harder and less intimate. It was an access of clarity and unfamiliarity that suited her task.

She waited several hours for the maid to come with her tea-tray and to attend to the fire which had sunk sulkily into a bed of grey ash in the small grate. The maid, who never spoke whilst attending her mistress, who was small and who kept huddled and averted, rose, face down, and bobbed to Edwina, turning to leave. Edwina called her back.

'The girl,' she said, 'Miss Clack's companion. Magdaline. I would like her to take tea with me. Send her up. And another cup. And some cakes, shortbread, things to eat.'

'Fresh pot of tea, m'm?' the girl asked.

'Did I ask for a fresh pot of tea? Do you think me incapable?'

The maid bobbed and left. Edwina became lost for a moment in the petty distress occasioned by this dull slut. They all sought to degrade her, to mock her incapacities. She wished she could inflict pain upon them. She wished she had the strength to strike at them, to knock away their prim little starch-caps and bring blushes of shame to their tight faces. The moment of this agitation was so forceful that she forgot her purpose entirely for its duration; the remembrance of that purpose coming upon her suddenly and frightening her. Coming upon it afresh, its enormity became apparent to her. She pulled herself from her chair and allowed the fear to move her about the room with unaccustomed, giddy energy.

Before she had realised, she had found the little phial in the pocket of her gown. She clutched it, drew it out hidden in the fat of her hand. She listened to the immaculate silence of the house. The girl would be here at any moment. If she arrived too soon it would be spoiled. The prospect of such a frustration propelled her to the table. She opened the lid of the silver teapot and the steam rose and clouded the metal. She unstoppered the phial, struggling again with the cork. The potion fell into the brew. with a single plop, seemed to be swallowed whole. She took a teaspoon which was not long enough for the purpose and stirred vigorously, almost upsetting it, slopping liquid down the side of the pot. She thought she heard a footfall, dropped the spoon with a clatter and snapped shut the lid. She returned hastily to her chair and sat, breathing violently, the empty bottle still in her hand, the remaining liquid gumming her fingers. She clenched herself tightly, waiting, afraid to move further. She was appalled, in a sequence of sudden rushes, at the magnitude of what she was about. It seemed out of proportion to her whole previous existence. But in a way it was already done. She sat and waited as the minutes ticked away.

The hunchbacked girl was in the stable yard behind the house. She had been walking in the garden, along the tidy pathways edged with little hedges, ankle-high; feeling the early strength of the sun upon her. She had walked in a long quadrilateral of paths, moving and breathing but unable to enjoy her awareness of the wider world, for the house and its atmosphere had invested her profoundly with its lethargies. She had trodden the monotonous gravel, grey and wet, each footfall producing a multitude of small sounds, complex and individual, but finally the same, uninteresting and precise. The air had been thick and damp and had seemed to clog rather than expand her as she breathed. She had been walking for over an hour, the same quadrilateral of paths, lacking the courage to alter her course or to run across the lawn through the gateway into the wood beyond.

The quadrilateral came, at the most acute of its angles, within reach of the open stable yard and, eventually, she had become aware of some activity in progress there. She had heard these sounds from the first, but it had taken several circuits for her to register them distinctly and even longer for her curiosity to take hold of them. She had distinguished then the sounds of a carpenter at work – the shifting of wood surfaces, the rip of a saw-blade, the sweep of a plane, the clump of a mallet. She had stopped to mark the sounds before she had been conscious of doing so. She had become aware of herself caught, attentive, bird-like, head cocked. She had felt the urge to resume her walk but had defeated it. She had walked carefully, quietly, across the open gravel towards the corner of the open stable yard.

She had peered in to see a large man, a bulk of a man in moleskin trousers, aproned and shirt-sleeved, his back towards her, bent over some large box structure. She had thought at first that it was a coffin but closer attention soon dismissed this morbid cobweb. He was making some sort of cupboard. On a bench beside him, in neat order, lay his tools. Around his feet in orderly piles were shavings and offcuts of wood dropped precisely. His head was dense with black hair as were his bared arms, bristling and muscular. She could not see his face clearly, but he reminded her at once of the large man she had seen in the prison office, the man who had come from the Governor as they had waited there.

She watched him unobserved for a while, ready to slide back out of sight should he rise from his work and turn. He was engaged in a detailed examination of the edge of his cupboard, marking with a pencil which he took from behind his ear, and peering closely at the wood, touching it minutely, planning his next incursion upon it. She withdrew silently from the entrance, retreated a little, then thought better of it, became bold, strode back firmly into the stable yard. The man had heard her, had risen and turned. He wore a pair of spectacles which distracted her for a moment, but the expression that opened his face as it met hers clarified him at once. He was indeed the man from the prison. So, he was a carpenter. She wanted to greet him as a friend, for his recognition of her was certainly as clear as hers was of him, but she restrained herself: his contemplation of her was not as simple as her greeting him would have been.

His surprise was succeeded by a large grin. He unhooked his spectacles, folded them and slotted them under his apron, producing a handkerchief the size of a small towel with which he wiped his face. From behind the handkerchief he watched her, his eyes bright. He wiped his lips, picked at a mote on them and spat it delicately away. He regarded her, put his head on one side which, she realised, was an imitation of her, a mockery. She pulled herself straighter, set her chin up; she was, after all, of the house. He was a servant. She did not impress him; he failed to notice her attitude, looking through it cleanly. His teeth became visible in his grin and his tongue, pale pink, peeped out between his teeth. He disturbed her.

She tossed her head and turned to see the maid waiting behind her. She felt as if she had been spying upon her, had peeked at an intimacy of hers and this angered her. She advanced upon her directly.

'Mistress wants you, miss. Up in her room. Now. You'd better go. You'd better go now.'

She pressed on past her, but a strangely high, single laugh from behind her kept her thoughts in the stable yard. She obeyed the call upstairs unthinkingly.

The girl knocked three times at the door of the mistress's room before there was a response. Her thoughts, busy with the carpenter, had not fully settled into this strange summons. The pauses between her firm, even raps on the door panels allowed her time to wonder what lay in store for her. She did not relish the prospect of this encounter.

The door opened and the fat woman surveyed her with druggy eyes that burned red in the atrophy of her features. The woman took her arm and drew her in, closing the door behind them, leading her to a high-backed chair set by a small table at which tea was laid. She sat where she was bidden and the woman stooped over the table and, with slurred movements, slopping and knocking the cup, she poured her a cup of tea, indicated dismissively the plate of shortbread and then retreated to a little chaise-longue upon which she perched, staring forward, watching the girl.

No word had been uttered and the strangeness of the whole proceeding alerted the girl, who glanced about the room at the musty hangings, at the heavy religious pictures. The chair and table were set strategically in a shaft of light which fell in through the long window. The chaise-longue was in a shadow close to the grate. It was not easy to distinguish the woman from the artefacts of the room, apart from the eyes which were upon her continuously.

'Won't you take some tea, child?' she said at last.

She raised the cup. The liquid was barely warm and raising it to her face she immediately drew back. The liquid was muddy and it stank like a stale drain. She put down the cup and faced the woman out.

The woman was staring back, trembling visibly, her redundant flesh, her redundant clothing beginning to wobble about her. 'Take some tea,' she said, pleading.

The girl reached out, took a finger of shortbread, broke a piece and put it into her mouth, keeping her eye upon the woman continually.

After several long moments of silence, disturbed only by the girl's chewing of the dry shortbread, the woman made a sudden shuddering effort, rose and advanced to the table. The girl clenched herself, ready to overthrow her in an instant, to push her back on to the chaise-longue and flee. But the woman's purpose was otherwise. She took the teapot, trembling, and poured herself a cup.

'You must drink, child. You must drink your tea. Look. I will drink with you. We will drink together.'

She was mad. The girl raised her cup again, but even had she wanted to, she could not have taken that foulness into her mouth. She made a hideous face and put the cup down firmly. The woman moaned, turned away; then turned back and tipped her cupful into her mouth with a sudden jerk, swallowing and gasping.

'Go on. Go on. It's all right, girl. Why will you not . . .?' Then she fell on all fours as spasmodic bolts of pain shot through her. Then she rolled on to her side and vomited, a thin, sour-smelling liquid dribbling from her mouth and nose.

The girl went at once to the bell-pull and tugged at it furiously. She knelt then beside the woman and, her sickness eased, she took her in her arms and cradled her carefully. The maid came, saw and ran off. The housekeeper came, saw and ran off. Then there was wailing, the house alive with distant shouting. The housekeeper returned to take command, but the mistress was rocked in a delirious trembling, and the hunchbacked girl held her so strongly, so kindly, that the housekeeper retreated and closed the door.

The fading of the afternoon drew the light from the

room. She held tight the lumpy little woman. It was not serious, she had voided the toxin from her; had it been that fearsome there would have been other symptoms by now. The woman lay in her lap panting fitfully, apparently unconscious, but the girl felt a tension in her, knew she was awake and pitied her. Her body felt so weighted, so formless below the massive drapery. The girl wondered soon what she had involved herself in here, in what position she now stood in the woman's obese mind. She foresaw another long servitude, another closed companionship. She wanted her freedom.

The doctor arrived and she took the first opportunity to slip away, went to her room and changed her dress, went in to see Miss Clack who was quite unaltered, quite closed. As the girl sat by her and took her dry hand for a few minutes, she realised that it did not matter her being here. She did not have to wait for her to die; in effect that had already happened. The whole house surrounded them with atrophy and decay. For Miss Clack this was probably appropriate, but it was not so for her.

John Stone returned that evening. His arrival brought a moment's release to the weight of the house as he busied himself inquiring into circumstances, dressing down loudly his senior servants, attending closely to his wife. The girl was required to attend dinner and had expected to see them both there, putting on some sort of unity for her; but he was alone. The meal was served and progressed through its first two courses in silence. She glanced across at him often, but he was winding himself up to speak to her and was resisting any glance at her whilst he did so.

He began at last. 'I understand that my wife attempted to kill you this afternoon, and then herself when you would not drink from her poisoned chalice. Her hatred of you was, apparently, inspired by a fancy that I had committed infidelities with you; and further, that I sought to destroy her and to instate you in her place. She tells me that you saw through her design at once, had some sort of mystical awareness of her great evil. She says that you are good and she is evil. She wants to beg your forgiveness. She wants to adopt you as her child, as the heir of this estate.'

He paused and, in the pause, she considered carefully his tone. It was without a sardonic edge. Its sarcasm was propelled only by anger, a repressed fury that might have risen against her physically at any moment. She held herself very still and did not look at him.

'However,' he continued, as if clearing his mouth of it, 'you are not a sainted child of nature; you are a partially reclaimed and superficially civilised whore. Your position in my household is as companion to my aunt who, in truth, has little further need for you. I would turn you out, if I could, but it would not be convenient for me at the moment to give the neighbourhood evidence to support their legends of me as a monster of all sorts of cruelty. You will be tolerated here, fed and sheltered. I see no easy way of disburdening myself of you and I will therefore maintain you as a memorial to my beloved aunt who found you, I understand, a fruitful symbol of the world's corruption, a perfect victim. However, I will not have my wife, a greatly disturbed woman, find a similar use for you. She has a weakness for parasites to which I will not pander. You will keep away from my wife. You will ignore any approach made by her directly or through any of the servants. You have a very sharp awareness, as we both know. I shall watch you very closely and if you disobey me in any particular, I shall have you confined in an insane asylum. Do I make myself understood?'

She raised her face to him and dipped her head once, her mouth straight, the dignity of her response catching him a little. He rose and left the table. She finished her meal attended by the servants with an active solicitude she had never known in them before.

— 2 —

The next morning, after breakfast, after a short vigil beside Miss Clack, she left Palmead House intending never to return. She took nothing but a purse with twelve identical gold coins in it; an object she had in fact stolen from Miss Clack. She had no idea of their value, or even if they were current coinage. She took them not so much as a means of support, but as a token, paying herself off.

She set off boldly across the lawn towards a gate in the dense hedge beyond which was the wood she had contemplated so often from the house and from such of the garden as was in the house's immediate shadow. It was a clear spring day, the sky bright and cloudless, the air edged with a little wind. Clarity was everywhere: it was the perfect day for a new beginning. She did not look back at the house and did not speculate on who might be watching her. None of them had any power over her now. She attained the gate and she unlatched it. It swung open with a whine. Before her was a stream which she crossed by means of a plank bridge, old and little used. It bowed under her weight and for a moment she expected it to split and drop her into the water. She strode over this expectation and stepped safely into the wood.

There was a path from the bridge. It was overgrown, choked with the dead tangles of previous years and invaded by the first growths of the new spring; but it lead onward and she stepped onward, following it as it turned through the trees and enclosed her in woodland. It was heavy going. The undergrowth snagged at the hem of her dress continuously and she was soon involved in picking her way, stepping high, hoisting her skirts. Her boots became saturated with an unpleasant green dampness. Frequently she disturbed unseen creatures and she would be startled by a sudden frenzy of movement close by her. She would go rigid, expect to be attacked, imagine something small and dark-furred with blind teeth and claws clinging to her. Frequently insects fell into her hair or on to her face or, worst of all, into her clothing where they were unnoticed until they had squirmed down to some hidden expanse of her flesh. She had once to bare her breasts in a panic to remove some frail little mite that had slipped down her neck. The trees rose high above her, detached, their trunks massive and ominous. Birds battered through their high boughs, screaming and flapping. The clarity of the day held but it was outside, above the trees, beyond her. It was apparent soon enough that either the path had been swallowed entirely, or she had strayed from it. With a moan she abandoned herself, her purpose gone. She felt small and stupid. She struggled through to a fallen tree and sat upon it, gathering her calm or trying to, trying to reassert some direction, some motive, something to do next.

The stillness of the wood came down around her and, gradually as the struggle and its futility receded, she began to experience a peace. The clinging of the undergrowth, the claustrophobia of exertion, these faded. Her fear of the swarming creatures of the wood-floor went. A brown bird with beautiful dappled breast hopped out from a bush and stood, not three yards from her in a small space, its head cocked, its body shifting in small jerks, responding to a precise and balanced tension within it. A small beetle suddenly appeared on the back of her hand, hopped in from nowhere, its antennae testing the air, its legs in strange concert rotating its body; then its back broke open and black wings appeared briefly before it was gone. Above her the sky was excluded; the wood filled with its own light, a greeny-brown shadow into which, at various distances, shafts of soft, amber sunlight fell, irregular in size and density, but all magically parallel. The wind moved the trees with a continual, high rustling. Twigs fell; creatures rattled through dead leaf piles. There was a pattern of sounds which was never repetitive and yet its very multiplicity, its infinity, its continuance, brought behind it the most perfect silence she had ever experienced: a silence beyond interruption, a silence that was not an absence; a stillness that the attentive ear could always make pregnant; an active and generated silence. Around her feet, and everywhere she looked, were the beginnings of the new year's profusion – the uncurling of miniature ferns, the upthrusting of flower stems, the burgeoning of new leaf-buds on dark bushes. The sodden density of the past, compacted by the winter into a rank, decaying compress, was mastered by the extrusions of growth. It was simple and obvious. She sat and watched it, imagined the opening of the buds, the stretch of the flower-petals, the larvae struggling from their eggs, peopling the wood, filling its spaces with a multitude of perfect worlds. Such a moment was the childhood she had never been given.

She sat thus for some hours, rapt, until the insistence of her own biology asserted itself: she was very hungry. She glanced about in an inspiration, looking for something to eat, a dream of woodland existence flickering up before her but soon overwhelmed by her ignorance and squeamishness. She considered the prospect of a night out here and this brought her quickly to reality. She must return to Palmead. It had not been a wasted journey. If she had not found her freedom here, she had at least clarified it. It was not yet but it would come soon.

Within a quarter of an hour of tentative advances in various directions, she realised that she was lost. The wood was, in every aspect, every ten yards taken, a different place: no way out, no way back, no direction, no guarantee that any progress was possible because even if that progress ended where it began the beginning would be unrecognisable. She moved on anyway, growing aware of all this, accepting it, a little afraid, falling back on her great tolerance of the world which did not, at this time, desert her. She trod through the easiest parts, letting the wood lead her. She found stretches of young bracken which crumbled into dust as she broke through it. She had no sense of time. It might, after all, have only been an hour since she had left the house: at times she believed that she had slept and had been gone days. Her hunger was real, a substantial emptiness in her guts and consequent lightness in her head. She looked longingly at the luscious greenery about her but never quite found the courage to eat. She found a nest in a bush, betrayed by a panicked bird, with five tiny white eggs in it; but she could not bring herself to attempt them, a sense of sacrilege rising in her at the thought, which she rationalised with the image of the eggs full, not of succulent yolk, but of wet little embryos, all beak and claw. She began to dream of curling up and sleeping in the soft bracken but she resisted this determinedly even though the dream grew intoxicating, filling her weakened mind with longing.

All at once she became aware of a change in the light. Ahead of her the density of the forest seemed to diminish. She advanced and, sure enough, she was approaching an edge of the wood beyond which was a solid fall of sky. The ground had been rising for some time and perhaps this was only the crest of a hill she was approaching, with the wood rolling on continuously on the other side. Nevertheless, the prospect of release gave her new energy. The ground cover did seem to be thinning, the trees to be spaced a little further apart as she advanced to the light.

She came to the brow of the hill and to the edge of the wood. The ground fell away sharply, a closed sweep of tussocky turf down to a little rivulet crossed with a plank. Beyond the stream was a thatched, stone-walled barn, a large building with shuttered windows and a stout door, with other buildings behind, stacks of logs and timber, a pen for chickens, a horse tethered in the pasture beyond, a small area of tilled earth. Behind the buildings, close against them, the wood rose up another, steeper slope. To her right, beyond the horse pasture, the stream disappeared up into the wood curtain; to her left it ran widening down a widening valley, followed round a bend and out of sight by a worn cart track that led from the buildings. A column of grey smoke rose from the large chimney in the barn's roof. She searched the prospect for the sight of the inhabitants, but could see no one. Presumably they were inside the barn, perhaps at a meal. This possibility removed all her reticence and she began to pick her way down the slope.

It was a difficult journey: the ground was deceptively uneven and steep. She had not gone ten yards before she tumbled over and found herself rolling painfully against a stone, her ankle wrenched. She hauled herself up and proceeded, stooped over, ready to use her hands to steady herself, coming down almost on all fours. At last she was at the stream side. She knelt on the plank bridge, cupped her hands and filled them, immersed her hot, dirty face in the brilliant water. Again and again she brought water to her face, drinking and dousing herself until her hair and clothes ran with it and she breathed in its sharp crystalline light.

She rose from her immersion refreshed and clarified. She glanced up at the barn. It seemed more compact from this vantage, slightly below it. She could see details now – the thatching tidy, showing patches of renewal. The smoke still rose enticingly from the chimney straight up into the sky. She wondered if she had been observed yet, felt self-conscious, ashamed of her dripping head and shoulders, aware of her deformity out here in the open world. She glanced back up the slope, but could not face a retreat. She glanced along the cart-track and considered taking flight thence – but from what? She rose and made her way up the tidy pathway from the stream, past the garden with its young plants in neat array, towards the dark doorway. It was a solid door, half-closed. She peered in but could determine no detail. A smell of woodsmoke and bacon drifted out and her expectations, her hunger, rose. She rapped on the door, but she made little sound. The chickens in their paled run skittered about and prodded their necks through the slats, pushing and squawking with excitement. She turned back to the doorway and waited, but no one came. The desertion grew into an alluring silence, a temptation forbidding and irresistible. She was certain that she was being watched.

She pushed the door and it swung soundlessly open. She stepped over the threshold stone and found herself in a rough room, low-ceilinged with a wooden staircase leading up directly in front of her to another storey. The floor of the room was neatly boarded, a little dusty, a little damp. The further half of the building was cut off behind a partition that was part stone wall, part wooden panelling: an open door lead through to the other part, but she could not see beyond it. Light came into the building through narrow windows, glassless but strongly shuttered; today the shutters were wide open, admitting the spring. In the stone of the partition wall was the fireplace, built up solidly through the low ceiling. The fire was out, apparently, which puzzled her until she had deduced the presence of another fireplace on the other side of the wall feeding into the same chimney. Bacon was hung in a large ham from the ceiling, showing signs of rough knife-cuts; not much left on the bone. There were also strings of onions and dried plants and, on the wall, a pair of heavy cooking vessels. Before the fireplace was a chair and table, roughly finished, but solidly built. A candle stood in a turned wooden stick. There was a bottle and a wooden tobacco pipe. Everywhere she looked there was something – a box, a little keg, a brass bowl hung on the wall, a jug, a pair of tongs, a stack of small logs, another of kindling sticks, a chest of drawers and cupboards and slots of all different sizes. Everything was in its place. Nothing was decorative. It awed her. She could not have touched anything without marking her presence clearly;

indeed, she had probably already done so. The room was undoubtedly male, had the whole intensity of single-minded, self-enclosed masculinity to it, and that disturbed her. Everything was burnished with hard use. It was a place of intense solitude. She felt for the first time that she was trespassing here.

She turned and, as she did so, the doorway was filled by the bulk of a very large man, obscured against the light, looking in, there all at once. It was the carpenter.

After a moment's surprise, he leant himself against the doorpost and regarded her closely. She turned away from his scrutiny, ashamed of herself, of her fears and fancies, feeling foolish to have arrived at his place above all others, sensing herself to be in a trap of her own making, completely at his mercy.

'Hello there, miss?' he said.

She looked up to find that she was crying with her weariness and shame. He came into the house. She thought he might touch her and she shrank. He kept clear of her, however, as far as the small room would permit. He pulled out the chair and offered it. She sat, clasped her hands in her lap and stifled the tears which perplexed him.

'You're a mess, my miss,' he said. 'What's brought you here then? Have they sent you? What d'you want?'

She looked up, pointed to her mouth, extended as much of her tongue as she could and pointed.

'What . . .? What? You've no speech? Is that right?'

She sat still, her point made.

He scratched his beard. 'Can you write your words?'

She shook her head.

After a moment's thought, he broke into a great laughter which alarmed her. He sat on the edge of the table which wobbled with his mirth. Tears came into his eyes as he tried to order his merriment, as it rose and spluttered out again.

Still laughing, he brought down the ham, drew a knife and hewed her a slab of it, put it on a platter and fetched bread, drew her a beaker from the little keg. He placed each of these objects with a thud upon the table before her as if they were the tokens of some rough bargain. Hungry though she was, she did not touch them yet. She watched him, wanting to offer something in response. He leant on the mantle and regarded her with his head on one side, the laughter still rumbling up into his face now and then. She felt amongst her skirts for the purse she had taken, drew it out, fumbled with the clasp and then spilled the coins in a clatter across the table-top. He was surprised at this. He came forward and picked up a couple of the coins, frowning, taking them to the window to examine them more closely, back and front, rubbing his thumbs over them. He returned and placed them on the table with the others, serious now. She considered the coins, picked one up also, but could not go through the pretence of finding it significant. He shook his head solemnly, sucked his teeth, turned his back upon her and burrowed in a box on a shelf, giving her time to scoop her little booty back into the purse and to conceal it back under her gown. She would have to go back and replace the purse before they came after it, and her. She had a sudden glimpse of the world set against her. She recalled John Stone's threat of the asylum. She recalled the prison. She began to feel the tears urging into her eyes again. She looked at the platter, at the bread and the slab of sweet meat, at the beaker full of dark liquid. She dared not reach out for them, submitted to the hurting ache in her belly and built her wretchedness around it.

He turned back. He had filled a pipe. He looked at her.

'Eat. I'll take you back to the house.'

He left her, went through the door into the far part of the building.

In his absence she wept again, the tears burning her cheeks. She covered her face with her hands and hunched down.

The man returned with a lit spill. She smeared away her tears but could not face him. He applied the spill to his pipe, the clean air suddenly coiling with tobacco smoke, a smell that took her back with a fierce clarity to the Inn, to the stall, to Old Mag late at night, to the beginning of things. She looked up at him, amazed that he should have been able to effect this magic upon her, that he should know so much about her. She looked at him intently to try to find a clue in his face.

He seemed still uneasy. He regarded her with caution since she had offered him strange coins, since she had wept, since she sat there still before his hospitality and failed to come into it.

'I'd best harness the trap and get you back,' he said. 'Since you've no appetite.'

She denied this at once, gave in with a sudden delight, breaking the bread, tearing at the meat with her teeth, swilling at the beaker which proved full of heavy cider. Her mouth was crammed and she swallowed in thick lumps which eased down into her hunger. The ham was as sweet as it looked, the bread dense with bran, the cider sharp and cleansing the mouth, rising almost at once into a lightness at the top of her head. The pleasure of eating and drinking, once it was begun, was irresistible and enormous, more than she had mouth and throat to contain. She finished every last fragment, drained the beaker and held it upside down for the final drips. She looked at him and smiled guiltily.

He laughed again, once, clearly, an expression of his relief and pleasure, his satisfaction at her.

'Did you come to find me?' he asked, relighting his pipe. He looked at her for an answer but, as she did not like to deny him, nor to deceive him, she held steady. Now she was here, she wanted it to be a deliberate arrival. Perhaps it was. It was easy to think that; it made her feel strong with a strength beyond her. He watched her and she smiled a little at him, coyly probably, perhaps suggestively; anyway, the effect of it was to unsettle him again. He knocked out his pipe in the empty grate and collected her platter and beaker.

'Shall I show you about a bit?' he asked. 'Would you like that?'

She nodded and slipped from the chair at once, wiping her greasy hands on her gown, a movement she made without thinking but which he noted and it amused him.

He opened the door into the further part of the barn and she went through, to find herself in a large workshop. At the far end were double barn doors, one of which was ajar and through it she could see further buildings, a yard full of shavings. Within the workshop was a long, solid workbench, about eight-foot wide and some fifteen- or twenty-foot long. In its surface were slits and holes for his tools: vices, stops, brass gauges, worn and grooved patches, patches cleared and polished deeply, a whetstone countersunk into the surface at the far end, trays sunk into the middle full of various nails and pegs, twines and wires. It fascinated her with its complexity and its order. He stood back whilst she walked round it, reaching out to touch its surface, its implements, a little apprehensive. Around the walls, about her head, hung further tools, long saws, axes, frames, coils of rope, hanging bags and sacks. In the roof hung, by means of pulleys, strange objects, heavy, half-shadowy, half-made objects. The window sockets were empty and through them poured bright, cool light. It was all so purposeful, so personal and yet, as with the living area, so functional. It intimidated her and intrigued her.

She had wandered as far as the end doors, then she turned back to see him standing by the fireplace which was where she had expected it to be, alight, a glue-pot bubbling upon it. Beside it, on the other side to the door through which they had come, a flight of stairs led up to the storey above the living quarters and he moved across to the foot of these stairs to indicate their next area of exploration. She came to him and mounted the steep stairs. A door unlatched into a bedroom which contained only a large, wooden-framed bed, its bedding coarse and rather musty, thrown back to reveal a rough mattress. A small window in the gable-end lit this room. Various suits of clothes were hanging about the walls and from the ceiling. She felt him behind her, following, watching, but pleased to let her find her own way. She saw the second stairs, down to the living room. She went to the window which, unlike those downstairs, had panes, fixed. She found a small chest in the corner which she pulled across to the stairhead and climbed up on to peek through the window, having a view down the valley with the trees thick on either side, enclosing, the stream wandering down and away.

She turned to see him standing with his arms folded, across the bed from her. She turned back to the window, expecting him to close behind her, ready for him and glad, recklessly, of the idea of him, her pleasure in this place swelling inside her. She longed to belong here. She longed to have its closeness and neatness about her, if only for a while, an hour or two, a little now. He was the embodiment of the place, not separate from it, not from its precision, nor from its woods and trees. Her previous encounters with him, in the prison and in the stable yard at Palmead, were irrelevant except in so far as they had led her, somehow, here. She waited for him to come and place his craftsman's hands upon her. The sweetness of this anticipation made her light and animated.

He did not approach. She glanced back and he was still watching her. She caught a curious distance in his eyes, a consideration of her as some strange creature of which he was unsure, which he was considering in a light which she did not understand. She stepped down from the chest and felt her fantasy go cold upon her. She considered an advance upon him, an offer of herself; but his strange scrutiny precluded that. She felt her deformity and shrugged irritably as if she might shift it off her back. A wave of tiredness came over her in a rush. The complexities of the day caught up with her and her eyelids began to droop, a gulf of sleep yawning for her. She turned and sat on the edge of his bed to recover herself a little, which she did, briefly. He moved round the end of the bed and stood next to her. She looked up weakly and he smiled, seeing her weariness, seeing her safe. She caught herself leaning over, pulled herself up, but began to lean again, gave in to it, rolled on to the bed. He came forward and eased up her legs, pulled up the cover. She was aware of his hands upon her, the decision with which he moved, laying her down and covering her up, but she was aware of nothing else.

Night fell. He harnessed the horse into his trap and waited below in his living-room, the fire bright, the breeze mustering in the woods under a starless sky. He heard the shift of her weight on the bed, took a candle and climbed the stairs promptly, lest she took a waking fright at her strange surroundings, at the darkness.

He found her indeed looking wild and alarmed, drawn back at his approach.

'D'you not remember where you are?' he said, setting down the candle in the window. 'Come on now. I've the trap ready. We must get you home. It must be gone nine.'

She did not move and he felt that he ought to leave her, to allow her to tidy herself or whatever.

'Bring down the candle when you're ready then. Don't be long. They'll be sending out for you.' He spoke softly, almost whispering. It was strange for him to hear his own voice in these tones in this place.

Soon he heard her moving to the stair head, beginning to descend, the candle-light throwing great shadows around her. He went to the bottom of the stairs to help her down. She came awkwardly, gripping tight on to the banister rail, her body unsure of the space about it, the candle held away. When she came within reach of him, she thrust the candle out at him. He took it, turned to place it on the table and she had gone through the door and out into the night.

He stepped quickly after her, went out on to the path but could not see her ahead. He wondered what she was about. Had she fled? What was she afraid of? Of him? Of returning to Palmead?

'Where've you got to?' he called.

He turned about slowly, listened and detected a movement at the side of the house. He stepped round and saw her crouched down, huddled up in the dark.

'What've you to be afraid of?' he said. He saw the pale shape of her face turned up to him. He came forward and squatted down before her, reached out a hand and then realised what she was doing there, rose in confusion and went quickly back into the house to wait for her, sitting down in silence, turning the chair to the fire.

She returned shortly and stood waiting. He mastered his confusion and faced her. She was playing demure, but her face rose and registered a sarcastic flatness. He rose, cleared his throat and, picking up the candle, led her through the workshop and out into the yard beyond where the horse waited, covered with a rug. He did not meet her eyes again, felt increasingly foolish. She waited for him to help her up on to the trap, which he did awkwardly, going to lift her bodily when all she needed was a supporting arm. There was a confusion in which her backside, unmistakable beneath its folds of stuff, pushed into his face.

He climbed beside her and they trotted out along the uneven cart-track. The horse knew the way and paced smartly, the trap rattling and jangling, sounds defeated by the surrounding woods and the blanket of the night. He kept silent throughout the journey, aware of her as a weight of body beside him, aware of this aspect of her and made uncertain by it. They came out of the valley, rounded the bend and joined the public thoroughfare that led down into the village.

When they came into the village, she knew where she was. She viewed the cluster of squat houses that night with relief. She had not gone far really, just wandered round and round in the wood. She saw the church, the attendant rectory and a terrace of better houses standing away from the main street of the village, solid and black in the night. The village houses proper seemed by contrast round and soft, with lights gleaming in the windows and smoke rising from the chimneys, mingled and dispersed in the breeze. The night air was alert with the woodsmoke and the promise of rain. They passed the inn and a group of men came to the door, stood in the wide pool of lamplight that poured from its openings and watched them pass.

'It's Jasper Catch!' one called.

''Evening to you, Mr Catch.'

He did not turn his head, but she watched them, twisted back to look at them and saw them huddle together at the sight of her. She eased herself back to face forward again. She had liked their deference to him, cocky with drink though it had been. She smiled to herself.

As the trap swung into the gates of Palmead House, her spirits sank. The buildings loomed low and dark ahead of them, no lights showing. She was not certain how they might receive her back, if they would receive her back, what he would do with her if they would not. She expected him to take the trap round to the rear of the house but, with what appeared to be a sudden decision, he pulled the horse round and they ran to a standstill before the porticoed front door. He glanced at her and, with another resolute movement, he jumped down, mounted the steps and tugged at the bell.

There was a while to wait before the sound of bolts and locks was heard and the door was opened by a manservant. She could not hear what was said, saw him shadowed in the light from the hall, saw the manservant peer past him then close the door and leave him there. He did not turn back, waited with his face to the closed door. It began to rain, small spots blown by the breeze, the precursors of a heavy fall. It would be a wet ride home for him; for her too perhaps.

The door opened again and John Stone came out, looking past the carpenter, coming down the steps to her, the carpenter moving down behind him. He came to the trap and looked up at her.

'We thought you'd left us,' he said. He had a cigar in his mouth which he did not remove as he spoke. He was far gone in drink, his voice slurring and his eye unfocused. 'We thought you'd fled into the wild woods forever. You mustn't leave us quite so suddenly. My good lady wife thinks I've done away with you. It's raining, isn't it? Won't you come in out of the rain, miss? I must slip this fellow a guinea for fetching you home.' He reached up and helped her down. 'I hope you've been behaving yourself. Mr Catch is an upright fellow.' The carpenter had closed in by the time this was said and she could see the resentment stiffening in the darkness of his face. 'I'll find you a guinea, my good man,' Stone said, guiding her past him.

'That won't be necessary, sir.'

'As you see fit. Goodnight to you. I hope you don't get wet on the road home, although I fear you will.'

What his parting reaction was she did not know, for Stone had her inside by then and, as she looked back for a parting glance, Stone closed the door upon the carpenter and slammed home a bolt.

'Will you come and have some brandy?'

She shook her head and left him in the hall watching her up the stairs.

She reached her own room without incident, looked longingly at her bed but remembered the bag of money and realised that she had to return her stolen treasure before she could sleep easily. Miss Clack had risen from the bed and had returned, in her nightgown, to sit in her chair before the window. Perhaps she did this every night. Perhaps she had risen to observe her return to the house. Whatever it was, Miss Clack had taken her day-time vigil into the dark of the night, sat staring out of a rain-streaked window through which the black landscape writhed and shifted under the driving weather. She did not turn. The girl went to the chest and replaced the purse, making noise as she did so. Shutting the drawer with a thump, she turned to Miss Clack; but she had not reacted to the disturbance. The girl could hear the old woman's even breathing, slightly rasped, with a conscious catch in it that precluded her being asleep. She wondered, as she had wondered often before in this room, of how much the old woman was aware. From her refusal, since her brother's death, to make any substantial communication, the girl had turned as from a wall, a mausoleum: it had no interest for her. But, because of what had gone before, she was never at ease with this turning away.

She was glad that she had brought back the purse, blushed at the memory of its taking, the petulant defiance of a child. She felt a smug warmth at its replacement. She could go to bed now. Before she left she went to look at Miss Clack to make sure all was well.

Miss Clack sat in her nightgown only, her back straight, hands gripped on the arms of the chair. The girl was aware as she had never been before of the old woman's body, the skeletal rigidity, the insignificance of the etiolated flesh that clung to this frame. She placed her hand upon Miss Clack's forearm, and it was alarmingly tensed. She would grow ossified like that, her joints rigid, fixed before the life left her: the measured, unreal breath came steadily. She looked into the face, mouth tight, eyes open, staring ahead. She went to the bed and fetched a blanket to drape about her shoulders, although it did not seem possible that Miss Clack could feel the cold.

As she tucked and tidied the blanket, she was suddenly stopped, aware of a change. She raised her face slowly and found Miss Clack's face turned towards her, the large staring eyes upon her. The night was black with the rolling of the rainclouds, but her eyes were accustomed to it; a faint luminosity filled the room. It was possible to believe that the light emanated from that face. The expression was without emotion, or rather, beyond emotion – clear, penetrating. The girl, resisting the initial guilts which impelled her to flight, held that face upon her own face, looked and was looked at.

It was a moment of clarity that was to last her the rest of her life. What it betokened, she could not have begun to imagine in any articulable shape – it was beyond expression. It gripped tight about her soul, that most intimate part of her that she could never stand away from. Suddenly, there, in the light of that look, she was clarified, stripped, examined minutely, confirmed, approved, blessed.

She leant forward and kissed the cold brow, then left quickly, went out into the landing where the candles still burned deep in their sockets. She hurried into her room, to her bed like a lover. The dreams plunged into her and filled her; she awoke in a morning that gleamed with the refreshment of the rain, the light twinkling through her window. She rushed from her bed to look out on a new, bright world.

She had to wait a week, a decent enough interval. She knew that there would have to be such an interval and she was patient, sitting mostly in her room or beside the stony Miss Clack. The weather held, bland and bright, the spring burgeoning under it. She waited, contained and certain.

At last the summons came. The maid knocked and entered with the nearest thing to a smile she had ever seen on a domestic face in this place. She was informed that the master would be pleased to see her in the drawing-room. Pausing only to smooth Miss Clack's hand, she rose and followed the maid downstairs. Out in the front of the house, she could see his trap waiting. She was pleased at his applying at the front door, felt her status and strength.

She expected to meet him beside John Stone in the drawing-room, but Stone was alone, standing formally with his back to the fireplace. He indicated for her to sit, which she did, away from him on a sofa.

'I am applied to by the carpenter, Jasper Catch,' he said. 'He asks my permission to come courting. Do you understand what is implied by this?'

She nodded.

'You are under no obligation to listen to this man, nor indeed even to receive him. I do have a responsibility towards you in the illness of my aunt whose ward you are.

Catch is a secretive man, not much liked in the parish, without relatives or friends.' He paused. 'Marriage into the village, or into the lower classes anywhere, I suspect, means a submission to your husband which, unless he actually kills you, and possibly not even then, no one will interfere with. Perhaps we do not manage these matters well either, we gentry, but at least we allow ourselves our little spaces into which we can withdraw. Catch will not, I think, afford you much space. You will be a servant and, unlike one of my servants protected by a hierarchy here, a servant absolutely.'

She did not look at him but knew that he was watching closely for her response.

'As to the other duties of marriage, you need little advice there, I think.' His tone had grown nastier. 'I have made it plain to him that you are no heiress. It did occur to me once to dower you up and see which of my respectable neighbours found you beautiful, but it was a point hardly worth the proving. Well, he's waiting for you in the library; and he ought to be grateful I didn't send him round to the stables. Make a decision quickly, will you. I won't put up with him at my front door again.'

She waited, assumed he'd finished, rose and went to the door without looking back.

'I took the liberty,' he said, halting her, 'in all honesty, of indicating to him a little of your unique upbringing. But I expect that will have made you all the more enticing, don't you? Your true inheritance!'

She banged the door behind her and strode across to the library door, pausing before it to allow the petty anger he had induced in her to subside and the warm expectation of the carpenter to reassert itself. She opened the door slowly, hoping to come upon him before he was aware of her. He stood with his back to the window, however, waiting for her appearance, hat in hands, wearing the foolish suit in which she had first seen him, constricted and awkward in his formality. He was smiling and she walked into his smile. She wanted to leave with him at once, but he did not register the desire in her look. He drew out a chair for her, had a little scene prepared for her in which she would have to take her part. She sat and looked up at him, smiling progressively. He stood away.

'Miss Magdaline,' he began. 'Mr Stone has been good enough to sanction my . . . my approach to you on er . . . He has spoken to you? He has explained . . .?'

She nodded and re-emphasised the smile.

'Ah. Well. Well, I must . . . You must be clear what it is I'm offering you. I live a simple life. You've seen how I live. You would share, as I say, a very simple, very quiet, very . . .'

She nodded and smiled away his exposition, by which he was obviously relieved; but there was something further.

'Another thing I must explain. The duties of a wife, the intimate duties of a wife to her husband, I . . . I do not understand such things, you see, and I don't think I could bring myself to an understanding of them. Mr Stone has told me how you were brought up, in a foul and sinful time and place; but I respect you, Miss Magdaline. I would not seek to burden you with that; no, not in any way.'

She did not know how to take this; her face clouded a little.

'Don't you be troubled now, Miss Magdaline. Forgive me. It was necessary to speak of it. We will say no more. You understand me though? You understand what I ask of you? Can you . . . Can you show me some indication? I ought to have spoken of love. Such a thing is expected, but . . .'

She rose and went to him, silencing him, leaning against him, her cheek against his stomach, her arms about him as far as she could reach. She heard his gurgling innards, felt his constrained breathing lifting her. He put his hands upon her and all was settled.

He explained thereafter that he would have to see the parson, to arrange everything. It would be simply done and soon. She interpolated, amongst his planning, a desire to have her out of Palmead as quickly as possible. She concurred with this expedition, felt her sympathy with him growing every minute they were together. She was allowing herself to be enormously glad of him. She did not think in any specific detail about the sort of life they would lead. She was glad of him and she would build on that gladness day by day. She felt that life in that valley would be good. It would be free in a way she had never been free before, in spite of all

John Stone's fancies. Life out there would be close and it would be an end, a resting place for her at last: somewhere to belong. It was a potent prospect. He was part of it, but it was not he alone. She had not felt it before she had seen him in his context. He had seemed, both in the prison and in the Palmead stable yard, an ominous figure. In his own house, in his own valley, she had seen a complete figure and whatever darkness he concealed, it could not be monstrous and still be contained within that beautiful and intimate little dwelling-place.

He took her out there again the day he made his proposal. The village was called Cutchknoll, or more properly Cutch-knoll St Mary, the church asserting its difference over the woods which were properly Cutchknoll, at least, where they cloaked the hill behind Catch's valley. He had lived there all his life, with his uncle and grandfather, and in his earliest childhood, his great-grandfather also. His father had gone off into the town before he was born. His mother had been a village girl who had been taken into the family, had been delivered of her son and, whilst he was still an infant, had returned to the village and had soon moved away, off into the town, perhaps even after her husband. His grandfather and uncle had been taken in a bout of smallpox when he had been nineteen and he had been on his own ever since, many years now. There was another uncle, Uncle Job, who had lived in the city and about whom he was reticent and embarrassed, as if wanting to explain something, some family secret, but failing to. She didn't mind what he told her, nor what he chose not to. He had, anyway, been bred up as a carpenter, Catch of Cutchknoll, inheritor of the valley. The village was new in comparison to him and his forebears, an excrescence upon the heart of the place. He was its heart, he and the forest space he maintained. He spoke of this freely, with a pride and fluency that made her grateful to and proud of him.

He spoke of the people rather than of the place but, as he spoke, he took her round and showed her everything. The living quarters she had seen, but she looked at them with a new interest, placing herself amongst them. They were very small. They would live very close together though, and she wouldn't mind that. His cooking was done in an iron mess-pot hung over the workroom fire. There were other pots but they were for glues and varnishes. Through the workroom, across a yard of compacted earth, was a stable, an airy building of wood, high, with space for the trap, a stall for the horse and a loft above with a stairway leading up. He had slept there as a boy, he told her. New wood was stacked here in the stable, some of it planed and planked, some uncut – raw trees – but all in ordered, distinct stacks. She noted the different timbers, the heavy, close-grained hardwood, the light, soft pines which still bore the tang of the woods. Beyond the house and stable was a steep bank with steps cut into it, the earth firm and planked into position, leading to a steep meadow across which a path led off into the wood. She wanted to go into the wood with him but he had other things to show her. Around the front of the house was the vegetable garden planted with roots and a couple of rows of early cabbages. The tillage was neat, the earth well tended, dark and wet. She stooped and sank her hands into the tilth, a gesture which puzzled and intrigued him. The hen-run was sturdy, the birds looking plump and arrogant. He showed her a flap at the back of the hen-house, let her work it out for herself: she lifted the flap and a couple of hens scuttled off nests, one leaving a heavy brown egg which she picked out carefully between thumb and forefinger. She offered it to him, her hands turned up. He took it and held it as she had held it, and smiled. They returned to the house.

He sat her down, took her bonnet, took her shawl, busied himself in a way that suggested he was masking a nervousness, as if he had thought about this too hard over the preceding week and was too keen for it to fit his aspirations for it. She tried to see how she should behave, what he was expecting of her; or what she could do that he was not expecting but which would nevertheless please him. She could think of nothing but to sit quietly, demurely, attendant upon him.

'Magdaline,' he said thoughtfully. 'There's not room here for that. It'll have to be Mag. Will you care for that?'

She would indeed. It was an unexpected gift. It brought together her pasts and her present in one sweep and it made her happy.

She looked at him for the first time that day as a man,

trying to clear her view of him from all the atmospheres that he had generated around her. He was so much bigger than she was, so thickly covered with flesh, his skin burnished and bristled. She found it difficult to accept him as a man like the other men she had known. His eyes were brown, the whites shaded, hidden in the shadows of their encasing bone and the thickets of hair and beard that massed about his head. His teeth, when he revealed them, when she made his smile broaden in surprise, which was not often, were dark and widely spaced; but there was a point of operation here – the stimulation of that surprise in him that out-manoeuvred the reticence, the detached smile that was bestowed upon her generally. When he was perplexed, the line of his mouth tightened. It was a delicate business, surprising without perplexing him; for she was well aware that he was not to be approached by any rush of sensuality.

She stood up and moved from the chair. He looked concerned, thinking she was in some need, but she smiled reassuringly and indicated that she wanted him to sit, which he did, moving around the table and easing himself down, expecting perhaps some domestic ministration, prepared to be well pleased with her. She smoothed the seat of her skirts and sat herself down upon his lap, shuffling her bottom backwards until she was well placed, able to look up from around her back at his face. His first reaction was to lean back abruptly, causing the chair to hit the cupboard behind it with a crack; had there been space they would have tumbled on to the floor and that would have been a catas-trophe. She looked at his startled face, ready to slip down if he registered any serious displeasure. But he was only startled, without a reaction. She set her face seriously and looked closely into his. At last he eased forward and the chair came right again. She smiled, careful not to be coy. She put her arms about the bulk of his chest. After a while, very carefully, he brought his arms about her, not holding her, but resting upon her, not exploring her shape as she explored his, but steadying himself upon her.

They remained thus for some while. At first she shifted herself about a little, snuggling, hoping faintly to stir within him the tension which stirred within her; but soon she rested, relaxed, was content with him. She rested against him as if he were a hillside in a cool and pleasant landscape. She listened and outside she heard the stream and the shifting of the trees, the passing buzz of an insect, the call of a bird, other sounds unidentifiable.

Catch wanted his marriage to be quiet, a quick formality before he would have her home and safe, but when the banns were read the village activated itself with gossip and lewdness at the prospect of this uncouth coupling. Catch's intention had been to collect her from Palmead in his trap, to take her straight home by way of the ceremony, a brief halt; but the village was not to be denied. A spontaneous holiday was declared and there broke out a great making of bonnets and pinafores, a stocking up of ales and meats. The squire heard of it and joined in with its spirit, laughing widely. He would bring the bride to church. He would found a wedding feast, hire fiddlers, release his labourers and servants for the day, obliging all his tenant farmers to do likewise, the hay harvest notwithstanding.

The day arrived. The sun glared off every surface. Spring had flourished into summer. The village green was peopled shortly after daybreak with those setting up tables and bringing out the pies and loaves, the joints and fowls, the cakes and sweets, the barrels and bottles and jugs, all covered with ghostly veils of muslin. The preparations drew the children out tumbling. The old took their places at the shady edges. The anticipation bustled prodigiously.

At nine-thirty, the green was hushed as Catch drove his trap into the village and drew it up outside the lych-gate where space had been left respectfully for him and for the squire. He backed his trap in ready for departure and defied, with a glower, any of the village urchins who came too close. They stood away and admired its new paint, green superstructure, black wheels and fittings, a new brass rail behind the seat and new leather cushioning. Catch, suited stiffly, prowled about his chariot for a while, then pulled straight his clothing and went into the church, strode up the aisle unswerving. The village crowded in after him in a flutter of finery, feathers and flowers everywhere. A high babble of excitement flowed down the church path but once

247

inside the building it ceased. They took their places quietly and sat as silently as they could under the irresistible prickling of expectation. The restraint was primarily due to Catch whose solid black back on the front pew seemed somehow ominous. Perhaps their frivolity had been misplaced; perhaps he might suddenly rise and abolish them all.

The vicar waited in the vicarage until he saw the Palmead carriage trot up, then ran out to meet it. Stone was dressed most elegantly, foppish almost. His wife was there, looking half-drugged as if brought out from a long, closed quarantine. Miss Clack was there, sitting like an obelisk beside the bride who was lost amongst her betters, a tiny figure in light blue silk, lots of it. Stone descended first and handed the hunchback down. The gown was absurd upon her, like some gaudy pantomime costume, a spoiled child dressed up to imitate some lady. The vicar greeted the family with a dignified inclination of himself and led them through the lych-gate, past the gawping rabble and into the church.

As they entered the church, the organ was belaboured into a jerky voluntary and the congregation rose to its feet with a great rustling, rising like banks on either side of them, pushing and shuffling to catch a sight of the procession. The vicar led with a slow prance. Stone followed, his eyes set at a sardonic distance, the little bride hobbling beside him, her arm tucked into his, weighted down with her finery; and, behind them, the quivering figure of Edwina Stone who looked as if she might dissolve at any moment, her eyes darting about for the rush at her that would finish her; and beside her, the great black upright of Miss Clack who did not take her eyes off the girl for one instant. As they advanced, Catch moved without looking back to take his position at the chancel step. The congregation settled as the procession reached him, affected after the initial curiosity by the underlying, still strangeness of the occasion.

The bride was placed beside the groom. She did not think of him. He was too large and vague. The dominant presence for her was Miss Clack. She had allowed herself, that morning, to be dressed in this extravagance, ribboned and laced tight, and, with ten minutes before the carriage was due to leave, she had slipped away to Miss Clack's room for a moment's silent valediction. She had found Miss Clack as usual in her chair, staring out. She had come beside her and had touched her arm, had knelt and had put her cheek upon the rigid knuckles; and when she had looked up, Miss Clack had been looking at her again. She had stood up, away from the old woman, half-afraid, half-proud; showing her finery. Miss Clack had risen then from her chair and had come forward, had taken the girl's arm and had come downstairs. Greeted with warm surprise by her nephew, she had not said a word. Edwina's maid had lost her place in the family carriage and Miss Clack, dressed as she was, looking all the while at her protégée with unalterable features, had silently taken over the whole proceeding; was still there as the girl stood at the altar and as the vicar wallowed into his rubrics, and with that bulk that was her new life beside her; was still watching her with the rigour and purity of her love. The girl did not know whether she was betraying Miss Clack or not: it was a real concern and it tempted her, at sudden moments in the protracted rigmarole, to turn and flee, to shake it all off. But the thought of those eyes upon her back, those eyes which seemed to animate such impulses within her, pinned her paradoxically where she was.

There was a pause in the proceeding and she looked up to find the parson glaring down furiously at her. She nodded strongly. She heard John Stone's voice behind her and Catch's voice beside her. Her hand was lifted and, in a gesture which she had not in the slightest expected, a thin golden ring was slid on to her finger where it beamed against her flesh. It was a beautiful gesture. She looked up at Catch who stooped in front of them all and bristled a kiss upon her cheek. Tears of embarrassment and pleasure filled her eyes and she was borne away on his arm in a mist of emotions with the organ squeaking and clattering and the people in the church all humming with approval; and out into the sunlight and a roaring cheer with petals and grains cast into the sky and cascading about them.

She recalled little of the ensuing revelry. She heard a fiddler who, at one point, touched a tune that she remembered from long ago. It bewildered her and she wanted to go in search of the tune but found that large weight upon her arm, upon which she leant hurriedly. They gave her wine to drink which was sour in her throat and heavy behind her eyes. They brought her morsels to eat, mainly sweet, cloying things that went down into the nervousness of her belly and induced little waves of nausea. Above all there was brightness in the air above, blue brightness, clarity and birdsong; but on the ground, all about her, were gaudy bodies, red faces, profusions of hair and flowers and ribbons and little sparkling bells; faces that came close to her with kisses and curiosities. Catch had his arm hooked about her and held her close.

They were not there long. Soon he lifted her up and she was in the trap with him sprung up beside her, flicking the reins. The crowd were below them now, moving against the movement of the trap. They seemed small, a thin bunch, cheering and shouting and throwing their little tokens up from way below her. She was up in the air now. She looked around for Miss Clack as they passed through, raised her hand in response to the raised kerchiefs and caps, but looking for that tall black certainty with the eyes that were always upon her. She could not see her, and they rose quickly out of the village with the stillness of the woods spreading around them.

They came to the house and only then did her awareness settle fully upon him – her husband. He was silent, looking ahead, his face stern but held so, she felt, deliberately, restraining a pleasure within it. She leant against him to support and receive that pleasure. She would have to take her pleasure in him as she found him, be glad of him as he was, and as he would make her.

He pulled up at the door and sprang down from the trap. Walking round he reached up his arms for her and she let herself down into his strength, was lifted up and borne across the threshold, a gesture which, for a moment, promised everything. He placed her down upon the hearth and stood away from her.

'You are Mag Catch of Cutchknoll now,' he said admiringly. 'This is your home. I am a man of my word. What is mine is now yours too.'

She registered her appreciation of this clearly.

'I've a present for you.'

He went to a cupboard and returned bearing a large white chamberpot. She accepted it and leant up her face for a kiss, which she also received.

Her few belongings had, by arrangement, been transferred
from a Palmead wagon into Catch's trap, a couple of bundles
of clothes, which he collected and bore upstairs to the
bedroom. Edwina's maid had come into her room the night
before and had traded all her formal gowns for more service-
able smocks and underlinen. Catch came down and said that
he expected that she'd want to change now. Bearing her
present, she went up and struggled to find a way out of her
finery: she had had two maids helping her into it. She
considered going down to ask for his help but decided, in
the end, to find her scissors and to unseam her way out. She
put on a plain brown dress, rough, tight about her upper
body, full below; and she freed her hair from its braiding,
brushing it out and plaiting it in the long hank which, next
to its flowing free, she preferred.

He had placed a small ungainly pot of wild flowers in the
window. She was touched by this. She wondered how else
he had prepared his house for her. The bed had clean, if
musty, linen, and a bar had been fixed up, other pegs where
presumably she was to hang her clothes. She set to to undo
her bundles, discovering that the girl had put in much more
than she had traded, had interleaved the many, many garments and lengths of stuff with little bags of fresh lavender;
here was a whole plundering of the depths of Palmead,
packed with detail, with affection. She felt the sorrow of its
silence.

At last done, she came downstairs into the living-room.
He was not there as she had imagined him, waiting for her.
She went out in search of him. He was round by the stable,
brushing down the horse which stood patiently, its head
down, its eye languid, its brown flanks relaxed. She came
beside it and touched its forequarter which was warm and
tough. She looked at Catch who looked up briefly than
continued his grooming. The brushing, she felt, was not
strictly necessary but was a task to keep him from the house
whilst she attended to herself. She stood in the workshop

doorway, noting how he moved in awareness of her, whilst ignoring her superficially. She waited awhile, then wandered away, sauntered down towards the garden, looking down towards the stream, up into the woods beyond with the afternoon sun beginning to throw shadows down to fill up the steep meadow. So much of the day had slipped away unnoticed: there had been a blur and here she was again, starting off again.

A sense of peace and distance grew in her. She could barely now recall the hurly-burly of the village green. She wanted to be busy, to immerse herself in the work of this place, to establish her belonging here. She went back to the stable but he had gone. He had led the horse out to the meadow at the head of the valley. He smoothed its flanks and slapped, and the horse moved away to browse in the thick grass. He came down towards her, removing his jacket and unfastening his collar. She held out her arms and received the jacket, folded it over her forearm. They walked together into the workshop. He paused by a half-barrel full of water and she watched as he dipped a broad basin in, set it on the workbench, rolled up his sleeves and plunged in his face, pulling back gasping and snorting, scouring and saturating the depths of his hair. She looked for the towel which must be to hand, found it and had it held out open ready for him. He glanced at her, pleased by her attention, smiling but, she thought, wary of her, uncertain of proximity, her power, burying his face in the towel for a moment.

'I bring water up from the stream,' he said. 'There's the bucket. You could do that if you like.'

She took the bucket, which was heavy enough empty, and went through the living-room, down the meadow to the bridge, kneeling upon it and swinging the bucket into the bright rush. Its weight then was startling, all that brightness suddenly become a black unbalancing, a depth that pulled and slopped as she toiled back up the path to the house. He was undoubtedly watching her. She reached the water barrel gladly and felt suitably proud of the thick shoot of water as she tipped her load. Although her muscles shrieked, the barrel would hold another bucketful. She turned to go back.

'That'll do us tonight, Mag.'

She looked round to see him at the top of the stairs, at the bedroom door. He was barelegged, a coarse working shirt down to his thighs.

'Fill it in the morning, that's best.' He went into the bedroom but, by the time she had rehung the bucket, with difficulty, he had reappeared. 'You can manage that old bucket? I'll get you a pail.' He pulled up his working trousers and stuffed his shirt into them. 'Can you light a fire, Mag? No? I'll show you how when I've got my boots on.'

She collected his jacket and ran up the stairs with it, wanting to be with him in the bedroom again, eager for the nearness of him. He sat on the bed lacing his boots. She dropped the jacket and knelt down to help him. He permitted her, amused again, watching her fumble with the spare length of bootlace before stooping over and showing her how it was done, binding the lace round and round the high sides of the solid boots. She watched his adept fingers and she touched his hands, tracing the sinews, smoothing the hair. She seemed to still them with her touch, render them purposeless: he did not draw them away, but they grew strange under her touch. She lifted his hands to her face, placed them on her cheeks but did not look up at him, resting her face in the curves of his palms, closing her eyes.

He showed her how to light the fire in a nest of shavings under a bivouac of kindlings, how to coax the flame into a little rage that would achieve its own perpetuation. There was an old oven by the workshop fire that he said he would refurbish for her so that she could try bread and pastries. He had known these things as a child but, living on his own, he had given up such refinements – bought his bread in the village, bought salty bacon, snared a rabbit, culled out a chicken now and then. His vegetables did well. He had a couple of strong apple trees in the meadow round the back which fed his cider press.

She went into the hen run on his directions, watched over by him, and scattered the corn into the run. She collected the eggs and took them to the house in the basket he always used. They would eat eggs that evening with a mess of boiled cabbage and bone stock. She had a specific open glance for him that he interpreted quickly as her admission of ignorance, and he at once showed her whatever it was. She had no culinary skill; but he was a cornucopia of ingenious dexterities and she was minutely attentive. As the sun sank deep down behind the trees and the swaddling shadows filled the valley to the brim, they sat down to eat.

She refused the chair, had noticed a small stool tucked away under a bench in the workshop and she ran to fetch this. The fire in the workshop, upon which the cooking had been done, was carefully dampened, the unconsumed logs withdrawn. The fire in the living-room was kindled and before it they sat and ate. He spoke in slow, disconnected sentences suspended between long, replete pauses, smoothing her with his voice. He spoke about the woods, the mushrooms and the berries that were to be gathered there, the herbs and roots. The life ahead of her seemed miraculously detailed.

The meal was plainly good and she matched him beaker for beaker of cider. He had acquired a new, matching pair of pewter cans for them. They were capacious cans and her head, consequently, began to blur and, when it was dark and he lit the candles, her retirement was inevitable. He gave her a candle and she made her way up, concentrating upon the fragile little flame, aware as he had made her of its perils amongst drapes and linen in a crowded wooden space. Upstairs she undressed quickly, burrowed into a nightsmock and waited for him to come up. She heard his moving, listened for a long time while he went out, came back, went into the workshop, clattered about, bolted and shuttered; by which time the candle had burnt down and she, lying on the unopened bedcovers, was asleep.

She awoke thus at the dead of night in utter silence. She was alone. She slipped from the bed, cold and numb, and fumbled her way to the stairhead. She was aware of him in the living-room before she had come down far enough to see him. She had woken him in her descent. He was rousing. She could hear his chair creak. There was still a tiny glimmer deep in the grate. She stood at the foot of the stair, isolated by the cold. He struck a match and lit a candle. He was sitting unbooted and unbuttoned. He looked caught out, unsure.

'You go back to bed, Mag,' he said. 'I'll look after things down here.'

She stood where she was but he did not come.

'Go on, now.'

She came across to him and, gathering her nightsmock, she settled at his feet, her head in his lap. She had to set herself against the shuddering cold and damp night; but she was not going to let him off. He sat rigidly under her weight, but he did not extinguish the candle. She could hear its flicker, hear his restrained breathing. Finally, though, she could not control the shivering. When the chill had been on the surface of her flesh, she had been able to hold it, but it had gone beneath the surface, had penetrated muscle and bone and she had to submit to it, clinging tightly on to his heavy knees, shuddering through and through.

'You're cold,' he said at last.

She did not think this worth a response.

'Go on, then. You'll be warmer upstairs.'

She looked up and glared at him, keeping her grip, exaggerating the shudder.

'Shall I carry you up, Mag? Would you like that of me?'

She sighed, extricated herself and rose. He heaved himself from the chair and reached out his arms, stooping to her, one arm under her legs, one at her back. She folded neatly into his support and he swung her up, stooping down again to blow the candle out.

Swinging up in his arms through the darkness with the wall-bulks about her, light and loose against him as his heavy steps found the stairtreads one by one, warm upon him with the cold clinging at her feet and face, the discomforts fell at once from her, and a dreaming half-sleep took her. He moved up the narrow staircase and under the low joists with the assurance of custom.

At the bedside he lowered her. She clung on but he unwrapped her arms from his neck. She was awake again at once and ready to follow him back downstairs, dropping off the bed and catching at him, pulling him, or at least his clothes, back.

'Very well, then,' he said, 'very well. I only thought you'd be easier on your own for the first bit at least. If you want . . . Get in now. You'll be frozen. I'll . . .'

She clambered into the bed and shivered, turned and twisted herself about to try to generate a little warmth, as well as to master and direct her expectancy which stirred under the slow sounds of his undressing. She heard his trousers fall, the shirt rustle over his head, the struggle into the nightsmock. He drew back the covers, admitting a vast cavern of cold air which he filled with his bulk, lowering himself into it and lying on his back. She drew away, letting him settle, and then, in one quick movement, she nestled herself against him, her head upon his chest, her arms across him, her leg cocked up across his flank. He remained massively still and she had to dream of his rising to her; but it was an easy, fluid dream, at first awake and then quickly into sleep where it took over and was a long, slow rush to fulfilment; and after this fulfilment she awoke at once, exactly as she had fallen asleep, with him lying awake as she had left him, breathing seriously and closely, now with the dawn light streaming in.

She eased herself away from him. He stared up at the ceiling, hands behind his head. She slipped from the bed and baptised the chamberpot loudly. When she looked back his head had turned, and he was watching her. They exchanged a smile that began uncertainly but which developed into complicity. Her life at Cutchknoll was properly begun.

Her days were now filled with activity, with hard physical work: she drew the water and scrubbed the floor of the living-room; she peeled and pared the vegetables; she washed clothes; she cooked; she learnt to skin rabbits, to pluck chickens, to pick out the edible offal from the fowl in drawing. She watched him kill the birds which he did one-handed, ostentatious, picking them up by the neck and silencing the flapping and squawking with a slow, cruel tightening of his fist, the eyes going wide then dead, the head lolling, the legs paddling the air briefly. He would then catch up the legs, dangle down the head and open the neck with a knife over a basin which she held ready. He did not, mercifully, expect her to learn this craft.

Under Miss Clack she had learnt a competence with a needle and thread, and she patched his clothes, made curtains out of the satin of her wedding-dress. She wandered into the meadow to pick flowers. She busied herself infinitely on the edge of a circle of which he was the centre. Everything she did, she did with the awareness of him there, in the stables or the garden, in the yard or up in the meadow, and mostly in the workshop bent over his making. She would often be drawn in to watch him and felt that this pleased him. She felt that she pleased him in everything. Even if she did badly, it pleased him to come and show her where she was wrong: to show her how to sprinkle water on the dust before she swept, to soak the greens in salted water to dislodge the tiny slugs, to hoe the rows of vegetables neatly, quickly and with the minimum effort. She learnt well.

He went into the village every few days and brought back bread and bacon, brought the promised pail, some oilcloth for the table, a cushion for her stool: over the weeks, item by item, nesting round her. He also went, for longer times, to his work. She never went with him, but when he was absent she felt her motivation sag. She frittered away the time in trivialities between long minutes spent standing out in the garden, looking down the track for his return, ashamed of having been caught thus. During the early weeks of their marriage he was never gone for more than a few hours.

He made her many things over those weeks. He replaced the stool with a chair, a perfect little companion to his, with a stout back and arms. He repaired the oven and spent a morning up on the roof cleaning out and repairing its chimney. He spoke of building an extension to the house, a washroom and a larder, an extension to the living-room, an extension of the bedroom storey out over the workshop. He spoke of such things speculatively, setting himself problems to solve, walking round and calculating the work, the materials, the processes and preparations required, constructing with gesture and enthusiasm, performing for an intent and avid audience. Next year, he said, he would build for her: he would make a manor-house about her. Meanwhile he built cupboards and tight, deep shelves for the new plates and new cups he brought back from his excursions. He set up a washing tub, a mirror for her in the bedroom in which she found her tanning, tightening features growing strange.

She began to wear her hair hung loose over her shoulders and back, her long, red hair, braiding it with flowers, brushing and plaiting it with much attention, much joy. Her dresses were clean and bright; she enjoyed their cleanness, their freedoms. When at work, she tied her hair in a scarf, but in the evening when they sat to supper, she would loosen her hair and loosen her bodice, sitting in the chair at his feet and feeling the toils and strains of the day easing from her.

This was the best of the day, with a jug of cider drawn and Catch sucking at his pipe and a replete silence between them, with the pull of sleep coming with the dark and the settling of the fire which grew grey at the edges of its final knots of heat. She would gaze into the complexities and shifts of the fire but conscious always of his regard of her which was as solid as his silence. Now and then, particularly in the early days, she would glance up and smile at him. His watching would not usually register these smiles: the final contentment which had settled into his broad, dense features would only be confirmed by these smiles; and soon enough they became unnecessary for her too. She knew how he looked at her and she was as easy in the glow of his regard as she was in the fireglow.

Her presence in the valley, so far, was a passive presence; but she did not despair of bringing soon some aspect of its life under her active influence, rooting herself independently. But so far she was caught up in it and carried through the bright days to the soft, sinking evenings, a succession of strong waves of living that seemed, if not actually propelling her from without, to be supporting her clearly.

She would rise from the fire eventually and go before him up to bed, rinsing her face and neck in cold water that woke her surface, briefly, making it burn and then subside more rapidly towards warmth and sleep. She undressed quickly in the darkness, afraid of the night air upon her solitary nakedness, burrowing herself into a thick nightsmock and burying herself in bedclothes. She could not, would not, submit to sleep until he came, however. At the sound of her settling, he came up slowly, and undressed, and lay down beside her. She gave him a few moments' silence, and then spread herself quickly to sleep up against him in a posture that soon became customary and easy, and at last, natural. She could not sleep otherwise.

Although she washed every morning, sharpened herself after he had gone down with more cold water, she missed the long tubs of Palmead and St Thomas's. Such indulgences were long behind her, and she did not regret them; but she did feel the need to bathe, to douse and scour herself in a full tub of hot water; a need that was particularly acute after her menstruations. She wanted to soak and sponge her flesh, thoroughly loosening the grime that she felt gathering in its crevices, beyond the numbing of any cold douche.

She had noted in the workshop a large copper hip-bath and her desires began to take practical shape. It would have to be the operation of an evening, before the living-room grate. She was at first deterred by the possibilities of his reactions to her nakedness. He would probably go out into the meadow or into the workshop: she didn't want to drive him away from their evening. He might not go, though, he might stay and watch her; and the imagining of that was the reverse of a deterrent to her. It took her a while to summon the resolution for this but, fixing on a day, and aware of her resolution as the afternoon developed, as evening came and supper was partaken, she grew progressively nervous, progressively excited, feeding on that excitement.

After supper, after the clearing of the table, instead of settling she went to the workshop door and beckoned him. He had already seated himself and had begun to fill his pipe, but he rose and came to her. She led him into the workshop and indicated the hip-bath. He comprehended, at least on a practical level, what she was about, looking up at where it hung, considering whether it would be difficult to bring down; which she knew it would not be. He fetched a step-ladder, climbed and cut down the bath, lowering it to her. It was heavy and it clattered down, pushing her over. He laughed but she was not to be daunted. It had a handle at the back and she tried to pull it across the dirt floor. He asked her where she wanted it and she made a feint of considering to have it before the workshop fire, changing her mind after a moment, indicating the chosen ground, the living-room hearth. He looked at her slyly, distrustfully, but she was all practicality and he did as he was bidden. He sat back at his pipe, not lighting it, but watching her, pressing down the tobacco and bringing the stem frequently to his mouth.

She meanwhile wiped out the dusty interior of the tub, determining to polish it up tomorrow into an object of prestige. She heated a kettle at the living-room grate, but soon realised that it would be a very long process before the bath would be full enough to make her operation credible. He appreciated this and went through to the workshop fire, stoking it back to life, putting a great copper on the large grate and bellowing up the flames under it. When it was ready, he bore it through and tipped it into the bath, a great steaming rush of it, leaving her to apply pitchers of cold water to take it down to the level of fleshly tolerability. It was a satisfyingly full tub by the time she'd finished; and a large tub too, in which she could immerse her small frame. She had brought towels, began to prepare herself, unlacing her boots, unrolling her stockings, but not yet unloosing the central reserves of her modesty. She waited until he was seated, until the pipe was well lit. If she was preparing to perform for him, then he seemed willing enough to be audience. The little room was hung with dampness and it grew cold and clammy at the edge of her excitement. She stood with her back to him as she unbuttoned and unlaced.

She did not face him at all, stepping from her garments and laying them neatly upon her chair. The first real nakedness she presented him then was the hill of her back, her protuberant spine. She had not designed it thus, but she was glad of the idea when it came to her. She was not trying to entice him with her flesh, not directly: she was trying to present him with the fact of her, to arouse firstly his curiosity. She was trying to breach not the denial of sexuality which he tacitly maintained, but the ritual of modesty they had together unwittingly established. Naked and with the hand of her deformity pushing her over, she stepped and sank into her bath.

She revelled in the water, in its sensuality. She ran a soapy cloth about her breasts, in the cleft of her arse, amongst the soft complexities of her sex. She did not neglect the other areas of her flesh, but to those places, their secrets at last out, she paid particularly indulgent attention. She did not look at him but felt, now and then, coming up from the absorptions of her pleasure, the steady weight of his watching. He was watching her as he watched her always, from a distance; closely and warmly but from his solid distance.

She washed her hair, tipping cupfuls of the water over her scalp and burrowing her fingers into the matted length of it, scratching the grime out of its roots. This was an awkward procedure for her in this cramped tub, and she needed his assistance; but she was quite unable to indicate this need to him. She finished quickly and rose dripping and shining, wrapping herself in towels, burnishing herself dry and slipping into a clean nightsmock, her wet hair turbanned up. Only then did she look at him, to see him considering her just as she had known he would be, precisely as she had known he would be.

But there was something more, an idea on his face which she questioned at once.

'Shame to waste all that fetching and carrying and brewing up,' he said. 'I've not bathed myself like that in years. Looks fine enough.' He rose and began to undress.

She was alarmed by this, an extension of her ploy. She tidied her clothes and took them up to the bedroom, towelling her hair in the dark up there and taking time before coming down again with a clean nightsmock for him.

He was in the tub soaping himself fiercely but patchily. She did not come too close, finding occupation in the tidying of his clothes, the laying out of dry towels; but she could not keep away for long, drawn by the involuntary glimpses of his great hairy torso crammed into the tub, pressing against the sides with much water slopped out on to the floor. She came to him and stood over him.

She rolled up her sleeves and plunged her hands into the water. He drew back, wondering what she was about. She found the soap down by his toes and took it and set about soaping him systematically. He submitted, leaning forward. She tipped water over his head and thrust her fingers into his thatch as he spluttered. She raked into his scalp, down over his shoulders and across the whole sack of his body which was taut with packed muscle and dark with shag. He remained quite still and she delighted in touching him, her fingers only ostensibly working, far keener to receive than to bestow. She tested the texture, solidity and breadth of him. He was exactly as she had known he would be. He was beautiful, a great beast. She resisted the temptation to nip into his shoulder muscle with her teeth. She did not prolong this indulgence, had soon rinsed him down and was holding the towel out for him.

He heaved himself out of the tub, unjammed his hips from its sides and rose to face her. She saw how the broad span of his chest was betrayed into a little roundness, a little sag at the belly; and she saw how the hairs swept together down that belly into a little tufty crest of hair that was lost in the mass about his fat cock which was surprising in its baldness and its childish simplicity. She noted how the little complex of his private parts, upon which was her curiosity could hardly in these brief moments be satisfied, was dominated by the massive pelted thighs upon which his frame was supported.

He submitted to this brief inspection, wiping the water out of his face, but watching her. He accepted this curiosity in her as a part of the same need that had driven her to display herself to him, and he thought little of it. There was no need of the modesties of manors here. He had been glad to have a look at her womanly parts, had himself been curious – about the swell of her breasts particularly, with which he found himself pleased. He had been surprised by the hairiness at the arches of her body. She was more comprehensible to him now.

The bathing was thereafter established as a weekly ritual, the modesties abolished between them permanently. Their life together attained a unity of action and an acceptance of each other's presence which expanded to fill the brief and busy hours.

As autumn drew on, he began to take her into the woods, showing her mushrooms and berries to gather, familiarising her with paths and clearings within reach of the house that gave her a new freedom to explore on her own. She grew to love the woods, reaffirming the responses she had discovered on her first flight from Palmead. Autumn brought its deep russets into the woods and she would find an hour or two, now and then, to sit alone on a favourite fallen trunk to breathe in the damp and decay, the melancholy of the year's decline. He knew where to find her and would appear suddenly beside her, standing away from her and watching her. She usually sensed his approach but rarely heard him until he came into view. She felt that he was nowhere more appropriately met than amongst the trees, in the shadows, his boots deep in leaf-litter and his breath hung in the permanent mist of the trees. She would never have that completion here. She loved the woods, the solitude and the absorption, the unreflective purpose. She came here to look and to enhance her awareness of it and of its power in him, but she could never be possessed by it as he was. She belonged in the house and, although when deep in the atmosphere of the woods she might regret, distantly, that it would never be hers, it was a sentimental regret. She knew that, at least for her, what had to be done was to be done indoors, across the hearth, to him from her; and that it was finally a far more complex thing than anything that rose and flourished and fell in the seasons of the wood. She stood and crossed the clearing to greet him. They returned together, silent and close, coming out above the valley and the house, as if breaking from a trance, returning from a journey.

— 4 —

Winter came. Their lives were contracted more closely into the house and its immediate vicinity, about the fireplaces which devoured log piles which he cut and she carried. In the stall of the stable they made the cider, mashing the apples and the straw, setting up the press, casking the sour juice to ferment. The first real frosts came making the grass and the air brittle, the water in the stream acid to the touch. Mag felt the cold. The layer of soft flesh that had swaddled her when she had arrived here had been used up. She was lean and growing knotty, and the onset of winter caught her loose in her clothes, her skin continually subject to shiverings, her fingers to numbness as she worked amongst the chickens or in the vegetable patch, or fetched up the water. The evenings became a thawing time, her flesh recovering its substance briefly before the warmth of sleep lulled her. Catch seemed quite oblivious to these difficulties in her. She spent more time in concentrated mastering of the cold and less time, therefore, in developing her awareness of him. They grew more solitary in winter: Catch didn't mind and she had no energy for resentment.

It was a surprise when their first visitor arrived after so many months in which they had been their own entire world. She was out in the garden, tugging fat roots out of the unwilling soil, labouring hard against the wind which ran down the valley in a constant bitter rush. She was aware of the horse distantly, but was too absorbed to stop, too cold to break rhythm. Only when he came close did she look up and see him. He was a thin man on a thin horse, a man with a blue face and thick, wet moustache. His eyes were small and greedy. She disliked him at once. He wore a heavy greatcoat and some official cap, the brim of which he touched in a minimal salutation. He did not dismount.

He observed her standing there amidst her turnips, and then he laughed, once. He beckoned her. She struggled towards him, but not too close.

'So you're what he's married. I'd not've believed it, not in a hundred years.' He laughed.

Catch suddenly appeared, coming rapidly from behind the house, his face animated and his approach fired. The rider leant up and his horse stirred under him, causing him to rein in and turn the creature round to master it. Steam rose from its flanks and jetted from its nostrils: it seemed more machine than creature, strapped and tackled and jangling.

'Mag, go inside,' Catch said. 'Go on. Quickly.'

She resented this, hung back a little; but he was not to be provoked in this and she slopped back to the house, leaving her spade lying in the soil in flagrant disrespect. She went to the window and saw Catch reading a paper the rider had brought him. When he had read it, he looked back at the house and she withdrew from the window into the middle of the room, knowing that she would be invisible now, keeping him still in sight. He nodded at the rider and stuffed the paper down into his breeches pocket. The rider turned at once and trotted away. Catch came straight to the house.

She was busy at the fire when he came in, chafing her hands before it.

'You'll rheumatic yourself if you warm yourself so close after cold work, Mag. I've told you before.'

She retreated sulkily and sat upon her chair, waiting to be enlightened.

'Today's Wednesday,' he said. 'Thursday week I've to be in town. Town business. I'll be back Friday, before dark. You'll manage by yourself for the one night.'

This was dogmatic and it betrayed a secrecy against which she bridled. She had to endure it: he would not tell her. She sulked continuously over the intervening days, not dramatically, but restlessly and pettily, refusing his smiles, lumping her body against him in bed. She was certain that he was receiving the signals of her disaffection; but he drew himself up tightly and did not speak of it again.

On the Thursday, after the midday meal, he went up and changed into his suit. He went into the depths of the workroom and appeared, ready for his journey with a small black box with a carrying strap. This she had never seen before. She thought he would just leave her to it and she regretted her week's churlishness; but he paused, came in to her and touched her face kindly.

'I'll buy you something pretty,' he said. 'Lock up tight and sleep well. I'll be back before nightfall. Think of me specially as the dawn breaks.'

She could not help herself, after an initial resistance, from running out to the track and watching him striding out along the path, weighted by the black box, solid and silent. He was someone else as he went, someone she did not know. She ran after him a little way. She saw him reach the road. He turned away from the village and she turned and ran back to the house, oppressed by its solitude, by its strangeness in his absence, and by her helplessness there. She sat down before the fire and wept.

*

It was to be a double execution. Two lads, Crowler and Tush, had got drunk and had smashed their way into the house of a solitary old coal merchant to demand his money, and Crowler had ended up stoving in his skull with an iron crow. They had bashed about the house in futile rage and the constabulary had had a considerable struggle to subdue the raging Crowler. Tush, overcome by the drink, had come quietly if messily.

The trial and sentence had been routine. Tush howled loudly from the dock and continued, through the intervening days and nights, to howl against Crowler, against the warders, the Governor and the approaching inevitability. Not only did he himself fail to find any dignity, he effectively prevented Crowler from finding any either. Crowler brooded in silence but could not avoid the incessant wailings from the adjacent dead end. They had originally been exercised together, Governor Bosker hoping that they might find some mutual resolution; but Crowler had torn from his escort and had nearly deprived Catch of his double fee. Seven men had been necessary to subdue him. They would meet only once more, on the way to the scaffold.

Catch was advised of all this as soon as he arrived at the prison by the officer whose thankless task it was to officiate with him in the morning. Catch at once went to Bosker and respectfully insisted that they should go separately, at an interval of half an hour, Tush first. The Governor had determined on the double-drop, however, had had the carpenters checking beam and trap. It was just and proper that they should go together. It had been done thus before. It was decided. He glossed over any difficulties, but Catch sensed his evasion.

As he made his preparations, peered into the dim cells to appraise them one by one, calculating their individual drops, as he prepared the ropes and straps, he thought mostly of the Governor's obstinacy; and he concluded that it was a plot against the immaculacy of his craft. He resented it profoundly, thought of putting his disquietude down in writing, having it witnessed, handing it, and thus the responsibility of it, to Bosker. But this, of course, would be to kiss defeat. Let it happen as it would. He would take the consequences. He felt himself go hard inside.

In the event there was no incident. Crowler was awed at once by the hangman's confidential bulk as it elbowed into his cell. Catch had him led out first and had made sure that the wrist-straps bit into any tension before he went in for Tush who shrank back, wailed briefly then collapsed and had to be lifted lolling from his cell, his feet pedalling automatically all the way out and up. Only on the trap did he find a brief strength to support himself. Catch trussed and noosed them back to back, dropped them perfectly, the snapping of their separate falls indistinguishable.

Catch was greeted with warm effusions of relief, hand-shakes, offers of conviviality from the gathered warders, an unnecessarily large number of whom had stood nervously attendant upon the event. Catch acknowledged them but shouldered solidly through them. He finished his work in the gallows-yard and made his way up to the Governor's office to sign the papers and to collect his fees.

Bosker seemed preoccupied and hardly stirred at his entrance. Catch signed and countersigned the waiting forms with the waiting steel pen. The Governor wrote in a fat ledger. Catch watched him, amused, took the man's refusal to countenance him as a sign of his having been thwarted in his desire to see the hangman faulted. Catch was gratified, stretched his muscles in the confines of his suit until he creaked insolently; after which he sighed loudly. The Governor continued to write, evenly and precisely.

'No troubles, then, sir,' he could not resist saying.

'You find satisfaction in your work here, don't you, hangman?' Bosker said without looking up, without ceasing the neat sequences of his pen, dipping and dotting and curving along an invisible but rigid line.

'I do my duty, sir,' Catch said. 'I take satisfaction in the perfection of my office, sir.'

The governor looked down at his ledger again, reached into a drawer and dumped the money in a little paper packet on the desk-top.

Catch waited a little while, then stepped up smartly and collected his fee.

'Will that be all, sir?'

Bosker nodded and Catch turned to go.

'You're married now, they tell me, hangman.'

Catch halted, turned back. The head over the ledger had not lifted.

'Sir.'

'Does your wife approve of your official craft?'

'Sir.'

Catch felt the tightness again, and underneath it the violence of which it was the instinctive control.

Bosker looked up to dip his pen. 'Forgive me, hangman. I'm curious. I wonder how hands that have strapped and noosed and hooded and dropped a man, two men, in a morning, can touch a woman in the way of love in the evening.'

Catch faced him squarely, this hideous man with the melted face, its one clear eye wet and distant, the mouth jerked to one side in a permanent parody of a grin.

Catch turned abruptly and barged out. He left the prison vowing he would never return, that he would never again put himself at the risk of such defilement as he had endured that day. Nothing had gone wrong. He tried to reassure himself with this but could not – it felt as if everything had gone wrong. And although he could not have identified it, everything *had* gone wrong. Catch's anger was without limit. He felt as if the Governor had touched him intimately, obscenely. He strode out into the bitter streets, seething.

Finding his way to one of the main thoroughfares that ran out through the outer clusterings of the city, he strode homeward, the icy day clearing and calming him. He recalled his promise to fetch Mag a present and, fingering the twist of guineas in his pocket, he glanced about for a shop. It was not, however, a distict of shops, and the grimy provision stores, cluttered ironmongeries, dirty butchers' and grocers' shops offered him no incentives. He wanted to be extravagant and here was only meanness. Turning from shop front to shop front bred a frustration in him. His impulse to delight her sank into an obligation, a chore, a weight that held him there in these dismal environs, stopped his flight for the open roads, for the safety of his valley. Eventually, stymied, he turned into a side alley and found a drinking shop.

He sat at a table, his black box upon his knee, and was plied with glass after glass of oily gin. The barman viewed him avariciously. Catch knew that he was being cheated; it made him angry, but it was an anger he nursed and nurtured, and fuelled with more gin. Very few other customers visited the place and he grew drunk in solitude.

After an hour or so Catch's brain was sliding about in the gin, and he knew that he would soon have to go and vomit somewhere. A thin woman with a black satin dress that opened to expose the ridges of her collar bone and the sad cleft of her breasts, a whore with hardly the strength to lift her face to him, came and sat at his table. He was too drunk to rouse against her with anything other than physical violence: he sat mute. She too sat mute, watching him, waiting, feeding his slipping glances at her with thin smiles.

In a succession of discrete clarities, he found himself out in the street with the whore swinging at his elbow. Later he stood over a drain and disgorged his poison. Later he was backed into an alley corner with the whore at him, her hands busy and functional, in and out of his pockets, at the front of his trousers. At the latter rifling he pushed her down. She sat on the ground below him and laughed at him, her skirts up over her knees. The laughter filled the whole alley, became part of its texture of mould and brick and refuse. He swung his black box at her. Somehow he still had it, clamped rigid in his left fist. As it swung it connected with nothing and he was swung off his feet, crashing on to his knees. Later he was on the road home, the icy air like a hoof-mark in his chest, his limbs working automatically, sometimes numbed, sometimes thick with aching. The road was steeped in icy mist and at times he felt that he had lost his way, that he was wandering towards an infinite end of the earth. The road was puddled and uneven and frequently the momentum of his stride was thwarted by stumbles, by the jag of stones or the slip of mire. He did not see, or was not aware of, another creature on the road.

The ache of the gin in his brain was clarified and stilled by the cold. The events of the day returned to him, not in their specifics, but in a general disgust and fury. A surge of degradation had risen up around him, had broken over him now. He drove himself on towards Cutchknoll with the thought of solitude, of concealment before him. He would not serve them any more. He would write his resignation. He would plough up the road into the valley, would plant it with young trees, would allow the wood to close around him.

Later he remembered Mag and the thought of her halted him at once. He burrowed into his pockets but the money was all gone. He was cheated even of that. He was returning to her befouled. He would disgust her. He could not bear it. He began to move forward again because he had no other course open to him; but he was advancing not upon solitude, not upon concealment, but upon continuing shame and failure. He began to resent her, to wish her gone; began to realise that she was a part of that from which he was fleeing. She had invaded him. She deprived him of his peace, of his sanctuary. He would give her money and would send her away. The details of their months together crystallised within him, involuntarily, and he grew angry again, walked faster, felt the outrage swelling him, felt it fire him with purpose again.

He would purge his home of her. He would find her and destroy her. The extremity of the law held no terror for him above all men. She must be destroyed. He would take her to the stream and he would drown her. He imagined the holding of her in the water, felt her under his strong hands, her head and her back, pushing her into the black water, the bubbles gushing up through the wreathes of her floating hair. He felt her grow sodden and still. Strangely, his imagination of this scene, vivid and intense as it was, was set in the valley at the height of summer with the woods thick and laden, the wood-pigeons calling through the trees and the meadows thick with flowers. He lifted himself from the lump in the stream beneath him and gasped in the density of the summer twilight.

It was night when he came again into his valley.

Mag had spent a wretched night, clustered by dreams and strange sounds half-heard, half-imagined. She had broken from her sleep time and time again in a panic, haunted by images of falling trees smashing through the roof, the stream flooding and sucking her away on its flood, the house dissolving in torrential downpours which washed away the thatch, liquefied the mortar, soaked and burst the beams. Her waking had been into a night that was utterly

270

cold, utterly still, but without reassurance: what she had dreamed seemed on the very edge of happening. She had woken, finally, an hour or so before dawn, with a stabbing pain in her belly. The pain faded quickly once she had risen and urinated, but its shadow remained, the space where it had been, as if it was waiting for her to relax and forget about it before it struck again.

She had intended to prepare a great pie for his return, but had not managed to connect herself with its making, had drifted through the morning waiting for his return. She spent hours out on the track looking for him. The mist, which had lifted at dawn allowing a brightness to invest the valley for a few hours, returned, the sky seeming to sink down over the earth. It was pointless then to watch for him. She went in and found both fires out. It took an hour of frustration and weeping to rekindle them, but she achieved it at last, banked up the grates until they roared up the chimneys, frightening her. Close to the fires was an aura of heat which hardly extended two yards. The rest of the house was icy, filled with the icy darkness into which the afternoon began to sink.

She sat dumbly by the living-room fire, on her chair, huddled into a blanket and slept, awaking abruptly, finding him there amidst a swirl of darkness, slamming the door behind him. She roused at once on an impulse to run to him, but she could not see his face, only his bulk and that deterred her: the darkness defeated her. She fumbled with a taper in the fire and, with hands that shook, she brought its fierce light to the candles which flickered and guttered and then sent an even softness of light out into the room. She looked at him but he still seemed shadowed. Although she could see his features now, she could discern no expression: his eyes seemed lifeless. She recalled her good intentions and their failure. She ran guiltily to the windows to close the shutters, shoved staves into the grate. He came forward into the room and she dodged behind him to bolt the door and to draw the heavy curtain she had stitched to mask the draughts. She slipped back past him to lay the cold fowl on the table, to put the soup pot on the fire, to bring the loaf and the cider jug. As she moved about him, brushing quickly past him, she had noted a tension in him. She kept busy to keep herself from being afraid.

He lumbered forward into his chair. The black box was still clamped on to the end of his arm. She noted the reek of alcohol about him, and the rankness of vomit. He sat solidly, staring straight ahead. He made no move at the food she brought him, flickering his glance down at it once then away again. She stood back wondering what to do next. She thought that he might be going to faint, expected him to slump at any second, wished for it to happen.

Summoning her courage, she came to him, knelt down by him and touched his arm, smoothing, touching his clutched hand. She felt again, distinctly now, the tension in him. It brought a metallic taste to her lips. She lifted the black box and tugged at the fingers. They remained clamped. She tried lifting the box up on to the table and she found that the arm bent easily, that she could place the box on the table. She wanted to touch his face but did not dare to. Something in him had not arrived yet. Or he had brought something in with him that was obscuring him. He was not with her. But, trying his fingers again, they fell from the box strap and she lifted it away and placed it on the floor.

When she looked up again, his face was upon her. She stood and he stood, abruptly, and swayed, staggering a pace forward to catch his balance. She watched him suspended between movements, unsteady, uncertain, about to lunge at her, or fall down in a heap where he stood, or clump back down into the chair. Catching a breath, she rushed boldly at him and clasped his middle; hardly supporting him – he would only have to topple forward to crush her – but giving him some sort of buttress upon which to steady himself. She buried her face in the coarse, damp, reeking cloth of his suit through which his flesh was hardly imaginable, certainly not as the warm, supple masculinity against which she snuggled and dreamt. He was solid, tight and unyielding, his hands loose at his sides. She pressed herself closer against him, willing him to relax upon her, to be as he was, to be returned home safely.

It was then that she became aware of the intrusive lump pressed into her side. She remembered the present he'd promised to bring her. And then she realised what the lump was. She gasped and looked up for his face which she could not see, drawing back a fraction, quickly pressing herself upon him lest, heaven forbid, he should think her unamazed, lest the opportunity should subside, which would be tragic.

As the minutes expanded with the situation no further developed, another extraordinary realisation came to her. He was quite unaware, consciously, of the state that he was in. He showed no urgency, no purpose, just a contracted physical endurance. The fact of it, whatever he imagined it to be, had simply blocked him. She would have to be very, very careful. She would have to make all the moves. She could expect no assistance. She would have to move him into position and find some way of clambering on to him. Speculating on how this might be achieved, still chafing softly against him, still clung tightly to him, she felt her own pleasure, and the thrill of possibility made her thick with urgency, held delicately, painfully, only just.

That it would be dangerous, she knew certainly. He was charged with something that he did not apprehend, and violence would be the quickest way out for him if, in any way, she bewildered or affronted him too soon. Although, until today, she had never seen him in any mood but placid self-absorption, never in the valley at least, she had always known him to be capable of violence. She must be very, very careful.

She relaxed and drew away, taking his hand and pulling. He came with her. He moved in heavy starts, registering her briefly then lurching forward, threatening to overcome her. She reached the foot of the stairway gladly and drew him up behind her. His fingers curled round her wrist and gripped painfully. He forgot the beam, for the first time ever in her knowledge, and she heard his head clump, felt him caught. She found that she half-expected this and she had stopped to allow him to absorb the hurt. She felt him pull at her suddenly as if he was about to go crashing backwards. But she held and he held and, after a moment, he was coming up again after her. She had to scurry on to be ahead of him.

Once in the bedroom, in the darkness, he again grew ominous and still. She clasped herself around him again quickly to reassure herself that he had lost nothing of his condition. She was reassured. She clung tightly and moved against him closely, quickly, then deftly slipped away and, as she had planned, he buckled down on the bed, sitting for a moment then falling straight back, his legs dangling over the edge. Something in the bed frame cracked as if it was about to splinter. She was at his feet, undoing his boots, opening them and pulling them off. She rolled up his trouser legs and rolled down his stockings. She brushed her face against his cold, lumpish feet which twitched and sent a tremor up his torso.

Thinking and planning quickly, one move at a time, holding the excitement between her legs like an animal, she ran downstairs, closed up the fire which was burning now fiercely again, put a couple of things away. Then, taking a deep breath, she burrowed her skirts and undid the underdrawers that clad her rump, dropping them down and kicking them away into a corner. She stood with her legs apart then and untied her hair, shaking it out thickly and vividly, feeling then as if her head was ablaze. She took up a candle, blew out the others and rose, in a halo, back up to the bedroom.

He lay as she had left him, his feet dangled bare-toed over the bedside, palms lying opened by his sides, his face upturned and lost in beard; and the extrusion at the front of his trousers plainly visible. She placed the candle on the chest and went round to the far side of the bed. With much struggling, but not without his participation, albeit heavy and creaking, she removed his jacket and waistcoat, shaking them out and hanging them up. His eyes were open, blinking now and then. She peered close over him and unfastened his collar stud, pushing into the flesh of his neck and causing him to gurgle somewhere. She undid the buttons of his shirt, starting at the neck, coming to the trouser band. Below the superficial stink of his debaucheries, rose the stink of him as he was, the animal reek of him coming off loudly. She unbuttoned his trousers lifting the material away delicately, as if from a wound. She paused and looked to see if he was still awake. He had to be awake. He was still staring upward, unfocused, breathing in controlled sighs. He was settled into his own weight now, accepting her ministrations peripherally. He was about to be taken by surprise. She was at the point of it now.

She was no longer afraid. She no longer cared. She rolled him from side to side to unseat the trousers. She went down on to the floor and drew them off, shook and hung them, keeping her glance deflected. At last she came to it. His thick drawers still contained it, but it was pushing out the material. She reached over and with her fingertips undid the cords, folded back the cloth and out it rose, his long, thick sex, muscled and soft, straining clear of its shaggy nest, the foreskin peeling from the tip. He sighed. It lay back along his belly, a pulse clearly discernible along it.

She bundled her skirts up about her waist, kneeling on the bed beside him, watching his face. Her breath held in tight, she straddled him, which was difficult; and she had to bring her knees forward. At last in position, she reached down for him. As she took hold of him, the light came back into his eyes suddenly and he was looking at her. His mouth opened and she saw his teeth come together under the lips. She had one long moment of terror then, closing her eyes, she slipped him into her, placing her freed hands flat upon his chest.

The conscious willing of each moment which had led her to this was no longer needed. She was adrift. She allowed her body to take control. She rose and fell slowly; perhaps not actually, but a rising and falling sensation spiralled in her belly. Precise sensation was diffused as this spiral swelled in her. Before she had even had a moment to register the clear sensation of him within her, her completion was upon her. It had taken so long to arrive at this moment. It was the actuality of so much hoping and pretending ever since she had arrived here; before she had arrived here, stretching back to the rectory and beyond. The whole of her sexual apprehension had been primed, consciously and subconsciously; the moment she had taken and had sheathed his sex in hers, she was released. She was only aware of the spiral, her whole awareness was lost within it, slow and dark and burning deeply. At its centre it was obliterating, but as it wound outwards from that centre, the intensity dispersed into long, easy pulses. Her awareness seeped back gradually, moment by moment to reclaim the situation.

She began to distinguish the individual physical details, the tightness across her splayed thighs, painful but offset by the liquidity of her sex, the slithering clefts of tissue that moved about the precisely runnelled swelling of his. She could feel a pulse about its bulbed tip; whose it was, she could not have said. She became aware of the space between them as she lifted, the cold air entering between them to be pushed out again as they closed, flesh to flesh, her meagre tufts of sexual hair mingling with the promiscuous landscapes of his.

As her pleasure began to subside, as a warmth and dazzlement succeeded, as the movement continued, as a drip of sweat ran coldly over her shoulder and down between her breasts, she sank back into the quotidian, becoming aware of the body beneath her palms, the man spreading into reality about the dominance of his unshot cock. She didn't care anymore about anything he might say or do to her. She looked into his face and found it open still in its first alarm, his mouth wide, his eyes wide and staring at her as if she had grown too big for him to encompass. Her triumph was complete for he himself acknowledged it. She laughed aloud, the sudden sound dominating the room. She bounced up and down in her triumph. She reached up with her right hand and touched his face, touched his beard, closed his eyes.

'Mag!' he shouted as if appalled and, as he did so, she felt the rush of his semen, great hot spurts of it. She slowed to a stop as he completed, relaxing her arms and laying down upon his chest as a sequence of spasms played through and his cock began to grow supple, to retract. It happened rapidly and suddenly he was too small for her and, with an audible plop, slipped out. She drew her legs together and he opened his. She dropped down between the flannelling of his thighs and snuggled, the aching of her crotch and its warmth, and the awareness, or imagination, of the threads of his ejaculation, combining and contrasting.

The candle began to splutter and, rousing quickly, she slid down from him, went and extinguished it. She heard him sit up. She pulled off the rest of her garments and put on her nightsmock. He did not undress, just heaved himself under the bedclothes in his shirt and drawers. She scrambled in beside him, reaching down, snuggling up, but was asleep almost at once.

*

He woke first in the morning and remembered it all, all of it he comprehended. He went down in the dawn light to relieve himself outside the front door, as he always did, lingering out there in the icy mist to examine his delicate and tacky member as if it might explain to him what had happened. He knew the country biology of it, but in that lore it was the man who took the woman, the woman who suffered and bled for it. He had no inkling that it could happen the other way round. She was suddenly revealed to have power. He reascended to find her still tousled deep in sleep, her lower lip extruded slightly by the tip of her tongue. It was unusual for her to stay sleeping after he had risen: it concerned him. She looked there the model of smugness. She had stolen his manhood from him and now slept on, self-sufficient. He should have killed her last night as he had intended. His instinct had been right. He should kill her now, quickly. No sooner had he articulated the idea than it emptied like a fart, ludicrously. He had no strength big enough for her anymore. He felt weak, sucked out. He stood and waited for her.

She woke with her eyes big and her face shining, stretching out her arms. He drew back but she patted a space on the bed for him to sit. He obeyed and she slung her arms about him, sank her face into his face, slung her leg across his lap and clung to him. He submitted, held her up, lifted her up at the buttocks so that she could reach up. Her gladness for him, the softness which she imposed upon him, reassured him, made him feel stronger, more himself again. He smiled tentatively when she leant back to look at him. She shuddered a little as the cold caught her and slipped off to be ready for the day.

He watched her with a new awareness throughout the day, and for all the days thereafter. She had become lighter, happier, running to touch him at odd moments, often intimately. When she scrubbed him down now on bath nights he noted the lingering of her touch upon him. He noted how she liked him to touch her; how, whenever he placed his hand upon her, she would stop and settle herself about his touch, valuing it seriously. He touched her shoulder and her head lolled aside to enclose his hand. He touched her back and she bent her neck forward for him to stroke her whole lumpy spine. He touched her breast and she smoothed his forearm, hung from it, her face down. He touched her belly and a tense stillness came into her, as if he had found the absolute centre of her and by touching it had stopped her. He took no conscious personal pleasure from touching her, beyond the pleasure of curiosity; but he gradually began to be reassured. What had happened that night did not betoken the onset of any strange subservience to her. She was more devoted than ever, more closely attentive, more intimate: he did not resent this.

The winter was long and wet that year. There was no snow but long weeks of freezing fog, the days greying faintly for a few hours then subsiding into a long dusk. He struggled in the workshop with timber grown moist and intractable in the cold. He had a sheaf of commissions from surrounding farms and houses at which he toiled, but it was difficult. Winter was to be endured. For the first time he felt it weighting him, felt a longing for the spring that grew fierce at times. Although she certainly felt the cold more than he did, she seemed to be less oppressed by the endless succession of grey days. He watched her little bent body in its continual busyness, her fingers quick and her labours intense. When she bathed he studied the lumping of her spine and marvelled at how she could carry that distortion of herself so fluently. As a boy he had broken a leg, badly, falling from the stable loft, and the months of disability had made him mad, this flaw, this halt in his vital liberty. He needed the full range of his body, sometimes needed more, and he marvelled at her who could manage so well without it.

Spring came suddenly. One morning the day broke with the mist dispelled and a warm, pale sunlight filling the valley. He stood before the house and his spirits rose at the sight of it. He could almost perceive the life before him begin to rouse. He went in to fetch Mag but found her caught in a small sickness. It was soon done and it did not seem to bother her. She came down with him, leaning against him and shivering a little. He took manly gulps of the sharp air and laid his hand upon her shoulder. He did not look down upon her, but out across the valley, his estate. A bird called in the woods, a distant twittering. The stream rushed urgently. The grass gleamed and the trees seemed open to the light.

'We'll get a dog,' he said. 'Clayman has a litter.'

She slipped from under his arm and went inside. He came in shortly to find her lighting the fire, still shivering. She smiled at him reassuringly, but it was a reassurance that alerted him. The sense of the rising spring outside had come upon him so strangely that he had perhaps grown too large for her. He came to her and touched her bent back, touched her head which turned up to him, open and frail, its sharp little features blurred, trying to sustain the smile.

He watched her closely in the succeeding days. The sickness came upon her often, filling the bedroom with its sourness. She roused again quickly after it, but he noted a weariness tugging at her movements, watched how her bustling often slowed, stopped as if she needed a moment to regather her strength. He tried to believe that he was being over-scrupulous in his observations but, by the end of the month, when the warmth was firmly established in the meadows and the woods, a year almost since her first journey here, he accepted the truth: she was ill; and not only was she ill, but it was an illness deep-seated and progressive, clogging her energies, weighting her whole presence.

He dreaded such illness. Pain, injury he could comprehend, but not the secret machinations of some gnawing, tumorous possession. He drew away from her, not fearful of contracting the sickness himself so much as from a sheer revulsion against the proximity of such a decline. It was an obscene irony that it could come for her with the spring. He found her increasingly repulsive to contemplate.

And yet, drawing clear of her, he did not find an independence: the reverse, he found himself growing morose, bewildered. He found that she had invested his life so thoroughly that drawing clear of her was a retreat into a half-life, a continual awareness of an incompletion. He suffered spells of listlessness at his work, left things half-done, started new work before completing old work. He forgot things, forgot to see to the horse, was late sowing his carrots and seed potatoes; forgot where he had left things. The rhythm of his life was awry, and yet he could not approach her. He watched her, petulantly wanting a way through to her; but she seemed to be absorbed in her need for rest, to be too absorbed in the failing complexities of her own body to respond to him.

The sickness subsided but the sluggishness remained. She was growing stout, bloating. He could not bear to see her nakedness now, turned away as she bathed, as she preened and squeezed her flesh with morbid inquisitiveness, as she began to walk about adjusting her balance to her new shape. He endured all this with growing resignation. He had expected her to slump into the final decline, pitied her her blithe ignorance of the dark weight gathering about her; but it took so long. He dogged on through days that were rainy or bright, but for which he had lost the relish. He grew automatic in his responses, in his work. The precision to which he used to rise was so far from him now that he no longer understood in what it had consisted.

And then one morning, planing down a plank which he had forgotten why he needed, lulled by the repetitiveness of the movement, all at once he was enlightened by a bolt of spontaneous clarity. He dropped the plane and yelled out at the enormity of his stupidity, walking about rapidly in a panic of embarrassment, so angry with himself that he bashed down his fist on to the workbench and split open the edge of his hand. The throb of this and the mess of it sent him instinctively in search of Mag.

He found her out in the garden, leaning on a hoe, having been worrying at the spring weed growth in between long spells of leaning and gazing across the meadow watching the movement of the trees beyond. He came close to her before she was aware of him and he paused, not wanting to disturb her from a confusion of motives: the withdrawals of the preceding weeks rising to be blown open by his new realisation, and the shame of that; but more, for a sudden profound respect he had for her, an awareness of her as the possessor of a great secret of which he could never partake; and then the respect tinged with envy, with fear. It was the most complex thing he had ever encountered.

She turned to him as if she had been expecting him to be there. He offered his damaged hand coyly. She came and took it, examined it, then, putting the hoe across her shoulder, she led him back to the house. She sat him in his chair and fetched water and cloth to wash and bind his hand, sitting down before him, dabbing away the dirt and exposing the rent flesh which beaded with fat drops of blood. These she licked away, sucking at and blowing on the wound.

'You're carrying a child,' he said. 'Aren't you?'

She smiled, rose and hauled up her skirts and smock to expose the taut belly. She was naked below them and he saw how the bulge was beginning to tuck her red nether pelt under her. She took his hands, one by one, and placed them on the bulge. It felt warm and strong and full, and he nodded, not quite sure how he was supposed to react, offering a general, if awkward, approval. Suddenly under his left hand, he felt a movement. She quickly covered his hand with her own to stop him pulling away before he had even realised he was doing so. The movement was an ungainly lumping of the flesh, a distension, sudden and large. He was amazed by this. He moved his face close to her belly and smelt the sweet, waxy smell of her, pressing his fingers into her girth and moving his other hand down between her legs as if to hold her up. He heard the gurgling and bubbling of the darkness within her, within which moved the child.

At last she grew weary of standing and drew away, dropped down her skirts and sat on her own chair, gone dreamy, contemplating, smoothing herself slowly. After a while he rose and went out into the sunlight, his mind crowding with all the things he must make for the child – cots and toys and a little chair – and all the things he must buy. He walked without thinking down to the stream and stood on the bridge with the rush below him clearing his mind, stilling him. He was held above the moving waters in a wide space grown heavy and solitary with the water running in its chaos of energy below him, seeming to sustain him. He was balanced, poised, perfect.

He was disturbed by the approach of the uniformed horseman who halted some way away and waited for him to rouse and come up.

She had not quite believed that he was unaware of her pregnancy, but she had considered it magically possible. She had been surprised herself by the first indications. Having never lived amongst breeding women, she had been puzzled by the lapse in her monthly cycle; and it had been only when the sickness began, the paradoxical churnings of her empty stomach and the strange well-being that lay below this, that she had guessed what was afoot within her. She was boundlessly content. She felt the strange realignments of her bodily processes, felt them, week by week, gathering themselves about that point in her belly where her child was coming slowly into being. The winter at Cutchknoll had been a long, physical struggle and, as the weight of that was eased, she felt able to stop, to rest, to allow her strength to work within her. He had certainly noticed this and yet he kept away, doubtful; removed instinctively, she felt, by the intense femality into which she was being absorbed. She had sensed, at times, an antagonism, a revulsion shadowing his reaction to her. These shadows frightened her at times, as she was frightened by the knowledge that it was possible for her deformity to be replicated within her womb. But such fear was peripheral to the swelling complacency which was sealed inside her; which, as it grew and grew, dominated her and centred her about the tight sac within which, in due time, the quickening had come, forceful and insistent, stopping her, yet gentle, an inner caress of soft cartilage and emergent freedom. Her breasts began to fill and her nipples stood out like thumbs.

She felt pain at times certainly, a catch at her spine as the new burden wrenched itself against it, a lassitude in her thighs and calves that grew to a dull ache, a watery swelling. Her head too, when the thin sunlight came too sharply in at the window or sent rods through the flaws in the foliage of the woods, grew dull and thumped. She submitted to these discomforts, letting them halt and possess her as they would, feeling them honing the profound fullness of her womb. She grew, under their whims, more inward, more solitary; as she had been before she came here. None of this she could share with him and he would have to find his way to her as best he could.

He had come that day with his broken hand, to be ministered to; and he had suddenly become aware of her condition, somehow; and she could hardly resist laughing out loud at his foolishness and at the pleasure she took in his bemused realisation; and she had placed his great, dry palms upon her belly and the child had stirred under its father's touch; and he had slid his hand between her thighs to support her; and she had been on the edge of opening herself over his fingers and drawing them into her.

Initially, in her scheme of things, the child would have to be a boy, a copy of Catch, a sustainer of the line. Later, she became certain that it would be a girl, mainly because of the new reaches of femininity that seemed to cloud and involve her. The child, her daughter, would be an extension of her, the unblemished version.

She kept close to him over the succeeding weeks, taking every opportunity to come within his awareness. She would come into the workshop and watch as he made the promised cradle, measuring and marking out, handling and cutting the wood, chiselling out complex dovetailing, shaving sharp edges into graceful curves, transmuting the brute slabs of timber into a softly shaped little box on crescent rockers that she longed to have filled with a nest of quilting, in which she imagined laying down her child in perfect security. As he worked, she would reach out and touch the backs of his hands which would pause in their work and wait patiently for her. Sometimes she would come at him in a rush and press herself against his aproned bulk, reaching round him. She had an enormous emotional surfeit which she discharged, at least partially, in such contacts as these, in the deep shade of his workshop with the buzz of a trapped fly and the sighing of the woods outside marking the edges of a silence that grew as palpable as her heavy womb.

She swelled prodigiously as the summer rose and the garden was tilled and cropped. She could not manage the buckets now, but she tended the chickens still and worked with her hoe between the beans and brassicas, feeling their growth clustering about her. She had no idea how long it was all going to take, how it would happen at its time. It had now taken charge of her and her days were made up of small knots of effort amidst long planes of waiting and resting, dozing and submitting to the enormity of it.

He went off for another of his mysterious journeys with the little black box and she felt faded in his absence, as she had felt before; but she was not entirely alone this time. He returned earlier than he had done before, with a bolt of thick blue tweed that was beautiful to touch and in which she could see shawls and blankets and real warmth. She sat on the floor with the cloth unravelled promiscuously about her as he undid his collar stud, laid down his black box and removed his jacket. He was sober this time, but roused nevertheless; and waiting for her. She re-rolled the cloth and wondered how she was going to manage him. She was beyond clambering over him by now. He grew restless, shifting his body when she came to him to express her gratitude for the cloth. She leant against him where he stood, unbuttoned and eased him manually, quickly and deftly. It first surprised, then embarrassed him to see his naked seed looping out across the room. She covered his confusion with smiles and winks, wiped him up and made much of sitting down in a pose of exhaustion. He loosened up at this. She would not present herself for him to take like a dog: she recalled all that from the Inn and she abhorred it. But it was a pity: she had at last received a sexual initiation from him and she wished she had been able to do more with it.

He made his weekly trips into the village to buy supplies and to do those jobs which regularly required and regularly paid him. One morning, abruptly, he asked her to come with him. She agreed at once and only later, after the surprise at being asked had subsided, did she suspect his intentions. He helped her up into the trap and they set off, her belly wobbling painfully down the track, and the awakening apprehensions unsettling her. She had been a long year in the valley and had grown into it. Her pregnancy was secure in its shelter, but might not be outside, with other eyes upon her. The responsibility she had been given, the child, made her vulnerable in a way she had never been before. As they came out on to the highroad and within sight of the roofs and chimneys of the village, and the heavy tower of the church, as the jolting of the cart-track eased into the smoother highway, her apprehension was revealed within her starkly. She leant against Catch and sought to alert him to her misery. He was, as usual, solid and unaware.

He drove past the church and then turned down an overgrown lane with a good hard surface to it where she had not been before, an avenue of new trees appearing about her. They came, behind the church, to a terrace of substantial new houses, iron-railed and brass-knockered, set back behind a stretch of well-trimmed grass. He halted the cart, swung down and came round for her. She had become very suspicious by now, a whole new set of potential dangers being embodied hereabouts. Here there was neither the decay of Palmead where she had half-expected to be taken, nor the slovenliness of the village street: here was something more assertive, more aggressively, successfully new. He waited for her to adjust at least to the surface of this environment, then he lifted her down.

They walked across the sward to one of the houses, passed through the line of railings and mounted the sugary stone steps. Catch jerked at a bell-pull. No sound reached them from within but they had not long to wait. The doors opened on to a peering maid. They were expected. They were directed into a massively furnished room. She shrank at once in this atmosphere, thick with polish and dried flower scents. Domes of glass covered ugly figurines. Everything was draped or fringed with faded maroons and golds. The sunlight seemed to stop at the window-panes.

Catch indicated her to a low couch spread with a linen sheet. She obeyed. They waited. Brisk footsteps approached and a tall man in a frock coat came turning into the room, closing the door behind him. He carried a black bag and he greeted Catch with a nod which was returned, balanced conspiratorially. He put down his bag beside her, opened it, drew out what looked like a small hearing trumpet, and various brown tubes, and a heavy syringe. She watched his hands nervously and only when he turned upon her did she register his face: fleshy cheeks supporting precise and full whiskers and, from these banks of hirsute complacency, two eyes met hers and digested her with one sardonic swallow.

She shrank instinctively from him but he smiled corruptly. He came towards her and took her shoulders and eased her down, back on to the couch. She was allowed to lie on her side as he placed his hands upon her stomach, smoothing his palms but probing cruelly with the tips of his fingers.

'We must look down into the depths of things, Catch,' he said without glancing away from her. 'If you'd wait in the hallway for a few minutes.'

She looked at her husband, begged him not to leave her. He was supposed to protect her.

'I'll stay,' he murmured heavily.

'My dear fellow, we can't have you prying into our secrets now. Your attentions down thereabouts are over with for the present. Off you go now.'

She slid from the couch and looked at her husband desperately. He was silent, motionless. He had withdrawn from the contention. This being so, she acted on her own, and, before the doctor could reach her, she had upset a large mahogany pedestal. He turned to see it topple in a moment of pure silence, the glass dome separating, exploding on the floor, the china figures, two pretty lovers at a bough of cherries, falling into fragments and dust. She looked briefly at them and then around the room for her next point of purchase.

They were seen out smartly. Catch was still solemn and silent. The leafy lawn, in contrast to the interior that they had just relinquished, seemed not formal but liberated: nature not constrained but assertive. Such a symbolism was smug and fitted her triumph tightly.

As Catch lifted her back up on to the trap, he said, without looking at her, 'When we get home, I'm taking off my belt and going to bare your little bitch arse for you.'

She wanted to laugh but feared lest she provoke this fantasy into reality. She sat demurely and contained herself, as they journeyed briskly home, about a sudden swell of her bladder which it needed all her concentration to control.

Once back in the valley, this pressure had grown into a sustained spasm that arched her back like an iron hoop. She had to gasp for air and clutch herself against the jolting of the trap. He pulled the cart to a sudden standstill and took her in his arms in an emotion that was as abrupt as it was inexplicable, and as it was irrelevant. The house was far off still, hidden all but its roof behind a shoulder of the meadow. She tried to urge him forward but he held her largely and, after a while, she just relaxed herself into his embrace.

Another spasm caused her thighs to gush. He started away from her. She struggled to straighten herself into some dignity against the back of the seat which cut into her back as the spasm drained from her.

How they got home she could not remember. The spasms came rapidly and obliterated everything outside them. There were brief flashes of lucidity between the spasms, but they were disconnected and unreal. Catch was there, his back to her, standing looking into the light, blocking it: she needed the light more than she needed him at that moment. She was on her wedding bed, naked. He must have brought her here, he must have arranged her thus. He stood by, attendant. She had no time to be grateful. She wanted him gone. The spasms which contracted the whole of her energy into her womb were the only reality, fierce points of sustained concentration into which the energy was rushed and devoured, rising to a point of oblivion; from which the drained energy flowed away again, her consciousness coming in behind it, the dreamy, watery lucidity in which her only task was to suck in as much air as might give her the energy for the next onset, the next assault. It went on a long, long while. Each spasm reached a point of intensity that seemed absolute, but which was always outstripped by its successor. Catch was still there, attendant and immovable. Soon enough he became unimportant, irrelevant, insignificant. Everything was put aside. The process, the rise and rise and the falling away, was everything. It was too total to be painful; for pain there had to be discrete awareness, an assailable self. Such niceties were suspended.

At last she felt the massive shifting within her, a dark downthrust of her womb, a rending and an opening; the process of parturition becoming explicit and logical. In the moments of respite, her sundered thighs throbbed, aching to be discharged. She had taken control of the contractions: this was possible, she found, by directing the energy downwards. She understood how it all worked and, with a sudden slithering, a sudden release, a child, purple and slimy, was expelled on to the bare bed, and after it its cluster of afterbirth, and gushing fluids. Catch was there, taking up the child, cutting it loose of its clutter, bundling it up. It

287

began to struggle and cry, was alive, a new voice, a sudden independence. She reached out for it, was weak and longing for the peace of her maternity, but she was thrown down again by another hideous spasm. What more was there to be done? She cried out. Catch drew back, appalled at the cry, the breach of her silence. She was racked and torn and bleeding and it was not over. She shoved down into the spasm to drive it and its process from her finally or to break herself upon it. She felt again that shifting within her, and then she understood. She calmed, and with the new understanding strong within her, she pushed out her second child easily. A rush of peace came upon her at once.

He had bolstered her up so that the ridge of her back was held between two stout banks of bedding. She lay back upon this support, her flesh drenched in the sweat and effluvia of her labour. He had drawn covers over her legs and belly. He had gone down, leaving her in the afternoon sunlight which fell leafily into the room. In the crook of either arm she held her babies, their faces smooth, their heads red, their eyes closed, their cheeks pulsing at her nipples. Her two sons.

He named them 'Rob' and 'Tom', and she acquiesced in this. She had imagined having her own secret names for them, real names that would mark them as hers; but 'Rob' and 'Tom' were clean and simple, thumps of sound, and they quickly grew into them. Rob, from the first, was more restive, more demanding; Tom was greedier, instinctively mouthing and scrabbling for the breast, after the achievement of which he grew entirely placid.

Her days were entirely consumed by their needs, by her need to tend and watch them. Each developed his own regime upon her and she had no time, during the early weeks, to impose her own life apart from theirs. She lived through hot and busy days, feeding them, washing them, and their linen, dozing when she could, rocking them as she dozed. They were tiny enough to fit one at either end of Catch's sturdy cot which had seemed too delicate when he had first made it, but which seemed heavy and crude when they were within it. The still points of her days were when she took them, one by one now, to her breasts, cradling and feeding them, feeling herself flowing out with the milk, feeling them grow tight and strong in her arms, watching the miniature fingers clutch, the delicate eyelids tremble and open to reveal the blue clarity of the perfect irises, the soft pulse of their fontanelles under which lay their embryonic individualities which she seemed to hold in her arms, and would go on holding until the cartilage hardened into bone, the minds gripped and they set off on their own. Most of the time, now, she could not distinguish between them. They were so full of potential for her that she was loath even to close them down with the specificity of names. She loved the handling of them, their burgeoning movement, loved the pout of their mouths, their cries of impatience, their digestive struggles, even the soft evacuations of their bowels. She was proud of her rent sex, proud of the flabby wombflesh that only slowly began to settle itself back within her, proud most of all of the fatness of her breasts and of the succulence of her dark nipples. She fed herself to them; she was inexhaustible.

Catch came up and watched her feed them sometimes. She would reach out his sons for him to take. He took them carefully, his whole size too gross for them: they awed him with their minuteness. He went away bewildered and grew obsessively constructive down there in the workshop.

By the time they had outgrown the single cot he had another made and, appreciating the lack of space in the bedroom, he made the rockers detachable and arranged for both cots to be slung from the ceiling. He fixed hanging hooks for them in the bedroom and in the living-room, giving her freedom of movement downstairs; for she would not, for months, be out of reach of them. She began to rejoin him, to settle them effectively and to attend to some, at least, of her usual work.

He meanwhile had begun to hack out a large section of the steep bank on the open side of the house, pulling down young trees and undergrowth which were consumed on great bonfires, shoring up with timber piles the steep earthen sides where he had dug. He was beginning the major extension of their house. It would become a manor-house, he told her; she would be its lady, their sons its heirs. He brought her sheaves of rough diagrams and explicated upon them at length. She understood partially – the concept at least. It seemed an impossible undertaking. It would add a whole new half to the house. It was work for a whole village of labourers, quarries of stone, whole woods of seasoned oak. How would he ever have time for the days of mundane craftsmanship by which, she presumed, they lived? Nevertheless, he had begun, and he seemed to extend his day in a fierce intention to accommodate the new work. By the end of the autumn he had levelled a great space about the house, a raw flat of earth that seemed frighteningly naked, that seemed to admit the rain and wind to lash the walls and windows with an unrestrained energy. He set to, through the deteriorating weather, digging out deep trenches for foundations and filling the trenches with compacted stone. Within a year, the shell of this first section would be up and roofed.

It was an obsessional occupation, fearsome in its potential to frustrate and devour him. She watched and waited but knew no way to slow him down and direct his energies back into her. He kept up his basic trade, nevertheless, extending it in fact, returning from days out with the trap with new timbers and with new orders. He was very tired in the evenings, slow and blurred with his tiredness. He ate quickly, slept briefly, smiling at her, touching her lightly, leaving her to her own life. She watched him from within the secure cocoon of her motherhood.

The boys gurgled and cried and worked their fingers and mouths around the little toys that he turned for them: shapes of polished wood, rattles and pegs and balls. She noted that Tom was the easiest satisfied, would nurse and gnaw at the same toy for hours, whilst Rob grew tired of the toys, found it difficult to settle to the enjoyment of any one thing. To look at they were almost exactly alike, flawless and chubby, many-chinned, with folds of flesh about their small eyes; both had tufts of black hair. She could almost be jealous of the marks of the paternity they bore so ostentatiously. She kept them to herself. Catch had no idea how to respond to them.

In the spring, Catch returned from his journeyings one day with a youth whom he presented to her as his apprentice. His name, apparently, was Fludd. He was thin and awkward, all bones, bulging head, long, wet nose and fingers like a corpse. He must have been fourteen or so, with the first symptoms of his maturity pimpling and patching his face. He gave the impression of being permanently frightened, debilitated with fear. He was appalled by Mag, would never meet her eyes although he looked at her continually. He ate his breakfast and lunch with them, but took his supper alone in the little room Catch had rigged for him in the loft above the stable. Catch promised him that if he set the place alight, he'd have to burn with it. The poor boy ate in darkness.

He was religious and would caterwaul thin hymns at the darkness to keep the demons at bay. Catch would cock his head, listen, wink at Mag and chuckle. She was uneasy at Fludd, and Catch's amusement made her more uneasy. She made efforts to engage Fludd with smiles and offers of apples and sweet biscuits, but she could never induce him to raise his eyes to hers. He moved about the buildings and paddocks as if hiding from something.

However uneasy she felt at his presence, Fludd was no idler. He learnt quickly and worked enormously. Catch gave him more and more to do, exploiting him maliciously; but he did not complain, was never noticeably defeated. He lacked the fineness of Catch's skill and could only do what he was told; but he could fit a joint, or turn a chair leg, plane a curve or gouge out a socket with precision and speed. The workshop grew busier and busier. Catch was increasingly away, delivering, fetching in orders, new tools, new supplies of timber and ironmongery. As the boys' first birthday passed, the workshop seemed to have acquired an energy of its own, to have become a spontaneously generating machine in which Catch and Fludd, at their different levels of operation, were consumed.

The extension to the house seemed forgotten under all this new work. Grass and weeds, tendrils and tiny flowers, crept out of the raw earth mounds, and the trenches hardly managed to dry out from their winter dousing. Then one day Catch arrived with a cartload of big stones and he and Fludd spent two days unloading and laying the first course of a wall, hardly taking it to ground level, but staking out a stark foundation, an intention. This was then abandoned as a set of twelve chair-frames were to be made to a peculiar design, ready for the french polisher and the upholsterer.

The boys, meanwhile, lifted themselves clear of the ground and tottered about the place, coming within reach of every danger. She was continually pursuing them, seeking them out, starting at the realisation of their ominous silence somewhere. Tom, generally, would blunder into things, bring all manner of clutter down about his ears, tumbled regularly into the stream, responding to every calamity with a strange hysterical noise that was neither laughter nor tears. Rob would be always more deliberate – reaching his hand towards a flame, prodding at the chickens until they turned, finding lethal implements and trying to imitate or discover their use. Her life at times seemed to move on a wave sequence of panics. She would rush instinctively and snatch one or both back from disaster: relief, then a moment of anger; then a moment of release, of tears and love.

They began to acquire a language, not of words as such. Tom expressed his wants and pains with increasing precision; Rob copied, using the sounds almost for their own sake, seeing what could be done with them, seeing what they could do to other people; or so it seemed to her, watching them acquire this great power that would pull them away from her and out into their own worlds. For the moment they were hers entirely: Catch rarely spoke to them and their voices were mere babble to him.

Catch announced, as autumn was well set into the wood and there were hosts of strange fungi to be gathered in familiar glades, that he was to be away again in the city, for another night with his little black box. He had not been there since the preceding winter and she had begun to assume that such excursions were passed now. No rider had come to call to her knowledge, and how he had received the call she did not know. But she was glad of what habitually followed, wanted to be with child again. She did not look forward to spending the night alone here with Fludd lurking about, but did not know why she felt this particular unease.

These suspicions were, however, exacerbated when the time came for Catch to depart, suited, his box in his hand, on foot as he always went. Fludd, at this incarnation of Catch, seemed to want to detain him physically. Such an attempt would have been ludicrous, of course, and Catch ignored him; although he was certainly aware of Fludd's agitation, grinning a little at it, to himself, telling Fludd to mind his own damn business.

When Catch had gone, Fludd stopped work and went out into the meadow on the far side of the stream where he stood for hours, or paced about as if tethered. She could achieve very little that day for watching the idiot apprentice, wondering what he was up to. Rob, in her abstraction, found a razor chisel and gouged a deep pit in his cheek which bled hideously and which needed all her attention. Fludd, meanwhile, as night fell, stayed out in the meadow, howling his hymns as if he expected the divinity to come down with lightning and sulphur upon the whole valley. She bolted him out with no supper, blaming him for Rob's injury, which she had to swab continuously, putting flour plasters on it which he kept picking off. Tom watched the renewed bleeding aghast, whimpering in sympathy. She put them early up into their cots.

She lay awake thinking of Catch's return tomorrow, needing her release. The boys breathed in their soft sleep, their exhalations almost exactly in time. She remembered Rob's wound, rose and lit a candle. She went to his cot and lowered the light over him. There was blood on the sheets but the wound itself seemed to be dry now. She touched him, and touched Tom, and returned to her own bed.

His victim this time, he learnt in the prison, was a pathetic little sodomite, a man well into his middle years, who had poisoned his senile old mother and had then run blubbering to the police. He had, by the time Catch came to him, fallen into the arms of the chaplain. Catch always felt that he and the chaplain worked against one another – the chaplain telling them that it was only a brief moment of travail to break forth into a better existence, Catch determined to fix their minds upon the moment itself, in all its clarity and awfulness. The chaplain dealt in swaddling illusions: Catch offered the dignity of the only reality.

True to his instinct this one was a messy affair, with the little wretch fainting and opening his bowels all the way up to the drop, begging for forgiveness and expecting to be let off: so much for the chaplain's consolations. Usually the corpse was pliant when they brought it down, softened by the bolt of death shot through it; this one was already rigid, the spine bent back as if set against the inevitable. Under the hood, the eyes and mouth were fixed open.

'Look,' he said to the assistant. 'That's what the chaplain does for you, traps the soul in. See?'

Once on the road home, this unpleasantness was diminished in his mind, reduced to a subliminal dissatisfaction. He thought of Mag and of his impending enjoyment of her. He strode home through a wash of blown rain with the purpose tight and warm within him.

Coming into the valley, ahead on the path, he saw a figure, a thin, black scarecrow which bolted away at his appearance. He halted, was surrounded suddenly by images of intruders and violence. He waited, alert, meditating a dash into the woods to come down upon the house from above; then he remembered Fludd. He had forgotten Fludd. He recalled the apprentice's behaviour yesterday as he had made ready to depart. Fludd had, he assumed, known where his master was going and had liquefied with vicarious fear. What did his watching and fleeing signify? A whole network of ideas opened like the branching of a tangled root system disappearing into the dark as he struggled to follow each thread to its end. He moved forward because it was all he was capable of doing in any difficulty.

He burst into the living-room to find Mag squatted before the fire with the twins, her hair down, nightsmocked. She looked warm and replete. The twins clambered about her legs and up at her arms, grabbed at her breasts and played with sprays of her hair.

'Where's Fludd?' he demanded, slamming the box down on to a table, shedding his oilskin in a heap on the floor.

She rose and was obviously about to set off in search of the little stoat in a parody of obedience.

'What's he been up to?' The words and the clotting of the ideas behind them began to spill out of him at random. 'Has he been in here? Has he been at you?'

She turned indignant, facing him, reaching out for the boys, ready to shield them from him. They had become still, watching, sensitive to the danger.

He strode across and snatched up one of them. 'How did this happen?' he said, jabbing at the scabbed cheek. 'This is my house. I am master here, not Fludd. Not you. Not these little runts. Get yourself upstairs.'

He dumped the child down and it began to whimper. The other joined in. Mag went to a bowl and fetched two fat apples, giving each a wipe on her nightsmock and offering them one by one, individually, to the twins. The fat little hands clutched and the fat mouths chomped. She stroked their heads and she lowered the metal grille he had fitted for her over the fire mouth. The calm domesticity infuriated him.

'Get upstairs, you lame bitch.'

She went upstairs and he lumbered after, unbuckling his belt as he went. Upstairs, she turned to him, her face contained and serious.

'Get on the bed, on your hands and knees, like a dog.'

He saw the resistance rise into her face and he hit at it, knocking her head aside. He waited for her to recover and face him again, ready to strike her again, boiling up for it; but she did not face him. She obeyed him, clambered up and gathered up her nightsmock, stuck up her arse at him. He struggled up behind her and made several stupid attempts to enter her. He was beginning to suspect her of a deliberate resistance when, with a sigh of resignation, she slipped her hand down and helped him in. With the cheeks of her arse buffering his bouncing belly and the arch of her back like a cat's up against him, he could feel her resistance, her betrayal. He came quickly, shooting into her venomously and pulling out at once. She rolled over and looked up at him questioning, hurt, but quite secure in spite of everything.

'Go and get my supper.'

She slipped away and left him kneeling awkwardly on the bed with his wet cock smearing his trousers.

When he came downstairs, Fludd was standing in the doorway of the workshop waiting for his supper to take away. As Catch came down in shirt-sleeves and thick braces, Fludd tensed, attempted to compose himself, looking down, trying to appear natural, a state he was anyway incapable of. Mag filled his can with rabbit stew and handed it to him without looking at him. He clutched the can with open palms, warming them upon it.

'Sorry you've had to wait for your supper, Fludd,' Catch said, seating himself expansively at the table, 'but whenever I go away into the city, spend the night with business associates, earn myself a little extra, a little jelly under the dripping, whenever I come home, first thing to be done is to give my little wife there a good servicing. Everything has to wait for that.'

Fludd had already gone, could be heard crashing through the darkening workshop.

'If he comes back because he's spilled his all over the floor,' Catch said, 'you tell him he's had his ration. More than his ration.'

Her eyes met his and were hard and angry. She brought him his meat and sat opposite, eating her own portion, feeding the boys; but she would look at him from time to time with a face of that set contempt. He had roused her and, at first, he was pleased with himself – smug bitch. But soon he became uneasy. He sensed the gap, the alienation that had been brought between them, made palpable now by him. He had the sense of being a stranger here, in his own house, at the hearth of his great solitude, or where that had once been. Even Fludd, thereafter, avoided him, kept his distance, shot uneasy glances, always seemed to be expecting his master to jump at him. He decided to bide his time, brewing in his silence plans to cast them all out, purging the valley of these aliens, these degenerates.

She had conceived again: she knew it almost at once. Catch became aware of it soon enough, watching for and noting the signs, finally asking. She knew that he nurtured the obscene fantasy of Fludd having beaten him to the paternity; but it was what he wanted to believe and there was no struggling against it. He had become embittered and removed. She did not know why. The way he had taken her had insulted her deeply: it had been deliberate and it continued to rankle. She stared her reproaches into him at every opportunity, but she only succeeded in driving him back. She began to be afraid of him; for her children, for Rob and Tom and for their unborn sibling. She wanted it to be a girl. She desperately willed it to be a girl.

Tom and Rob were now independent of her for much of the day. She stitched quilted jackets and caps for them and they strutted out into the winter meadows, fell over and found tiny, sometimes imaginary, points of interest over which they would stoop for hours. Tom would lead, would stay longest. Rob would orbit his brother, bringing him things, pulling him away to new things or back to old things. She watched them, was always aware of them. She made them aware of the dangers of the stream, and Rob at least understood, and through him Tom, too, was safe. Her life was beginning to contract itself again, about the new existence that was forming within her. She needed to have the twins independent, to be alone with her new child in its struggle into being – her daughter.

The only times she became apprehensive for the boys were when they ventured into the workshops, coming within reach of their father's whims and of the unaccountable obsessions of his apprentice. She had no power in the workshop and she did not trust the boys there. They were naturally drawn to the busyness, the intricacies and the skills of the workshop, as she had been, a long time ago, drawn to the offices of the Inn. That was in another existence, of course, but the potency of masculine creativity and cruelty was the same and she dreaded, at the back of her mind continually, a sudden shout, a sudden scream, a blackness.

One spring day, at breakfast, Catch made the following announcement: 'The doctor's got himself a practice in town. He's moving out, says there's no need of a doctor here now. Now the manor's mostly closed up, there's no profit in it. There's a lot of turning off of the servants going on. Some of them will have families who can take 'em back. A couple he'll take with him. The most of them'll have to beg and thieve and whore.' He paused again. 'There's a girl there might be useful here. She'd be handy and won't cost. I don't want you dead of work within a year and a scatter of brats going amiss about the place. She'll be someone for Fludd to play with too.' He leant back and bellowed over his shoulder. 'Fludd! Come in here!'

The apprentice appeared, sucked in unwillingly, shuffling about in the doorway.

'That room across the stairhead from yours, Fludd. Get it cleared and cleaned out. We're bringing a girl in. She's to help the mistress here, but you can make anything of her she'll let you.' He laughed.

Fludd laughed too, uneasily, joining in although obviously appalled by the idea. Mag cleared away the breakfast, breaking a bowl in her anger.

Catch fetched the girl that afternoon. Fludd was busy making room for her and Mag fussed over the twins. It rained, which allowed her to keep them in the house. She heard the trap returning, stopping below the door. She waited. The door opened and Catch ushered in the latest addition to their menagerie.

She was very small. This was all Mag could register at first as she was wrapped in a brown cloak far too big for her: a child. Mag was reassured, a little. Catch uncloaked her and she stood blinking, looking round quickly, a cat-like creature with sharp features and long, lank, black hair. Her body was indeed childish, her greasy smock was loose about her hollow shoulders; but as her eyes met her new mistress's, Mag's reassurance went. The thin face lifted and the chin set, the mouth curled and she shook her stringy hair. Mag looked at Catch whom she discovered watching her, watching to savour her reaction. She turned away and smothered her fury only by stooping to her sons who had come close to her under the presence of this stranger.

'Mercy, this is Mag Catch, your new mistress. Those are Rob and Tom. You'll soon tell them apart. Mag doesn't speak but she understands everything – more than everything, so mind yourself. She'll show you your duties. Get her bathed, Mag. I'll go and see what Fludd's managed to achieve.'

Mercy stood waiting, ignored by Mag who lifted the boys on to her forearms where they sat clinging to her. Three-headed, then, she glanced at her maid, up and down, dismissively.

'He says I'm to have a bath,' the girl said, her tone rough and lazy, 'and some clothes, some new clothes.'

Mag advanced and thrust the boys at her. She reached for them but, once transferred, they writhed and cried and the girl was forced down, trying to calm them with baby words which she spoke as if they were charms to protect her from them – from Tom's wailing and from Rob's potent little fists. Mag meanwhile hauled the tub in from the workshop, gathered the boys and indicated for the girl to follow her, which she was glad to do.

The girl was quick to comprehend, set coppers on the fire, brought the water through. It was work she was used to. She expected, once the bath was full, to be left private, but Mag had taken her seat, had picked up her sewing, stitching through leather panels with a disc of metal thonged across her palm, working and waiting. Mercy, after a moment's pique, understood. She pulled off her smock with a studied pretence of innocence that Mag knew to be display. She wanted to see, and the girl wanted to show, how much of a woman was present in her undernourished frame. There was enough. This was no child.

Catch came in amongst all this and Mercy shrieked and clapped her hands over her breasts. He chuckled, winked at Mag, and said the room would do for her tonight at least. When she was ready, he would show her. So she was digested into their lives.

Like Fludd, she was not admitted to their evenings, and Mag was thankful for this; although she was not to be lulled out of her suspicions of the girl. She was a willing worker: Catch had an instinct for ready drudges. Mercy scrubbed and washed and cooked and Mag was glad of the leisure now afforded her. She would have been prepared to show her gratitude to Catch if he had ever been in any state in which he could have received her tenderness. Mercy said little to her. The girl would occasionally hum melodiously, wistfully, jauntily, songs from another dreamworld; but would stop immediately if she thought Mag was within earshot. She was sullen but that was her natural bearing and Mag did not take offence even if she was meant to. She was personally sluttish, oblivious to the reek of her own filth. At times Mag could not bear her, pulled out the tub and insisted. Mercy submitted – another chore. She developed, as Mag watched her, a habit of straightening her back, demonstrating her advantage. Mag was not to be diminished, however, by a girl who could scrub a floor and drop her monthly blood on to it at the same time.

If Catch had seriously intended any sport for Fludd in Mercy, there was certainly no sign of it, nor of its possibility. Mercy had taken one look at Fludd and had dismissed him. She served the food at breakfast and lunch, and Mag noted how she placed Fludd's bowl without looking at him, as she might put down a dish for an animal. Fludd stared at her helplessly, open-mouthed and fascinated. He even came up to her on occasions, approaching her sideways when she was out with the hens or pegging up the washing. She ignored him, probably wasn't even aware of him. Mag saw him once approach her with a fistful of limp weed flowers, pushing them into her attention. She looked bewildered, then laughed a little, then shrugged and left him standing there in an absurd incompletion. Mag tried to feel sorry for him, but his awkwardness was so palpable, his intentions so lumpish that she found the whole lopsided courtship beyond sentiment, merely ugly. It was to Mercy's credit that she did not, at least in Mag's observation, exert any deliberate cruelty upon Fludd: she disregarded him completely.

Mag grew, as the day of her delivery approached, more isolated than she had ever been in her time at Cutchknoll. It was summer again and the boys were out discovering meadow life in their first full access of freedom, coming in dirty and weary to eat and to sleep, to be ministered to by their mother as a matter of course, accepting her caresses as part of the abundance of the world about them. She was glad for them, glad that the tangles that had sprung up about Catch and Fludd and Mercy did not involve them; rather, excluded them from the society of the workshop. She was glad for herself that they seemed to have acquired a self-sufficiency that allowed her to concentrate upon the growth of her new child.

This pregnancy was certainly different from the first. The child moved within her, but slowly. Sometimes she could not tell when the movement began or ended. Sometimes she felt movement so deep down that she had to sense, to imagine, rather than actually feel it. She grew a little fearful of the birth in a way that she had never been fearful about the birth of the twins. She no longer dreamed of her perfect, liberating daughter, her real self passed on and set free: now she just wanted it all to be all right, whatever it was, whatever she would have to go through to achieve it.

One day, at the height of the summer or just beyond it, when the greenness of the meadow and the greenness of the woods seemed infinite, and the sky in its blueness seemed perfect, a festival came into the valley. At dawn, although Catch had given no intimation of this, loads of stone were brought into the valley in a cavalcade of heavy carts, around the slow wheels of which came two-score loud workmen. Another wagon arrived later, with barrels of ale and meat and cheese and fruits. For three days they worked and ate and slept out amongst the foundations of the extension, over which the summer grass had grown thick. They were strangers, from another part of the country or perhaps from another country altogether. Their speech was deep and rounded and mostly incomprehensible, their hair dark and curly, their statures short, their capacity for work enormous – an appetite. Catch worked out amongst them, organising, cursing, commanding, aglow with purpose. The whole valley was alerted, possessed by their cries and blows, driving the silence and stillness deep into the woods. In the three days the walls of the extension were raised, window frames set in, roof joists fixed: the barn house was doubled in size.

For the two nights they slept out amongst their work, building a great fire and roasting roots and carcasses in its embers, drinking down tubfuls of ale and singing mournful songs. They had a pair of fiddlers amongst them and they danced. Catch was with them in their revels also, largest and loudest, their host and their guest, their employer and their apprentice. He abandoned the others completely, forgot they were even there, the inconsiderable natives of the place.

Fludd and Mercy kept well clear of this invasion, both for

essentially the same reason: the labouring force was all energy and consumed every task before them and would probably have consumed Fludd and Mercy had they ventured within reach. Mag, who also kept inside, watched Fludd and Mercy and saw that Catch's two foundlings at last had a common emotion. It was not obvious, not dramatic, just an expression exchanged, Mercy lingering a little, Fludd moving with a distinct decisiveness back to the workshop that was his for the duration.

The twins were naturally drawn towards the new excitement and Mag, who hated to thwart them, was nevertheless afraid to let them loose amongst the rout, the swinging beams and tumbling heaps of stone and mortar. After a morning of indecision, when Catch failed to come in for his lunch, she ventured out with them, one in each hand, one bulging out in front of her. She went out into the meadow, up across from the stream, well clear of them. She could see Catch there amongst them, larger than any of them, taking the weight of a huge lintel stone. One or two of the labourers saw her as they wandered from the main hub of activity, saw her there, the little bent woman with the bulging belly and the pair of identical manikins on each hand, and they stopped and pointed and laughed. The laughter spread and it reached Catch who looked up and saw its subject. He said something to the men near to him who bellowed with lewd mirth. She turned and took her children into the house, barring the front door on the lot of them.

The following day Mercy came and said she'd keep the boys with her, for which Mag was grateful: they had grown fretful at their detention. She went, freed now, into the workshop and exchanged a smile with Fludd who was pedalling at the lathe in a frenzy of spindly energy. She went out into the stable yard and saw Mercy in the high meadow with the boys gambolling about her. She returned to the house, the noise of the construction thumping into the thick end wall, but distant for all that. Almost for lack of anything better to do, she began to make ready the bed for the approaching birth. She had no interest in Catch's building; it was only noise, intrusion. She had no energy to be interested in it anymore. She had only one purpose now and she settled down to the fulfilment of it.

She woke on the second morning with the contractions beginning, a long way away, but coming closer. Mercy, the previous evening, had brought the boys into the bed where Mag had been dozing. She came in again early, as the labourers rose to work with the first light, to collect the boys again. She looked at her mistress and knew what was happening.

'Shall I fetch him? . . . What must I do?'

Mag shook her head, wanted to be alone with it and the girl understood, had no wish to minister to this particular mystery anyway. She took the boys down for their breakfast. She came up now and then, drawn in spite of herself, by duty and curiosity, coming a little way up the stairs and peering to see if there was anything to be done. There was not.

The contractions grew in strength, building up in clear stages, allowing her greater awareness, greater control than before. Her emotions as well as her body seemed to know what they were about this time. By noon the waters broke and, with a few mighty heaves, she had delivered herself. With a pair of sharp scissors she severed the umbilical. She fetched the new infant from the mess of its afterbirth, sinking back with it, another boy, strangely quiet but alive, and hers, hers alone.

Alone, after a moment's quiet, she pulled her numbed body from the bed and attended to the necessary ablutions. Alone, she washed and wrapped the new child, and fed it. Alone, she set it to rest beside her, swaddled and still. She slept a heavy sleep, slipped away from the weight of her solitude and her duty.

When she woke it was dusk and there was a strange difference. The baby cried thinly and she took it to her breast. The difference was the silence. The labourers had gone. Catch was there in the gloom, watching; so still that he frightened her. The baby sucked evenly and her breathing grew big in the silence. She wanted to be proud of her achievement, her solitary struggle to bring this tiny thing to life, but she could not be under the darkness of his watching.

'A girl now?' he said eventually.

She shook her head.

'Another boy then. I thought it would be. I'll call him . . . Ethelred.' He laughed. 'Ethelred is Fludd's name.' He rose and went down.

She suckled her new son. Ethelred. How could she subvert that? Eth . . . Elred . . . Red . . . Ethelred. Elred, she thought, for her at least – strange and secret. Catch could call him what he pleased. She sensed his frailty and wondered if she would lose him. She cradled him, afraid for him, prepared to throw herself in the path of the monster for him, glad of the idea, longing for the opportunity; and finally weeping for him, for her love for him under the truth of her frailty.

Tom and Rob came up later on, stood either side of the bed, registering their new brother, reaching out to him, allowed to touch him. She noted their instinctive delicacies towards him and felt easier. They would help.

That night Catch tried to compose himself to sleep down on his chair in the living-room, having been nauseated by the bedroom and all its milk and urine, all its clustering infancy with Mag sat in the middle, a humpbacked sow at farrow. He was conscious, at moments, of the poison that had entered his system, conscious of its clogging at his heart; but he could no more explain it than he could purge it.

Sometime in the hours before dawn he abandoned sleep, clattered through the dark workshop and out into the stable yard. He urinated and, as he did so, realised the impulse that was pushing him. He went into the stable block and climbed the stairs to Mercy's door. It was barred. He shook it but it remained solid. He set his shoulder to her door, pushed slowly, felt it ease against its sockets.

'Go 'way, Master Catch!' she called. 'Go 'way!'

'What're you afraid of, Mercy?'

'Go 'way!' She didn't sound afraid, more threatening, which set him on rather. He increased the weight of his pressure and heard the wood begin to splinter, the sound giving him an exact image of the fracturing fibres. He halted a moment to savour the silence, the moment of anticipation. Then a weariness came over him in a sudden swell. He drew back, clumped down the stairs and back out into the stable yard. The urgency was dissipated. He breathed in the cleansing night air. He went back into the stable and threw himself down on a bank of straw where he slept, waking with the day well begun, Fludd at the lathe and Mercy out with the twins gathering eggs from the hen house. They must have stepped over him on their way down. He resented this.

He shook himself, went out into the meadow, skirting the front of the house to view his new achievement. The new stone walls were clean and beautiful, the roof-beams strong, symmetrical and expert. His gypsy crew had been an inspiration of genius. He had revelled in their energy and companionship, and in his position as master, employer, director of all that power. After three long days he had begun to tire of their incessant appetites, but it had been a holiday for him, the after-effects of which were probably what were now cloying him. But look at it! He had completed, magically, in three days, what would have taken him, with or without Fludd, years. He had now only the fine tasks, the thatching of the roof, the dovetailing of the floor-boards, the hanging of the doors and windows, building in partition walls, staircases, an upper storey, knocking through from the old barn, releasing them into their new space, his family, Fludd and Mercy too. He felt briefly benevolent, purposeful, the provider.

The sourness was not to be dismissed so glibly, however. The building, the more he looked at it, seemed raw and ungainly; it broke the pattern of the valley he had always known. And as it stood, it was useless. Long, long hours of work waited. And for what? For whom? He realised that he wanted them to marvel at it, to run to him wondering, his servants, his wife, his sons; but they had shrunk back into their own concerns. They behaved as if he wasn't there. They had usurped his valley. He had worked for them. He appeared only to have united them against him. It filled him with incomprehension, a gathering bitterness and a grey rage.

He trudged out of the valley, went to the village and into the inn where he was treated with the deference he had always inspired in the village. There they still knew who he was – Catch of Cutchknoll. He drank acid brandy until it blunted him completely, and then returned home. As he came down into the valley, his drunkenness met his dissatisfactions and he slumped down in the damp meadow and slept there.

He made frequent excursions to the village inn thereafter, returning always dead drunk, slobbing himself and wasting whole days coming back into focus again. Sometimes he would not go for a month at a time; then he would go day after day. He showed no shame at his degradations, no desire to control his need; when it came he followed it. He alternated, when sober, between days of brooding lethargy and days of frantic energy; days when his old self seemed entirely absent and days when he was a helpless caricature of what he had been.

The work was still done, thanks to Fludd's steadiness. The new extension was left open to the weathers, although Catch would occasionally go out and brood over it, sitting on the bare floor-joists, staring up into the rain which poured down through the naked roof-ribs. He lived alone, his contacts with the others now perfunctory and without the slightest curiosity in any of them. He accepted the food that was offered him, he dealt with Fludd in matters of business, but he was no longer part of them. He lived in a limbo which they at first feared, as if it presaged some new outrage; but eventually they became accustomed to it. Mercy particularly avoided him. Tom and Rob grew wary of him, dodging off when he approached. Mag waited for him, patiently and dutifully, but she had neither the desire nor ability to go after him.

She, above all else, had her new son: strange and small, Catch's features clearer upon him than upon his brothers; in the eyes particularly, which were small and countersunk deep in his cheeks; and in the smallness of his nose also. He seemed an abstract of his father, a whittled-down imprint of the best of Catch's features. It would be perfect now to fold her life about her sons, to watch their burgeoning strengths, and to see them fashioning the world about them to their own growing understandings. This would be the perfection of her solitude, the consummation of her life. Catch was effectively gone. Mercy and Fludd were extraneous. She dreamed of setting off with her children into the woods, of the world fading behind their tight circle of growth and their hungry, nourishing love.

— 6 —

They had effectively ceased to use Catch's professional skills at the prison. They had sent for him once, but the messenger had found him incapably drunk, and the report of this had, unbeknown to him, put him on their reserve list. Bosker had retired, and his replacement was a faceless man, a professional of the prison service, limited and efficient, running the prison like a tidy business, going home to a wife and five children and musical evenings.

A woman's prison had been established in the city, but it was on a far more liberal plan, with facilities for re-education, moral and practical. There were no facilities for the ultimate sanction in this new institution, and the Gunwall Prison retained the apparatus, should it be needed for a woman.

Jenny Child was nineteen, at a college which trained up orphan girls in the rudiments of gentility, sending them off to be the wives of missionaries in far lands. Amongst one irregular clutch of scrubbed and oppressed young women, Jenny Child had blossomed into a rare grace and beauty which the supervising matrons of the college by turns prided themselves upon, and by turns distrusted and envied. Jenny took no offence at their envy, floated through their endless regimes with patience, humility and willingness. She accepted her destiny and longed only to be fit enough to fulfil it.

Then one day she went to the principal of the college and collapsed, weeping and weeping in a rush of abject emotion that terrified the Lady Principal with a raw humanity quite beyond her. When Jenny had cried herself out, calmed, she announced simply that she must leave the college at once. And when the Lady Principal began to comfort her with Christian maxims to soothe away her doubt, she announced bluntly, 'I am with child.'

The governors met, chaired by the bishop, and there was nothing for them to do but to send her away, to cast her out. To have done otherwise would have been to compromise the whole purpose of their foundation.

She was brought before them for the last time. They found her not the wracked figure as feelingly drawn for them by the Lady Principal, but serene and detached. She stood with her head bowed in formal deference. They begged her, as had been done many times before, to name her seducer. She lifted up her face in the perfection of its dark and golden beauty. She looked at the bishop.

'It would make no difference to your decision, my lord. I cannot tell you.'

When the stout front door of the college closed behind her and she stood with her little bundle in a cold street, she left behind her an emptiness. They felt disturbed by her absence more than they had by her transgressing presence. They felt instinctively that they would hear of her again.

Some months later she walked into the central city police station with a bundle of bloody linen in which was wrapped the corpse of her new-born child, a girl. She had slit its throat. There was a medical opinion that tried to establish that the child had been stillborn, but Jenny Child denied this, insisted on standing by her crime and its consequences.

'He would not come for me,' she explained. 'He was afraid to come. Now he knows I am not afraid. He will come to me now.'

She passed passively through the successive chambers of the law which closed round her. She attended and responded to all their questions, reserving her essential secrecy and perceiving and thwarting all their attempts to circumvent it. She bowed her head penitentially as the sentence was passed upon her, then lifted her face streaming with silent tears, silencing the buzzing court-room.

In the closed cell with the awesome wardresses who never left her, she was at peace, waiting, disturbed by nothing, waiting for her lover to come to her. Did she think he would dare to come to her now? Did she think that if he did come it would make any difference? The Governor, the chaplain, the wardresses, all tried to confront her with the vacuity of her dreams; but she retained her inner certainty and, all in their various ways, they were defeated by her, falling back from her and watching her dark, fearful perfection.

They had trouble finding an official for this sensitive function, until Catch was mooted and a discreet messenger was sent for him. He was not at Cutchknoll; strange children and women watched the messenger's visit. He was given directions and rode to a nearby lunatic asylum where a supply of durable coffins was being constructed and stored. The messenger found Catch in a yard between high walls, a pit into which the baying of the inmates tumbled. Catch worked intently with an apprentice, paying no heed to anything. He took the official note, calculated a moment, then indicated his acceptance and went back to his work.

'You know what this is?' the messenger asked, as instructed.

'No need to know,' said Catch.

'Jenny Child.'

Catch shrugged. 'A woman. It's a while since they've given me a woman.'

'It's important, Mr Catch. You'll not let the Governor down?'

Catch shrugged again, a ubiquitous gesture. 'A woman's easy.'

The messenger returned with a reassuring report.

The evening before the morning appointed, Catch arrived with perfect promptitude. It was dark November and bitter rain fell on and on. There were loiterers already outside the gates, in twos and threes, which Catch took as unusual, the hour being very previous and the weather what it was. The prison gates offered him security from such speculations. The Governor greeted him with visible relief, went on at length about the sensitivity of the case, the possibility of a last-minute reprieve, the discomfort of the whole prison at what must be done at dawn. Catch found all this tedious. He studied the medical details and then went to the trap. Amateurs had been at it and there was an hour's work to be done before it functioned to his satisfaction, in spite of the black rain which swirled about the open courtyard and the trembling of the two junior warders who stood by him holding lanterns. He felt more purposeful here than he had felt at any time over the previous eighteen months. He was at his secret craft: he was clear of everyone else.

He went to the condemned cell to take a sight of her, just

to be certain, to fix the image of her in his mind for the morning; to see if there were any chaplains about; to see how she was waiting for him. He was surprised in the outer cell by the sight of the wardresses, the relief pair who waited for any call from the pair within. The presence of women in the prison set a cast in the atmosphere. He remembered who had been the last woman he had seen in this place, his mind slipping into unwonted complexities. The wardresses rose at his appearance, knew what he was and averted their eyes: he was complimented. The inner cells such as these were dark, lit from greasy gas mantles which created as much shadow as clarity. The wardresses were bony and shapeless, but the presence of their sex was tangible: it clotted his breathing. He snorted to clear his head and went to the eye-hole in the door through to the last cell. He hoped she would be in view, that he wouldn't have to arrange to have her manoeuvred or, even worse, to have to don some ill-fitting warder's jacket and cap and go in there for himself on some stupid charade. He hated to be seen before the moment of revelation in the early morning.

She was sitting directly opposite the eye-hole as if positioned specifically, waiting for him. She looked straight at him as if the door did not exist between them. The light which flickered on the walls about her seemed to be held still in her face. Her hair was brilliant gold; it flowed loose across her shoulders. Her eyes met his one squinting eye, wide open, points of precision in their delicate white ovals. The nose and lips were lines perpendicular. The expression was held in an exact equilibrium. Catch found himself holding his breath. He studied the shape of her, thin beneath the shapeless prison smock, the hands in the small lap, knees together, the womanliness of her masked but implied in her tension and, above all, in that face, that perfection, that assertive purity that Catch felt was beyond any man, if only because of the blunt rousing it caused in him.

He withdrew from the eye-hole and turned to the wardresses who were still averted as if he had been performing some private function. He chuckled and shot the eye-hole cover across with a loud clack.

'Make sure you crop that hair before I come for her. D'you hear me?' The faces rose up at him, one on either hand, indistinguishably alarmed. 'D'you know what I am? Cut her hair short. I don't want to have to ferret through that bush to put my knot in place.' They gave no indication of having understood him. 'At ten before seven exactly, I'll be here for her. You have her ready for me.'

Next morning, a minute or two late, the Governor looked back at him – the signal. He stepped from behind the front rank of attendant dignitaries and advanced into the last cell, taking over. She knew him at once and smiled at him with a greeting that held him for a second. He reached out for her hand to clasp it and pinion her, but she ran her hands so firmly over his, exploring them with a brief minuteness, that he found himself leading her out of the cell on his arm, unstrapped, like a bride. He felt the rest of them stiffen at this breach of established protocol, but he was with her now and they did not matter.

They had cropped her hair hideously, making her look like some mad syphilitic. As they passed out into the court-yard, into the grey, wet morning with the daylight hardly established and vague, watery lights bobbing about them, a noise emerged, a broken sea of clamour against the surrounding walls, a roar from within the prison and beyond it, of frustration and outrage. Catch accepted it as an acknowledgement of his triumph.

She leant lightly beside him, but stepped firmly forward. The rest seemed to drain away from them. He noted her face rise to register the waiting platform, the beam, the noose, and as she saw it he felt a lifting in her which was surely not of fear. She understood. He put his arm about her as if to steady her, but really because he could not resist feeling the strength of her. They passed into the double doors, out of the daylight, to the foot of the staircase that led up to the platform. He halted, out of sight now of the dignitaries, now only with the frightened boys.

'I must bind your wrists now, Jenny,' he said softly.

She smiled and submitted, turned her back for him. He ran his hands over her shoulders and down her arms. He buckled the leather tightly about her wrists. She turned back to face him.

'I knew you would come at last,' she said and put her head against his shoulder. He held her briefly to him.

'Mr Catch!' He had forgotten about the chaplain.

He released her, looked across at the affronted priest and spat on the shed floor.

'We must go up and dance for them now,' he said to her.

She mounted the steps freely and came out under the rope still lifting. Even when he dropped her down through the trap she was still lifting, the snap of the rope like the discharge of a spring. He looked up into the sky, expecting to see her still rising, spreading her liberated, infinite soul above him; and although he could see nothing, could not have seen anything even if there had been anything to see, he knew she was there.

Catch's departure from Cutchknoll was observed with satisfaction by Mercy. In the days before, he had seemed positive and purposeful again, at last, rousing a new clarity about him in the workshop and in the new extension where he suddenly went to work again with a will, leaving the workshop to Fludd.

The day he left, she imagined Cutchknoll without him and it became an easy place. It could support itself, it had its own momenta. Catch had become unnecessary. She had been down at the stream washing, pounding large doughs of grey linen on a stone, when Catch had stridden out of the house, black-suited and unbalanced by his funny little box. She watched his going, sensed his strangeness today and found it easy to imagine him setting off for good with his miser's hoard in his little box: she was sure he had a hoard. Once he had gone, taken his echoes with him out of the valley, Mercy had risen, left her own work where it was and set off to explore the place in his absence.

She ostensibly went to find Fludd, but really she just wanted to see what the place felt like now Catch was lifted from it. She sauntered into the stables and went up the stairs. She peered into Fludd's loft. He was not there and she went in. It was a cramped and messy little box, smelly and full of mouldy bundles and papers. There was a stark, home-made crucifix on the wall. She glanced at some of the literature that lay about the bed but she couldn't read and the crude illustrations meant nothing to her. She thought about tidying up for him. Thinking she heard him in the stable below she stepped quietly across to her own box, waited, but she had been deceived in the sound. She went down into the stable yard again and crossed into the work-shop. The twins were playing with some off-cut wood blocks, one piling them up into complicated constructions, which the other, on a sign from his brother, knocked down in one quick move; at which both erupted in mutual glee. They did not notice Mercy and she passed on quietly, not wanting to intrude. She went into the living-room where Mag was playing with the baby, offering her fingers for its exploration. Mercy could not think of it as Ethelred. She noticed that the infant had a seriousness already in its features that Mag seemed to be trying to clarify in her patient play. She looked up and smiled at Mercy.

'I was looking for Fludd, mistress,' she explained, kneeling down beside Mag and attracting the child's attention, causing it to retract to its mother. Mercy regretted disturbing the moment.

Mag shrugged at her enquiry, indicated vaguely behind her and Mercy rose and left through the door out into the meadow, back into the grey daylight with her work still waiting for her down at the stream. The rain began to fall in large globules. The wind rose up the valley and shook the woods where the rain rattled. Mercy stood and knew the need of shelter, of belonging. She did not belong here: a shudder of profound inimicality shook the illusions out of her. She walked forward, away, on an impulse which fell as quickly as it had risen within her. She turned and went for the nearest shelter which was the empty door-socket at the end of Catch's new extension.

He had finished thatching the roof now and had nailed two-thirds of the floor-boards across the heavy joists. She stood in the doorway, uncertain of her footing, waiting for her eyes to accustom themselves to the murk. The wind blew in through the vacant windows and gushed about making strangely animated creaking and rustling noises. She did not like this new place. It had taken too long. It seemed like a ruin. He was building a ruin, empty like a blown skull.

The creaking and the rustling continued and it occurred

to her, with a moment of genuine terror, that these sounds were no longer consistent with the wind. She drew back. What she had assumed to be a bundle of Catch's materials in the far corner of the place, moved.

'Fludd?' she called. 'That you, Fludd?'

There was a murmur, a response. It was Fludd. He was whimpering. Keeping to the wall, stepping carefully on the boards and bare joists, she came up to him, not coming too close lest he should be infected, or deranged.

'You ill, Fludd?'

He shook himself, or shuddered. It could be taken as a denial, she supposed. She came closer, stooping down, but was ready to jump back at any second.

'You had me piss-scared for a moment there, you miserable little turd,' she said, as affectionately as she had ever said anything to him. His face lifted. She looked away, looked up. 'It's piss-raining out there. Least he can build a roof that don't dribble.'

'Has he gone?'

'Yuh. He needn't come back as far as I care.'

'He'll be back tomorrow. He comes back and does the mistress. He always does. I can't stand it. I want to die just thinking of it.'

'Does the mistress?'

'With his thing. Does her. You know.' He shuddered and shook in a spasm that made her pull back, expecting him to spew.

'Fludd, you really are a miserable bit of shit, aren't you? What's wrong with ... with doing her? They're married, aren't they. How d'you think they made the babies? I bet he does her all the time.'

'No, no. He doesn't. Really. I swear on the Gospel. He only ever does her when he gets back.'

'What are you on about?'

'When he gets back. When he gets back afterwards. It makes him want to do her. And I know who he's got this time. I was there when they called for him. I heard them.' He began to ferret about inside his shirt as if ravaging a violent itch.

'I haven't got the first notion what you're on about, Fludd. Nor have you.'

Successful inside his shirt, he produced a very grubby pamphlet and thrust it at her. She took it, glanced over it front and back, lingering, her eyebrows raised.

'So what?'

'Jenny Child, poor Jenny Child. That's who he's got. Don't you understand?'

She shrugged, affected a bored yawn, wanted to change the subject.

'Can't you read, Mercy?'

'At least I don't have to toss myself off twice a night.'

He did not respond to this, if he understood it. He took back the pamphlet, smoothed it out on his knee. He began to read, slowly, flatly, stumbling over words and muddling the pauses.

Through the haltings of Fludd's literacy, Mercy was caught up in the sad, sad legend of Jenny Child. Mercy's blunted emotions swelled to the story, rose towards the end in an agony of narrative expectation.

'"Shall Jenny Child be murdered shall the wheel make its final fatal turn",' Fludd read then stopped abruptly.

'Go on,' she demanded, 'go on, you pig.'

'That's all.'

'What happened to her? It can't end just like that.' She snatched the pamphlet from him and searched in the thicket of black symbols, certain she'd been cheated.

'They're hanging her tomorrow morning,' Fludd said flatly. 'Master Catch is the hangman. He's got his rope and his buckles in that little black box. I've seen him check them. They knew him in the city where I used to work.'

He fell silent but it was not his silence. It was a silence that seethed up about them, a silence that betokened a reality too big to deny and too big to comprehend.

'I'm getting out of here,' she said eventually, but did not move. The words had been specific, referring only to where she now sat; but in the inactivity that ensued, she knew that she would have to leave not only this particular, tainted shelter, but Cutchknoll in its entirety. The prospect of facing Catch's return was more than she had courage for. She would grab what she could and would fly to the city, lose herself there. The enormity of this frightened her also. Chasms opened either side of her. She held herself tightly to stop herself trembling.

315

'Can I come with you, Mercy?' Fludd asked.

She looked at him, becoming at once aware of him as something distinct, unknown, possible; knowing how much she was going to need him. Sharing this secret with him bound her to him. She was no longer free: it was a relief. She shuffled across the boards and nestled against him. He put his arms about her. She felt small waves of shuddering pass through his hard body. He made no attempt to caress her, just held her like a frame. The rain still blew about the hollowness of the building. In the woods behind they could hear the rush of falling leaves and the creak of the stiffening tree-limbs. From down in the valley came the rushing of the stream, distant but constant amongst the waves of wind and rain. They seemed completely alone.

'And I'll tell you something else, Mercy,' he said suddenly, very quietly. 'She doesn't know.'

She turned and looked at him. He was looking away into the distance.

'Who?' she said. 'Mistress Mag?'

'She doesn't know where he goes.'

'Ah, she must know.'

'No.'

'Then we'll tell her.'

There was a pause whilst this resolution grew and set within them.

'When?' he asked.

'Not now. First thing tomorrow. We'll tell, then we'll go.'

'What if she doesn't believe us?'

'Won't matter. We'll tell her. That's all.'

They sat a while longer, then Mercy rose and went to one of the window holes. He rose and came to stand behind her. She turned to him and faced him properly. He grew awkward under her look. Holding hands, they stepped carefully to the doorway; then, without speaking further, they separated and went about their work, resuming the lives which had been completely altered.

They attended Mag to receive their supper bowls. Sometimes, on cold evenings, they would sit and eat their suppers on either side of the dying workshop fire. Before, they had established a complete silence here. Fludd, for the few minutes of the day when he had Mercy alone, had never dared affront her with so much as a glance: here, they had been too close for the awkwardness to be concealed. Tonight they accepted the ladling of Mag's dark, homely stew as usual, said their goodnights and left her with the boys, the twins settling before the fire and exploring Ethelred who gurgled and moved his thin limbs. They slipped away and sat in the workshop in their usual places, silent but for entirely new reasons. Neither felt keen to eat, but both ate out of habit, and to stave off the implications of their new intimacy which were closing upon them.

Fludd finished first, which he always did, and waited for Mercy to finish, which he always did. He would allow her to leave first and would give her ten minutes to cross the yard, ablute and bar herself in, before going up to his own room. Tonight when she rose she waited for him, held out her hand and together they went into the stable yard and up through the stable darkness, past the shifting and munching of the horse which was restless tonight, having spent the day stalled. Fludd, who had forgotten about him, resolved to begin tomorrow by letting him out to pasture and mucking out his stall; but then he remembered that he would not be there in the morning. A sudden rush of excitement went through him. He reached the top of the steps just behind Mercy, almost shunting into her.

'Get your things together,' she said in a whisper. 'We've got to be ready at dawn.'

He nodded and went, deflected, into his own box to bundle together his few miscellaneous possessions into an old tool-bag. He could not see what he was doing and did not much care what he took and what he left. It was the mechanics of packing that moved him, aware that she was also packing with the same purpose. She had a candle in her room: the doors were open and its light danced faintly about him. Without considering really what he was doing he went out of his room and stood on her threshold. She knew he was there. She paused, but went on ramming clothes into a sack, ramming scraps of material and little objects, stones, wood-chips they looked like, small things that could have had no value but in her cherishing. It moved him to see these secrets.

'There,' she said, and turned to him as the next thing to be attended to.

In the morning, Mag was irritated that she had to rise into the dark dawn and stumble about in the cold to light the fire and tend to the boys. She had come to rely on Mercy: she felt let down. But the chores were not hard for her and she had the continual tumbling of the twins, the demands of Elred, as motivations for her usefulness. She accepted Mercy's negligence, speculated that she might have found comfort with Fludd last night, having sensed a difference between them at supper-time. She could not begrudge the girl her comfort. She got on with the day, cooked the porridge and stirred in the berries she used to spike its bland taste with sudden sharp bursts of blue acidity, the dark, woody berries she had discovered and collected herself.

The workshop door opened and they came in together. Both were dressed for the road. She might have wondered more at this had she not been primarily aware of how they stood together, not touching, too close for that to be necessary. She smiled gratefully at them and moved to the porridge pot: they would be hungry.

'We're going now, mistress,' Mercy said. 'Leaving.'

She stopped a moment, turned to them, looked, then moved to her chair and sat down, looking from one to the other, at both together, waiting.

'We'll not stay for him to come back,' Mercy started up again. 'You come too, if you like. Bring the babies. Don't be here for . . .' She had gone further than she had meant to and she turned for Fludd to rescue her.

Fludd came forward and stooped down to be near Mag, looking up at her, his head on one side, his face as fearful as she had ever seen it; but not cringing, facing her out. She drew back from him, suddenly apprehensive.

'Look in his box, mistress, his little black box,' he whispered. 'He's the hangman. Master Catch is the hangman. He's gone to do for a lovely, lovely girl. He's just done it. Now. Just as the dawn breaks. They always do it then. He'll be coming back to you, and then, then you know . . . He told me . . . You know what he always does . . .' Mercy was tugging at him, pulling him away; he was going too far, too far and she stopped him. They stood away, intending to flee, but held.

Mag looked up at them. A ball of fury against them rose in her, but broke when she saw them, frightened venturers out into the world. They had come to her on an impulse of honesty, a new and molten honesty that was heated in their discovery of each other. She could begrudge them their honesty no more than she could begrudge them their pleasure. The emotions defused and drained back into her, pulling her down with them, down and down.

They watched her rise against them and they gripped hands to be ready to withstand her. The boys' faces were upon them, big, serious eyes, widened to understand it all, not understanding, turning to their mother who sank down under the bow of her back and wept. Strange sounds broke from her dumb throat, a keening, a tearing, the low, pulsing howl of her new solitude, the loss of her last innocence. Her sons clambered about her, whining and clawing to try to reclaim her, but she was gone, a little old woman who had been cheated, always, of her body and now, finally, of her soul too. They stood and watched her.

The incessance of her children roused her eventually. She reached out to touch them, to see if they had any comfort for her. They had not: they were his children, the children of his cruelty. Only much later did it occur to her to doubt what Fludd had told her, and by then she doubted it only as a faint, lost hope. The moment she had heard it she had known it to be true; and looking at her children seemed only to confirm it. But they were real and she pulled herself up amongst them, went to the stove and brought the porridge pot to the table. Mercy and Fludd, exchanging glances, took their places. She ladled out the breakfast and they ate. They did not look at her. Had they looked at her face, they would only have seen a mask.

After they had eaten, they rose. Mag set down her child, came to them and clasped them briefly, Fludd and then Mercy. They took their leave, hurried down the cart-track with Mag at the doorway watching them.

When they had fallen out of sight of the house, Mercy said, 'Do you think she'll kill them? Do you think she'll kill them and then he'll have to hang her like poor Jenny Child?'

Fludd did not answer. The implications of this were too

real and would haunt them for the rest of their lives. Their only impulse now was to be as far away from it as possible. They headed north where, they had heard it said, you could take ship for new lands far away.

Catch came back into his valley triumphant. It could hardly contain him anymore. He passed the unfinished extension and it irritated him. He felt impelled to stop and finish it at once; after food, perhaps, and other appetites, which he felt stirring clear and strong.

He entered the living-room. Mag was squatted with Fludd's spawn by the fire. He glanced over her. She did not rise to him and he hardly noticed her. He slammed the box down on the table and took a wedge of pie from a plate. Cramming his mouth, he went into the workshop and called for Fludd who was not at his work. He decided all at once on Mercy. She hadn't been in the house or meadow. He went to the stable, which was a convenient place for her to be.

The emptiness of her room, the emptiness of Fludd's room, struck against him like an outrage. He grabbed a chair and broke it through the window in Fludd's room. He bellowed with rage. He went into Mercy's room. He sprang down the stairs and out into the stable yard, out on to the cart-track to see if he could see them fleeing. He would have pursued them and destroyed them, but they were obviously long gone. He shook them from him with the foulest curse he knew. He felt it leave him and echo back off their absence.

He turned into the workshop and made a complicated progress through, pulling things down around him, creating a flow of clattering and smashing: it was the noise more than anything else that he needed. He came to the living-room door and burst through it, rending its latch as he did so, the bits scattering down behind him.

Mag was at the table, her back to him. As he entered, she turned away quickly and took up the infant which clambered, whimpering, at her. She moved to the door. He would have stopped her, but he saw that she had forced his box. The noose had snaked out of its coil, the straps hung like flaps over the edges. Mag was gone, had left the door wide behind her. Catch began to cram the facts of his secret back into their box, but he knew that the secret itself had escaped and that it was all futile. He sat down on his chair and a cloud of enervation took rapid and total possession of him.

She must have known, he began, she must have known. But he knew that she had not known, that the whole point was that she should never know; and that now she did know, everything was spoiled. A sense, not of shame, but of mess came over him. He saw himself in a new image, a new nakedness. He shuddered. He wanted to call her, to confess to her and to receive her forgiveness; but this was an illusion. He was powerless against her knowledge of him, against her mastery of the source of his energy. A succession of memories took possession of him – shrieks of anguish, of despair, of terror in the prison yard, limbs writing against the cutting straps, the jump of the rope, the reek of shit, the flopping corpses with their swollen faces, their bloated pricks, their limbs distorted, unseated by the shock of death shot through them; the long sacks and the lime pit, the stench, the shame that remained sweating in the dark corners of the prison; the averted glances upon which he had feasted. It was the ecstasy of killing. He knew now. He had come home with the power in him and he had bred children out of it, the offspring of his darkness, children of death. He did not know what there was to be done.

Towards dusk Mag came back into the house. She had played with the boys out in the meadow or had watched them at play. She wanted it to be over. She wanted Catch to have hanged himself, wanted to be free of him. She kept the children waiting outside whilst she went in to see. He lay asleep sprawled across the table. The lid of the black box was closed but he had not repacked it, the contents bulged out. His arm was around it. She reached across and extracted it. His eyes opened but his head did not lift. She took the box and rammed it deep into the grate. She fetched in the children and closed the door. They stood together watching as the flames grew fat about the box and the chimney began to roar. The room filled with the glow. The varnish bubbled and cracked, the leather sizzled, the wood split and was consumed.

Satisfied, at least temporarily, she set about her evening work, fed her children, washed them and settled them up in bed. Catch remained sprawled across the table, his eyes at times open, at times closed. When she was alone with him she ladled out the chicken stew for him and for her, sat down facing the fire and ate.

She ignored him and went to bed. In the morning he was still there across the table, his suit drenched in his own filth. This was not to be tolerated. She fetched a stave from the workshop and prodded him awake. He stirred, rose and was, for a moment, dangerous. She struck him across the head, swinging the stave back and slamming it into him. He reeled and fell. From the stairway the faces of the twins watched, little moons. From above the baby cried. She drove him from the house and out into the meadow, down to the stream. She returned, scrubbed out and settled down to life without him.

He did not die and he did not leave. He took refuge in his new extension. She accepted this and took food out to him three times a day. It disappeared. He took in the few necessities she gathered and left on the new lintel for him. He was like a tramp, lodging alone in his ruin, accepting her charity. The children avoided him. He rarely emerged, never approached them or her. She wanted him to hurry up and be done with himself.

The winter was cold but he endured it, hibernating through it. Mag occasionally passed one of the vacant windows and caught the stink of his den, a mess of thick and filthy blankets and straw in a corner where the old wall met the new wall, not four feet from where she and the boys lived. She felt no compassion for him, but the hatred subsided into a dull disgust. It was not in her to prosecute any long-term design against him. She was by her long experience purged of vindictiveness, a vice bred in claustrophobias of a type she had only recently come to know. She wished only that he would go, or die. She wished that he had not fathered her sons, but was strong in their growing and, at last, he did not matter: anyone would have done.

Catch meanwhile lived in a world of corroding nightmares. Asleep or awake he lived constantly with the touch of twisting, knotting limbs; images of mouths opening, the skin drawn back from the teeth, back and back until it had uncovered the whole bleached skull beneath; images of large, clustering genitals lopped off and dropped into a slithering vat; of beautiful girls naked with golden hair as long as they were blowing about as they spread out in a stretching sexuality that suddenly gripped them like a rack, arching them up until their spines snapped; of buckets of cold, black blood drawn up from a well, tipped on to a dry, parching plain, turning it into a dark, steaming morass; a mountain of grey bones shifting and tumbling as if pushed up continuously from some vast necropolis far below. He had no control over these terrors. They endured for days sometimes. When he tried to move, to take food or drink, the images still surged, more lucid and moving faster as he moved. He was aware of Mag, of the children, moving in the meadows and rooms of another world, a lost world.

— 7 —

The winter was endured. She noted missing tools, missing timber, she had even heard him shifting as quietly as he could down in the workshop below her bedroom. Elred slept in the big bed with her now, and the twins had their box beds at the foot of the big bed. She awoke and listened to the rhythms of their sleeping breaths, reassured by them, safe with them, as she was with the stave that stood propped within reach. The monster below made no attempt to rise. She would break his head if necessary. The certainty that she could do this made her strong. Prepared as she was, she was still uneasy about him. He would not be gone. There was more to be done, more for her to face with him, sooner or later.

When, one bright, flowing spring day, she heard him at work in the hollow extension, for a moment she was caught off-guard and her spirit rose to him as it had done before in the days of her innocence, but the twins ran from wherever they had been playing, frightened by the noise, clinging to her skirts and bringing her back into the present. She turned to fetch the stave to go in and beat him down again, but she held herself, submitted to the fact of his activity, bustled the boys away, confirming their fear: she did not want them drawn into that. The new building was tacitly forbidden them. In it dwelt a monster too large for their infancies to encompass.

The noise of his work continued through the ensuing months, albeit spasmodically. There would be weeks when nothing seemed to be going on in there. The food she placed now in one of the window-sockets was taken, but there were no other sounds from within. She still expected, every morning, to find the food still there, steeled herself continually to the task of having to go in and clear him out for the last time.

A year passed. Occasionally she thought she saw him when the light was strong and fell into the depths of the house, a moving bulk in there hurrying into the shadows. The sounds of sawing and hammering came occasionally, disturbing when they first began again after a long silence, but soon blending into the sounds of the woods, the laughter of the children, the heaving of the wind. They lived in increasingly reduced circumstances, on vegetables mostly, and berries and mushrooms from the woods. The chickens provided eggs in their season and occasionally a broiling fowl was culled: necessity overcame her squeamishness in this. The horse died and she did not know what to do with it. With the twins' help she managed to scoop out a shallow pit in the meadow and cover the dead beast with a foot or two of soil. The twins were growing useful and inventive. They would go into the woods, spend whole days there, and come back with rabbits or squirrels, or some bird they had snared – a rook or jay or pigeon. There was a triumph at their first rabbit. They grew over-ambitious, however, and came home once with a sheep. She resisted it, hungry though they all were, showed horror at it and made them bury it as they had buried the horse. Elred was different. As he outgrew his infancy, she saw a wariness settle in him, a need for solitude, for distance. He would go into the workshop and explore the remnants of his father's craft. He never once hurt himself there, showing a caution that protected and sustained his curiosity. He was subject to dark moods, sulks and tears, for no apparent reason; but he would always come at last to her, from his solitudes as well as from his sulks, requiring immense amounts of concentrated affection, more than the twins had ever needed. She worried over him and she sought to spy on his privacy; but he would always sense her observation, always turn to her. He was as silent as she was. She felt that one day soon he would break the one law and go to his father, and that terrified her.

One day, when spring storms kept them all inside about the fire in a clustering that she loved – herself and her three strong sons sitting quietly together – they heard a burst of noise through the wall that separated them from Catch, noises of hammering and fixing on a large scale. The following morning, after a disturbed and fearful night of it, they found that the two big windows of the extension had shutters fitted tightly. Running round to the end of the building where she never usually went, she found a door fitted, ajar, hung solid, clean white planks with a hole ready for the latch. Looking up she saw smoke rising from the new chimney. In one fearsome burst of energy, in the midst of a gale, Catch had turned the empty shell of the new extension into a tight and functional dwelling. The smoking chimney altered everything. It was no longer a pit in there, the lair of an increasingly legendary beast, but a dwelling, a presence with its own assertions. She again considered going in with her stave and driving him off. She did not. It was too late for that now. She took his food round to the door, leaving it on the step; no longer in propitiation, an offering to a dormant malevolence – now the feeding of a neighbour, a stranger who seemed suddenly to have acquired rights in the valley. The months slipped past. The stocks of wood in the workshop were almost gone and it began to echo. Their living space was a cramped cabin between these two spaces which he had claimed. She knew that soon she would have to face him again. She began to charge up her courage and to imagine ways of taking the initiative.

The solitude of Cutchknoll during these seasons was absolute. The grass grew thick in the cart-tracks and no one ventured into their seclusion. The world beyond had forgotten them. Mag was glad of this, although she did not trust it. She would have been happy thus, but her sons were growing and their worlds would not be bounded by these meadows and wood fringes. She wondered how far Rob and Tom had gone, if they had encountered strangers, if they were known. She wondered how they would free themselves when the time came, feeling sick and sad at the thought of it.

One day she sat stitching, Elred at her feet playing with a collection of strange bits of wood he had gleaned from the workshop and from the nearby meadows: knotty, deformed objects which he explored minutely, piled and organised in strange configurations before his mother's gaze as if they held some message. Rob and Tom came running in, broke in breathless and gabbled and pointed and pulled Mag out into the wind.

Coming up the valley was a pony and trap upon which sat an old man with white hair and a long, black cloak, and a woman, also in black, with a tight, black bonnet. The woman held the reins. Mag advanced upon them, fearful, pushing the boys back. She recognised the man: he was the vicar. A surge of memory rose in her. She glanced back towards Catch's lair to reassure herself that he was keeping down. She advanced quickly down the track to meet her visitors, to stop them as far down from the house as possible.

The woman, seeing Mag's intent, pulled the pony to a halt, placed a protective hand on the old man's sleeve. Both looked down at the wild woman who approached them.

'Ah. Mistress Catch,' the vicar began. 'Are you . . . are you well? Are those your children? We . . . we hadn't heard that you'd been . . . been blessed with . . .' He halted, cleared his throat, looked up at the sky and shuffled down into his coat. 'May we . . . may we speak with you?'

She came forward and stroked the pony's hot nose. It was a docile beast and its eye fell upon her dolefully. She was not going to let them come any closer. The vicar had grown old. He'd been old enough before, now he was truly old. He did not frighten her.

'Miss Clack is dead,' he said.

Miss Clack? She had died years ago. Surely. She felt a pull

at her from her past, a sucking at her which she fought. She held the pony's bridle with both hands tightly, until the creature, sensing her tension, began to pull back. The woman tugged at the rein, Mag let go and the trap settled back a yard or two. Both its occupants looked increasingly alarmed. Mag could see her own ferocity reflected in their responses.

'Is Master Catch at home?'

Mag shook her head fiercely.

'There is to be a funeral tomorrow, which, if you would care to come . . . Palmead is to be closed up, sold perhaps. Mr Stone has been gone abroad some while. Mrs Stone . . . she too died. It is all most . . . distressing. But you will have heard all this.'

No, but she could imagine it. She shuddered and turned away. There was nothing for her in any of this. They had no right to bring it all back to her.

'There's also . . . a small sum of money,' the vicar called as she began to move away.

She turned back on an impulse of defiance, but she saw their fear of her, the trembling old man and his hard-faced companion who was ready to throw herself in front of any outrage. Mag sighed and came back towards them, came beside the trap and took the old man's hand, his long, bony fingers in a tissue of black leather, limp and surrendering to her touch with a tremor.

'A small sum,' he said. 'The remains of Miss Clack's property, willed to you or to your . . . your children, or to your husband should . . . should he . . . It is clearly stated. She was, it seems, remarkably lucid at the end, perhaps before the end . . . I am trustee, if you should require . . . Some two hundred and fifty pounds . . .'

She nodded her general acquiescence. It would give her something with which to arm her sons.

'Will you come tomorrow, Mistress Catch? I think she would have . . . Two o'clock?'

Mag nodded, stroked his flaccid fingers and left them, walked back towards the house, gathering her sons together as she did so. When she had herded them inside, the trap jolted forward, came up to the house, swung round fast and set off on the road away.

She sat up all night making dark garments for herself and the boys, inspired by the prospect of setting out with them, walking down the road into the village with them gathered round her. Had she detained him, the vicar might have offered to send a trap for them, or a cart at least; but she was content to walk, as she thought it out, content to walk the gauntlet of the village, a pleasing penance, an act of defiance, whatever. It kept her busy thinking about it.

At dawn she roused them and brought them down to the fire which had glowed all night for her. One by one she dressed them in their new formality. The twins seemed to take fright, to shrink within their new clothes, suspicious of the strangeness, of her strangeness as she cased their limbs tightly into it. Elred alone seemed pleased with his new persona. She fed them well, porridge and rough bread, stocking up their bellies. She looked at them and was proud of their chubbiness. The twins would always be stoutly built, and Elred had not yet lost the swaddling of his baby-fat. She went out with Catch's ration in good time, dressed in her own tight finery. The new-wood smell of the place was thinning and a mustiness that could only have come from him was asserting itself. The windows were shuttered and, although there was a dim fire-glow, she could distinguish nothing else. She turned away and the door creaked closed of its own accord behind her.

They set out. She had Elred saddled in a leather sling across her back. She could feel him resting his face against the rise of her spine. She walked with a tall stick. The twins walked ahead of her, holding hands and never looking back, aware of her close behind and stepping firmly. They passed up the gullet of the valley where the woods narrowed in on the path which turned, first to the right, then to the left sharply, and went down to the wide and rutted roadway to the village. The ground sloped gradually down under them and it was easy walking. She wondered how easily they would walk home, with the tumult of the village behind them and the slope rising against them.

It was a grey day but not rainy, a day that could belong to any month from March to November, a day when the business of the seasons seemed obscured in the greyness of the hanging sky. The village appeared before them, the houses at a distance, dark hulks shaggily thatched ranged on either side of the road like the carcasses of giant sheep. As they came closer to the houses their shapes became distinct but the oppression remained. They walked between them and they appeared deserted. Even the smoke rising from the occasional chimney seemed lifeless, the smoking of a fire gone out.

They reached the village green before the church, although it was only now green in ragged patches. She recalled it as wide and lush and daisied, coming across it on her wedding day. Now it was threadbare and mired, cut across with ruts and hoofprints. Something had passed across here, something had passed through the village of which she was unaware, and did not want to know about. Her children came close to her as she stood on the edge of this hurt space.

The church stood unchanged, its tower dark and four-square, standing above the surrounding cottages; its strength turned grey too, but still resolute. They crossed towards it, passed through the lych-gate and came to the nailed door. The handle was a great iron ring, corroded and icy. She wrenched at it and heard the catch rattle in the great space beyond. The door gave with a groan and she led them in.

The church engulfed them at once. She herded them on and pushed the door closed behind them. The silence was cavernous and perpetual, a heavy, stone-damp echoing. They moved down the aisle, tiny within the emptiness. She shuffled them into a pew and sat them in a row, the twins on her left, Elred, unslung, on her right. She began a long vigil.

She had no idea of the time: time had no relevance in here. Whether the service had taken place, or whether she had understood wrongly, it did not matter. She sat here with her sons in the presence of the God whom she knew from the long rectory hours – the clear, cold certainty at the centre of life. It was not a comforting, nor a reassuring presence. It betokened endurance and eternity, a light so great it obliterated everything and reassured only by its totality. She felt an urge, bred of the old days, to offer some devotion, but she could remember none of that. She settled into the stillness with the offering of her sons and that was enough.

At last, perhaps hours later, the doors opened and the vicar, supported on the arm of the woman who had driven the trap, entered the church. A couple of men in black followed, rattled at the long bolts on the doors and swung them open. The vicar and the woman, meanwhile, moved slowly up the aisle. Mag sensed an acknowledgement of her as they passed, although they neither turned nor paused. She kept herself still, her eyes ahead. Behind her came a shuffling and a lifting. The men who had opened the doors came slowly but purposefully past, bearing trestles which they set down before the communion rail. The vicar turned and faced down the aisle. Borne by more heavy men in black, the coffin came. It was plain and long, and Mag identified it at once as Miss Clack's, could feel her, long and bony, lofty and still, but present. The coffin was placed upon the trestles and the vicar began to read from a heavy missal. His voice was thin but it gathered deep echoes. The words were indistinguishable, the tone frail and helpless. Miss Clack lay still in her box and submitted to this small breeze of words blown across her, smoothing out a surface if nothing else. Soon it was done and the procession inverted, the coffin lifted by the black warders, the vicar leading the way back down the aisle, the woman beside him, keeping close.

Mag, herding her sons, followed them to the place of committal. The long box was roped and lowered to its rest. More words were puffed out to be swept up by the wind. Mag, releasing her sons, pressed in close and they moved away, making space for her to peer down into the grave. It was a deep grave, the wet earth crumbling at the sides, keen to be closed again about its purposes, its digestion of the dead. It made her giddy to look down but she had to see that shape, the long box lying there. It was right. It was final. She knelt and grabbed handfuls of earth, throwing them down, hearing their thump upon the coffin-lid. She rose and walked off to where her sons stood at a small distance, waiting for her to complete this oblation. It was done.

They were escorted to the vicarage. The woman, who was the vicar's niece, and a maid took the boys off to the kitchen whilst Mag sat in a gloomy and cramped room with the vicar. He gave her cake and a small glass of sweet, thick wine. She sat in a high-backed chair, her feet off the floor. He spoke of the money that would be hers, of registering the birth of her sons according to the law; he was frail and uncomfortable and she did not feel like making his task any easier. When he asked after her husband, she grew perceptibly hostile.

She rose when he had done with her, went through into the hallway to wait for her sons. They came with the niece who seemed keen to have them gone. Elred smiled up at his mother as if he had a secret to share with her. The twins looked sombre and hidden. The pony and trap waited for them and they were driven to the mouth of the valley by a young coachman who had boils on his neck and who smelt of drink. She trudged up the valley and found it all as she had left it, suspended and waiting for her return.

She undressed and bathed the boys, bundling away their formal clothes for rags. She fed them although they had filled their bellies at the vicarage and were pale and exhausted. They ate dutifully, silently, and went to bed. She stripped and bathed herself. The night grew blustery and she felt cold and lonely. She went up but, although she ached with tiredness, she could not sleep. She wanted to rise and go to Catch, began to rouse herself to go but fell back and let her tiredness possess her. She slept badly and was visited by old dreams of fear and tangling in living woodland. The past seemed to have come back for her on all levels, sucking her back. She woke with gritted teeth.

The grey season resolved itself into spring. Her work left her little time to brood. She cleaned and cooked and rationed out the food. The oats and the flour gave out and their staple was stewed cabbage, and fat, tuberous potatoes. The last of the fowls had been eaten. The twins brought rabbits and birds in from their snares, but their poverty was cutting close. She scrambled amongst the soil of the garden and planted the seeds she had prepared in the autumn, but the earth seemed tired and she waited tensely to see if they would germinate. They came up eventually, some of them, but were insipid, weed-like growths that promised little sustenance. It was a cold spring.

Catch stayed buried in his extension, taking in his rations, coming out at night to prowl. She heard him, a nocturnal

brute, growing harmless if only with familiarity. She sometimes heard him lumbering about down in the workshop and
once she woke to find the twins awake too, wide-eyed and
listening. She took them into her bed with Elred who slept
solidly. Their bodies were knotty and hard and gave her
little rest; nor did they really need her protection, having no
fears of anything, no nightmares; but it was a procedure, a
ritual that was repeated on other nights. Elred slept through
it all; or appeared to, for you could never be sure with
Elred. The boys began to watch more closely as she prepared
Catch's food. She gave him more than she allowed them, far
more than she allowed herself, an unvarying mound for
him, however little was left. She had to do her duty.

One evening, as soon as she had filled Catch's bowl with
broth, Elred took it up and went out with it. The twins rose
to stop him, looked to their mother for her assent, but she
let him go. It was inevitable. She dreaded most of all the
boys making an alliance with him against her. That would
break her heart.

Towards the end of that dismal spring, on the threshold of
what promised to be a dry summer, hot air rushing out of
the woods, the earth parching and crumbling quickly, the
vicar's niece arrived alone, in the trap. She did not like
coming there, held together only by her sense of duty. She
brought the promised money, a bag of fat golden guineas.
She looked around the place and saw the poverty. She
offered to take some of the money and to buy things, to
help them re-stock and re-plant. Mag was grateful and
rewarded the woman by making her feel that her charity
was appreciated, putting her at her ease a little.

So life at Cutchknoll improved. The promised supplies
were brought. The hen-run was filled with young birds,
startled, scrawny and greedy. A cow was bought, led lumbering and dragging into the pasture. The farm-boy who
brought it showed Mag how to milk it. The twins watched
and learnt too. There was to be cream and butter. Cheese
they brought in, and great jars of honey, and haunches of
smoked and salted flesh; and new seed. A cart-load of hot
dung was brought and the farm-boy spent two days digging

over a new tillage, breaking the soil and dunging it deeply. The twins worked with him, learning from him, growing in strength and working in the promise of their manhood. Mag watched and was happy for them.

Elred, meanwhile, took charge of the new hens. He searched out all the gaps in the old run and dragged out lengths of wood to bar them off. He knew each hen individually, studied them, moved about them with an authority to which they soon acquiesced, growing excited when he approached, scurrying into the hen-house at night under his tiny inexplicable shouts. He brought in their first eggs triumphantly. He set up a board to mark down the number of eggs laid. Mag watched this too with wonder and pleasure. Life seemed to be opening out about her again.

The valley filled with summer and grew lushly. The long meadow grass was scythed for the cow's winter fodder and life seemed certain, for a few months at least.

Winter came early that year. She awoke one night to find the house at the centre of a blizzard. The wind roared and the snow hurtled through the wood and up the valley in horizontal sheets, blanking out the world. She rose into the still, steel air of the bedroom. The boys slept in their huddles beside her, turning in the warmth of the quilt. She listened for Catch, but heard nothing but the mad fluttering of the snow as it piled about the house, and the drone of the wind behind it. She crept down into the living-room in darkness. She knew every movement of every board beneath her feet so well, although she could see nothing. The shutters were tight and the fire dead. Suddenly she felt him near to her, expected to blunder into him at any moment: this was why she had come down. She shivered and fumbled for a light, struck a phosphorus match which blinded her momentarily. In the dance of the candlelight she found herself alone and felt afraid, for herself and for him. She took the candle to the door of the workshop and peered in. She cupped the tenuous flame with her hand. The little light jumped about amongst massive shadows, filling the emptiness, but not making it any less empty. The blizzard pounded at the doors and shutters. She was now cut by the cold and trembling violently. She returned to the living-room and pulled on her boots, old padded boots Catch had fitted for her. They were cold and clammy, but her warmth was contained within them and they began to take effect. She struggled into a large sheepskin coat. It had been his but, last winter, she had unstitched it and adapted it for herself. It muffled her well enough. Her head was bare, but that would have to remain so. The candle blew out and her fingers were too numb to relight it.

She unbarred the front door and a rush of snow shoved it open, piling in around her, her fragile barricade against it breached. It would fill up her home, smother everything. She set her head down and pushed forwards against it. Once over the threshold she sank up to her thighs but, in a respite, when the force of the storm was pressing at some other weakness, she managed by grasping the handle and hurling her weight backwards, to pull the door closed and latch it behind her. It might hold.

The storm came back for her and tumbled her sideways into the soft abyss of a drift. The snow filled her open mouth and choked and froze her palate, and lanced the sensitive pits about her teeth. She writhed and struggled and came upright. She had little sense of direction but, heading instinctively against the storm, she felt the ground sloping down and, with what was hardly firm proof, she assumed that the downslope led away from the house, down to the stream and to what would obviously be death by freezing. She put her back to the blast and allowed herself to be shoved uphill until bashed blindly into the reassuring wall of the house. At least she knew where she was, approximately.

The storm was all paradox. It was white and black; it was soft as feathers and hard as spikes; it was roaring so continuously that it created a silence in which she could hear her heart beat, hear the breath hiss through her gripped teeth. She was soon entirely adrift – with no idea where she was, where she was going, who or what she was. The longer she was out in the storm, the less and less she knew. It would have been miraculously easy to slide down the wall behind her, cradle her arms over her head and let the storm envelop her. This had always been the first option: it always would be the first option. One day she would give in. Not yet. There was another pleasure, an older and deeper pleasure in pushing on. The living pain, the bruising stone against her spine, the soddening of her flesh as the blizzard penetrated her clothing, making it hard to tell where she began, reducing her to a tighter and tighter knot against the enormity of the weather, edging interminably along the wall face without any sense of it ever ending, her progress in small discrete pushes of energy which advanced her less and less at each push, the weight of the storm striving incessantly to still her, but not stilling her, not quite, not quite: this – yes, this.

And suddenly the wall ended and she was spun backwards into a deep drift. She had fallen off the end of something and it was all over. She writhed about, trying to free herself, to get upright, but she had lost the sense of what was upright. Something struck her on the head, a hollow thud, not stone, wood. The blow caused a clarifying bolt of pain to shoot down into her back. She clawed and found a door latch. Bending her thickened fingers about it, assuming she had somehow arrived back where she started, she hung on.

The door opened and she fell out of the storm into a place she had never been before: a long, bare room with a great fire roaring out over a great empty hearth. Her name was being called. She roused and realised that the storm was still with her, that she was perceiving all this from within the storm. She pushed herself along the floor and found that it was possible to leave the storm behind, that there were patches where the storm did not reach. Her name was called again from deep in the room, a squeaky monosyllable that might have been anything. First the storm had to be shut out. She found her way to the back of an open door and went for it, shoving herself against the door, moving it, pushing the storm back, pushing it out. She sat against the door, exhausted, frozen, bedraggled and gasping. She was in Catch's dwelling: the fire was his fire; the voice was his voice, calling her from beyond the shadows where, even as her vision began to clear from the whirling of the snow, she could not see him.

'Mag . . .? Mag . . .? Mag . . .?'

Had his voice really gone so squeaky? Why had he not come to help her? She felt the warmth of the fire and lifted herself up. She advanced towards it, unsteady, stumbling, going for the wall to support herself. It was a greedy fire. She might easily stumble and be pitched into it. Would he rescue her? Where was he? Why was he letting her fall about on her own here? Had she not come to him at last? She grew angry. She felt futile.

The fire roared into the chimney: great logs glowed and splintered, sap hissed from their raw ends. She left the wall and advanced into the heat. It began to overpower her. Her clothes turned clammy about her. Her flesh began to ache back to life. She sat down in the bed of the fire's power and struggled off her boots, pulled off her coat, pulled off her nightsmock, pushed them from her. The heat dried her nakedness almost immediately. She felt the skin tighten to splitting across her cheeks. She curled up and the heat swallowed her.

When she woke, slowly, she felt his heavy, living weight against her and, before regathering all the precision of consciousness, she thought she was back in an earlier time. She was glad of him then, glad of the way he lay against her, holding her intimately; surprised and pleased to find them both naked. This was how it always should have been. A weight seemed gone from her in the simplicity of his contact. As her awakening came clear to her, she re-membered, re-attired herself in the outrage of finding him there like this.

She did not immediately pull away. Her body was limp and raw and it would certainly be painful to pull away, to shed the coverings, for the room was full of iciness at which her exposed nose flared. Drawing a sharp, awakening breath, she felt her lungs fill with the cold. The wide room was lit with blades of light that came through slits in the shutters. The fire before her was a mass of ruined ash with a speck of gleaming and a faint savour of heat. She remembered the snow, remembered her journey, realised that quite possibly she was blocked in here; with him.

She writhed about suddenly, determined to shake him from her but not to lose the warmth. She felt him wake all at once, felt him retract guiltily from her and leave a massive gulf of cold at her back. She rolled over and clutched at the coverings to staunch this space, not caring about anything but staying warm. Only when she had struggled herself back tight did she attend to him. He was up, moving about the room, mostly in shadow, a shaggy figure, naked, reaching out with long arms and bringing things to him, touching them closely, bringing them to his face, putting them down. This behaviour seemed to her more animal than human, strange and primitive. She did not remember this at all. He came round her and squatted down before the fire, his long buttocks towards her and the arch of his back. His hair was grown wildly and came down his shoulders. It was white.

He prodded the fire and laid kindling chips precisely, laid logs, blew expertly and soon the crackling and flickering returned; not much warmth yet, but the promise of warmth. She sat up, shuffling in a little way towards the grate. He turned and stumbled against her.

'Mag?' he said, regaining his balance and reaching out.

She drew back quickly, avoiding his face, hiding. But he did not advance and she glanced up at him at last.

He had aged immeasurably. His flesh was sunken, the dark shag of his body was all quite white, the flesh sagging underneath. From the crown of his head the hair had fallen, revealing a dark dome, furrowed with lines. His beard was long and straggly. The centres of his eyes were obscured by white discs. He was naked and shuddering and the fire danced about him cruelly.

The sight of him broke her. She had done this to him, driven him into the spiral of himself, deep and mad. It was not shame she felt, nor even regret; but a terrible, terrible pity that it had to be thus, a terrible desire to fetch him back to her, a terrible desire for him.

She shed her covers and leapt at him. He stood as she came and as she jumped and clung to him, hung from his shoulders. He picked her up, held her under her buttocks and stood with her. He walked about with her until he realised how cold she was becoming; then he took her back to the hearth where the fire had begun to throw out its heat again. They sat before the fire and rediscovered each other, silently, blindly, a feast of touching, pure contact, all emotions subsumed in the touching.

*

Tom, Rob and Elred woke to the strange white silence of the morning and realised that they were alone. They dressed fearfully and stood down before the cold living-room hearth, troubled and undecided. Rob went to the door, before which there were strangle puddles of icy water, and opened it to find a solid white barrier confronting them. Tom cried out, ran to his brother and together they confronted this new emptiness. Elred came to them and looked at them for leadership. Not receiving any, he pushed past them and into the snowdrift which tumbled in over him. All at once all three of them were struggling through the snow and had scrambled through to a view of the new-made valley, a vast whiteness that they did not recognise, but which had devoured them and had presumably taken their mother. They floundered back, wet and shivering into the house, bringing great gouts of snow with them. Only Elred had noticed the smoke billowing from the extension chimney.

The twins were motivated by desperation now. They ran through the old workshop and found that, the snow having blown primarily up the valley, the stable yard was relatively clear. They heard the cow lowing in the stable and they went to her to draw her milk, which they knew must be done. They had hardly begun, Tom soothing the steaming brute and Rob fetching stool and pail, when Elred ran in and pulled them away. They trusted their strange brother enough to follow him, out of the stable, up on to the slope behind the house. Here Elred indicated, not only the smoke, but a way through, a runnel of black earth in the lee of the house, clear of snow. They ran along it, Elred tottering, but in front, the twins pressing behind him but keeping back to avoid careering into him, stumbling into each other instead. They came to the end of the house and another sheer wall of snow met them.

Elred turned and looked helplessly at his brothers, and beyond them at the shuttered windows along the side of the house. But they were gone now, had run back at a mutual interchange of looks and gestures and were working together. Back they ran to the stable yard, held off course for a moment by the distress of the cow, but going straight to the place in the stable where they stowed all their tools. They grabbed their shovels and ran back along the side of the house to where Elred stood, waiting for them, relying on them.

They hewed into the snow-wall, laughing at the warmth of the work and its ease. The sun was out and the snow glittered and crumbled and sprayed about them. It did not take them long to reach the door, although they were now surrounded by cliffs of snow which might, at any moment, have tumbled down over them. Elred watched from behind and waited, aware of the dangers of which his brothers were oblivious, fearful but holding close. They cleared enough of the door to make an attempt upon it, then they paused and looked back for Elred.

He came scrambling over the mounds of broken snow. They reached out and helped him, recognising his right. He reached the latch of the door and pulled upon it. It was too much for him. They helped him, all three of them, and the icy solidity of it broke audibly, the door sprung open and all three tumbled simultaneously into the open room.

Their parents sat naked on a bundle of covers before the blazing fire. The three boys stood before the doorway in a slope of fallen snow and saw the light of the fire dance on the warm flesh of this unimaginable pair. He was a man more vast and strange than they could ever have imagined. They had heard him, had their own legends about him, the twins even uncertain memories, but they could never have imagined this: great bolts of loose muscle, great shags of snowy hair; tiny white discs for eyes; his humanity gone entirely wild about him. But even more extraordinary was their mother, her essential familiarity turned as strange as her husband – bewildering. They saw, for the first time that any of them could recall, the nakedness of her humped back, the fullness of her breasts, the sheerness of her flesh, the unloosed redness of her hair. It glowed upon her head as if it had come from the fire itself. She seemed indeed entirely of the fire, raw and hot, nestling in the arms of the snowy man. She turned to face them, viewing them from a long way away, but calling them with her eyes to come and meet her, to meet their father.

They came slowly, respectfully, and gathered before the fire, the twins easily and gladly, Elred more circumspectly, sensing something wrong, not knowing if what he saw was wrong, or if how he felt about it was wrong; not knowing whether he turned his eyes from something too beautiful and intimate to be seen, or too hideous in its exposure. He came nevertheless and knelt before his mother, looking up at her face; sensing that the world was different now. The twins busied themselves with the warmth of the fire and laughed at the strangeness. Elred sat tight and waited, perhaps for the blessing he had earned, the birthright he claimed. Whatever he later became, the mould of it was made in those moments.

This tale has no other end than this. Mag finds that there is nothing anymore to be forgiven, nothing to be taken for granted. Nothing can ever be as it was, nothing changes its nature. She can only take into herself what belongs there: she can only give out what she is. She can always submit: she can never surrender.

She feels as she copulates that she is flagrantly defying death, if only for a sudden bunched instant. In winter she conceives again and by autumn she has given birth again, to a daughter.